To Alison

Hope y joy it

Syrup and Cyanide

Best Wishes

Dave

Syrup and Cyanide

Dave Copson

JANUS PUBLISHING COMPANY LTD
Cambridge, England

First published in Great Britain 2019
by Janus Publishing Company Ltd
The Studio
High Green
Great Shelford
Cambridge CB22 5EG

www.januspublishing.co.uk

British Library Cataloguing-in-Publication Data
A catalogue record for this book is available from the British Library

ISBN 978-1-85756 897-4

Cover Design: Janus Publishing Company Ltd

Printed and bound in the UK by KnowledgePoint Limited, Reading

For Dick
1958–2015

Back in the Day ... 1994

The market square was deathly quiet at this hour of the night. Unread newspapers that were blown about by the gusting wind and any old wilted and well-trodden cabbage leaves came to rest up against doorways or the legs of the permanently fixed market stalls. Pigeons sat roosting high above the shops on ledges covered in bird crap. The occasional flapping of feathers broke the silence as they shuffled about to claim their spot for the night. The light from the nearby streetlamps barely lit the desolate market stalls but provided just enough of a yellow haze to suggest where the cobbled road ended and the filthy, dirty old pavement began. Evidence of earlier drunken antics adorned the square, contents from beer bottles and stomachs.

A patch of bloodstained kerbstone suggested it was an unpleasant evening for someone, nothing new in this neck of the woods. As ever, the police around Whitechapel in London's East End had had a hectic time of it and would do tomorrow night too. Shops and pubs, their windows caged and covered with years of grime from the market activity, sat silently as if finally sleeping after another hard day.

At twenty minutes to midnight a van slowly crept into the market square. A black van, no lights on; hardly visible in the sultry light. For ten minutes it sat, engine off. Again, it was only the pigeons that could be heard.

There was silence in the rear room of The Fallen Oak public house which perched itself between the market square and the river to the south. Cigar smoke drifted and hung like an old 'pea-souper', reminiscent of the smog-ridden days of old London Town. A badly stained light bulb tried its best to help with the visibility through the disgusting atmosphere, only managing a token glimmer through the hanging smoke. The table was sticky from spilt beer and the empties were spread around the floor, every so often being kicked and trodden on by sets of booted feet.

As midnight ticked closer the mood in the back room of the pub grew tenser. The two men at the table were known as 'The Crew'. Never really addressed as much else and always seen together when it mattered ... and it mattered tonight.

They dressed in black leather overcoats, black polo-necked jumpers and black jeans, with the only exception being their dark red boots that they polished to a shine. Sometimes they were 'good enough' to let some of the local kids clean them for them. Most of the local boys knew it was a task they really didn't want to be given, as refusal wasn't a wise alternative and it often went unpaid despite promises from one or other of The Crew.

It had been two years ago when one of the boys had omitted shining the soles of the boots as instructed; he was found twelve hours later badly beaten by the side of an old warehouse that sat close to the river. He would not say who had hurt him and refused to talk about the event for a long time.

When he did speak about it, all he said was that he deserved it.

The bigger of the two men was Bernie, should you choose to believe it, and his counterpart called himself Oscar. Both men were intimidating and had the look of Albanians or Croatians, somewhere that way. Bernie sat leaning back with his chair tilted and his head resting against the wall. An attaché case was clutched to his chest and a chain ensured it could not go far from his left wrist. Oscar stood half in the hallway and half in the room, edgy, sweaty. Both men had maintained silence for the past two hours and listened to the sparsely filled pub gradually empty out into the street. The landlord had locked up and gone to stay with his sister for the rest of the night knowing full well that he should remain well out of the way. He had left the side door unlocked as instructed by his guests. If The Crew had business, he didn't want to know. It was a pleasure, of course, to allow them the use of the back room and a pleasure not to wind up with a finger missing had he refused.

John Garron had been running The Fallen Oak for many years and was well known by the clientele and by The Crew. He was to be trusted to keep his eyes averted from whatever business was 'going down' and to keep his mouth firmly shut. Garron knew the drill only too well. What John Garron knew and what he had seen over the years was his business and stayed stored away.

The black van sat as if it were stalking its prey. Engine off, lights off, but inside, cogs were whirring, plans were being made and checked and mentally rehearsed. The driver of the van stared across the market square towards the front aspect of The Fallen Oak. The building had suffered severe bomb damage during the war, so much so that the majority of it was demolished and rebuilt soon after

1945. Before the reconstruction it was called The Oak but was renamed in 1947 in memory of the original old pub.

The van's rear doors opened slowly and four men, gloved and dressed in dark blue boiler suits, disembarked. They gazed up and down the market square to make sure that all was quiet before gently closing the rear doors to, but not allowing them to fully close. Weapons of choice were concealed under their suits. The group walked slowly across the square towards the pub, knowing full well that their targets were in the back and unable to see the market from where they were. To the left of the pub was a narrow alleyway which led to the rear and was used to roll the barrels down to the cellar doors at the side of the pub. The four men didn't utter a word as they closed in, still glancing around and double-checking the square. Three of them walked towards the side alley and the other stood in the doorway at the front in the half-light and tucked under a protruding archway above the main doors, out of view. His job was important. He was to give a signal by banging once on the pub doors if the police rolled by or if there was any other awkward interruption. It would be heard in the back room, especially as everywhere else was silent.

Bernie and Oscar were going to make it big tonight, really big. This was the biggest and best deal they had ever been a part of. The attaché case was laden and spelt wealth for The Crew; riches, houses, cars, girls and more money than they had ever known. Two months' work and planning were about to come good. Bernie finally shifted his huge bulk in his chair and stood with a muffled groan. He stretched and began to move towards Oscar, who was smiling and gloating inside. A month ago, The Crew burst in on a delivery of diamonds at a jeweller's in Hornchurch and came away with more than they had bargained for. Twice as much as they thought they would be getting. The problem for The Crew was that the job became complicated in a couple of ways. There were three blokes delivering the goods instead of the two they had expected, which gave them a bit of a headache in so far as everything they had talked about worked around just two hurdles to overcome. In the shop there was a girl who wouldn't stop screaming despite all the warnings. They had come too far to bottle it and had to change their plan as they went along, making it up as they went, which left them feeling very uneasy and nervous, jumpy, trigger-happy. Shotguns were drawn and their faces were obscured by balaclavas as they entered the shop close behind the three delivery men. Both Bernie and Oscar were yelling instructions to the men, telling them to hit the floor and keep their faces down, 'Eyes on the fucking floor.' The cases they had carried in with them were still being held firmly to their chests, the goods were still being kept safe for now. Bernie was in a foul mood and didn't wait for the goods to be handed over. He struck the first man hard on the back of his head with the butt of the shotgun. Blood oozed out of the wound and the man collapsed unconscious, maybe dead for all Bernie cared. The other two men slid the cases across the floor towards Oscar who gratefully gathered them up. The guy that ran the shop had received more than he expected and had curled up on the floor, shaking like a shitting dog, but the girl was really getting on Bernie's tits and he gave her one more chance to shut up.

'Leave her alone and let's go … guv'nor, let's go … Now.'

Oscar knew they hadn't got time to mess around.

He had parked the Volvo around the corner just twenty-five yards away and they could be away from there in no time. Oscar stood at the door and felt the panic rise inside his gut. He wanted to puke, he wanted to go … now. In a moment of uncontrolled fury, Bernie stormed up to the girl and punched her full in the face sending her flying backwards into a cabinet, shattering the glass. Her limp body landed heavily, face down, and didn't move.

'Now,' screamed Oscar.

Bernie grabbed the third of the cases and ran for the door, stepping hard on the back of the delivery guy he had originally flattened. The Volvo made its way back towards Whitechapel and Oscar was more than a little worried. He hated it if a plan didn't work smoothly and this one had gone very wrong as far as he was concerned. It was supposed to be straightforward, in and out without any violence. The Volvo was parked briefly whilst Bernie and Oscar moved their prize into the flat and found a suitable temporary home for the goods. Five minutes later it was being driven away by one of Bernie's trusted little helpers and dumped in Newham beside an old derelict factory. It was doused with plenty of petrol and torched.

* * *

The alleyway at the side of the pub was a snug fit for three bulky men and their weapons. One carried a shotgun; the other two had iron bars. They waited by the side door and listened to the movement inside. Bernie and Oscar were expecting a visit from a 'businessman' who had contacts and knew how to move the jewels on. It was easy tonight; they handed him the diamonds and he gave them the £500,000. Easy.

One prize in exchange for another and everybody happy.

Except the load was light and the plan was corrupt.

Three cases of diamonds were brought home and only one case was to be exchanged. Bernie and Oscar had ideas, plans, schemes that ran around their heads. They weren't the best fences in town but fancied their chances with the big boys. They were playing with fire. They were out of their depth tonight. Oscar was impatient and decided to take a look outside to see if their man was coming for his collection. Carefully, he opened the side door, stepped into the alleyway and peered up towards the street, but couldn't see into the market or tell whether their man was waiting nearby. They wanted him to come into the back room where they could overpower him and take the money and the diamonds … a good night's work. Oscar took a few cautious steps up the alleyway and peered out into the square. All he saw was an old black van; probably belonging to one of the stallholders. He sighed and turned to go back inside, when something solid struck his face very hard and knocked him to the ground.

His head spun and he couldn't stand, as hard as he tried.

A hard kick to his ribs … and another … and another.

He was heavily concussed and could hear voices whispering, unable to decipher a word of what they were saying. He tasted blood in his mouth and felt nauseous. He puked and his head spun again. The warmth of his own blood was running down his face and pooling around his throat and neck. Oscar was going nowhere and knew he was in real trouble and tried hard to work out how to survive. He couldn't string two thoughts together. His vision was blurred and nothing around him made sense. The beating had stopped for now and as he breathed he felt a terrible pain in his chest. He knew they had done a job on his ribs, probably smashed several of them. They would be back to finish him off and he knew he had to move somehow.

If he didn't, he was a dead man.

Oscar stretched out his hand and groped around in the dirt and muck, his fingers scratching in the grit, simply feeling for anything that might help him pull himself upright. The taste of the blood in his mouth was sickening and he struggled to breathe without swallowing any. He gasped to get some air into his badly bruised lungs and spat blood onto the ground. Move … move … His hand reached out again and could feel some sort of latch, and as he pulled himself towards it, dragging his wounded body across the alleyway through the filth, he felt it move. Oscar's mind was beginning to picture what this could be. In the dark he wasn't able to make out exactly what he had hold of but it was moving … it was moving upwards … he was lifting some kind of panel or door. Oscar's brain clicked into gear … the cellar doors. It was his best chance to get away from whoever did this. He assumed it was the man that they had been waiting for that had turned up with a few heavies and was a step ahead of them, but he had no time to think about anything else other than getting out of the alleyway, and no option but to save himself and hope that Bernie survived the night. It took a huge effort for Oscar to raise the door just enough to get his arm underneath it to hold it open. All he could do was drag himself painfully under the door and wait until he reached the slope where the beer barrels rolled down into the cellar. His movement was hindered by his badly injured ribs and the blood from his face was like a sticky glue and impaired his vision even more. Before Oscar had any chance to control his landing his limp body slithered head first into the pitch-black beer cellar and lay unconscious in the murky dark.

Bernie called to Oscar in a muffled whisper.

'Hey, man, what are you fucking doing out there?'

There was no response so Bernie hauled himself to the door, attaché case in one hand and a jagged butcher's knife in the other; the hickory handle embedded in his huge and sweaty palm. The side door was ajar and he could see the dark and dank passage outside.

'Oscar?'

Bernie thought he must be having a piss in the alleyway and turned back into the pub. It was at that moment that he felt the shotgun being pushed into his back and heard the warning loud and clear.

'You try anything clever and I'll blow your guts all over the wall.' Bernie froze and thought about using the knife but couldn't be sure exactly where his assailant stood. Behind him, yes, but whereabouts? He was shoved forwards hard and ended up colliding heavily with the chair that he had not long vacated and dropped the knife under the table out of his reach.

'Sit,' the man ordered.

Bernie sat down and saw a masked man, who was followed into the room by two more men, also masked. Two of the men held his left arm down flat on the table with extreme pressure and without a word they proceeded to cut the chain attached to the case with bolt cutters. Bernie knew he was in no position to resist; his mind was full of confusion and he feared for his life. His heart raced uncontrollably and he didn't even have the time to wonder who these men were or how they knew to use bolt cutters, before one of them held a gag tightly in place around his mouth as an iron bar slammed down hard on his left hand, causing him to scream, almost silently, in pain.

'Now, where's the rest, Bernie?'

Bernie looked at the man who spoke; the masks were like woollen ski masks with just the eyes showing. He didn't recognise the distorted voice and had no idea who he was dealing with. Another of the masks smashed an iron bar against Bernie's chest and again directly onto his shoulder. The pain was like something Bernie had never felt before.

'Tell me where,' said the first mask.

Mask number two stood behind Bernie and grabbed a handful of hair, pulling his head back so hard that Bernie thought they were going to break his neck. An iron bar was pushed into Bernie's mouth, scraping against his teeth, and forced into his throat, choking him.

'Where?'

Bernie was trying to breathe and retch all at the same time. He thought he was dying there and then. The iron bar was pulled out of Bernie's mouth and he retched but nothing came up. He breathed rapidly and gasped for air, struggling to regain some composure. The first mask nodded to the second who delivered another massive blow to his ribs, followed by a sickening strike to his shin that crunched the bone and almost caused Bernie to pass out. Blood ran down his leg, which had gone numb all the way into his foot.

'Now then, Bernie, I hope by now you can see that we are not playing games. The next attack will leave you crippled for life and it's your choice. Where are the diamonds?'

Bernie's heart was racing and his head was in a massive panic. There was no way out … tell them … tell them. The mask with the iron bar raised it once more and Bernie gave in.

'The flat … the flat.'

'Where in the flat, Bernie?'

'In the airing cupboard,' he replied reluctantly but without any real choice, or at least not a nice choice. The first mask held the shotgun and pointed it at Bernie. Bernie's eyes almost bulged out of their sockets as the gun unloaded the shot into his chest, launching him back against the wall and killing him instantly. The masks walked out of the room, taking their tools with them.

The first mask said, 'Kill the other one on the way out.'

Outside in the alleyway Oscar was nowhere to be seen. Despite a quick search, Oscar had vanished. The mask at the front door had not seen him come out of the alleyway and the four masks knew they couldn't afford to hang around here for too long, so they began to make their way back towards the van.

'Fuck that Oscar, we'll get him. Let's get to the flat and get the rest.'

As far as the masks were concerned, Oscar's days were numbered.

Chapter One

The steeple towered majestically and dominated the grey and overbearing skyline above St Dom's, as it was locally known, as the rain drove sideways onto the aged and flaking stonework of the old church. The cold winter wind howled and whistled around the north side and challenged the ancient yews to yet another battle for supremacy. St Dominic's had stood since 1523 and the defiant yews had remained steadfast like loyal guards for 150 years. Many reverends, rectors, vicars and priests had come and gone over this prolonged period. Essentially, there is very little to distinguish one title from another. Rectors may have had others carry out certain duties in their place, which was known as doing the work vicariously, hence the word vicar. Revd Martin Brookes was one such vicar who lived just a few hundred yards from what had become his new place of work. He had spent the last eight years working as the vicar at St Patrick's, which was situated on Mile End Road, Stepney, in the heart of what was once the feared East London territory of the infamous Kray twins back in the good old, bad old 1960s. Martin had seen it all, or so he always said, during his spell in London. His congregation had diminished somewhat over the years but then many of his friends in the church were making similar statements about the falling attendances. Despite Martin's best efforts to raise the awareness of all things good about the church, the local residents would rather spend their time and money frequenting the local pubs and clubs before watching West Ham United play their Sunday Premier League matches for the benefit of Sky TV than come along to listen to him. It was an easy decision to flee the chaos of East London in search of a quieter existence, and when the opportunity arose to fill the gap that had been left by the previous vicar, he realised his chance and applied for the post immediately.

St Dominic's was the only church serving the village of Laurel's End, near Saffron Walden in Essex. Junction 9 of the M11 wasn't too far away which meant that he could easily go to visit the friends that he had left behind, but somehow he knew deep inside that that was probably not going to happen. Good intentions and all that, and when would he make the time anyhow? It was time, he felt, to change his focus and to adjust to the slower pace of village life. He had got used to the quiet evenings and had spent more of his time reading novels. He rarely drove very far these days so there would be lots of opportunity to walk and take in the scenery when the weather improved a little.

He was looking forward to the spring.

His home for the last five months was the rather weary-looking and slightly damp and discouraging vicarage, which was known as Deanbury House and was the only reference that remained of the Deanbury family that owned most of the properties in the village a long, long time ago. The Church offered it to him as his residence for the foreseeable future. It had been acquired around the same period as when the church was built. It had plenty of space as the rooms were quite generous and the attic was particularly huge. When he moved in during a particularly hot spell the previous August, he hadn't bargained for the challenge of the bleak January days that the people of this area were used to and that were upon him now. Martin gave the front door a hefty shove as it had developed a knack of sticking in the frame, which he blamed upon the winter rains. With his head down to defy the wind and rain, Martin trudged up the gentle incline towards St Dom's. Icy needles of rain hit his face and made him grimace. His cloak blew in the wind, endeavouring to make its way home again without him. The gentle incline may not have been too steep but it was always a welcome stroll down again at the end of another day's work for The Lord. This morning Martin had an appointment to keep with a gentleman who had said something about making a contribution to him, and although it was a very bad line, Martin had managed to agree a time to meet him at the church. As it was always quiet on a Wednesday morning, especially a very wet and windy one, and as he was doing nothing better for an hour or so, he decided he could make good use of the time. After all, a contribution to the church could not be turned down, especially at these times and with so much to maintain against the elements. Martin was completely windswept when he completed his short but nonetheless challenging walk to St Dom's. On days like these he felt his years. He was fast approaching 60 years old and had always dreamt of having just enough money and enough time to enjoy it when he finally retired. He so looked forward to spending time with those close to him and catching up with old friends.

As Martin opened the front door that had over many years welcomed thousands of people into the house of God, he clutched at the modest crucifix he wore on the outside of his cloak. St Dom's had a short passage that led you into the main part of the church, which opened up to allow a view of the rather impressive roof structure. Old wooden beams dominated and gave a definitive message that said St Dom's is here to stay, no matter what. The stained glass windows let in a charming reflection of green, purple and blue which filled the whole church with calmness even on days like this. Martin made his way towards the rear of the altar where a small but serviceable kitchen area was situated. He was a big fan of good, honest, strong tea and there was never a wrong time for a cup of tea in Martin's book.

It was 9.40 a.m.

The kettle boiled away merrily as Martin shuffled some prayer books around that had been left on a table in the kitchen area instead of being placed onto a shelf as he had asked the previous evening. Mrs Calderwood had helped at the church for thirty years and was a little forgetful at times but Martin didn't mind, he was glad of any help at all. The tea cups and an old teapot were set out on the table in readiness for his usual daily cup of tea with Mrs Calderwood around lunchtime.

He heard a noise that came from the main part of the church and assumed his visitor had arrived on time. Punctuality was a good habit, as far as Martin was concerned.

'I'm in the back, won't be a mo. Come through if you wish, I'm just getting us some tea,' he said.

Martin decided that he should really welcome the gentleman properly; the tea was fine looking after itself. He ventured out of the kitchen and saw a man whose waxy trench coat was just as wet and dripping as Martin's cloak had been.

'I'm sorry, I was in the back. Glad you found us OK, pity about the weather though, thoroughly dreadful.'

'The Visitor' turned. A distant, unwelcome memory gatecrashed into Martin's head and his inviting smile instantly turned pale. His mouth dry. Another look and his refusal to accept this horror became short-lived. Martin iced over.

'Hello, Martin.'

This was a terrible nightmare, and one that had been in the back of Martin's mind for many years but was never going to happen.

'You don't look very pleased to see me, hardly the way to welcome an old friend. Tell me, Martin, did you really think I wouldn't find you? Did you really think that leaving London would save you?'

Martin stood frozen to the spot. He opened his mouth to speak but there was nothing. This day was never supposed to come, never supposed to fill him with terror, never supposed to be the end of his life. But he knew it was. The Visitor slowly withdrew a pistol from his thoroughly sodden raincoat and with a clinical calmness, fitted the silencer onto the barrel that held Martin's destiny. Martin stood transfixed with his focus firmly on the weapon that was pointing his way. No words were necessary. Martin began to cry and prayed that it would all be over very quickly.

'Please …' uttered Martin.

'You are pathetic, Martin, always were. Do you know that?'

The Visitor stooped over Martin, who was on his knees looking up at the face he dreaded seeing. The weapon was all Martin could see as he began to shake with fear. Tears ran down his cheeks.

'I'm bored now and it's finally payback time,' said the Visitor as he aimed straight and true at Martin's chest.

In an instant the force from the first bullet threw Martin back against the kitchen door and it was very much over. Martin's lifeless body thudded heavily to the floor. Another bullet eliminated any possibility of a mistake. The Visitor had done what he came to do and looked for a minute at his work. Blood oozed onto the floor from the gaping wounds in Martin's chest. His eyes were staring straight up at his murderer, who casually turned away, satisfied, and left to brave the rain and get another potential soaking.

Chapter Two

I left the M11 at Junction 9 and followed the signs for Saffron Walden. When I turned right onto the B184 the rain finally stopped. My trusty new steed swallowed up the road with ease. I had just picked up a new car from Essex Police HQ at Chelmsford and driven straight up to meet Bob Hand, who was a detective constable the last time our paths crossed. That, however, was eight years ago when we both worked at Walthamstow nick in East London. Nowadays, I am reliably informed he is a detective sergeant and a much respected one at that, having done his time on the Serious Crime Squad for many years. Bob was meticulous in his work and very little passed him by unnoticed. We had got on very well back then and yet I hadn't seen much of him since he moved into the Essex force and I stayed put in the borough and worked from the Chingford station a few miles away. I enjoyed the life at Walthamstow and it suited me to hang around for a few more years before I too ventured out to Essex, which was part of a promotion package when I became a detective inspector at Chelmsford.

Now, when I say I was driving out to meet Bob Hand it isn't strictly true. Yes, I hoped to meet him but that wasn't really the purpose of the journey, albeit an incentive. I was cooing over my new Ford Mondeo when I overheard a couple of the lads in the yard talking about a rather nasty-sounding murder which had taken place in a church. I interrupted them and got some more details, even though they weren't exactly clear on the facts. It did sound 'juicy' and I just thought I would have a peep. I went upstairs to my office to grab my coat as it was still teeming at that time, and bumped into one of the detective sergeants.

'Terry, if anyone is interested will yer let 'em know I'm nipping out to take a look at this murder near Saffron Walden … and, Terry … who is on this job?'

Terry Brush was a good worker and I took to him in an instant. He would often keep the nosy so-and-sos out of my hair if I wanted to scoot out for any reason. I couldn't stand being glued to my desk any more than was necessary.

'Yes, guv ... one of your old mates from your days in "the smoke" ... Bob Hand.'

The combination of me being inquisitive and a chance to see old Bob again was too much to resist. Bob had started his career over in West London at Hendon before coming to work at Walthamstow via Tottenham and Hornsey.

I was off.

It was also an opportunity to give the new car a run up the M11 and see how it went. So I left Chelmsford and headed down the A414 towards Junction 7 and looked forward to blowing the cobwebs away. I parked my new toy adjacent to the sign that read 'Laurel's End Welcomes Careful Drivers' and decided to wander along towards the church, keeping the car away from prying eyes. I was still relatively new to the force and thought I'd take advantage of turning up unannounced without my nice shiny toy advertising that the DI had arrived. I like to get a true reflection of what is going on at a job and quietly walking up to the church would allow me to see which cars were here and maybe give me an impression of whether someone on scene had sealed the doorway into the church, or whether they were going to leave it wide open for any 'Tom, Dick and Harry' to go ambling in and potentially destroy valuable evidence. It was all quiet as I walked up the leafy path towards the church entrance, and as I got to within ten yards of the doorway a constable poked his nose out and saw me coming, not that he had any idea who I was. I had put my raincoat on that I had grabbed as I hurried away from the office when I left Chelmsford and although I had my shirt on underneath it he couldn't really identify whether I was on the force or just some local chap having a look in to see what was going on.

'You can't come in I'm afraid, sir,' he said with all the authority of a bowl of cold soup.

'What are you afraid of?' I said, picking him up on what he had literally suggested.

He wasn't quite sure what to say so I put him out of his misery. I didn't like to take advantage of him, he'd only hate me in the future and I don't need to make enemies of anyone.

'Pardon me, Constable,' I said, pulling my coat aside to reveal my name badge.

'DI Dave Calloway,' he read, '… sorry, sir.'

'No need for apologies, you stopped me coming in and that was the right thing to do, so well done, and remember, if anyone tries to step across this doorway, and it doesn't matter who they are or what rank they hold, you tell them they can't go in unless you tell me first, OK?'

He looked a little shell-shocked but he smiled and that was all I wanted to see. He'll feel proud that he did the right thing and that the DI has praised him. Simple. Why some officers find it satisfying to deploy the 'one-upmanship' tactics I don't know, but it's not my way, albeit I did put him on the back foot initially.

As I slowly entered the vestibule and made my way towards a group of officers that had gathered at the far end of the church, I looked around and had to appreciate the solitude. These places always give me a sense of calm and peacefulness but then I suppose that's how it works. Everywhere smelt fresh and clean. I stopped when I saw the stain of blood on the door ahead of me. Blood was smeared on the floor too and I tried to imagine the body of the unfortunate vicar slumped amongst it all.

I took a moment to allow the scene to sink in.

The body had already been removed, which I could see later if I thought it would make any difference. The importance of preserving the evidence at a scene such as this has always been drummed into every attending officer and yet nothing was cordoned off, and it appeared that people may have been wandering around here before my arrival, but I had also learnt that unless I have all the information I shouldn't go jumping to conclusions. It wasn't really my job and I didn't want to upset the guy in charge. Talking of which, where was the old bastard?

Right on cue, Bob Hand appeared at the doorway to the back room. I only needed one look and even after all these years he was unmistakable and so, it would appear, was I.

'Bloody hell, Dave Calloway. I don't Adam and Eve it.'

'Hi, Bob, it's been eight years, you know. Eight years.'

He immediately offered his hand and shook mine until I thought it was about to come unhinged. It was a strange moment and one that was very welcome as Bob and I had always got on very well back in our Walthamstow days. Bob was dressed in a smart navy-blue suit with a white shirt and a grey and blue striped tie. No rank markings but no-one really needed to see any because when Bob was around people just knew who was in charge; he had that sort of persona. Often, it isn't apparent who is in charge of a job unless there are clear rank markings on show. In Bob's case, there was an air of authority that is fast dying out these days.

'... and look at you, a bloody DI,' he continued.

'Yeah, well someone's got to do it, Bob. What's gone on here apart from the obvious claret paintwork?'

Bob turned towards the bloodstained doorway and wall. He took a few steps then stopped and turned back towards me.

'Some bastard did the vicar this morning. No idea as yet what it's all about. The ol' girl over the road came in and found him slumped in a big crumpled heap ... dead ... couple of bullets in his chest. She's at home being looked after by a couple of lady cops, if you'll pardon the expression.'

I did, but only because it was Bob and I didn't want to start putting him in his place in these circumstances ... didn't want him to think I'd changed that much, when I guess I probably had.

'Who was he, Bob?' I asked.

'Revd Martin Alan Brookes.'

'Do we have an accurate time of death?' I asked.

'They're saying around 10 o'clock which means he was quite fresh when she found him.' Bob gave me a quizzical look and said, 'Anyhow, are you here to take over or what?'

'No, no, just here because I heard that you were and I thought it sounded interesting ... you know me, inquisitive.'

'Nosy git, more like it.'

It was nice to see that Bob Hand had not altered one bit. There would be time for catching up later but for now there was an investigation to get to grips with ... it just wasn't officially mine, although that has never stopped me before.

'Look, Bob, I know this is your job but ...'

'Of course I don't mind, mate,' he said, interrupting me.

Doreen Calderwood sat whimpering and dabbing her tears in the front room of her house which was just a stone's throw from St Dominic's. A paramedic had been with her for the last hour and had managed to calm her with some oxygen and lots of 'TLC'. The police officers had been making her some tea and generally giving as much support as possible. Not much else could be done. It was a dreadful shock for poor old Doreen, who was 82 years old according to the casualty assessment form that the paramedic had been filling in that I'd spotted perched on the arm of the sofa nearby. Doreen's house was what I considered typical of an elderly lady that had lived in the same spot for fifty years. Old photos and pictures adorned the walls, mostly of family members I assumed. The shelves and window sills were busy with knick-knacks and vases with old flowers that probably needed throwing out but had not been.

As Doreen had discovered the body so soon after the killing had taken place, it was imperative to get whatever information we could from her, but I also knew that we must respect her age and the fact that the shock had still not worn off completely. I asked the paramedic whether he thought that Doreen would be able to have a short chat with me and I got what I deserved from the lady herself.

'I'm still here you know. I'm not in the ground yet.'

I realised that if I had wanted permission to talk to Doreen I should have asked her and not talked around her.

'Mrs Calderwood, I am sorry. You are quite right. My name is Dave Calloway and I'm here to investigate the ... er ... situation at the church. I'm sorry to have to ask you so soon but it is terribly important that I talk to you as soon as possible. I understand that you found the vicar this morning.'

'Yes, dear, but the church is over the road.'

'Of course, Mrs Calderwood, but I would like to speak with you, just for a moment.'

All I managed to do was to prompt another flood of tears, which duly streamed down Doreen's cheeks and I did feel for her.

'Poor Martin,' was all she could manage before slumping back into her chair and letting out a big sigh, 'he was always so lovely to me.'

I pressed on.

'Mrs Calderwood, can you tell me whether everything looked normal when you walked across to the church this morning?'

'I think so ... what do you mean?'

'I mean did you happen to see anyone in the church grounds or nearby that caught your attention?'

'No dear, it was all pretty quiet as usual. It's always pretty quiet on a Wednesday morning and most other mornings for that matter, unless there's a market or some other thing going on.'

'Mrs Calderwood, when you first entered the church, what did you see straight away?' I asked.

'Well …' Doreen took a big, deep breath, '… I saw Martin on the floor. I asked him what he was doing down there and then I saw all the blood everywhere, all over my nice clean floor.'

Doreen seemed equally disturbed that the floor was a mess. But then after devoting so much time to looking after things at the church over the last thirty years, I suppose she was very proud of the cleanliness.

'So, I cleaned up as much as I could.'

I thought I was going to drop dead myself.

No, no, Doreen.

The two PCs and the paramedic both stared at me as I in turn stared at them. There was a deafening silence as the enormity of what Doreen had done sank in with an enormous thud.

Oh my goodness, what had she wiped away?

What sort of crucial evidence had gone into Doreen's mop bucket?

'Erm … Mrs Calderwood, what exactly did you clean?'

'All those mucky footprints, of course. I might have slipped over on them,' she said as innocently as anyone could imagine.

Doreen Calderwood did not have a clue what she may have done.

No wonder the bloody church smelt so fresh.

Oh, bloody hell, Doreen.

* * *

The first thing I did when I got back into the church was to look at the blood on the door and wall where it had dried as it had on the floor, what was left of it. I found Bob sitting in one of the rows of pews looking at his mobile. He turned to me as I approached and slipped it into his trouser pocket. I must have been displaying a look that said 'you won't believe it but guess what she did'.

'What's up? How did you get on over the road?'

I told Bob the story. Basically, she had little to offer except for the bombshell. Bob put his head in his hands and mumbled something indeterminate. Whilst I was with Doreen, Bob had been talking to a few of the locals that had amassed at the end of the path, all straining their necks for a look inside. No-one had seen or heard anything that morning. They had not seen Martin go into the church, much less his assailant. It was, as Doreen put it, a quiet Wednesday morning. Bob and I sat for a moment and recapped what we had to go on. Or what we didn't have, more like it. No witness, no known motive, no assailant as yet, no-one heard a sound, no break-in. I assumed that it would be usual for the church to have its doors open at that time … or would it? I hurried back over to see Doreen again. When I got to her house the paramedic was just leaving. He jumped up into the front of the ambulance and waved to me as he slowly drove away. Doreen was at the front window and saw me approaching down the path before I saw her. I knocked. One of the PCs opened up and let me in.

'How has she been?' I whispered for fear of getting another reminder from Doreen that she wasn't dead yet.

'Much better, sir, and I was wondering how long we should stay. I've asked a neighbour to come and sit with her for a while, so if it's OK …'

'Yes, yes. Thank you for your help. Providing you've got all the details you need then get yourself away. I just need to have a quick word.'

As I walked down the passageway, Doreen appeared from the front room.

'Mrs Calderwood, I'm sorry to bother you again but there's something I'd like to ask,' I said softly.

'Ask away … and don't take all night. I need to get the fire lit, it's going to be cold again, you know.' The priorities of Doreen Calderwood were a world apart from mine and I suppose they should be too.

'Mrs Calderwood, is it usual for the church doors to be unlocked at that time of the morning?' I enquired.

'Oh yes, dear, always, although not usually on a Wednesday. Martin would always be doing some jobs in the vicarage until lunchtime when we'd meet at the church for a nice cup of tea.'

Poor Doreen sobbed and I felt awful again, but what could I do. Right on time her neighbour pushed the front door ajar.

'Only me, Dor.'

So, not on a Wednesday. So the question was, what was Martin doing in the church so early? He may have genuinely had things to do but they could surely wait until after his routine visit with Doreen.

Was he expecting someone?

What brought Martin Brookes to church that morning? I wondered as I walked across to the church again. I nodded to the constable at the doorway and it was nice to see him smile with a respectful acknowledgement. I walked in and saw before me a rather different scene. The Scene of Crimes Officers (SOCOs) were gone and so too were the team that painstakingly collected fingerprints from almost everything, or so it seemed. Photographs were still being taken of where poor Revd Brookes had been discovered earlier and it appeared that a number of people were making themselves very busy, so I decided that I should leave and have a re-think back at the office, where I could write some notes and contemplate what to do next. I looked around for Bob and didn't see him. I was going to check in the kitchen to see whether he was hiding in there but with the all the activity going on around that area I decided it would be better if I kept out of the way, so I began to take a stroll back towards my car. As I ambled away I turned to look across to Doreen's house, and strangely enough there she was, just seeing her neighbour out and waving as she went back indoors. A tough old stick like Doreen will be alright, I told myself. Back in the car, I felt a sense of excitement again at looking forward to enjoying another luxurious ride back to Chelmsford. As I drove away and began to join the M11 to head south, I wondered what on earth had really gone on at the church. Why would anyone want to murder a vicar and in such a clinical fashion? It just had to be premeditated.

As I journeyed south I found that my mind kept on conjuring up the gruesome picture of the heavily bloodstained door inside the church. I had seen numerous murder scenes during my career and many of them were far worse than this one, and I decided that it could only be that this particular crime had involved a vicar in a church. That, itself, was unusual and the combination of that and the fact that there seemed to be nothing much to go on, made me more determined to try to get to the bottom of it. I pictured poor old Doreen and wondered what she would do with herself now that she had lost a friend. It was always much more than just the shock of what she had witnessed, it was the fact that her routine had been fractured and those cosy cups of tea with Martin would never be enjoyed again. I liked Doreen and pledged to myself that I would visit her whenever I was in that neck of the woods. I would be back to see her soon anyhow; after all, who knew more about the church than she did?

Doreen Calderwood might just prove to be very useful.

* * *

I was approaching Junction 7, which was my turn off to Chelmsford, when my mobile phone blasted out some awful noise at full volume that scared me half to death. I knew it was not my usual ring tone and quickly realised that someone had decided to take the opportunity of changing it whilst I had left it unguarded on my desk. I would probably never find out who played the prank but it didn't matter to me; as far as I was concerned this little trick just said 'welcome to Chelmsford'. With my heart doing about eighty miles per hour, I answered as calmly as I could in order to not give away the fact that I had been caught out, but then the prankster and any others that might be involved would know that I had been.

'DI Calloway,' I said, trying not to sound alarmed.

'Guv'nor, it's Terry.'

This immediately made me wonder whether he was at the bottom of the skullduggery. As I drove along the A414 ,Terry explained to me that Bob Hand had been asking to speak to me at the station. It occurred to me that he wouldn't have my new number, which had been changed in the last eight years. Apparently, he was keen to put our heads together regarding the murder details. I was too, and told Terry that I wouldn't be too long and to let Bob know I was on my way back. This phone call got my mind whirring again and I began to think hard about where to begin. What I knew was that somebody had carried out a cold-blooded killing and that Martin Brookes was dead. I hoped that the SOCO and the fingerprint team could give me more to go on, because right now my investigation was as cold as Martin Brookes.

Chapter Three

He sat checking his latest emails and picking greedily at a bowl of mixed nuts. The TV in the other room was on but had been muted. The altering picture offered a flickering light that reflected into his room. Dinner was cooking in the oven and he was filled with a confident satisfaction that always made him feel unbeatable; he loved being one step ahead all the time. The Visitor had remained one step ahead for some time now, ever since he removed Daniel Grainger from his little list of problems. The police were miles away from ever catching him and he was adamant that they never would. Grainger had made a very similar mistake to dear old Martin and it had all been so unnecessary. He simply didn't tolerate dealing with untrustworthy people, which is what Martin, and Grainger before him, had become. Two years ago, Daniel Grainger left his house in North Weald Bassett, Essex, at 6 a.m. sharp to make the short journey to the golf club where he had the responsibility of ensuring that the cleaners were busying themselves prior to the arrival of the first of the club members, who would turn up at 6.30.

It was the occasion of the President's Cup and Daniel was on the list of players who would be teeing off a little later in the morning. He parked his car in his favourite spot outside the window to the members' lounge where he could view it whilst socialising with the other players. He was very car conscious and he always ensured that it was clean inside and out. His golf clubs and bag were in the boot and his cap and a thin jumper were on the back seat, which was covered with a soft blanket to protect the leather. Everything about Daniel's golf equipment suggested that he was very particular in his appearance and it all looked as though he had just bought it. He carried his golf shoes in one hand and pushed open the door, which led him into the rather plush reception area, and savoured the smell of the recently laid carpet. To the left was the trophy cabinet which housed the President's Cup and an assortment of other less valued awards.

'Maybe today,' he muttered quietly to himself.

The sound of the antique clock, which sat proudly over the doorway leading to the members' lounge and bar area, abruptly reminded Daniel that it was 6.15 and that it was time to hurry along. He made his way along the corridor and could hear the sound of vacuuming, which seemed to be coming from the bar ahead of him. He pushed open the double doors and was met by the bustle of determined activity.

The guy in charge of the cleaning crew was Roberto. He had left his beloved Italy ten years ago and followed his dream to travel across Europe and see all the beauty spots he had only, previously, read about in books. He had simply fallen in love with England and the countryside and decided to make it his home, although ensuring he made regular trips to see his family back in Naples. He and his trusted team had been nurturing the members' lounge, corridors, changing rooms and toilets of the club for the past five years.

Roberto ensured that everywhere was shining like a new pin each morning, especially on the occasion of the President's Cup. Daniel and Roberto exchanged pleasantries and once Daniel was happy to see that everything was in hand, he left the bar area and wandered outside into the sunshine that had just began to break through. It looked as though a dry and wind-free day was ahead of them. Slipping on his golf shoes he stood and looked across the practice green and towards the first tee, imagining himself driving a ball as straight as a die onto the centre of the fairway. As Daniel turned back towards the clubhouse, someone inside the members' lounge was waving frantically at him through the window. He could see it was Roberto but couldn't make out a word he was saying. Daniel stepped back inside the building and was met by Roberto as he opened the door to the lounge.

'What on earth are you flapping about, Roberto?' asked Daniel.

'Look, look ...' said Roberto, pointing towards the fairway beyond the first tee, '... smoke.'

Daniel turned in horror to see the wispy smoke drifting across the fairway. It didn't look too bad to him and his heart steadied a little but the President would be arriving at any minute and Daniel had promised to have everything organised. His first thought was that it was a bonfire in a nearby garden. He simply couldn't afford for this to cause any sort of delay to the proceedings and take the risk that the President might blame him for not having everything under control. He knew he would have to go and see what was causing this and whatever it was, it would have to be sorted out straight away. Daniel briskly walked up the fairway from the first tee and before long he could see where the smoke was emitting from.

At the back of the green on the first hole was a large shed that was used to store a couple of mowers, some bunker rakes, a box of spare flags and tee markers and a few cans of petrol for the mowers. Daniel worried that the whole thing might go bang as he approached and gingerly peeped into the shed. It was difficult to see exactly where the smoke was coming from but it was definitely towards the rear of the shed. With the door wide open, the smoke dissipated quite quickly and his vision improved. At the rear of the shed was one of the old mowers that was clearly giving off some fumes. Daniel wandered carefully over to it and realised that the smoke was coming from a few old rags that were lying on the engine of one of the mowers. He bent down to pick up a spare flag pole to knock them off with and as he did, he felt an intense, sickening blow to his face. His knees buckled and he crumpled face first onto the burning material. He barely had time to make a sound as a second blow struck.

It was more like a kick.

Blood poured over Daniel's face and he felt terribly afraid. Something cold splashed across his face and stung his eyes. Whatever it was had a strong, pungent smell and the small amount that had entered his mouth made him retch violently. A heavy kick to his stomach made him expel any breath that was in his lungs as more of this vile-tasting liquid began to soak his clothes and splash once again over his face and into his mouth. Daniel struggled to breathe as he retched and curled up in agony from the acute pain in his abdomen. A solid object struck his back and shoulders very hard as if it had been delivered from a great height. He heard his bones creak. He gasped for breath and managed to catch sight of someone leaning over him as he tried to prepare himself for another attack. When he didn't feel another blow he looked up with stinging eyes at his attacker. He knew the face and the last thing Daniel had any recognition of was the tiny glow of something that resembled a shooting star as it landed near his head towards the rear of the shed.

* * *

The Visitor reflected on his success. Daniel Grainger had really upset him and as he reviewed the gory scene of Grainger's body ablaze and recalled how he had swiftly and stealthily slid away around the back of the shed and into the trees that formed a part of the boundary of the course, he closed his eyes. He allowed his twisted mind to picture his latest revenge and he could clearly see the body of Martin Brookes lying pathetically against the kitchen door at the rear of the church. Blood had dripped down the door and puddled where he sat, creating a pool of the red, sticky mess.

'Bloody Daniel Grainger … that pathetic Martin Brookes … and just two more to go … when I'm good and ready,' he said to himself, pulling himself up from his chair and ambling tiredly into the kitchen to check on his dinner.

Chapter Four

Bob Hand and I had gathered for a meeting with Detective Chief Inspector Nicholas Corrigan at his request. He always referred to himself as Nicholas, never Nick or any other variation of address. No nicknames. I always had found him to be quite stuffy on the few occasions that I had crossed paths with him. Bob and I stood side by side in the lift and as I selected the 3rd floor Bob broke the silence.

'Wonder what old St Nick will have to say for himself?'

'The usual, I suspect. He'll want to know how much progress has been made on the Martin Brookes case. That will be the moment when we tell him that we haven't actually made any,' I replied.

Bob turned sharply towards me, agog.

'You are joking, I hope. Tell me you're joking. There's not a chance we're saying any such thing. I am not giving that stuck-up ponce any opportunity to start giving me grief over this case. I don't want him thinking that we're dragging our heels, otherwise he'll be sticking his nose in all over the place and that is the last thing I need.'

Bob had a red glow to his cheeks that wasn't there a few seconds ago. I could tell he meant every word. When he gets ruffled, he gets ruffled pretty quick.

'So, what are you going to suggest then? We can't lie to him.'

'You watch me.'

'Ah, come on, Bob, he's gonna know,' I said.

'He's gonna know nothing and don't forget it. Listen, we'll get the bloke who sorted Martin Brookes soon enough and he doesn't need to know everything about it. Just follow my lead,' Bob insisted with the air of authority that usually got him listened to or into deeper trouble.

When the lift doors opened we both almost walked head on into Nicholas Corrigan. He happened to be passing the lift just as we came wandering out.

'Ah, gentlemen. I won't be a moment, please go straight on in and make yourselves comfortable. I won't keep you waiting too long.'

'He's far too happy,' said Bob with a sneer and probably a little too loudly. I looked towards the DCI and it appeared that Bob had got away with it. That would not necessarily have been the best start to the meeting. Corrigan's office was one of the largest on this floor and had the benefit of a huge window which overlooked the Essex countryside. I immediately noticed a comprehensive collection of books which on closer inspection were actually autobiographies by different chief constables from around the country. Sad git, I thought. His impressive collection also included encyclopedias and a number of volumes about the railways of Eastern Europe. I turned to Bob.

'Have you seen these?' I said.

I could hardly believe what he was up to. All I could see of Bob was the top of his head as he bent over and appeared to be digging deep into Corrigan's desk drawer.

'What the bloody hell are you doing, he'll be back in a minute.'

'Guard the door then,' he said, as if it was the simplest of tasks.

A shudder of terror ran through me as I expected Corrigan to appear at any moment and explode into several pieces at the sight of Bob raiding his desk.

'What are you looking for, anyway?' I enquired nervously.

'I wanna know what he's got on the Martin Brookes killing. If I'm gonna bluff I wanna know what he knows first.'

Before Bob had the chance to find what he was looking for, I heard the DCI muttering outside in the corridor and told him to get the hell out of there. Bob shifted everything back into place and stepped around the desk as the door opened and DCI Nicholas Corrigan entered the room.

Corrigan was a tall bloke and stood at around 6 feet 4 inches. When he sat at his desk he looked as though he was taller than we were, and we were still standing.

'Sit, sit, sit,' he ordered.

As we sat down, I glanced at Bob as if to say 'that was close'. Bob was always one to take a risk and I recall getting a sweat on regularly back in our days at Walthamstow, watching him do something ridiculously risky. Still, that was Bob Hand for you.

'Now then, gentlemen, what can you tell me about your progress on the Brookes case?'

Here we go, I thought. Bob shifted in his chair and crossed his legs.

'What would you like to know, sir?' Bob asked, trying his best to buy time whilst he came up with a plausible answer or a believable lie. Corrigan stiffened and stared at Bob and said in a rather condescending tone, 'If it isn't too much trouble, I should very much like to know just who put a big hole in his chest. Are you able to assist me with that, Detective Sergeant?'

'Of course, sir,' Bob answered. Of course not, I thought. This will be interesting. 'We have a couple of possible suspects that we are working on but it is early days, sir.'

I was all of a sudden a lot more uncomfortable than when Bob was riffling through Corrigan's desk and then it got worse.

'DI Calloway, can you elaborate for me?' said Corrigan.

Oh, cheers Bob, I thought.

It was time to think very quickly and to sound very convincing and then kill Bob Hand later.

'Er, well sir, we have a couple of ideas that we are currently working on and hopefully we'll have something a bit more concrete soon,' I offered weakly, hoping he would be placated just enough to leave it there.

Corrigan stared and frowned slowly. I felt as though someone had just lit the blue touch paper and I was waiting for a rocket to rip straight through his collection of autobiographies and probably straight through me too.

'You haven't got a fucking thing, have you?' Corrigan said with a tone that said we were rumbled and about to receive a huge bollocking from a very agitated detective chief inspector. Bob looked at me and I looked back, both as guilty as each other although none of this was my idea. Corrigan's bollocking took a very different form to the one I expected. There was no explosion, no bloodshed, and no fear of being reduced to tears.

He simply looked at us both alternately and quietly said, 'If, by the time I review this case in a couple of weeks, you can offer me nothing more than a pathetic response such as the one you gave today, I shall have to think long and hard about which direction your careers are heading and which department might benefit from the level of competence that you are displaying. Do I make myself clear, gentlemen?'

We left Corrigan's office with our tails between our legs and made our way down the stairs to the canteen for a calming cuppa. Nothing was said as we made our way down the three flights. Then I had to say something.

'That went well then,' I joked sheepishly.

'Yeah, OK. Tell you one thing though, he hasn't got a clue about the Brookes case either,' said Mr Cool.

Bob was right about that but it didn't actually do us much of a favour. The problem now was that Corrigan would be watching to see how we got along and if the way the investigation had gone so far was anything to go by it wasn't going to be pleasant. We sat down in the deserted canteen and had a chuckle at the sight of Bob delving into Corrigan's desk.

'Did you find anything after all that?' I asked.

'No, but that's not a bad thing. Like I said he hasn't got any more idea than us right now, not that it's his place to, I suppose,' said Bob with a grin.

'Maybe it's time we pulled our fingers out and got some ideas. I'll go back to the church in the morning and have another dig around. There has to be something,' I said.

'Wasting your time, I reckon. Whoever did this knew what he was doing. No witnesses, no weapon, no nothing,' said Bob.

'Just a body on the floor and an over-enthusiastic lady on the end of a mop,' I said with some resignation.

Diamonds

The flat was in East Ham, not far from the tube station and close to Plashet Park. It was situated on the ground floor with the front door conveniently to the side of the block, out of sight from the main drag. The masks had done their homework well and they knew where to come. It was just a matter of collecting the jewels that were attached to Bernie's arm first. It was always a consideration to kill them both, remove them from the streets forever, but it didn't quite work out that way. Two of the masks jemmied the door to the flat and bundled their way into the hallway. They stopped dead in their tracks. They could hear voices coming from the living room and could see there was a light on too. Maybe Oscar had made it back.

Whoever was in there was about to get a big shock.

Slowly and as silently as possible, the door was edged open. They listened and the voices remained constant, nothing changed. Armed with the iron bars that had been so successfully put to work earlier on Bernie, they barged the door wide open and stormed in like something from an SAS movie. They had made enough of a commotion that anyone present would have shit themselves on the spot. No-one was in sight so they split between the bedroom and the kitchen and again it was all quiet. One of them headed to the bathroom and burst in wielding his iron bar but it was empty. They both realised that Bernie and Oscar had left the TV on and that was what they had heard. A size 10 boot put the TV on its back and they got on with checking the airing cupboard. One of the masks opened the door and found himself juggling toilet rolls as they fell onto him. He batted them out of his way and cursed. All he could see were towels, all bundled into the cupboard haphazardly. He grabbed at them anxiously and dragged them out and onto the floor around his feet until he could see just what he had come for. There in front of the masks were two black attaché cases. They pulled out one each and stood gawking at them for a few seconds in wonderment. They felt heavy and laden with lovely, sparkly stones. They wanted to open the cases and be able to stare at their swag but that wasn't in their brief.

'Get in there, find the stuff and get the fuck out,' were the clear and precise orders.

'Not surprised this place is a shit-hole are you? Pair of wankers. They've left the back door open as well, look. Not very security conscious of 'em is it? C'mon.'

As they carried the cases out towards the front door a noise from around the side of the block startled them. Kids. It had been a long night already and the last thing they needed was to be seen coming out of the flat. They could safely assume that most people who lived around the area knew precisely who lived here. Another bloody delay and they could bet their lives on it that the blokes waiting in the van were asking themselves what was taking so bloody long. After a few minutes the kids started to disperse and it fell quiet again.

'Right, let's get the fuck out.'

Back in the van, the tension built as the remainder of the gang wondered just how long they would be. One of them was talking about going into the flat to hurry them up a bit but that suggestion was squashed.

'C'mon, c'mon … Here they come,' said the van driver as he spotted the shapes in the gloom approaching the van at last. He started it up and was keen to get away from this place. They had been here too long and just being seen here would very likely tie them in nicely to the murder; singular unfortunately. The masks got on board in the back and showed the others the cases as the van crept away unnoticed from the garages and onto High Street North, past the tube station and down to Barking Road. From there they turned right and made their way through the murky darkness towards Poplar. Back to more familiar ground.

Oscar would have to wait until another day.

Chapter Five

As the morning sunlight glinted through the tiny gap in her curtains, Kim Fisher could make out shapes and even recognised some of them as the cloudiness of sleep faded and she opened her eyes and began to endure another day. A day that usually began by waking around 8 a.m. and looking to see whether her mother, Debbie, was there waiting to give her a big cuddle and whisper softly to her. Kim loved her mother very much and she was always the first person Kim wanted to see when she awoke. Debbie Fisher was a saint, at least that's what her friends and neighbours would say of her. She walked into Kim's room as soon as she heard her stir and spoke softly.

'Hey, Kim. Hey, beautiful girl.'

Debbie had one of those very kind faces, the sort that belonged on an angel. In many respects she had become an angel to some degree but took this all in her stride. Debbie helped Kim dress into her favourite 'Boyzone' sweatshirt and a pair of warm tracksuit bottoms. Kim could walk but had some difficulty with her balance, so managing the stairs alone wasn't always possible.

It hadn't been entirely possible for many years.

The stairs were quite steep and turned at right angles about halfway down. Debbie supported Kim downstairs and helped her into the kitchen for her breakfast. She would sit opposite Kim at the breakfast bar and watch her eat; only helping when she had to but trying mostly to allow Kim to manage as much as she could on her own. Eating at any time of the day was often an uphill struggle but nobody could say that she didn't try. She didn't get dressed into anything else very often. It would depend on whether she was going out or not. Going out invariably meant another visit to the hospital or maybe the doctor's. Just occasionally a schoolfriend from years ago would pop in to see how she was, or maybe a neighbour, but all too often they would end up watching the TV and talking with Debbie because communication with Kim could be rather a challenge some days if you weren't used to being ultra-patient and concentrating on what Kim was trying to say.

It wasn't always that way, Kim had some really good days but the excitement of seeing someone she knew and loved would cause her to try to speak too fast and consequently the words became a little jumbled. Pictures of Kim were all around the living room. Pictures of a beautiful, fun-loving young lady. There were pictures of Kim on the beach in Minorca when she had gone abroad with a friend's parents and without her mum or dad. The one above the fireplace was of her and her old faithful dog. Bentley was a Briard who had lived a long and full life. Kim did a project for college about him and explained all about the French history of the breed. She had adored him. Another was taken at her best friend's 18th birthday celebration at the local church hall. These were all memories of another life, a much kinder life, one that seemed an age away.

The emotional and behavioural effects that had altered Kim's life as a consequence of her injuries had also weighed heavily on Debbie Fisher. She had aged a little quicker than she ever intended and although Debbie was, unarguably, a very attractive woman, one look in the mirror or even a passing glance would remind her that her best days had been cruelly left behind. She remembered the long days and nights in the neurology unit as she watched over Kim and wept many prayers, silently, almost pitifully.

The consultant would tell her that Kim 'will be back with us soon'. A part of Debbie was terrified, but she had an incredibly strong resolve and she hoped that Kim did too. She talked to her daughter almost non-stop apart from when the doctors needed to prod and poke around. Debbie forced herself to take a break and get herself a coffee and every time that she did, she felt that she was deserting Kim and hurried back to her bedside, peering to see whether the doctors had finished with her.

Leaving the hospital and saying goodnight to Kim would break her heart. It was always a tearful journey home and she absolutely detested the silence that awaited her when she walked into the house. Home wasn't home without Kim but after a very gradual recovery, with the improvements taking tiny steps towards some semblance of hope, Kim finally made it home. The consultant had spoken to Debbie about something he called Post-Traumatic Amnesia and explained the difficulties associated with how Kim may behave from time to time. He said that people that have suffered a coma such as Kim did could not be held responsible for their behaviour during the period following such a traumatic experience. It was perhaps a blessing in many ways that Kim was mostly unaware of what was happening around her, at least in the early days, and this alone helped Debbie to cope a little better as the thought of Kim being fully aware of her plight was too awful to contemplate. The warnings of what to expect frightened Debbie to the extreme and kept her awake at night, listening in the silence of the night for any sound that may come from Kim's room. She was told that Kim may become very agitated and emotional, have difficulty with her speech and become explosively angry without warning, and that Debbie should never forget about her own welfare and that she could call the support group any time she needed them. Debbie felt as though she needed them every hour of the day but she also knew that Kim needed her more.

Her world revolved around Kim.

One person visited her every weekend and sometimes during the week too. He hadn't missed a visit in many years and was very close to Kim, even before the incident that so cruelly changed her whole life. He would read to her and show her photographs of when she was younger to help her with her memory loss. Kim's speech had been all but lost during the initial few months following her injuries. Injuries that almost claimed her entire life. Nowadays, she would speak slowly and usually quite clearly unless she was traumatised or frightened for any reason. When Kim was experiencing those types of emotions she would revert to a stutter and became difficult to understand. The stutter led to frustration and the whole thing got out of hand to the point where Kim had to be held gently and spoken to very softly in order to calm her and enable her to regain control once again. She would sleep for long periods on days when she wasn't being stimulated by a trip out or by a visitor or some other activity going on in the house. One thing that was certain was that Kim was loved by many people: aunts, uncles, cousins, neighbours and friends. But for them to be able to maintain the level of attention that Kim required was too much to be expected. When Debbie wasn't being a mum and a housewife or a nurse and a godsend, she would take the time to sit and read but always ended up nestled with Kim for a cuddle on the sofa and said anything she could to bring a smile to Kim's face. That was always a reward in itself.

The shock of what happened ripped through her family like a hurricane and the pressure within the house was, at times, almost intolerable. Her coma lasted for a whole month and not many people thought that she would ever recover and be a part of the family again. It was very difficult not to give up hope during the darkest moments and, apart from Debbie, one man never gave up, not for a second. Kim's uncle was the closest thing she had to a father since her real father kissed her forehead before he left the house for work five years ago and never came back.

'The truck driver couldn't have seen him ... he never stopped' was the explanation given. The only consolation was that Kim didn't fully understand but it wasn't much of a consolation in reality. No-one in the family ever forgave the truck driver.

Chapter Six

The weather that welcomed us back to St Dominic's was a far cry from the strong winds that blew us along the street and up the path to the doors of the church the last time we were here. We were still in the midst of a fairly cold winter but thankfully the sun was shining on us today. St Dominic's looked very different. The side of the church was glowing with the reflection of the low winter sun and the huge yews looked so much more majestic when they weren't stooping in defiance of the wind. The stained glass softened the harsh stone walls and I found myself slightly mesmerised by the beauty of the building as a whole. Bob clearly had no time for the finer points of the architecture of this magnificent building as he was already at the front door and was soon disappearing inside. I ambled up the path and enjoyed the remainder of my time outside in the warm sun, albeit short-lived. When I entered, after a fight with the door lock that seemed to have a handle that turned entirely the wrong way, I stood in the entrance to the main part of the church and once more found it hard to contemplate that someone had so clinically murdered a vicar, and inside the church too. I slowly walked towards the area of the church where Martin Brookes had been discovered by Doreen Calderwood. Bob was poking around in the kitchen and seemingly making himself busy, although I had no idea what we were expected to find here. Then behind me, I heard the front door to the church clunk shut. A large man approached and asked who we were. We showed him our ID and explained that we were following up our investigation into the murder of Martin Brookes. The man didn't seem moved or bothered by this and continued past us and into the kitchen area, where he opened a cupboard door and brought out a black cloak and an unmistakable black and white 'dog collar', or clerical collar, to give it it's proper name. It was then that the penny dropped and it became clear that our rather rotund friend was indeed the new vicar of St Dominic's.

'I don't feel right unless I'm dressed properly. My name's Paul Archer and I'm the replacement vicar here at St Dom's. Please call me Paul,' he said, rather proudly.

'I'm DI Dave Calloway and this is DS Bob Hand. Pleased to meet you,' I said politely.

He looked like a jolly sort of chap although I'm sure he would have nothing useful to add to our lacklustre investigation.

'Have you found it?' he asked, with a cheerful expression.

'That depends on what it is. Have you picked anything up?' Bob replied, a little sharply.

'No, no, I've been spending my time cleaning up after your people but haven't noticed anything that I wouldn't expect to find. What is it I should be looking for?' said the enthusiastic vicar.

'We don't actually have any particular object in mind, Paul, but if you do happen to come across anything that doesn't belong, you must call me,' I said handing him my card with my mobile number as well as the station number. He promised that he would and began to wander towards the kitchen area.

'Would you like me to put the kettle on?' he asked, but before I could answer Bob appeared at the kitchen door and butted in as usual.

'I'm going to talk to the old girl over the road and see if I can get any more out of her.'

Alarm bells immediately rang in my head.

I was concerned that Bob's approach would not work with Doreen and felt that I should go instead. Anyhow, I would like to see her again. It took a good few minutes for me to persuade Bob that it would be much better if I spoke with Doreen and eventually Bob reluctantly gave up the argument.

I squinted as I stepped out into the bright light that came as a bit a shock to my eyes, which had become entirely accustomed to the gentle, subdued lighting inside St Dom's. I stood for a moment and allowed my pupils to adjust themselves before venturing down the path, which was covered in damp leaves and grit lying in wait for an unsuspecting DI to skid and fall on. I looked across in the direction of Doreen's house and saw her looking straight back at me from her front-room window. I raised my hand and there was a distinct delay whilst Doreen gave a more definite stare in my direction before raising her hand and waving. I smiled and made my way across the road, quite looking forward to seeing her again. As I stepped across the road I had found myself thinking about visiting an old friend rather than conducting a police investigation. The front door opened as I reached for her gate and she seemed pleased to see me. I went inside and followed Doreen through to the back room, where she offered me a seat near to the fire that was burning merrily and providing some much-needed warmth. Before I could say a word, Doreen was off into the kitchen and very soon after, I could hear the kettle being filled for tea. As I sat and waited for her to return I looked around the room and once again studied her photographs and pictures that adorned the fireplace and the walls. Weddings, groups and some of children seemed to be the theme. Family stuff I supposed. Then I saw a photograph that made me go cold. Martin Brookes was staring back at me from the sideboard. He was dressed in civilian clothes and it looked as though he was holding a stick of some sort but it wasn't clear, so I got up to have a closer look just as Doreen walked in with a tray of tea, biscuits and cake.

'Here we are. Oh, it is nice to see you again. I did wonder if you'd turn up before you finished all the investigating. Have you got him?' asked Doreen innocently.

'No, I'm afraid it'll take a little while longer, but we are trying to do what we can,' I said, wondering exactly what we were achieving.

Doreen was busy cutting the cake, which looked like a Victoria sponge. I loved sponges like that and was looking forward to enjoying a piece. With my mind still choosing which piece I fancied, which of course was the biggest piece, I thought I should try to see what Doreen may have remembered from the morning she found Martin.

'Mrs Calderwood, I have to ask you a few questions. I hope you don't mind?'

'Do I have a choice, dear?' she replied.

'I really could do with asking you about a couple of things, if that's OK with you?' I said.

'Oh, of course, dear. I'm only kidding, fire away.'

'Thank you, Mrs Calderwood. Now then, firstly I have to go back to the morning when you found Martin.'

Doreen studied me closely but on this occasion there were no tears, just kindness in her eyes, which looked as though she really wanted to help. I was hopeful that I could refer to things without upsetting her this time. Although I knew I should tread carefully, nonetheless.

'Mrs Calderwood, how did you used to arrange that you would meet Martin at the church on Wednesdays?' I asked.

'He used to give me a call in the morning to confirm that I wasn't busy doing something else first and then we would decide whether we would have the time to meet for a cuppa. We usually did though,' she said.

'Did he call you on that morning too?' I asked.

'No, actually, I called him but I couldn't get through so I had to try again a bit later.'

'What time was it when you tried to call him?'

'Well, let me see. I took the ash out and put it in the dustbin. I'm always careful to make sure it has cooled down enough before I put it in the bin and then I sprinkle some water on it from the watering can that I keep by the shed. So, I came back in and washed up my breakfast things. Then I realised I had not heard from him so I rang him, but the line was engaged,' said Doreen graphically.

'And what time was that?' I asked patiently.

'It must have been just after quarter past nine 'cos I heard the clock in the front room chiming away. Anyway, dear, don't let your tea get cold. Would you like a biscuit or a nice piece of cake?'

Doreen didn't have to twist my arm at all as I gratefully accepted a piece of her Victoria sponge. Whilst I sat enjoying the sponge and watching Doreen pouring the tea, I tried to put together the little snippets of information I had relating to the murder of poor old Martin. So, if Doreen called at about 9:15 and found his phone line to be engaged, then I can fairly safely assume he was on the phone. Or it was off the hook. One scenario places Martin at his house, the other doesn't necessarily. Doreen went over to the church at 10:30 and found him dead, according to the report from one of the police officers who comforted Doreen at her house that morning. Clearly, I needed to do a bit more digging.

'Your sponge cake is absolutely lovely, Mrs Calderwood.'

'Ah, thank you, dear. It isn't bad is it?'

'Forgive me for posing another question but once you found the telephone to be engaged, did you try to call again?' I asked.

'Well, I was going to but I wanted to see if I could catch the weather on the radio so I left it for a while. That blessed rain had woken me up, you know, and I was looking to see if it was going to finally blow away. I waited for around twenty minutes and thought I would try again but then I thought I may as well go over and see if Martin was at the church, sometimes he was, but then my phone rang and it was the lady down the road just seeing if I was alright after all the thunder. I don't like it much, dear.'

'No, I'm sure you don't,' I said, trying desperately to remember what I wanted to ask and after a moment I realised where I was up to and continued. 'After your neighbour called, what did you do then?' I asked tentatively, half expecting another long-winded answer.

'I put my coat on. It was still raining and blowing, wasn't it? I couldn't decide which to wear for the best and then I remembered what my old husband used to say. He would say "there is no such thing as bad weather, only bad clothing", so I put my new one on.'

'Very sensible … and then what did you do?' I persevered.

'I made my way over the road to see whether Martin was at the church, although I was in two minds whether to go along to his house and see if he was there. I started to walk towards his house but changed my mind as the church was closer and I wanted to get out of the rain as soon as I could,' Doreen explained in detail.

'Do you know what time that was, Mrs Calderwood?' I asked. I actually already had the answer from the report that had been collected by the police officer on the day but wanted to check anyway.

'I think it was half past ten by then, that's what I told your young lady.'

'So you did. Now, when you walked up to the church did you see anything or anyone else?'

'I wasn't really looking, I just went in and, well, you know the rest. I still can't believe it really,' she said.

I didn't think that Doreen was going to be able help much more right now and decided I would leave her in peace and get back to see whether Bob had found anything interesting. I thanked Doreen and said goodbye for now. I strolled into the church to see Bob on his hands and knees by the kitchen door just where Martin had fallen. He seemed to be in a world of his own as I crept right up behind him and laid a hand on his shoulder with the expected result.

'Jesus Christ,' he yelled and banged his head on a bookshelf as he sprang up, totally startled.

'Sorry, mate,' I said with absolutely no conviction.

I glanced in the direction of Paul Archer, the new vicar, to check whether he had heard Bob's outburst and wasn't surprised to find that he had heard it loud and clear. I offered an apology on Bob's behalf.

'I'm sorry, Paul. My fault.'

'I've heard worse, although not usually in the church, I must say.'

Paul was a little upset by this, especially coming from a respectable and professional officer of the law. Oh, well. Never mind. Bob stood rubbing his head and grumbling away to himself as I perched on a pew at the front of the church.

'Anything, Bob?' I asked, hopefully.

'Nothing,' replied Bob with a sigh.

I suggested that we return to the station and take another look at the SOCO report to see whether anything in there helped in this dead-end investigation. We had driven to the church in my car as I was still enjoying the newness of it. As I turned into the station yard I immediately spotted that our friend DCI Corrigan was walking across the yard from where he had just parked his car. I was keen to avoid being spotted by him as our last rendezvous had not gone too well and coupled with the fact that we hadn't learnt anything else from our visit to the church, I didn't want to have to further explain that we were no closer to discovering who had committed the murder of Martin Brookes. I managed to steer the car towards the covered area reserved for any vehicle in need of attention from the guys in the workshop attached to the station. Fortunately, that little manoeuvre did the trick and kept us out of sight until he had gone inside. Once we had the all clear, we sneaked in stealthily.

Chapter Seven

The Visitor paid close attention to the news reports and the newspapers just in case anything about the Martin Brookes investigation was reported. He didn't really expect to see anything other than the usual. He was confident that he had done such a good job that nobody was going to ever track him down. He reflected on his earlier conquest when he had 'removed' Daniel Grainger from his short list of problems so efficiently. The police investigation at the time had concluded that dear Daniel had died at the hands of an unfortunate run of circumstances. Clearly, he had noticed some smoke coming from the old shed at the rear of the first green and gone to check it out. This was confirmed by Roberto, the man in charge of the cleaning firm. Daniel had ventured inside and in the smoky atmosphere had stumbled over a petrol can that was standing in the shed. He had kicked the can over ahead of him as he made his way into the shed and towards the rear where the smoke was thickest. Daniel had fallen and struck his face on one of the lawn mowers that had been used that morning by the head groundsman in preparation for the event that day, and had fallen onto the petrol that was spilt, soaking his clothing.

The small fire that had begun to take hold on the engine of the mower had been sufficient to ignite the strong fumes and Daniel had been engulfed in flames. The injury to his face had disabled him to the degree that he was unable to get himself up and out of the shed. The attending Fire Service had confirmed that a body had been found in the shed when they had extinguished the fire, and the sad news reached the clubhouse that Daniel Grainger had had a dreadful accident and died in the fire.

The Visitor was content that there was no news of Martin Brookes, at least not yet. Something was bound to come out at some point but he wasn't really too bothered. He was in control as always and he grinned to himself at the prospect of fooling them again one day soon; when he was ready.

Chapter Eight

As I drove up the M11 towards Laurel's End I reflected on why
Paul Archer had been so keen that I should see him at the church right
away. He had called my mobile, which again blasted out an unfamiliar
ring tone that startled me even more than the last time. Someone at the
station was ahead of me at that game. One day I would find out who
it was. In the meantime, I really must stop leaving the mobile on my
desk where it could be tampered with. Paul had found something that
he wanted to show me, so I agreed to go up to see him. I did wonder
what he might have found and how it might make a difference to the
investigation, but I guess I wouldn't know until I got there. I parked
outside Martin Brookes' old vicarage, which, I suppose, was where
Paul Archer resided nowadays, and strolled along the street and up to
the church. I glanced across the road to where Doreen lived but I didn't
see her. I wasn't sure whether she was going to be of any help to me or
not. The church door was open and Paul Archer was standing at the
entrance waiting for me. He waved as I approached the end of the path.

'Good morning, Detective Inspector. I hope you don't mind me
calling you out this morning but you did insist that I should get in touch
right away if I had anything to show you.'

'Yes, I did and I shall be interested to see what this is all about,'
I replied.

'Come in and I'll get you some tea. We've just made a pot this
minute.'

'We?' I enquired with an air of puzzlement.

Paul led the way into the church and I once again experienced my
eyes adjusting to the change of light inside. The church looked pretty
much the same to me as far as I could recall, and as I walked towards
the kitchen I found myself glancing down to where Martin Brookes had

been found. It was then that I noticed that the once bloodstained door had been repainted. Hopefully the blood had been washed off first.

I followed Paul into the small kitchen at the rear of the church and immediately recognised Doreen, who was pouring a cup of steaming tea; just for me. After the niceties were over we all stepped out from the claustrophobic kitchen and into the church, where Paul insisted that we sat on the first row of pews and continued with our tea. Although it was all very nice just sitting, sipping tea, I was very keen to establish why Paul had called me in the first place, so I interrupted his story about when he worked as a builder before pursuing his life as a vicar, interesting though it was. I managed to get Paul and Doreen back onto more important issues and finally got around to why I had been summoned.

'Ah, yes of course,' said Paul, 'I'll hand you over to Mrs Calderwood for this part.'

'Well,' began Doreen, which always made me feel that I was in for a long, drawn-out story. However, she seemed to get to the point quite quickly for a change.

'I found it over there,' she declared proudly whilst pointing over her shoulder, which could have been indicating just about anywhere.

'Isn't that wonderful?' interrupted Paul with equal enthusiasm and a broad smile.

'Isn't what wonderful? What did you find?' I said, already losing the will to live.

'The thingy ... you know? This.'

Doreen started to dig deep in her bag, which reminded me of the one that Julie Andrews had had in *Mary Poppins* in 1964 when she brought out a standard lamp and a birdcage, I think. I wondered for a moment whether Doreen was going to upend herself into it and disappear.

'Here,' she said.

Doreen held out her hand and in her palm was a rectangle of card. I asked her to let me hold it so that I could see what the fuss was all about. Doreen passed the item into my open hand and pressed it firmly into my palm. I studied the object with a look of uncertainty and puzzlement.

'A card?' I uttered to myself.

'Yes, isn't that lucky? It could have been there forever, couldn't it?' said Doreen.

Paul rejoined the excitement. 'Does it mean anything?'

I was rather dumfounded that I had driven up to see Paul, who was full of urgency on the phone, just to have Doreen hand me a playing card.

'Where did you say you found it, Mrs Calderwood?' I asked.

'Behind the bookcase when I was getting at all the cobwebs down there, dear. After that day I found Martin I didn't want to clean around there, not with all that blood that had been on the floor, although I did manage to get most of it up.'

I turned the card over so that I could see the face of it.

'The ace of hearts?'

I sat looking at it blankly and began to think I had just been wasting the morning on some sort of wild goose chase. What happened next was something between spooky and surreal. Doreen leant forward and tapped my knee, saying, 'Martin was shot in the heart wasn't he?'

For a moment I felt a coldness run through my veins and then my mind started to work overtime but wouldn't allow my reasoning to accept that the card had anything to do with what had happened to Martin. Too much of a coincidence, surely, or was it? One thing was for sure: however obscure the idea might be, this ace of hearts didn't really fit at the church and Doreen did find it very close to where Martin fell. Maybe Doreen didn't wash away all the evidence after all. If I could somehow make some sense of this then Doreen might just have turned up something significant.

Or was I hoping for a miracle?

* * *

When I arrived back at the 'nick' I made my way through the front doors and headed for the stairs. The old grandfather clock that sat proudly in the entrance hall boldly chimed away as I began to ascend the stairs en route to my desk.

Half past four, it told me.

I wondered whether Bob had made a sharp exit and got himself away home early, something he had always planned towards through the day providing the DCI wasn't watching his every move. Some people would question some of Bob's antics from time to time, but not me. I knew Bob Hand and on some days nothing surprised me with regard to the tricks he would try to pull. I looked across the office to where

Bob usually sat and began to scan the array of empty desks including Bob's. I sighed and turned towards my office just as Terry Brush called me over to him.

'Hey, guv, you're missing all the fun.'

'I doubt that, Terry, what do you mean?'

'Corrigan's got everyone in his office, reading the riot act about how he believes the department is dragging its heels over the recent Martin Brookes murder. He listed a number of unsolved crimes and got rather hot under the collar. I've just managed to nip out for a slash, any excuse to get out of there.'

'Can't say I blame you, mate. Sounds like so much fun. Is Bob in there?'

'He was but not now. He got a right grilling over it. In front of all of us too. Hardly fair but I think Corrigan is watching him, if you ask me.'

That is something I wouldn't be surprised to learn after Bob's last performance in Corrigan's office. Not that my performance went down too well either, but still.

'If I were you, guv, I'd keep my head down and make myself scarce.'

'Way ahead of you, Terry, I'll slip away and maybe shoot round to Bob's place on the way home. I can catch up with him then. Cheers, mate.'

Terry approved of my tactics and kept an eye on Corrigan's door until I could get out safely. He's a good lad, Terry. I wish I had had the pleasure of working with him years ago. He's a star. I ventured down to the canteen and decided on a black coffee in a feeble attempt to try to sharpen my mind and help myself understand what this bloody card was all about. I sat looking at it and pondering, wondering and letting my mind run wild with all sorts of weird concepts.

Did our killer leave it there?

Had it been there since the last service or ages before? Has it got nothing to do with anything? I don't know, but it is all I have at the moment and it appears to be of interest, maybe only to me though.

Why was it there?

* * *

Bob's flat was a few miles to the east in Chelmer Village so it didn't take me too long to get there. The door to Bob's flat was already ajar when

I got to it. It was certainly modest to say the least, with no real homely features to speak of. The curtains at the front windows looked like they had not seen a washing machine for quite some time, if ever.

'Saw you coming,' called Bob.

I made my way inside and immediately noticed how dark it was in the hallway. A light further on was the only suggestion of where I was supposed to be heading to find Bob. I pushed the door open and found him sitting in his living room with a can of beer in one hand and the TV remote in the other.

'All set for the evening, I see,' I said.

'I was. What do you want?'

Straight to the point. Why was I surprised?

'Can I sit down?

'Why, are you staying?'

Clearly Bob wasn't in the mood for guests and he could sometimes be such an obnoxious swine, so I thought it would be best if I explained why I was here and then hopefully he might be a little more welcoming. I reached into my pocket and offered the card to Bob. Bob held it without saying a word. He seemed to be studying it and, I assumed, wondering whether I had gone daft.

'And?' he said.

'… and, this has come from the church, from inside the church, and I believe it was there on the day Martin Brookes was killed.'

'So?'

Bob was clearly not impressed, and for that matter I wasn't sure that I was.

'So, it was found by Mrs Calderwood, the one who kindly cleaned the floor when she found Martin Brookes.'

Bob shifted in his chair and took a closer look and for a moment I thought he was going to treat the finding seriously.

'Got any more, we could have a game,' he said dismissively, 'So, tell me then. What has it got to do with a dead vicar?'

'I wish I knew the answer to that,' I said with an air of defeat.

Bob took a long drink from his can of beer and then threw the empty can across the room towards a wicker bin. The can hit the wall and bounced back across the room towards him. He lashed out at it and kicked it hard and cursed.

'Bollocks,' he said.

'Would you rather we talked about this in the morning?' I asked, already knowing what the answer would most likely be. But I got a surprise.

'No, let's talk about it now. This card was found by the old lady, right?'

'Right.'

'So, if it was left by our killer then the question is, what is the connection?'

'Bob, I don't even know if there is a connection but it does seem like a strange object to find in a church, especially as it turned up where it did, precisely where Martin Brookes fell.'

Bob was almost lying in his chair having slowly slipped down. His eyes were closed and he looked as if he had fallen asleep. I kicked his foot but there was no reaction and I guessed that the beer had finally got the better of him, so I took the card out of his hand and let myself out, closing the front door as I left.

I got home at about 8 p.m. and wanted nothing more than to get something to eat and have an early night. I ferreted about in the freezer for something quick and convenient and found a shepherd's pie that would do just nicely. After I had eaten, I opened a bottle of red wine and sat in comfort for a while and relaxed.

Only I couldn't relax.

I couldn't stop wondering about what Bob had said about the killer leaving the card at the scene. Then a thought struck me. What if there was anything in the archives about someone who had left their calling card at other incidents. I would have to wait until I got in to work tomorrow to check possibilities. It was a long shot but I didn't have anything else right now.

Chapter Nine

For now, I sat in silence. A silence that I still struggled to get used to even after all this time. I still missed her terribly; Ana Carvalho, my Portuguese beauty.

Ana and I had attended the same night school classes at a primary school in Ilford. Both trying our artistic hand at pencil drawing. I wasn't bad with wildfowl and birds generally but that was all I could do. Ana was amazing with everything she attempted. She left everyone in the class way behind and was soon lending a hand to the other students. Ana used to help me too but I spent the whole free lesson staring into her dark brown eyes and watching how her thick chestnut hair lay on her shoulders. I found myself lost in her bright smile and consequently never learnt a thing. I stuck to my self-taught attempts at different birds and never dreamt that I would ever be anything other than one of Ana's hopeless pupils; until one evening after class.

I had left as usual and turned right along Cranbrook Road towards where I had parked my car. It had begun to rain quite heavily and, although my car was no more than 300 yards down the road, I decided to step into a shop doorway until the worst of the sudden heavy shower eased a little. That was the best decision of the evening as it turned out. I stood for five minutes watching the rain come straight down like stair-rods; bouncing as it hit the pavement and splashing at my feet.

'Is there room for two?' I heard and looked up to see Ana standing as if she was waiting for permission to come aboard.

'I thought you had gone,' I said.

'I waited inside the school for a while to see if the rain would stop. Then I decided to try to get to the bus stop before the bus went without me.'

'I'll take you home if you like,' I said with far too much enthusiasm and making myself look completely transparent. Fortunately, Ana took up my offer and we scurried along to my car and made our way through the dazzling headlights of oncoming vehicles towards her flat. She shared with two other girls that were attending a college in the area. The girls were from Leeds and Ana explained that they had allowed her to stay with them when she was pushed out of her rented place in Redbridge. The girls were home and Ana was reluctant to invite me in but I didn't mind. We stood in the porch just out of reach of the rain, which had started to ease off a little more and looked as if it would probably stop in the next ten minutes or so. I was almost at the gate and heading for my car when something made me turn back towards Ana, who thankfully was still waiting in the porch and looking straight at me, watching me go.

'Ana, could … would you like to go out for coffee some time? You don't have to if you don't …'

'Yes please. That would be nice.'

Wow … I had a date with Ana Carvalho.

* * *

She always managed to make me smile and now the memories of that wet and dreary night were working their magic again. We dated for a fairly short time, I suppose, before she moved into my house in Woodford. After a few years there we moved to a house in Loughton, Essex. I could get to work at Walthamstow quite easily and Ana was working locally at a beauty salon in the main street. If beauty was a qualification for working there she had the job in the bag. Ana had that lovely olive skin that many of the Mediterranean girls are blessed with. She was a joy to be with, whatever was happening or even if nothing was happening. As you might expect, there were plenty of examples of her artwork to adorn the walls in just about every room. Sometimes she would copy freehand and by the time she had finished her work in pencil it mimicked the original picture or photograph beautifully.

She certainly had a talent.

The trouble was, I didn't; at least I never had the time to improve my skills. Due to the police work my leisure time was minimal, and that became more and more demanding as time went on, to the point where the stresses of the job started to creep invasively into our lives and our relationship. Strange how slowly and unnoticed these things seem to happen. Sadly, the poison seeped deeper and I would come home from work occasionally to find that Ana had gone to bed rather than wait for me to get home. Not that I was very late, but I guess the unpredictably long days were always going to take their toll in some way. Ana would look forward to the weekend and I would be at work more often than not. I felt as though I was stifling her and blocking her chance to have fun. Far too often I would spoil her plans by having to respond to the call of duty at the last moment, and I could see the disappointment in her dark brown eyes as I, once again, shut the front door behind me.

What time would I get home?

God knows.

I couldn't ever be angry with Ana because she was such a lovely girl and such a special person. I blamed myself, or perhaps I should blame my job, but I always considered that that would be cowardly. I had to take it on the chin, as they say, and when Ana sat across from me as we ate breakfast one Sunday morning I knew that her adorable, watery eyes were trying so hard not to tell me the truth about the future of our relationship.

'I know,' was all I could say before I began to cry too.

We sat gazing across the breakfast bar, both lost for the appropriate words. We remained silent and held each other's hands for what seemed like an eternity, as if neither of us wanted to have to speak first. But it wasn't us that finally broke the tension, it was my mobile phone and we both knew precisely what that meant.

'Sorry,' I said and began to offer the excuses again.

'Don't. Just go and do whatever it is they want you to do.'

I stood and answered the infernal thing, knowing exactly what would happen next. As usual I left Ana alone but this time it felt as though I was leaving forever.

Another murder.

Another destroyed relationship.

Once Ana and I had endured the dreadful pain of separation I decided to move away from Loughton. Ana stayed with some friends back in Woodford. I didn't want to keep returning to the house and find her missing. I had to until it was sold, of course, but thankfully that went through very quickly. I moved back to Woodford and was foolish enough to think that I would be able to cope better just because it was a different house. I was wrong. I saw Ana in my sleep, I saw Ana across the road, in the supermarket, even in the police station.

Not once was she ever actually there.

One day I heard from a friend of hers that she had returned to Portugal to study her beloved art, and for some reason I felt a degree of relief and release. I knew that Ana would be happiest of all if she was creating in the way only she could. To be lost in my work fast became a way of coping without Ana. I absorbed myself in it and found that I would work at home as well in order to blot out any thoughts that threatened to destabilise my world. I don't know whether it was the right thing to do or not but it seemed to work and get me through a difficult time.

One Sunday, when I actually found myself some time to spend at home and attempt some of the more mundane jobs that had built up when I wasn't looking, I heard a repeated knocking at the front door. When I opened the door before the over-enthusiastic neighbour knocked it down, he was already on his way back towards the front gate.

'Hey, Michael, I'm here. Sorry, I was out the back.'

'I thought you'd gone to work or something. Anyhow, this came for you yesterday but I didn't see you come home before I went to bed so I thought I'd pop it round this morning. The postman said he didn't want to try to shove it through your letterbox in case he did it any damage,' he said.

'Oh, right, thanks.'

I went back into the house and wandered through to the kitchen, putting the package down on the worktop and flicking the kettle on. I had been working in the garden since finishing breakfast and decided that this timely interruption had given me the chance to have a cuppa and sit down for a moment to inspect just how many thorns I had got stuck into my stupidly gloveless hands. When I'd made my tea, I turned my attention to the mystery package. It was one of those padded envelopes. I turned it over and studied the rear of it and my heart almost jumped through my chest when I read the words written on the back … From Ana xx.

It was a very good job that I was sitting down because my legs turned to jelly and I went quite light-headed. Looking at the front of the package, I could see that the stamps and postmarks should have given it away but it took me by surprise. Then, when my brain began to function again, I wondered how she had known where to send it. I could only think of her friend Tina who had kindly told me where Ana had gone and what she was doing. I sat staring at it and found myself wanting to tear the package open and yet, at the same time, I was unsure of what it contained. I realised that I was being stupid and got on with opening it. As I carefully slid out the contents I could see that I was looking at the back of a frame. I turned it over and momentarily didn't appreciate what I was seeing. A pencil drawing of the front of a building and a street. I let out a spontaneous sigh as tears filled my eyes when it dawned on me what the picture was showing me. It was an amazing drawing of a shop front but not just any one; it was the shop doorway that Ana and I had huddled into to keep away from the downpour on the night that we first got together. She must have done it from memory, and knowing how clever she was, I wouldn't put it past her. I looked inside the package again but there was no note, no message. I held the frame and studied every line on the drawing, knowing that Ana had carefully drawn every one. That was the end of my work for the day, I had no inspiration left. I took the picture into the living room and decided where to place it. The fireplace? The wall? Nowhere seemed good enough. Eventually I settled for simply resting it on the coffee table in the middle so that I could see it from anywhere in the room. I sat down on the sofa and, through teary eyes, I looked at the drawing until my eyes had worn all the lines off. Fortunately, that didn't happen. It was wonderful and has remained a treasured possession since the day it arrived. It was my part of Ana that nobody was ever going to take away.

Chapter Ten

When he decided to take the train to Upton Park and walk the rest of the way, it wasn't without a great deal of preparation and consideration. Everything needed to be just so. Poor preparation produces poor performance.

The 'Five Ps', he called it.

Up to now everything had gone to plan, every step was covered, he was ahead of the game. He boarded at Bow Church and saw that the carriage was pretty empty. He sat and gazed at the underground map above the seats opposite him and counted the number of stops. Someone had left a newspaper on one of the seats so he grabbed it for a quick look at the football results from last night and stretched his legs out. His end of the carriage was quiet, which is how he would prefer it anyway. To his left, about ten seats away, was a woman with long shapely legs and several bags of shopping at her feet. He sat looking at her and she was seemingly more than a little uneasy at the attention she was getting. She barely glanced in his direction for fear of appearing to approve of it. Once in a train carriage he felt as though his audience were captive. It was a game to him, one he enjoyed very much. It prepared him for what he had to do, for what he knew he must do. Today was different though. He was known in the area, or at least had been some years back, and any slim chance of being recognised had to be eliminated. The false beard and moustache felt weird and he found himself constantly touching it as he travelled. Tinted glasses were perched in front of thick eyebrows which also felt odd. He had a hooded coat just in case he spotted someone he knew, as if the false looks were not enough.

He noticed how the pattern on the seats was almost indistinguishable from the grime upon them. A man got on at West Ham and walked towards him, sat down opposite and pulled out a book to read. The Visitor took a quick glance at him and looked down again.

Only a couple more stops, he thought.

He looked back in the direction of the woman; she had gone. Either she had got off at the last stop or had moved further up the carriage to get out of his line of sight. When the train approached Upton Park the man opposite stood and made his way towards the doors, and The Visitor followed slowly. He had no interest in him. By the time he reached the top of the steps and ambled into the main part of the station his mind was absorbed by more important issues. He stepped out into Green Street and headed towards the Boleyn Ground, the home of West Ham United, whom he had followed as a boy and into his early adult life.

The area hadn't altered that much; maybe there were a number of new dialects and languages that could be heard these days but essentially it looked familiar to him. The shop fronts looked 100 years old and desperately in need of a lick of paint. Buses queued at the traffic lights as if waiting for the flag to drop, enabling them to storm off only to grind to a halt a little further along the road. The Visitor began to feel quite glad that he didn't have to spend any time around here any more; it just wasn't his patch nowadays. He glanced at the houses and couldn't help but notice the bars at the windows and the gated front doors.

Keeping them in or keeping them out?

There were no flowers in the front gardens, only rusty bikes, old rain-soaked armchairs and general rubbish. As he walked opposite the football ground he could almost feel the energy and atmosphere of the games he loved to remember. Manchester United, Chelsea, Millwall, the fighting in Castle Street, the chase to the tube station and more aggro on the platform.

Then there was the Boleyn Tavern public house on the corner of Green Street and Barking Road. He'd been in there a few times on a Saturday before the match, singing 'Bubbles' with the rest of them. But he wasn't in the mood for singing today, not one bit. He turned right at the traffic lights and went past the bank on his right. The road was fairly busy and still as noisy as ever, maybe more so. Across the road was a music shop of some sort with an awful noise blaring away and a group of black youths crowding in the doorway as if they were trying their best to block it. A fish and chip shop had its front window boarded up; glass could still be seen on the pavement outside. He crossed the road and headed towards Prince Regent Lane, turning left. As he passed the pub the odour of stale beer lingered in the air. A bloke stood having a fag at the doorway instead of inside the pub like in the old days. He nodded, acknowledging The Visitor as he passed. The Visitor didn't reciprocate; he just kept on walking, head down, almost marching; full of purpose. No time for pleasantries.

He crossed over the road, doing his best to avoid a bus that wasn't looking like it was going to change course just for him, and stepped up onto a walkway that would lead him around to the side of a block of grubby flats. The smell of a smoky bonfire was drifting around the block and getting in his eyes, making him turn his head and waft his hands in front of his face. As he looked up he saw the imposing sight of Mulberry Towers, and pressed on towards where he expected to meet his target. Around to the rear were the allotments. The Visitor pulled out his mobile phone and, as promised, announced that he had arrived at the allotments, albeit a little late, and then, doing as he was told, he followed the path ahead that led him to a beech hedge, where he turned left to follow it along to his meeting point, and waited by the big shed at the end of the path ahead of him. It was just starting to get dark.

Chapter Eleven

I sat in the snug waiting for Bob to show. He would of course; it was a pub after all. It was 8 o'clock on a chilly Thursday evening and the fog was getting thicker. I could see out of the window and found myself watching people who were either still travelling home or on their way out to the local off-licence for a few cans and some kettle chips. Bob could walk the short distance to the pub without the concern of how much he had to drink. Sometimes I wondered whether he was just as likely to use his car anyway but I never asked. I had arrived about half an hour ago and got myself a coke, which was probably not going to last a lot longer. I had come along to meet Bob and an old mate of his. I didn't know him but Bob seemed to think that it was going to be worth us talking to him. Bob had kept his reasons all a bit secretive, even though I had tried to prise it out of him at work in the day. All he would say was that it might be worth our while to talk to this mate of his and it might help us to piece one or two things together. I wasn't so sure but I didn't really have anything to lose either.

The windows were starting to steam up as the pub filled with more heat-generating bodies and the open fire spat embers onto the hearth. A crowd of darts fanatics could be heard in the other bar, their noise competing with the old-style juke box that stood not too far from where I sat. I was never any good at darts. Now pool, I could play. It was one of just a few things I could beat Ana at without cheating. Well, maybe I cheated a little bit, often by tickling her as she was about to pot a ball that had sat nicely for her over a pocket. It backfired badly on one occasion when we visited a friend of hers who had been bragging about her and her husband being able to beat us easily at doubles. We were winning and there were only a few balls left on the table when Ana stepped up to play. We had all had a number of drinks and were struggling to see which ball to hit, when I slowly crept up behind Ana gave her bottom a friendly pinch. Much to my surprise, and undoubtedly hers, she thrust her pool cue at the cue ball and promptly put an awful tear in the cloth. I'll never forget the sound of the ripping material and the deafening silence that followed. Ana spun around and looked at me, cracked the biggest smile and immediately got the giggles. Our hosts didn't see the funny side but the moment served to give us plenty of laughs for a few days to come.

The pub doors banged against the wall as a rather large man wearing a West Ham shirt came bowling in, looking flustered and a little anxious. I watched him head over to a group of men who were standing by the bar. While they were deep in conversation and busy knocking back a jar or two, he looped his big arm around the neck of one of the men and dragged him backwards and down onto his back. He held him there and put his chunky hands around his throat. The copper in me was just starting to stir and I was considering how unwise it might be to get too close to a load of alcohol-fuelled men. Just as I was waiting for the blood to fly, 'West Ham shirt' lifted his 'victim' back onto his feet and planted a big, sloppy, wet kiss on his forehead. The others laughed and howled, and I was quite relieved too. Boys will be boys.

'Dave, can I get you a pint?' said Bob as I snapped out of it and realised that he and his mate had sneaked in without me noticing.

'Hi, Bob, no, just a coke, mate.'

'This is Andy Potter, the bloke I told you about,' said Bob.

Andy Potter looked as if he had played a lot of rugby. He was very thick-set and had one of those lived-in faces.

'Hello, Bob has told me that you two go back a long way.'

'You could say that, Andy.'

'Sorry about the mystery, his idea, not mine. Still, it's nice to get away from the Gestapo isn't it?'

'I suppose so, not that I have anyone at home these days.'

'Cor, lucky old you. Still, at least I don't have to cook for myself and do all those bloody housework tasks. You know what they say; why keep a dog and bark yourself.'

'Yep,' I said half-heartedly, as I immediately thought of Ana again.

'You been waiting long?'

'No, not long, maybe half an hour or so. It's a lot warmer in here anyway. Where are you from? What nick?' I asked.

'Now, I'm at Enfield, but I did most of my time at Cheshunt. Twenty years there, I was. Liked it too; mostly anyway. You know what it's like, the job changes so bloody fast, don't recognise it these days. Still, not a lot we can do about that, eh?'

Before I had a chance to answer Bob was back with the drinks; a pint of bitter each for him and Andy and a coke for me.

'You sure that's all you want? I'll get you a pint if you want.'

'No, Bob, I'm fine, honest.'

I have never been much of a drinker and unlike Bob, was more than happy to have a soft drink. I made myself a rule many years ago that if I was driving I wouldn't have any alcohol at all. Some people would call it boring but I always felt better for sticking to it. If anything went wrong then at least I knew I was never going to have any problem in that area.

The darts match sounded as though it had got underway as there were bouts of sporadic clapping and cheering coming from the bar area behind me. It certainly provided some atmosphere in the pub. Bob and Andy were in full flow, chatting away, not that I was taking too much notice. I looked towards the window but it had completely steamed up; the only reference to the outside world being the occasional change of colour from red to green as the traffic lights nearby continued in their monotony.

'So, Dave, Bob tells me you've got yourself a mystery,' said Andy, his voice a little lowered.

'Oh, yeah, just a bit. I suppose he's filled you in on the details that we do know.'

'Yeah, he told me on the phone the other night. Found something though, didn't you?' he asked.

'Well, I didn't but someone else certainly did. I doubt it means anything though. It was the old lady who helps out at the church. She lives opposite. She was unfortunate enough to find him,' I explained.

'So I hear. Well, I don't know either, whether this is just an odd coincidence or what, but I had a similar article turn up on a body of mine a few years ago and it wasn't until Bob mentioned it that it made me wonder whether there could be any connection. Like you say, I doubt it but you never know, I guess.'

'What was it?' I asked.

'Do you remember hearing about a body that was found at the golf course in North Weald? In a big shed, involved in a fire?'

'Actually, I do. I remember thinking what a bit of bad luck it was.'

'Bad luck, alright. At least that's what everyone thinks it was.'

'Are you saying it wasn't?'

'I don't know. But what I do know is that there was never any explanation given or discovered as to why he had a playing card folded in his shoe.' I looked straight at Andy and then at Bob, who had a silly grin on his face.

That was nothing out of the ordinary when he had had a few drinks, but still.

'What d'ya reckon to that then "Sherlock"?' said Bob.

I wasn't really sure what to think immediately as Andy jumped in.

'Your boy had a bullet in his chest, right?'

'Yes, he did.'

'And your lady-friend found the card, right?'

'Yes,' I said, hoping that the pub wouldn't close before Andy got to the point.

'What card was it?' he asked

'Ace of hearts,' I replied, and as I said it I recalled what Doreen had said that day in the church. '*Martin was shot in the heart, wasn't he?*'

'So what card was in this bloke's shoe then?'

'Ace of clubs,' said Andy.

'Golf … club …' I said under my breath and looked at the two silly grins in front of me.

All of a sudden I had a jolt of adrenaline that finally gave me some hope, but what I couldn't be certain of was whether it was just false hope. I sat sipping my coke and pondering for a minute. Bob got up and went to the toilet leaving us with the parting words: 'It's probably all bollocks anyway.'

Andy smirked as Bob ambled off.

'That's bloody typical of him.'

'Yeah, I know. He might be right though,' I said.

'Might not be too, Dave. I could never really work out whether the card in his shoe was just packing that made it more comfortable or what. It was clean too and that kept making me think, but then the fire had badly charred the top half of his body and his legs and feet were relatively unscathed. I just kept imagining someone posting it into his shoe when he was ablaze, or more likely once he was flat out before the fire. But then I would keep rejecting the idea as silly and I hadn't an ounce of proof. I asked his wife about it and she said he did all sorts of funny things and put it down to the fact that she wouldn't be surprised if he had put it in there himself for comfort. Not a lot of help. I even went into the clubhouse and found a pack of cards on the table by the window and got one of my PCs to scan it for the ace. It was there.'

'So, it went to ground then?'

'It did … so did he.'

'Who was he, Andy?'

'… er … Daniel, somebody … er … Grainger, yes, Grainger. Daniel Grainger.'

'Cheers, I'll do a bit of checking up if you don't mind?'

'Fine by me, Dave. I've got absolutely nowhere but you can have a dig if you want.'

The West Ham shirt spilt his beer down his jeans as another in the crowd pushed into the back of him just as Bob was on his way back to the table. I watched as the two of them squared up for a brief, tense moment. Then I noticed Bob was heading straight over to them both and as he got close, they both turned towards him as if they were listening to what he had to say. The conversation was fairly short and the pair both glanced over to our table as Bob came back and sat down.

'That's that sorted then,' he said smugly.

'What did you say?' said Andy.

'Oh, nothing much,' said Bob.

Now, I knew enough about Bob Hand to know that he had a knack of poking his nose into situations where his nose did not belong, so I pressed him for an answer.

'Oh, come on, what have you said? They both looked over here. I hope you haven't told 'em we're the law.'

'No, nothing like that. What d'ya think I am, daft?' The first word that sprang to mind was 'yes'. 'If I did that they'd grab us and throw us out, probably.'

'So what did you come up with?' asked Andy as I prepared myself for what was to come.

'I told 'em you two were SAS and you came in for a quiet night. Said you'd been fighting "rag-heads" for months and wanted a rest.'

'You are fucking kidding me,' said Andy

'He's not,' I said.

'Well cheers, Bob, I can always depend on you.'

'Stopped it, didn't I?' he said ... ever the diplomat.

I had walked into the pub as a harmless citizen and now, thanks to big mouth, I was an SAS hero back from a stint in Afghanistan or Iraq or heaven knows where. He's a bloody menace.

Chapter Twelve

The next morning, I woke at 03:15 and found myself thinking about the two playing cards which may or may not be connected. Questions were whirring around in my mind, a mind that didn't really want to start the day quite so early, especially when I had to be at a reunion this morning. It took place each year and, as usual, fewer and fewer people managed to find the time to go. I have to say I have always enjoyed seeing the old faces crop up and it was always nice to know they were in good health and still marching on regardless. Some of them were great characters too and I did tend to think that the mould was broken, as they say, when they joined the force.

There was Ted Seabourne, who was my old desk sergeant when I was at Walthamstow. He was a lovely fella and could charm anyone who ventured through the doors into the station reception area. He played a very important part in calming people down who were sometimes irate, to say the least. Equally, if they were frightened, he had such a caring way with people too and always managed to put them at ease with a soft, strong, comforting voice and a cuppa.

He was a proper, trustworthy, old-fashioned copper.

My mind allowed me to doze for another hour and a half before I finally gave up trying to sleep and went downstairs for a cup of tea. The morning hadn't quite woken up either as it was still pretty dark, but I didn't want to have any lights on so I took my tea into the living room and sat on the sofa looking at Ana's picture of the shop front, in the half-light, where we had escaped from the rain. I didn't need much light to see it; I think I knew every line off by heart. Today was one of those few days when I didn't have to wear uniform to a function as this one was always a relaxed affair. I was quite glad to be able to chill out for a while and simply enjoy the company and not worry about perfect creases and shiny shoes or who was checking them. After breakfast I went upstairs to get ready. It wouldn't take me more than fifty minutes to get there and it didn't start until 10 o'clock, so I wasn't exactly rushed off my feet. I decided to be ready in good time, nevertheless; I have always been a bit of a stickler for timekeeping. I had treated myself to an aviator flying jacket and thought I would give it an airing. The leather was black and really soft. It had some smart buckles and zips that gave it a retro look too. I dug out a respectable pair of jeans and a pair of workmanlike shoes with steel toecaps and a good thick tread. A white shirt seemed to set off the jacket well and although I had myself looking a little bit like 'the Fonz' from Happy Days, I thought I would get away with it Ok. The 'Old man's do', as it was fondly known, was a chance for some of the retired coppers to meet up with a few of those still serving and catch up on how everyone was getting along. This year it was decided that the venue would be an old working men's club, one that most of the local retirees could still get to without too much of a problem. Every year there was a discussion about where to hold it and whether everyone who wanted to go could get there. It was impossible, of course, to please everyone, so the venue would get moved from one place to another each year. However, usually sixty or seventy people managed to come along. I turned up just before ten and made my way into the club. A sign had been put in the foyer to say that the retirement party, as they called it, was upstairs. Not really a retirement party, more of a party for the retired.

As I made my way up I heard somebody shout out from behind me. It was a guy named Ronnie Deacon, who would rarely miss an occasion such as this. Ronnie left the job before he had done his time. He was unfortunate enough to be retired early through injury. I remember the job that finished his career only too well. It was a standard break-in at a house in Leyton. Ronnie was only a street away when the call came in. One of the neighbours had been spying out of her curtains when she saw a youth jump over a side gate at number 17 and disappear around to the back of the house. The area had been victim to a number of similar goings-on recently so she decided to call the police. The information had been passed on to Ronnie via the radio in his car and so he thought he knew what to expect. Ronnie was too adroit to make silly mistakes and knew not to go charging in.

He parked his car about fifty yards from the house and walked calmly along on the opposite side of the street until he was able to get a good view of the property. Another car was already on its way and Ronnie knew that help would not be too far behind. He stood and looked through the windows of the ground floor but couldn't see any movement. He was scanning all the windows at the front of the house when one of the curtains upstairs moved. He could clearly see a man and a woman near the window. The woman grabbed at the curtain and was immediately wrestled away from the window by the man, who seemed to throw her to one side. Ronnie didn't know whether this was a domestic argument or whether the burglar had found the woman upstairs while he was busy searching the house. Either way, this woman was in danger and Ronnie couldn't wait for the support car to arrive. He made his way quickly across the street and decided that banging on the front door would probably do no good, so he clambered over the side gate just as the man had done, according to the report. When he got around to the rear of the house he noticed broken glass on the patio and that the door that led into the kitchen was open. Just as Ronnie took a step inside he heard the woman scream and also heard the man shout something indecipherable. There was a loud thump from upstairs which sounded like someone landing heavily on the floor and Ronnie knew he couldn't just do nothing. With the situation unfolding into something more than a quick burglary, he realised it was decision time. As one voice was telling him to wait for the support car, which surely couldn't be too far away, another voice was telling him to make his presence known. Ronnie stepped further into the house and into the hallway that led to the stairs. When he got to the foot of the stairs the woman cried out even louder this time, and her plea for help was followed by a much harder crash onto the upstairs floor.

'POLICE. Stay where you are.'

There was a strange, eerie silence and then he heard the man shout.

'Shit.'

Ronnie knew he was right about that bit.

He heard the support car roar towards the house and the flicker of blue lights was visible in the hallway. Support had arrived and Ronnie felt that the man had nowhere to run now. As Ronnie put a foot onto the bottom step of the stairs in order to crane his neck for a better view of the upstairs landing he heard the unmistakable sound of breaking glass and it sounded as though there was a lot of it. Then a thump, which seemed to come from the back garden, painted the picture of the man leaping to make his escape. Ronnie ran out through the kitchen and saw the man in next door's garden still struggling to get to his feet properly but nevertheless moving quickly as he prepared to straddle the next boundary. The two officers from the car appeared at the back door. Ronnie was half in pursuit and half turning to tell the guys about the woman upstairs who may need help, even medical help, when something heavy slammed into his left leg and completely knocked him off his feet. He fell hard onto his side and had all the wind knocked out of him; but then came the pain and it was almost unbearable. Blood ran down his leg and was visibly spurting out from the wound that had been exposed by the torn-away material. Mick Yelland saw it first. The dog was big and snarling and looking for a fight with these invaders of his territory. Then he noticed the other one chained to a huge kennel at the side of the garden. Ronnie was in a bad way and needed to get to hospital as soon as it could be arranged. He was curled up in pain and holding on to his leg, which was bleeding heavily. The dog that had done the damage was growling away almost under its breath but it sounded menacing enough and was certainly close enough, but didn't seem as though he was about to launch into a second assault. Mick sidled slowly towards the kitchen with both eyes firmly on the dog, which thankfully hadn't moved. Upstairs, Phil Sutton had found the woman unharmed but for a few red marks which would no doubt present as bruises soon enough.

She was shocked but OK.

He stuck his head out of the broken window and saw the chaos below. Ronnie, his hands red with blood, Mick, stepping out of the rear of the house with a bundle of tea-towels, and the biggest dog he had ever seen watching them intently in the garden. Phil told the woman he would be back shortly and made his way hurriedly down to the rear garden. Remembering the dog, he stopped at the doorway and asked Mick if he'd sent a message yet.

'No chance, mate. Can you do it for me? I need an ambulance for Ronnie and get me something to tie this lot round his leg with. And see if the woman can get this dog tethered up sharpish.'

'What about our burglar friend?'

'He's long gone, mate. Forget it; just get me something to hold this lot on.'

By the time the paramedic arrived, the woman had secured the dog by a chain and Mick had just about managed to stop the bleeding with all that was available to him at the time. The ambulance crew, with the help of Mick and Phil, managed to put Ronnie onto a scoop stretcher and carry him to the rear doors of the ambulance. When the doctors had a good look at Ronnie's leg it could be seen that the dog had sunk its teeth into the back of his knee and that the wound was more like a tear which had caused an awful lot of damage to the soft tissue and the tendons. The wound gave the impression that the dog had been travelling at speed and had dragged Ronnie over without letting go, continuing to bite hard as he fell to the ground. Most of the damage was due to a tearing action rather than a puncture. Ronnie was out of action for almost a year.

After a lengthy process of recovery that included regularly attending clinics and the out-patients department of his local hospital, he was finally able to walk unaided but not without a certain amount of discomfort. Throughout his recovery Ronnie had his suspicions that he may not be able to return to operational duties, and if that was the case then he would most likely take an early retirement. He had almost done his time anyway. Ronnie Deacon was not the type to amble around in an office or be sat for long periods at a desk; he was lost in that world. It was the streets or nothing.

We ventured into the function room on the first floor and began to see the old familiar faces from other years. There were a few nods in our general direction and a wave of a hand or two. We got ourselves a drink and were soon mingling with the others. The atmosphere was always pleasant at these meetings as old friends caught up with the latest gossip and swapped stories of bygone days; probably the same ones as last year. Even a group of the 'old school' were playing cards together; they were members of a bridge club that had started up as part of the sports and social and sometimes they sounded very serious about it all. They were an amusing bunch, the way they squabbled over the scoring and regularly accused the other pair of sending secret signals across the table to each other when the bidding process was underway. It was all in good faith and they had found a pastime that they enjoyed, so it was all good in the end and harmless fun. Ronnie was chatting with a couple of the guys that had been at his station around the same time as him, and no doubt the story of the incident with the dog was bound to be one of the subjects they would be talking about. I wondered whether Ronnie enjoyed telling it or whether it was wearing a bit thin by now.

Either way, he was pretty much stuck with it, I guess.

Chapter Thirteen

The body was discovered by kids at about 9 p.m., half buried on the allotments at the back of Mulberry Towers in Plaistow. His head had received a heavy insult which looked as though it had been delivered by a sharp-edged weapon. What hair he had was covered in congealed blood. The earth around him cannot have been there to conceal the body; far too much of him was still exposed. Maybe, the original idea was to bury him but it didn't give that impression.

Trevor Eaden was the inspector in charge of the crime scene. He had arrived shortly after the first officer to arrive, who had confirmed the details to him of a somewhat patchy telephone call received by the Control Room. The scene was secured and a tent had been erected around the body of Stan Elms. Fortunately, there was no clear view from that side of Mulberry Towers so the residents weren't able to peer down at the scene.

The few people that had gathered were quickly dispersed back inside and would soon become part of the investigation with regard to what they may have seen or heard. It was common in these parts to discover that nobody saw or heard anything. Inside the tent, Inspector Eaden was studying the body of Mr Elms. He didn't touch a thing, he just looked on. He wasn't about to upset the forensics people. The wound on the deceased's head was very deep and had been delivered with a reasonable amount of force. There was another deepish cut to his neck, more like a slice.

'Guv, can you pop outside a minute? Looks like we've got a weapon.'

Inspector Eaden went outside and was led to the rear of the tent where another police officer was standing, shining a torchlight onto a spade which had a short handle that had been reduced in length by a straight, clean cut; probably sawn off.

'You see here, guv, it's got hair on it, just there look, and blood.'

'Right, well done. Let's get this bagged as evidence. Cheers, lads,' said a grateful inspector.

Chapter Fourteen

I finally got to sit with a couple of the bridge team and Ronnie Deacon. We tucked into the generous buffet as though we hadn't been fed before, as though it might run away if we weren't quick. As we ate I scanned the room for old Ted Seabourne, but I couldn't see him anywhere and wondered whether he was OK. That's the trouble with these sorts of events, if anyone doesn't turn up you always think something's wrong. The noise level from all the chatter was pretty high and was accompanied by the sound of cutlery tapping and scraping against the plates. One of the bridge players asked me how I liked retirement and I had to tell him that I was still doing the job. I told him about my move to Chelmsford and how they all seemed a good bunch to work alongside.

'Out in the sticks, eh? Don't know whether I'd fancy that, bit quiet, ain't it?' he asked.

'Not too quiet really. We have our moments too, you know. I walked straight into a murder almost from the start,' I said.

'Still, you're used to all that lark, ain't yer? Seen it, done it, got the T-shirt, as they say. 'Ere, shall I tell you something funny?' he added. 'See old Tom, over on the next table? Well, he's always playing the part of a bit of a rogue and one night we all met down the local for a game of bridge. Well, Tom was playing with me against the other two and he said to me beforehand that we would win tonight no matter what. I didn't know what he was alluding to but I knew he had something up his sleeve, so to speak. So, we played and when it got down to the last round of cards we needed to win it to seal the match. So, the cards went down on the table and last of all Tom lays the king of clubs and wins the hand, which gave us the win we needed. Anyway, Barry Healy gave him a right look and he said that couldn't have possibly won it 'cos the King had already gone. Tom disputed this but Barry was insistent and said that he could prove it. So, he picked up the last hand and turned all the cards face down on the table and, guess what, three of 'em were red and the one Tom laid was blue. He had brought one from a different pack. They had nothing to do with each other.'

A proverbial penny dropped in my mind with a thump. I made my excuses and found a quiet corner to give Bob a call and ask him for Andy Potter's number. I wanted to know whether Andy knew the whereabouts of the card he had found in the shoe of Daniel Grainger. If the back of the card that Doreen discovered at the church and the one from Daniel Grainger's shoe were identical, then just maybe I could link the two deaths together. Another hopeful long shot, I know, but definitely worth a go in the absence of anything more substantial. After several attempts to get Andy to answer his phone I left a short message, asking him to return my call as soon as he got it. All of a sudden and due to the recent injection of inspiration about the cards, I felt that I had lost interest in staying too much longer at the do and decided that I would look for a convenient opening to slide away unnoticed. On my way out of the main room I stopped briefly to say goodbye to Ronnie Deacon and then slipped out and down the stairs, through the reception area and out into the afternoon air.

As I drove up the M11 the traffic began to slow. Ahead of me was the familiar glare of red brake lights as the other vehicles slowed gradually to a halt. I could see a flicker of flashing blue lights and thought that I might be in for a tedious, unscheduled stop. Sitting in lane two and not really admiring my view of the rear of a new and shiny Mercedes wasn't what I had in mind at all. It's strange what things you find a weird interest in when you have nothing else to look at and no way of changing the view immediately in front of you. I found myself staring at the number plate and trying to remember where vehicles that displayed the International Registration Code of SF came from. In my desperation, that particular challenge occupied my mind for just long enough before the traffic began to trickle forward again at a snail's pace. The illumination of the area courtesy of the flashing blue lights grew ever brighter as we crept towards the incident that thankfully appeared to be on the southbound carriageway, the other side. SF? South?

I don't allow myself to get flustered by these sorts of traffic problems because I know I cannot do anything about them so I was quite chilled as I sat pondering my number plate conundrum. A fire engine thundered by in the hard shoulder lane to my left, its lights whizzing around the interior of my car like one of those 1970s disco glitter balls that would be found suspended above the dance floor, and disappeared out of my view. My mind had been so occupied by the thought of the cards finally shedding some light on the murder of the unfortunate Martin Brookes, coupled with the number plate puzzle, that the shrill of my mobile phone caught me completely unawares as it shattered the silence and sent a jolt through me like a lightning bolt. Once again, I had fallen foul of the mobile phone prankster, who this time had chosen something resembling either Led Zeppelin or a squealing pig, I couldn't decipher which as I shuddered in my seat and instinctively switched to the hands-free facility, as much to bring the torment to an end as to answer the call.

'Dave Calloway,' I answered as the beat from my heart bashed away inside my chest.

'Dave, it's Andy, I got your message, how can I help?'

'Andy, thanks for calling back. Listen, I was wondering whether you knew where that playing card you found in Daniel Grainger's shoe might be? I think it could be important after all, although I can't prove anything just yet.'

'Blimey … er … I think that what happened was that it was decided it had nothing to do with anything and it went back to his wife along with his possessions, at least those that where salvageable following the fire. As you know, the whole thing was closed and his death was recorded as accidental, so no more came of it. Everyone seemed to think that it was just some superstition that he had, you know, a lucky charm almost. Not so lucky on that morning though, eh?'

'No, OK thanks for that. I'd really like to see it. Can you tell me where he lived?'

'I can but you'll be lucky if it's still hanging around. I tell you what; I'll text you the address. I'm in the office so I'll dig it out straight away.'

'Thanks, Andy. I'll let you know how I get on.'

'SF' had changed lanes and managed to gain some ground so I let the poser go with it and concentrated on what I would say when I got to Daniel Grainger's house, providing his wife still lived there, of course. With the traffic moving a little better, I decided that if Andy did text me the address soon then I would go straight there; it was only about four-thirty so I wouldn't be too late. I could see what the commotion was all about on the opposite carriageway now. A bus was glowing underneath, where the engine had obviously caught fire. Two fire engines were doing what they do and the traffic on this side of the carriageway drove on as if nothing had happened. Once again, the delay and the endless trail of red stop lights was caused by the drivers on this side of the road slowing to peer at what was going on opposite. It's something that happens with great regularity and causes chaos.

A gentle bleep told me that a text message had arrived. I managed to put the postcode into the onboard satnav and headed off towards the house of Daniel Grainger. I was approaching Junction 6 and so all I had to do was come off at 7 and take the road that would eventually lead me back to Chelmsford, stopping off briefly at North Weald Bassett.

Chapter Fifteen

Inspector Trevor Eaden gazed out of the window and wondered if the apparent need for seemingly senseless killings would ever wane. Somehow, he didn't really believe it would. His career as a police officer had seen him serve the areas of Bow, Hackney, Islington, Shoreditch and finally Plaistow. He had lost count of the number of murders that had happened on his patch over the years. Then there were the robberies, the beatings, the fraud, the extortion; the list was pretty much endless. The questions always outweighed the answers too. Now another batch of questions had landed on his desk. Stan Elms was his latest puzzle and 'why?' was, once again, the latest question. Why had someone attacked him at the allotments with a spade and left him half buried and very dead? Stan Elms' wallet was still in his trouser pocket and contained £40, so it didn't appear that he had been robbed. He had retired a few years ago and liked to spend some of his time at the allotments tending his vegetables and flowers. Trevor Eaden wondered whether that was too much to ask.

The list of possible individuals who might fit the bill for this sort of violence was too long to simply point the finger at anyone in particular. Eaden sat down at his desk and rested his head in his hands, and not for the first time today either. The coffee on his desk had gone cold an hour ago but he took a sip anyway; maybe it would shock his brain into coming up with an answer that made some sense for once. All he knew for now about Stan Elms was that he had owned Elms' Electrics, a shop that had been around for a lot of years and could be found at one end of Prince Regent Lane. Elms had spent most of his days in and around the East End of London and was, by all accounts, a quiet sort of man with no known enemies that sprang to mind. Perhaps this was just some kind of random attack on an old man by someone who had a cruel and twisted idea of fun. As Eaden pondered the possibilities and tapped his pen on an empty page on the A4 pad in front of him, there was a knock at his door.

'Come in.'

'I got the report from forensics on the spade at the allotments, guv.'

'Tell me the worst then,' said an already deflated Eaden.

'It's confirmed as the weapon that killed Elms. His hair, his blood, but no prints, no nothing really.'

'Well, I guess that was to be expected. What about the residents of Mulberry Towers, anything from them?'

'Nothing, guv.'

'Surprise, surprise,' said Eaden with a certain irony.

'There is one thing, guv.'

'And what would that be, a signed confession from our killer gardener?'

'No, guv. Me and PC Harrington went round to where Elms lived and were tasked with the job of taking a further statement from his old lady. Anyway, while we were talking to her about it all she showed me this, and said it had been popped through her letterbox about an hour after Mr Elms had gone to meet some chap who wanted to join the allotment group, supposedly.'

Grosvenor, a fresh-faced PC of 5 years' service, all of it at Plaistow, searched inside his jacket pocket and handed over an envelope to the inspector. Eaden thumbed the flap open and turned it upside down over his A4 pad. Out dropped a playing card, face down. He picked it up and turned it face up and looked up, in silence, at Grosvenor. He turned his attention back to the card, allowing the sick irony of it to sink in.

'Ha, fucking ha. Someone with a sense of humour, eh. The ace of spades. The fucking death card ... how lovely.'

Eaden slumped back into his chair and excused Grosvenor, thanking him for what he had done so far. He felt as though the killer, providing he was the one who left it, was not only callous but was confident enough to purposely leave behind some kind of a trail. The ace of spades and a spade to kill Elms with. Eaden shook his head as he sat quietly, taking it all in. He drummed his fingers on the desk and ran the scenario through his mind again as he scribbled on the empty pad.

Chapter Sixteen

Debbie Fisher got home at about 6 p.m. after stopping off at the supermarket on her way back from her mum's. The house was in darkness apart from a gentle light that came from the rear room where Kim was. She let herself in through the front door and dropped the door keys into one of the shopping bags that she was carrying.

'I'm home, sweetheart,' she called to Kim.

Kim was keeping quiet and playing a game with her visitor. Debbie lifted the carrier bags onto the worktop in the kitchen and unbuttoned her coat as she turned towards the living room to go to see Kim, flicking another light switch on as she did. When Debbie got to the living room door she could see a man sitting close to Kim and holding her hand. For an instant Debbie froze and felt a cold chill run through her.

'You stupid sod, how long have you been here? Where's Jean?' she said.

'Well, that's a nice welcome for your own brother. I let her get back when I got here. Me and Kim have had a right nice time, ain't we, babe?'

'You should tell me when you're coming; you know how it makes me jump. Pair of monsters, you two are.'

Kim smiled and her eyes sparkled as they always did when her Uncle John came to see her.

'You still jumping, Deb?' said John as he followed Debbie into the kitchen.

'I can't help it, John. You know how alike you two always looked. It gives me a fright every time. I just wish you'd call, that's all. You want a tea, I suppose?' she said as she switched the kettle on to boil.

'Yes please. Look, I'm sorry that I made you jump. I know we looked alike but I thought you'd got over that by now.'

Syrup and Cyanide

'Over it? How am I supposed to get over it? It was the biggest shock of my life. Well, one of 'em anyway,' Debbie corrected herself as she looked in Kim's direction. Debbie popped back into the living room and asked Kim whether she wanted a cup of tea.

'It shouldn't have happened, you know. Wasn't his time. He was only fifty-three, for Christ's sake.'

'Stop it now, John; I'm not in the mood.'

Debbie's eyes glazed a little as she prepared the cups. She looked out of the kitchen window and down the path. She used to stand and stare at the gate at the end of the path and wish he would walk up to the front door. Tearing herself away from the view she went back into the living room to sit beside Kim.

'Pull that blind down for me will you, John?'

It was dusk by now so John obliged, and once the kettle had boiled he poured the water into the cups, each with a waiting tea bag.

'Come in here and let it sit a minute,' said Debbie.

John sat on the sofa and winked at Kim, who smiled back at him and emulated a crooked wink. Debbie closed her eyes momentarily and let out a sigh. There didn't seem to be any such thing as an easy day any more, not since everything changed. It had been seventeen years. Kim was now 34.

'Why don't I go and fetch the tea for you and your mum, eh, Kim?' John eased himself up with a groan and wandered to the kitchen. Kim's eyes followed him until she couldn't manage to stretch her neck any further. She reached out and rested her hand on Debbie's, who opened her eyes and looked lovingly at Kim.

'I love you, darling.'

'I love you, Mum,' replied Kim.

71

Chapter Seventeen

I was driving with one eye on the satnav as I tried to understand the layout of the road ahead of me on my way to Daniel Grainger's house, albeit it hadn't actually been his for some time. I didn't really like to drop in unannounced but felt that I needed to follow this thready lead whilst it had presented itself to me. The roundabout 100 yards ahead was where I needed to turn right at the area known as Tyler's Green. As I did so I was routinely informed that my destination was only 800 yards further on. I noticed a road sign that indicated the direction to the golf club where Daniel had perished. The High Road led me into North Weald Bassett and ultimately I turned into the road on a quiet estate where Louisa Grainger lived. At least I hoped she still lived there but I didn't really want to think about that scenario. All the front gardens were well manicured and all the fences were well maintained. Louisa Grainger's house looked just as prim and proper as any of them. I walked slowly up towards the front door, mentally rehearsing my opening line which sounded more and more inappropriate with every rather unsure step that I took. As I got close enough to the house to see my reflection in the front-room window I realised that I was, obviously, still dressed in my civilian clothes and looked nothing like a police officer whatsoever. Not only was I faced with digging up a very painful past for Louisa, I had also to explain my attire and lack of uniform, or at least a suit. With the realisation that there was nothing I could do about it anyway, I rang the bell. I fumbled for my warrant card and waited. I stood patiently for about a minute and began to think that I was going to be out of luck. A woman walked along the pavement towards the house and stopped to open the gate to the house next door, never taking her eyes off me. My 'good afternoon' received a fairly cautious and frosty response.

Just a nod and mumbled 'hello'. I was about to enquire whether Mrs Grainger still lived here when I saw a shadow out of the corner of my eye and turned my attention back to the front door.

Someone was in, it seemed.

The woman from next door was still watching me closely as the front door opened slowly and an attractive woman in her late fifties peered around the chained door. She took a good look at me but didn't speak. I held my warrant card so that she could see it clearly and explained who I was and where I worked from. Trusting my explanation, she unchained the door and asked what I wanted. Having confirmed that she was Louisa Grainger, I asked if I might come in, as I glanced across to the ever-attentive neighbour who was even more interested now. Mrs Grainger agreed that I had better and raised her eyebrows as if to understand my concern for privacy. I was ushered into the hallway and told to go through to the front room.

'I hope nothing awful has happened. I couldn't stand another shock.'

'No, nothing like that, I assure you. Although my reason for being here does relate to your husband in a way,' I said.

'I don't know how I can help you, not after all this time. I answered all the questions years ago. What on earth is it now?'

'Mrs Grainger, I promise I won't keep you long and I'll try to come straight to the point.' I took a breath and tried to be as concise as possible. 'When your husband's personal items were returned to you was there a playing card in amongst them?'

Mrs Grainger gave me a quizzical look and screwed up her face as if she was trying to remember some mysterious fact.

'I believe it was found in his golf shoe at the time,' I offered by way of a memory jogger.

'Oh, I haven't got those any more. No, I gave them to someone over the road. They had just started to play so I thought I might as well let him have them,' she said.

'It isn't the shoes that I'm interested in, it's the card. Do you remember it, by any chance?'

'Oh, yes I do now. It was in one of the shoes wasn't it? That's right, yes. Don't know what he put it in there for. Perhaps he did it for luck. Couldn't have been more wrong could he, as it turned out? Oh, what a dreadful business it all was. I've tried to forget it, you know.'

'I'm terribly sorry to drag this up again but I think it might be important.'

'Do you? Well, I'll have a look for you but it's been a while. I might have thrown it away, I can't remember.'

With that she wandered out of the room and made her way upstairs. I sat in hope more than in expectation and wondered where I would go from here if she returned to tell me she had thrown it out years ago. Maybe I would walk into Corrigan's office and voluntarily put my head on the chopping block. As I sat in silence I found myself admiring a picture of what I thought resembled a French café scene which hung above the fireplace. It depicted a tranquil setting in what looked like the autumn. A few people, a few parked bicycles and a number of tables situated beneath a brightly coloured cherry tree outside in the afternoon sunshine. The waiter stood in the doorway and looked out across the square which was encompassed by quaint architecture. In no time my imagination had me sitting at one of the tables with Ana. France had turned into Portugal and I was lost in the solitude of her world once again.

'Haven't found it,' were the words I didn't want to hear as Mrs Grainger walked back into the room, shattering my daydream and sinking my heart with despair all at once.

'Not yet anyway. I've got to face up to all his things and have a good scout through them soon, so it could turn up yet.'

'Have you not gone through the items yet then?' I said with a little more hope that perhaps the card will still be sitting there.

'Not properly anyway. I'll have another look when I can and let you know if you'd like?'

'I would. Here's my card and the telephone number is there at the bottom. If you find it please call me straight away,' I almost begged.

One part of me wanted to ransack the whole house in search of it and yet I still wondered as to the likelihood that the cards would be anything more than a strange coincidence. With that I left Mrs Grainger in peace and said my goodbyes. As I started the car I noticed our nosy neighbour peering, once more, around her front-room window curtains. I smirked a little as I imagined her with a glass to the wall, eavesdropping on our conversation. Although the visit didn't really give me quite what I wanted, I have to say that all was not yet lost and that I was pinning my fading hopes on Mrs Grainger's search techniques. Within thirty minutes I was back at the station and avoiding going anywhere near Corrigan's office, at least for a little longer.

Chapter Eighteen

He watched John Garron check his pockets and heard him cursing out loud as he fumbled around for the keys to the front door of The Fallen Oak. Garron scanned the street around him as he turned the key and gave the door a hearty shove, which only opened part of the way and yet still enough for him to squeeze his large frame through the available gap and into the darkness of the pub. He had no intention or need to follow him in just yet. Garron wouldn't be leaving any time soon, not with last night's takings to count up.

He knew Garron's routine.

It was 6 o'clock in the morning and the distinct lack of activity and light from the rooms above the pub the night before had told him that Garron had spent the night away. He pulled another cigarette from the half-full packet and turned his head away from the pub as he lit it under the darkness of the arched steps. Only a wisp of smoke could have given his position away but he was willing to take the chance. Quietly, he studied the front of the pub and watched Garron through the grubby windows of the lounge bar, noticing the deep red of the ancient flecked wallpaper. A single light had been switched on behind the bar, just enough light for Garron to see what he was doing as he began transferring the glasses from their overnight position on the sticky table tops to the comparative cleanliness of the dishwasher.

He dropped his cigarette end and trod it into the dirty pavement. A final exhalation of the stuff that would probably kill him one day, albeit he hadn't necessarily expected to live this long, and out of the shadows he came. He knew that it would all be about the timing, something he was quite proud of getting right, most of the time. He took a good look around the market square before he crossed the street towards the pub. No market stalls today; all part of the plan, of course. Sunday morning was always like a morgue around here and he knew Garron would be nice and early. Isn't routine a wonderful thing? he thought to himself as he wandered closer to his target.

Closer to his prey.

And yet he would not take his prey today. He would not see him dead today. Today he wanted to make him think. Today he was playing nicely, but that would change in time.

Garron had emptied the contents of the safe onto the floor behind the bar and was counting the takings that had been gathered from the till at midnight and placed into a small holdall, when he heard a loud bang that made him jump and instinctively swear out loud. With his heart pounding in his chest he held his breath so as to listen hard for any noise in the pub. He heard nothing but knew it wasn't just the wind blowing something over or blowing a door shut. He had to check. His arm squeezed between the safe and the wall, rucking his jumper up his forearm and causing the exposed skin to scrape against the rough brick. His fingers felt for the gun. Instinctively, he managed to loop an index finger into the trigger guard and slowly draw it towards him. He stood up as quietly as possible and took very careful steps into the corridor behind the bar that led to the rooms at the rear of the pub. He was sure that the noise had come from somewhere towards the back of the building. It definitely wasn't upstairs so he concentrated his efforts on searching the rear rooms. He stood in silence outside each room before gently pushing the door open with his foot, ensuring that he kept his body out of the way of the entrance to the room in case anyone bounded out and tried to knock him onto his back. The two rooms at the back of the pub were empty, which left only one place to check … the cellar.

He could see Garron's shadow and hear his breathing now; closer, closer. It was dark and murky in the cellar and it was going to stay that way. He had unscrewed the bulb that dangled from a single piece of flex from one of the old beams and had secured it safely into his pocket. Perfect … c'mon Garron; closer, closer.

Now it was his turn to take a long, slow breath and hold it, waiting for the right moment to spring his surprise. Garron looked down at the old rickety wooden steps that led into the darkness and reached for the light switch. Click … click … nothing. Bloody bulb has gone, he thought to himself. Garron half-turned away from the steps and was about to return to the bar to fetch a torch when he heard another noise ... something clanged against a barrel and the echo sent a chill through him. His trigger-finger was squeezing ever so slightly and now he knew he had a guest. The creaking of the old wooden steps couldn't be avoided so he took a leap down onto the cellar floor and landed flat-footed with his gun pointing into the unknown.

'Come out, yer bastard,' he yelled.

Silence, absolute silence.

Garron tried to focus but it was pitch black apart from the small amount of morning light that entered the cellar from the top of the steps behind him. His mind was trying hard to understand what had made the first loud noise. The second noise could have been a rat scurrying into a barrel but even that didn't make much sense. Confused and feeling helpless, Garron relaxed his stance and dropped the gun down by his side. That was when something smashed him in the face and sent him reeling uncontrollably into a stack of wooden pallets. The gun he had been holding was no longer in his hand. Garron felt blood trickle down his chin and before he could properly react another hard blow hit the side of his head, almost rendering him unconscious. The kicks and punches rained into him and were so fast that they all blurred into one huge attack. He felt himself being lifted by his head and struck with a terrible force. His stomach and ribs were being kicked and he could barely breathe. The second of the next two firm thumps to his face turned his world to darkness.

When he came to he simply couldn't move for quite some time, he just lay in his own blood and slowly moved his fingers and toes, which all responded satisfactorily. Garron was alive but had taken a severe beating. He felt pain almost everywhere. He could just about focus and was able to see a shaft of daylight coming down into the cellar, brighter than before and just enough light to see something stuck on the back of his left hand. He dragged his hand closer to his battered face and saw exactly what it was. A postcard; not stuck but nailed into his bleeding hand. He starred in horror at the picture of a huge church and the words printed diagonally across the picture ... Welcome to Bratislava. A gasp of breath stabbed into his ribs as Garron winced at the realisation of exactly who was back in town. It took another whole hour before Garron got himself to the top of the steps and into the hallway.

Opening time was some way off and he was extremely grateful for that. He didn't want anyone to see him like this: later OK, but not right now. He slowly put his hand into the pocket of his trousers and managed to get two fingers to draw his mobile phone out. As he tried to focus properly on the address book he felt a cough take over. He couldn't stop it and had to endure a dreadfully painful couple of minutes as his bruised and battered body retched, constricting his breathing even further. John Garron panted and deliberately breathed as shallowly as he could and yet still get some oxygen, in order to control the pain in his ribs. He crawled back to the safe and it was no great surprise to him to see that the money that he had begun to count was gone. He lay behind the bar, out of sight, and made a call to Mandy, who worked as a bit of a fill-in at the pub when it was busy. Garron told her that he needed her to cover later on and she was more than happy for some extra money. The blood on his face and hands was drying. He avoided seeing his reflection anywhere at the moment but he knew he wasn't a pretty sight right now. As he caught his breath he remembered the gun and began to feel his pockets, but realised it had gone. He turned himself very carefully and glanced back down the corridor towards the cellar. He could see smears of blood on the floor and shook his head at the thought of the clear-up operation he had to do before he managed to leave.

He couldn't leave a trace. No-one must know. The more he eliminated the possibilities as to the whereabouts of the gun, the more he realised that it must be in the cellar and he couldn't leave it there either. The little rest he had afforded himself would have to come to an end as there was some tidying up to do.

Garron didn't relish hauling himself back down the cellar steps but he had no choice. With the aid of a small set of steps that he always left behind the bar he slowly got himself upright, and as he took the first step of what was about to feel like an epic journey he glanced down at the open and very empty safe. 'Bastard' he muttered as another droplet of blood dripped down onto the wooden floor in front of him.

Chapter Nineteen

The office prankster who had been sabotaging my mobile phone by changing the ring tone and increasing the ringing volume appears to have got bored at last. I had actually forgotten about it and had left my phone on my desk from time to time with no adverse effects. Sometimes the prankster gets to the stage where they feel that their actions no longer have the desired effect and they simply give up with it. Conversely, Bob and I didn't have the luxury of giving up with our task of discovering who had killed Revd Martin Brookes and had been doing something that we called 'stirring the porridge'. It was a term we used years ago when we worked at Walthamstow together. As an analogy, it was a comparison between stirring porridge and getting the lumps to come to the top and delving into the Martin Brookes case and seeing whether anything substantial showed itself. We painstakingly revisited everything that we knew from the moment that Doreen Calderwood phoned Martin before she popped over to the church and found the grisly scene. After two hours of probing Bob came out with another of his little gems.

'Well, we've got it surrounded; I'll go get us a coffee.'

'Surrounded' like a wagon train being encircled by yelping Apache or Cheyenne or Sioux Indians, I never knew the difference. I was only pleased when Richard Widmark came to the rescue.

As Bob disappeared out of the office, I thought I should call Andy Potter and at least keep him up to date with the Daniel Grainger ace of clubs fiasco. I searched my phone and found his mobile number. I called.

'Hey, Dave, how ya doing mate?' said Andy in his own jolly way.

'Hi, Andy. I'm OK mate. Just thought I should let you know how I got on at Grainger's house the other day.'

'Ah, yeah, I did wonder. Did she still live there?'

'She did, thank goodness ... and she was in.'

'That's a bit of luck, how'd you get on? Did you get any joy?'

'Sort of. Her name's Louisa and she didn't mind me turning up unannounced, so that was good. I asked her about the card and whether she still had it. When she told me that she had got rid of his golf shoes I feared the worst but she thought the card was upstairs with his other stuff; she still hasn't cleared it all out. So, she went upstairs to have a ferret about. When she came down she said she couldn't find it but she promised to have another look and let me know if it turns up.'

'Oh, well, I suppose that's something. Dave, I was thinking ... what good will it do if you do find it? We all thought it was nothing more than him being superstitious. Like a lucky charm when he played. We assumed that he saw himself as the ace of clubs, y'know ... the best player.'

'That could be true, Andy. I might be wasting my time but it's not the face of the card I'm interested in; it's the back.'

'The back? What about it?'

'I want to see whether the pattern on the back of the card matches the one that was found in the church, remember ... the Martin Brookes case?'

'So, if it's from the same pack, which I doubt ...'

'Then we might have the same killer ...'

'Well, good luck with that, Dave. Think you're gonna need it.'

'Worth a go, Andy. I'll let you know.'

I put my phone back down onto my desk and rubbed my eyes. A sigh quickly followed and I was wondering all over again where this was heading as Bob returned and swore out loud as the hot coffee spilt onto his fingers.

Chapter Twenty

The news of the death of Stan Elms hit Derek Bladen like an earthquake. A '10' on the Richter scale. He felt a chill run down his spine and he became instantly light-headed. He felt a sense of nausea and needed to sit down. His kitchen radio had delivered the news, now that the dead man's name could be publicly released. He staggered into his living room and sat ashen-faced for twenty minutes before he could regain his composure.

Bladen lived with his elderly wife, Joyce, in a small house close to the doctor's surgery in Writtle, Essex. Joyce was bedridden and asleep, oblivious to the bombshell that had just rocked her husband's world. His head was suddenly full of confusion. He needed to call someone, but who? Derek was sixty-nine and was known as 'Grandad' by all his old mates. He was easily the oldest of the bunch that used to roam the streets of East London in their heyday. He was born in Hackney and went to school there, when he was at school, that is. After a number of different jobs, he worked for a greengrocer in Bow and got to know his way around the area well. His mates would taunt him by saying, 'How's the boy doing, Alfie?' The greengrocer would reply with something like, 'He'll be fine when he grows up a bit.'

Derek Bladen was at least fifteen years older than the greengrocer but he never minded. At least they were all mates. He always said that if they were taking the piss then they liked you, if they weren't, then something was wrong. But due to one thing or another there weren't many of his old friends left that he could turn to. They all seemed to have either moved far away or he had lost touch with them during and after their spells in 'Her Majesty's', or some other fate had got the better of them. Derek had been suffering with emphysema for a number of years and his condition wasn't improving, not that he really expected it to. Shocks like this one made his breathing more difficult than usual as his heart rate quickened and his lungs demanded more oxygen. With long, slow, deep breaths he switched on the oxygen bottle that sat by his armchair with all the necessary tubes connected. He fitted the nasal cannula to his nostrils and took a few steady breaths. He spent a lot of his afternoons and evenings 'getting topped up', as he called it. From where he sat he could see out to the road where his pride and joy was parked. He had wanted a BMW ever since he used to see them gleaming at him from the showroom in Whitechapel Road opposite the greengrocer's shop. He had had a few years of enjoyment from it but his current condition dictated that he wouldn't be flitting off without a care any more. Not unaided, and not without his bloody bottle.

He considered waking Joyce and telling her about old Stan but decided that she probably wouldn't recall who he was, what with her failing memory that had been getting progressively worse in recent months. As he looked out to the road outside, a group of schoolchildren caught his eye as they marched along in twos like a procession of animals ascending onto Noah's ark. He could hear their excitement at being taken on some outing, probably down to the church hall for the book sale that had been advertised in his local magazine recently. Derek reminded himself of how he would pass the time when he lived near Whitechapel Road as a boy. He lived with his mum and grandma not far from the River Lea and if the weather was OK he would go down to the river and wander along, talking to the fishermen and watching them catch perch and roach, and sometimes one of the men would drag out a pike.

The River Lea started life in the Chiltern Hills not far from Luton and meandered its way for about forty-two miles towards the capital through Hertfordshire, and after working its way in and around East London it would eventually make it to the River Thames. Derek would venture along towards Hackney Wick and back again but not a lot further than that. There was a group of boys that were older than him who used to be knocking about along that stretch of the river too and Derek, having fallen foul of them once, didn't relish a chance meeting again, so he always turned back in good time. But Derek wasn't averse to a punch-up when the numbers were fair, and all his mates knew that even if they were his mates they still needed to afford him a certain amount of respect when it came to asserting yourself in the pack.

His attention returned to the present when he snapped out of his daydream and felt the horror that had previously consumed him return. He didn't know the details of exactly what had happened to Stan Elms but he knew enough to appreciate that someone out there had planned their move carefully. He knew in his heart that this was not just any old random attack, he wished it was. Again, he thought about calling someone to try to find out a bit more. There was only one person he could think of that might have had their ear to the ground lately and might just know some of the details, or at least know how to find out; Garron. But it wasn't going to be straightforward to simply start up a conversation with him, not since they had a huge fall-out some years ago. He thought hard about what he would say if he called him and sat silently for a number of minutes before electing to shelve the idea and just wait patiently to see what information drifted through on the grapevine.

Maybe it would be better not to know after all.

Once more, he reflected on the sad news and felt his eyes fill with tears. But his emotional response was not so much for Stan Elms. Nor was it for Daniel Grainger or Martin Brookes.

It was for himself.

He was the only one of the gang left alive.

Chapter Twenty-One

The more Bob and I tussled with the Martin Brookes case the more we both thought that there had to be more to it. Maybe we hoped there was more to it, but either way it was starting to be a thorn in our side and one that we wanted removed sooner rather than later. Could someone have simply entered St Dominic's with the sole purpose of shooting the vicar without a motive? Neither of us thought so and therefore we had to prove it to ourselves before DCI Corrigan completely lost his, already threadbare, patience. Our problem was not only that nobody caught sight of anything unusual or that SOCO and forensics had turned up nothing substantial or significant, it was also that Doreen had done such a splendid job of clearing up that any shred of useful evidence ended up in her mop bucket. I shall never forget the faces of the two PCs and the paramedic that day in Doreen's living room when she announced what she had done. The stunned silence that fell around the room said it all.

My phone buzzed away in my jacket pocket and made just enough of a vibration against the chair leg to get my attention. I had switched it to vibrate when I was in a meeting earlier in the day and forgotten to switch it back again. I reached in and picked it out.

'Hello, Dave Calloway …'

'Oh, I'm sorry to bother you, this is Louisa Grainger.'

'Ah, Mrs Grainger, how are you?' I said with an extra beat or two to my heart rate at the anticipation of whether she had found the card.

'I'm very well, thank you.'

I don't care, have you found the card?

'Good, how can I help you?'

Have you found the card? Have you found the card?

'You said to call you, I hope it isn't inconvenient. I know you're very busy.'

'No, it's fine, Mrs Grainger, how can I help?'

'I was upstairs looking through Daniel's things and I found that card you wanted so I gave you a call, is that OK?'

Oh, God … I love you.

'Yes, of course it is. Is it alright if I drive up to get it this afternoon?'

'You can, I suppose, or I could post it to you.'

'No, no it's fine. I'll come up now if you don't mind?'

'Alright then, I'll see you soon.'

'Thank you, Mrs Grainger, bye.'

* * *

With the ace of clubs in my possession I was keen to get back and compare it with the ace of hearts that I had locked in my desk. When I returned to Chelmsford it was getting dark, and as I drove into the yard I saw Corrigan driving out. Timing is everything, I thought.

Although I knew the back of the heart was blue, I still needed to see them side by side to be sure that they had exactly the same pattern and I just couldn't be sure purely from memory. I stood beside my desk and laid the ace of clubs face down. It was certainly blue but was it the same pattern? I unlocked my desk and lifted the ace of hearts out, laying it beside the club. I studied them and could see that the patterns were both blue, and both seemed to be showing an identical zig-zag design which ran across the card, but to me they differed in some way. The zig-zag was blue with white and the edge was a slightly darker shade of blue but what was it that I didn't like? My eyes flickered from card to card, comparing, checking and studying. Then it dawned on me, the edges of the cards were imperfect; they were not exactly the same. It was almost as if the darker blue edges had been drawn on individually afterwards. The more I stared at the darker colour, the more I could see the difference between the two cards.

It wasn't a great difference but it was there. Why?

I sat down, trying to comprehend what this meant and whether the cards were linked in some way or not, other than the fact that they were both discovered in suspicious circumstances. I tapped one card against the other as my mind whirred through the possibilities.

Did they come from the same pack?

Where is the pack?

Were they left by the same person?

'What d'you reckon then?' said Bob after a long, quiet pause.

'Well, they are very similar. The pattern is definitely the same and the colouring too. Both have this blue edge to them although it doesn't look original, but I reckon they are too similar to be anything other than connected. I reckon this is good, Bob.'

'Could be, mate. So, if you reckon the cards are connected in some way then that raises another poser. Do we have ourselves a double killer or is it more complicated: are the victims connected too? Is someone doing the rounds?'

Chapter Twenty-Two

When she woke and reluctantly tried to focus on the green light that provided the only glow in the room, Debbie Fisher just knew that the digital figures on her bedside clock were going to be displaying some unearthly time that spelt out that she had once again been robbed of a good night's sleep. Sometimes she blamed the fact that she had gone to bed too late and couldn't get her mind to relax, other times she had eaten too late and caused herself to dream all sorts of stupid, nonsensical, weird and wonderful craziness.

It was 02:29.

Her first thought was always regarding Kim in the next room, just along the hall. Debbie could never simply turn over and fall asleep without taking at least a quick look in on Kim. She stepped out of bed, her feet fumbling for the cosiness of her slippers, and ambled slowly towards Kim's room. The door was open, as it always was at night, so that Debbie could always hear Kim if she were to cry out whilst having one of her bad dreams. Kim was sound asleep. When she slept she looked so peaceful and was free, temporarily, from the tragedy that controlled her life. Debbie pulled Kim's quilt up a little more and glanced around the room, noticing that the curtain at the bedroom window was not pulled completely across, allowing the light from the streetlamp opposite to invade Kim's solitude. She took a few careful steps towards the window, trying to avoid treading on any of Kim's CDs that seemed to spend more of their life on the floor than in the rack on her table next to the mirror. Debbie put her hand onto the edge of the curtain and looked across the street at the offending streetlamp and along the rows of cars in the sleeping neighbourhood. It was then that she saw him looking up at the window, his eyes filled with a hateful, demonic stare. Debbie jumped back and kicked a CD casing across the room. She looked at Kim but thankfully she was oblivious to the sudden noise. Debbie was two feet from the window and could no longer see down to the pavement outside her house.

She didn't want to look … she had to look.

What if he was still there?

What did he want?

Why was he staring up at the window like that?

Debbie was shaking all over as she peered through the gap in the curtains, aiming her gaze downwards to the pavement. He was gone … no, across the road … a man with his back to the house. She couldn't be sure whether this was him or not … and then he turned to face her. Debbie was frozen to the spot. She wanted to step out of sight but her legs were going nowhere. He looked hard at her face and then did something that caused Debbie's legs to finally buckle.

He pointed at her and smiled.

She spent the next five minutes shaking and whimpering on the floor in Kim's room, quietly so as not to disturb Kim. Debbie managed to get onto her knees and sat to one side of the window, not knowing what to do next. Somehow, she plucked up the courage to take one more look.

Nothing … just a peaceful street scene in the middle of the night.

Debbie went back to bed and lay awake but for a few moments of dozing off, each time waking with a jump, until she could hear the dawn chorus beckoning to the steady pace of sunrise.

* * *

John Garron ached. He let out a deep groan as he turned onto his back and stared up at the ceiling in his bedroom. It had been another night of broken sleep and discomfort. He slid one leg towards the edge of the bed and hooked his foot over the side of the mattress in order to get some sort of purchase before he tried to slide himself further across to the edge. He had got used to this routine and found that it was still the best way to get himself out of bed. Once he was all the way over to one side he allowed one leg at a time to reach down to the floor. With two feet on the floor he slowly lowered his body over the edge, simultaneously turning so that he ended up on his knees beside the bed with his body on the top of the mattress.

That was the worst and most painful part done and from here on it was comparatively easy. Once he was upright he wandered slowly into the bathroom and stood leaning against the wall. As the hot water steamed in the cold sink, Garron looked into the mirror and inspected the damage. The cuts were healing but the bruising was still there. He lowered his gaze and could see the variety of colours that now adorned his sturdy upper body. His ribs were still reddened and his abdomen blackened. At sixty-one, Garron was still a formidable man, fit for his age, which he knew would make a big difference to his recovery time. He wanted to shave today and smarten himself up a little. He thought it might make him feel better. As he shaved off five days of beard growth he noticed the very sore-looking scab on the back of his hand where the 'calling card' had been left. He sneered in the mirror and repeated his daily promise that one day he would get even. He had been cooped up for a few days and really wanted to get some air, so he dressed and decided to visit Debbie and get the lecture out of the way.

Garron knew precisely how Debbie was going to react, the same way she always did when he got in a spot of bother. Debbie had seen him come home displaying war-wounds a number of times over the years, although usually he had won the battle. Not this time though. What he didn't want was for Kim to see him like this. As he was about to leave home he remembered Debbie's plea last time for him to call before he came. He recalled the anxiety she felt whenever he turned up unannounced, and how she would jump out of her skin because of the resemblance he had to her husband, who had been hit by a truck and killed. He sighed and switched on his mobile phone. As soon as it had become active it rang, startling him slightly, but he didn't speak; he just listened.

Debbie's voice was fraught, 'John, are you there?'

'Deb, yeah, I was just gonna call and let you know I'm coming over.'

'Can you hurry up?'

'What's the matter? Is it Kim?'

'No, she's fine. It's probably nothing but there's been some bloke standing across the road and he kept looking over here. It's got me worried.'

Garron froze momentarily. He thought of the beating and who had delivered it. Was it him?

'Debbie, lock the doors and windows, close the curtains and do not go outside or answer the door to anyone. I'll be right there as soon as I can.'

'You're frightening me, what's going on?'

'Just do it, please. No questions; just do it. I won't be long, I promise.'

'John? Give me the code when you get here ... you remember?'

'Yeah, course. Now do as I say.'

Garron didn't give Debbie the chance to ask for any sort of explanation, he just cut the call off, grabbed a jacket and locked the front door behind him.

On his way to Debbie's his mind tussled with conflicting emotions. He hated hearing her so fraught and so scared. If it was him, he knew it wasn't Debbie he was really getting at.

She was just part of his game.

She was a weapon he chose to use to create the desired effect and get at Garron. He shuddered with anger at the fact that he had got so close, the fact that he had found her ... and Kim.

If he ever touched either of them ...

As Garron got to within a couple of miles of Debbie's house he knew he ought to slow down. If he didn't he would end up in some woman's front garden or worse. Although it was still quite early the traffic was starting to thicken, and people were milling about and hustling to bus stops and reversing their cars off of their driveways. He glanced to his left and his attention was drawn to the entrance into Hornchurch Cemetery, where Brian Fisher was buried five years ago. He had been on his way to get the District line train at Hornchurch Bridge but never made it. Garron drove past the spot where it happened, where the truck mounted the pavement and struck him from behind before leaving Brian to die against a shop front. The rain that morning created a river of blood that spread across the pavement and into the gutter.

The police investigation was cut and dried. The truck had lost control in the rainy conditions; it was dark and the road was greasy. They hadn't any idea where the truck had come from or where it may have been heading, it just vanished. There was no CCTV in that area and no-one saw a thing that helped. The truck never turned up again, which didn't entirely surprise Garron, he never thought it would. He felt that he knew the truth but had never told, and would never tell, Debbie. Brian Fisher and John Garron looked alike. That was all he needed to know. He had never been able to find out who the truck driver was but something ate away inside him and had done ever since that dreadful day.

Unfinished business.

He called it the tipping point.

Debbie heard a gentle tap on the front door and listened for a friendly voice.

'My toys are your toys,' he said.

Debbie unlocked the door and all but dragged him inside the hallway, grabbing him in her clutches, so relieved that he was there.

'What's the matter?' she asked as he winced and moaned in pain, the ribs still very tender.

'Nothing, it's nothing.'

'Oh, look at your face. What the fuck have you been doing now?'

'Let's get inside, Deb. Put the kettle on will ya? I'm drier that an Arab's jock strap.'

Chapter Twenty-Three

'I'll get Andy Potter to come in and meet with us, see if we can't tie up a few loose ends,' said Bob.

'Yeah, you do that ... Coffee?'

'Please, mate.'

As I walked away from the desk I could hear that Bob had successfully got through to Andy and was urging him to come and see us. The office was bustling today which usually meant one thing; DCI Corrigan was in the building. Some people responded to that by making themselves scarce and others would want to be seen to show just how busy they were. It seemed that most people were playing that particular game today. Various ranks had been in and out of his office today doing their own brand of 'brown-nosing', something you wouldn't find me and Bob doing. They would walk around with a folder or maybe an A4 piece of paper that made them look, or perhaps feel, important. Some would be jotting notes onto a pad as they hustled along corridors. I, on the other hand, had two dirty, empty coffee mugs.

'Mr Calloway, busy I see.'

I turned sharply and there he was, peering through a crack in a partition between his office and the printing and photocopying room.

'Yes, sir,' was all I could think of immediately as the coffee mugs clinked together as if to declare exactly how busy I was.

'You can make me one whilst you're at it.'

With that, he returned to his office, and vanished inside.

'Bugger. Bloody basic error,' I said to myself.

Now I couldn't get away with simply handing the coffee over, I would have to go into his lair. I made my way back to my desk first to drop off Bob's coffee for him and explained that I had been snared. All Bob did was snigger. I knocked and waited for the command to enter Corrigan's office, then went inside, leaving the door wide open in the hope of having created an escape route.

'Close the door, please,' he said.

I put his coffee down on his desk and turned to leave. I knew it was an unlikely plan but worth a go.

'Now then, Mr Calloway.' It was never good when he addressed you as Mr. 'Please enlighten me on your progress with the murder of that unfortunate vicar in Laurel's End, would you?'

How did I guess?

I told Corrigan all about the theory that there may be some connection between the cards found at the scenes of the two murders, if Daniel's was a murder, and how I was intending to follow this up. He looked down his beaky nose at me with a sort of suspicious intrigue. I didn't know whether this was good or bad but I pressed on with my thoughts and explanations as to why Bob and I felt that it was worth following, as it was the only decent lead at the moment. I tried to sound as convincing as possible but his expression didn't alter one bit.

Then he surprised me totally.

'Well done, it sounds as though you may have something there. I'm not convinced, I might add, but I'm happy, as much as I can be with you and Hand, to allow you to push on for now, but don't take forever, will you?'

'No, sir, we're working on it now.'

'Really,' he said sceptically, '… and the coffee, is that helping too?'

'As much as it helps you, sir.'

Corrigan's face reddened slightly and he shook his head gently from side to side in disgust, no doubt.

'I can tell you're working with Hand. Go on, out you go and keep me up to date. I don't want to be chasing around after you two, I've got enough to do here.'

* * *

'Well?' said Bob enquiringly.

'Well, he told me to push on with it. Seemed to think it might be getting us somewhere at last.'

'Huh, how nice.'

'So, what did Andy have to say? Is he coming?' I asked as I slumped back into my chair and took a sip of coffee.

'Yep, he's on his way. He seemed keen to help out and he said he liked the idea. He should be able to shed some light on things, I reckon. He's bringing a folder on Daniel Grainger for us to go through. See if we can match any details of him and Martin Brookes.'

'That would be handy to say the least,' I said.

* * *

Andy Potter arrived about two hours later and made his way up to the floor where Bob and I worked our fingers to the bone. As promised, he had with him a folder containing as much detail on Daniel Grainger as the original investigation had gathered. It was Grainger's past that I was interested in, his work, where he lived when he was young, which school he attended and all that sort of thing. If there was nothing significant in this folder I could check again with Louisa Grainger to see whether she could help. But before I pestered her again I wanted to go through the history that we had. Andy guided Bob and me through the information that was set out in front of us. He started with the initial investigation into Daniel's death and as expected, there was nothing new to add at this time. The photographs of Daniel's body showed how the top half of him had been severely burnt, rendering any recognition of his facial features impossible. He was pictured face down with his head turned to one side. It seemed that the lower half of his legs were virtually untouched and his golf shoes were clearly visible. I wondered whether he had put them on with the intention of spending a bit of time on the practice green or the driving range before the match started. We also looked at the investigation from the aspect of it being a murder rather than an accident but it was difficult to prove as our prospective killer had left no indication that he had even been there. The footprints that were imprinted into the rough ground immediately outside of the shed were mostly those of golfers, studded treads. His injuries matched the original scenario of him falling forwards heavily and causing a blunt trauma to his face and head. The damage to the top half of his body was represented by full thickness burns over almost all of it, leaving his legs with partial and superficial burns which included some blistering.

Once we were done with going over the details about the scene in the shed at the rear of the first green we began to study Grainger's history. His wife, Louisa, had provided most of the information about his youth but only as far back as she could recall. They had met when Daniel was in his late 20s and gone through the usual courtship rituals. She hadn't known him during his school years and by all accounts he moved from school to school. He hailed from the East End of London originally and was a member of a boxing club in Bethnal Green. The rest was sketchy but it was a start. We went around in circles a couple more times before deciding to call it a day for now. Andy promised to keep his ears and eyes open and call me or Bob if he heard anything which might be of use. In the meantime, I was keen to delve into Martin Brookes and see whether anything of his past crossed paths with Grainger's.

It had been established that Martin had worked at St Patrick's Church on Mile End Road in Stepney, East London, for a number of years before venturing into the Essex countryside and taking over at St Dominic's in Laurel's End. I needed a way into the life of Martin Brookes prior to his days with the Church but I didn't seem to have anything at the moment so, to my mind, the only way was to go and get it. Bob had seen Andy off the station and had come back upstairs.

'Well, it's a start, eh? We know a bit more now. All we have to do is some digging into the vicar's past and see what turns up.'

'Yep, just what I was thinking.'

'How far back can we go so far?'

I took a glance down at the Martin Brookes file and said, 'We go back as far as his job in Stepney, that church … St Patrick's.'

'Let's start there then,' said Bob.

I began to check on whose station ground the church was on in order to phone the local station and speak with the officer in charge to let him know, just out of courtesy, that we would be sniffing around on his patch. I explained to Bob what I was doing, which I felt was the right thing to do in the circumstances.

'Fuck that. I'll pick you up first thing in the morning, we'll go in my motor. C'mon let's pack up and go home. We'll get down there early and see what we can find out.'

A leopard never changes its spots, does it?

Chapter Twenty-Four

Bob was bright and early and before I knew it we were heading off into East London. His old Vauxhall Cavalier rattled its way through New Wanstead and picked up the A12.

'You got any idea who the vicar is? This one we're gonna see?' Bob asked between bouts of swearing at other, really quite innocent, motorists.

I had checked him out on the internet last night and discovered who he was.

'His name is Chris Fragakis.'

'Indian bloke?'

'You'll find that's Greek, you wally. Honestly … don't go and upset him, will ya? Let me do the intros, eh?'

'It'll be alright. I like the ol' "bubbles".'

Bob's reference was straight from the cockney rhyming slang … Bubble and Squeak – Greek.

It said on the net that he lived directly off the Mile End Road so if he wasn't in church we might find him at home. Hopefully he'd be in church and we wouldn't have to go searching for him. We turned off the A12 and onto the A11 which would lead us nicely into Bow and then on to Stepney and the Mile End Road. Bob was whingeing that he wanted a fag but I was insistent that he waited until we got there so he could light up before we went inside St Patrick's. Besides I definitely didn't want to be filling my lungs with smoke whilst I was trapped in the confines of Bob's old Vauxhall. The traffic became heavy as we approached our destination, which only served to wind Bob up a little bit more. He began muttering at other drivers and slapping his hands against the steering wheel as his stress levels bubbled towards boiling point. I was, not for the first time on this journey, wishing that I had come alone. Finally, the traffic came to a halt. A bus had tried to squeeze through a gap that would barely accommodate a car and jammed itself very close to a removal lorry that was coming in the opposite direction. From now on it was going to develop into a 'Mexican stand-off' and one that would not be beneficial to Bob and his already strained and frayed nerves. The bus driver got down from his cab and made his way towards the driver of the removal lorry. With one very rotund and irate bus driver peering up at the open window of the removal lorry we had the makings of being in for the long haul. St Patrick's Church was about three-quarters of a mile further down the road and I was very tempted to wish Bob farewell and walk the rest.

But I didn't.

'C'mon, sort it out,' Bob yelled, now a fully-fledged member of the newly founded 'hang out of the window shouting club'.

Thankfully, before Bob had any ideas about getting involved, the bus driver got back on board and began waving at the removal lorry to come through the gap. There was just enough room for it to crawl by but not before a quick round of four-letter words and V-signs had been exchanged one last time.

'About bloody time and all. Go on, sling yer hook,' was Bob's parting gift to the removal lorry driver and thankfully his only contribution to the whole fiasco.

There was enough space immediately outside the front of the church to park the old Vauxhall. Bob stepped out of the car and lit a cigarette. I looked up at the building and lost myself in the architecture for a moment. I always found these sorts of buildings mesmerising. The huge blocks of masonry, the intricate stonework and the figures that peered down towards the street. People often misquote them as gargoyles but they have water spouting from them. These, I believe, were grotesques.

'One of 'em reminds me of my ex.'

'Remember to behave yourself and don't call him a bubble.'

We entered the main part of the church and could see three men perched at the front of the rows of pews, sitting in silence with their heads bowed.

'D'ya reckon he's one of 'em?' said Bob.

'Don't know but let's not disturb them, eh. Just wander up the aisle and see if we can find somebody to ask.'

Slowly we walked past rows of bench seats on either side of us and made our way closer to the gentlemen at the front. There were two impressive crimson drapes at the far end of the church, hanging at a very large window of stained glass that allowed a few beams of sunlight to intrude. Statues that stood proudly in the alcoves to left and right seemed to watch us enter as if they were deciding on whether they approved or not. Hopefully they approved of me, Bob was another matter.

'Can I help you, gentlemen?' said a voice from behind us.

I turned to see someone that I recognised as a vicar and assumed that this might be our man.

'Yes, I hope so. I'm Detective Inspector Calloway and this is Detective Sergeant Hand. We are hoping to be able to have a chat with Chris Fragakis.'

'Ah, well you've found him … call me Chris. Can I get you anything to drink … tea, coffee?'

'That would be lovely, tea for me.'

'Tea please,' Bob said

Chris called to someone out of sight at the back of the church and organised the tea.

'It's a good job you caught me, I was about to go down to the shops for an errand or two. Still, no problem, I can do that later on. So how can I help you?'

'It's about the vicar who was here before you, Martin Brookes?'

'Ah, yes, I heard about this. What an appalling thing to happen. Everyone was so shocked and so saddened by such dreadful news.'

'Yes, it must have been a shock to you all. As part of the investigation we would like to know a little more about Martin's past. How well did you know him?'

'I only met him about five years ago but we got on famously and he helped me settle in here at St Patrick's before he left. I don't know if I'll be able to help very much but I shall certainly do my best.'

'Thank you, we can't ask for any more, after all.'

We sat at the rear of the church on some rather rickety wooden stools that looked as though they belonged in an old Victorian school. The roof was much lower here and it certainly felt quite cosy. An ancient-looking electric bar fire was churning out as much heat as it could but most of that must have headed straight up to the roof or out to the street. Leaflets sat on shelves and Bibles were piled up on the dusty floor.

'I must thank you for your time and apologise for just dropping in like this,' I said.

'Oh, that's fine, don't worry. It's an open house after all. People often pop in and out throughout the day and if I'm here, I'm here. It's fine. Now what would you like to know?'

Before I could get into my stride I saw an elderly gentleman creeping along towards us with a tray of tea cups and saucers and a rather generous plate of chocolate biscuits. He reminded me of a Ronnie Barker character, stumbling along with more tea on the tray than there was in the cups. Everything halted before it had really begun as we were handed our tea. The plate of biscuits was fortunately out of Bob's reach.

'Right, Chris, can you tell me what Martin may have mentioned about himself before he became the vicar at St Patrick's?'

'I'll try. Let me see. He said he was born in Newham and lived there for most of his school life, but when his father died he and his mum moved to somewhere near Limehouse, or it may have been Shadwell, somewhere close to there anyway. I remember him saying that he had a job near Leadenhall Market when he first started work but it didn't last. I think the Church is the only thing that he had done for any length of time. He used to chat away quite happily about his friends although I got the feeling he didn't see them very much any more.'

'Can you remember any of the names?'

'Goodness, erm ... I'm not sure about the names. He said they were a formidable bunch and used to joke that they rained terror in the streets. Can't imagine that, can you? Not dear Martin.'

'What about the places that he visited when he was younger? Do you have any recollection of that sort of thing?'

'He was keen on fishing down by the River Lea. He told me a number of times that he and his pals used to fish down there. And he said once that he was a dab hand at darts and used to play for money in the pub. That's about it really, I can't think of anything else immediately. If any of this is true then he must have had a real change of heart when he decided on a life in the Church.'

Bob had been busily jotting everything down and keeping quiet ... until now.

'What about any other family, brothers, sisters?'

'He never said. He used to say his mates were his "brothers", a sort of a club it seemed to me. One of them was a bit of a boxer, I think, Martin used to watch him fight sometimes.'

Bingo ... Daniel Grainger attended a boxing club at Bethnal Green.

'If you could remember his name ... it's important,' Bob asked.

'Oh dear, now you're asking me. I'm rubbish with names.'

Chris sat in deep thought for a moment and I allowed him as much time as he needed.

'Martin used to refer to them as a group mostly. He would say "we did this" and "we did that". I'm sorry, I don't know. I wish I did.'

'OK. Thank you for your time, Chris. Here, take my card and don't hesitate to call if there's anything else that springs to mind.'

We said our goodbyes and left. Bob and I sat in the car for a moment outside the church and Bob looked over the notes that he had made.

'Doesn't get much clearer does it, mate?' he said

I had to agree with him. As Bob turned the key and brought the car to life I saw Chris coming towards Bob's window with an anxious look.

'Cheshire Street,' he said.

'Pardon me?'

'Cheshire Street, it's where the boxing club is. Repton is the name of it. They might help you more.'

'Thanks, Chris, well take a ride over. Bye.'

All of a sudden, we had a little bit more to go on and just maybe someone at the gym could link our boys together. We programmed the remotely fixed sat nav and were on our way.

Chapter Twenty-Five

Repton Gym has been an historic part of the local boxing fraternity. It had been established in 1884 and had over considerable time witnessed some memorable fights and produced many memorable champions. Some had become Olympians; others held world titles. Even the Kray twins had attended back in their heyday.

Repton was the real deal.

As soon as we walked in through the front door we could feel the atmosphere … it soaked into your skin. You could almost hear the crowds roaring as the fighters battled for victory. The white tiled walls and parquet floor caused footsteps and conversation to echo along the corridors. A plaque was strategically placed at the end of the corridor that led you directly into the gym itself.

It simply said 'No Guts, No Glory'.

As we passed underneath the heart-felt message we could see the boxing ring and hear the punches landing on punch bags and the unmistakable sound of whipping skipping ropes skimming the floor at ridiculous speeds. Shouts of encouragement were being directed at sweat-soaked bodies as they pounded bags and dodged and weaved. Sparring partners, protected by head guards, also resembled punch bags as they repeatedly absorbed blow after blow. The walls of the gym were adorned with pride and respect. Photographs of past members and past champions filled the walls all the way around the gym and echoed the history of the club. The ring itself was empty and yet full of the ghosts of gargantuan conquests that spanned the many decades. We noticed one of the trainers, rigged in the obligatory tracksuit, sitting on the canvas at one corner of the ring on the far side of the gym and

Syrup and Cyanide

made our way round to him. He must have been about 70 years old and he looked as though he had been there for a lot of those years. He had an old, wrinkled face that bore the evidence of many years in boxing, and a thick grey beard. His hands looked enormous and would be even larger wearing gloves.

His tracksuit bore his initials on the left breast: GD.

Gerry Dawson was the boss. He had been here at Repton for more years than he cared to remember and had had a hand in the development of numerous young boxers. During his career as a fighter he had gained the utmost respect from his fellow pugilists across Britain as well as many parts of Europe. Bob and I hadn't a clue who he was but we knew we wouldn't want to end up on the wrong side of him even at his advanced years. He peered over his glasses at us.

'Afternoon, gents, what can I do for you?' said GD.

'Good afternoon, we are trying to track down a couple of old friends that used to box here some years ago and wondered whether you might remember them,' said Bob.

'If they were here then I'll know 'em I expect. Although the old memory ain't what it used to be.'

'One of them is Martin Brookes.'

'What weight was he?'

'Weight? No idea.'

GD scratched his woolly chin and sighed.

'I don't recognise his name but if you knew what weight he fought at it might jog the old memory.'

'Well, we don't know his weight. Can't you remember him?' Bob's agitation was not going to work with GD.

'Nope. You gotta give me a bit more than that. I would know him if he was any good.'

I thought it was worth trying another name with GD in case he could help so I tried our other 'ace in the pack'.

'How about another name then ... Daniel Grainger?' I offered.

'Grainger ... yeah, I remember a Grainger. A nippy little bloke. Full of himself but a tidy little fighter. Never all that successful but he was a good trainer as I recall.'

'So, Daniel Grainger definitely came to this gym?' I confirmed.

'Yep, he was here. Him and Elmsy.'

'Elmsy?'

'Stan Elms. Welterweight he was. Not bad either. They were always in here together.'

Bob noted the new information as we listened to GD.

'But you can't place Martin Brookes?' I asked once more.

'Well, he could have been one of the others I suppose. There were four of 'em that used to come along together but only Grainger and Elms were any good so the other two got asked to leave. If you're not up to scratch you won't last at Repton. There ain't any room for slackers here. There are plenty of good boys out there who would love to have the chance at club membership, ya know?'

'Do you know the name of the fourth one?' I asked.

GD puffed out his cheeks as if he had just been on the receiving end of a low blow, although in reality he probably wouldn't flinch.

No guts, no glory.

'He was taller, heavier too. Older than the others, can't really say what his name was. Like I say, the other two didn't stay here very long. We've got our reputation to consider, ya know?'

'Of course. That's an impressive display of photos you've got on the walls,' I said

'Yeah, ain't it just? Some old photos amongst 'em too. Title challenges, some of our best fighters ... some of the best in the country. Lot of 'em went on to make a name for 'emselves and not just as boxers either. Some went into films, some still run clubs north and south of the water.'

'Would you be able to pick out Grainger and his mates?' Bob said hopefully.

'I might do, but I ain't got all day. Gotta class starting in ten minutes and there's a bloody lot of pictures up here. Still, if they are here ... they'll be ... somewhere in this section, I reckon. Not the oldest and not the most recent. If the boys start coming in early I'll have to leave ya to it.'

'I understand but it's important to us ... we'd really like to catch up with 'em and maybe if we see a photo we'll remember what they look like ... erm ... not seen 'em for a good few years,' said Bob.

GD removed his glasses and gave them a clean on his handkerchief as he wandered around the ring and led us to the start of a row of photos that would hopefully be the right era. Each photo was framed in exactly the same way; a pale green border. Every one was perfectly lined up, perfectly spaced apart. Another wall had black bordered frames and another further round the other side of the ring showed gold frames, most of those looked like certificates of some sort.

'Here we are then, gents. If they're anywhere they'll be amongst this lot.'

Without GD to lend a helping hand we wouldn't have known where to start, there must have been hundreds of photos. Floor to ceiling on some of the walls. The problem we had, of course, was that unless GD located them before the next class started to roll in we would never find them. Unless, of course, we showed our warrant cards, but so far, we hadn't had to. GD seemed happy enough to show us so we thought we'd let him carry on. We had no idea what they looked like in those days ... all we wanted was to find them together to get some sort of a link between them that we could work on. GD strolled along, reminiscing over title fights and belts and trophies, mumbling names as he went. We followed behind, gazing in admiration at the size of the trophies and the width of the belts that were slung over their shoulders, gloves held up for the photo. Finally, a bit of luck ...

'Here we are ... here's one of Grainger ... on the right of that bunch.'

'Who are the others?' I asked.

'Daly, Henderson, Collins, Franklin and O'Shea. None of the other lot you mentioned but they could still be here.'

We wandered some more and GD muttered some more.

'Ah, Grainger again ... and here is Elmsy after a training session with that Brookes boy you mentioned. Elmsy liked to pop ya in the ribs and then swivel his hips and catch ya with a short, sharp uppercut. He tried it on me once ... only once mind you. He soon recovered ...'

Bob and I took a look and stared intently at the photo. It was definitely Martin Brookes, much younger but unmistakable. We glanced at each other and nodded. Now we could tie Martin Brookes and Daniel Grainger together. The two aces were looking like key factors in potentially two murders. We couldn't be absolutely certain but things were coming together at last. Bob asked GD if he could take photos of the ones that included Grainger and Brookes. Elms would appear too, of course. GD had no problem with it so our badges stayed in our pockets again.

'Look, here's another of 'em in that crowd. That was the farewell do for one of the guys who had been at the club for twenty years. 'Minty' … good lightweight. Got 'imself injured in a fight in Milan and was never quite as sharp again. Good do, that was. Anyway, I've gotta fly … next class is here. Good luck with ya reunion. Hope ya find 'em in good health and say Gerry says 'ello.'

GD strode off towards a group of youths; all of them togged up and ready.

Chapter Twenty-Six

Our trip to 'the smoke' had been quite enlightening and given us just the kick-start we needed to progress with the investigation. Bob had downloaded the photos from his phone and printed them off onto 7x5-inch photo paper. The photos of Grainger, Brookes and Elms were spread out on my desk. As well as those there were a few of the group photos in case we needed to try to put names and faces together later, albeit the faces were on the younger side.

'Didn't Chris Fruitcake say that Martin Brookes used to watch the fights?' said Bob.

'Fragakis. Yeah, he did. Obviously, he did a bit more than watch. Maybe he never mentioned it to Chris. Perhaps he was embarrassed that he wasn't all that good and didn't want to tell him.'

'According to that bear in the tracksuit he wasn't up to much, was he?'

'No, but Stan Elms was. He might be able to clear up a few things; maybe he can tell us whether Grainger and Brookes had any particular enemies,' I said.

'Yeah, that might be handy. I'll have a "butcher's" round for him and see if I can dig him up from somewhere.'

I decided to let Bob do the searching while I let Corrigan know that we had found a link between the two aces. I was feeling quite smug that Bob and I had turned up some useful information and that we could now move on a bit more in our search for the answers to a few questions. Before I could gather the photos together and report to Corrigan, the DCI came out of his office and made a bee-line for me and Bob.

'Ah, sir, I was just coming to see you.'

'Voluntarily, Detective Inspector? Whatever next? Right, what have you got for me this morning?' he said with an exaggerated cheeriness.

I explained about our trip to visit Chris Fragakis and how that had led to us sniffing around at the Repton Gym. I showed him the photos and explained who was who, and that we were continuing to search for more information. Eerily, he seemed content for now that we had made some advances into the case.

'Keep me posted,' he said and retreated to his office.

'Bloody hell. Don't say we've done something right,' said Bob.

'You never know and what's more, it might keep him at bay for a bit too.'

I sat looking at the photos and wondering what the connection could possibly be between Grainger and Brookes other than them being old friends years ago. The worry was that that may be all it was, just old mates. Although it certainly seemed far more than an innocent coincidence that the aces had been involved and especially as they had both got some coloured marks around the edge. It was all very well thinking that both Grainger and Brookes had been murdered by the same person, but why? Louisa Grainger had routinely been asked whether she knew of anyone who might have wanted to cause harm to Daniel, although at the time it appeared to be a tragic accident, but after yesterday I wasn't so sure. If Grainger had been killed it had been well covered up at the time. I pondered as to whether the killer had worn golf shoes to disguise their footprints. Maybe.

Did Grainger know his killer?

Likewise, Martin Brookes may have too.

As yet we had no motive for the murders and no other link between the two men than Repton Gym. I got a coffee for myself and Bob and resumed my study of the photos, hoping that something else would jump out at me. Grainger, Brookes, Elms and many others.

Then a thought popped into my head ...

'Bob, didn't GD say there were four of them that used to go to the gym together?'

'That's right but he couldn't remember the other one.'

'No, he couldn't but I wonder if he's in any of the group photos? When you find Elms we'll ask him to have a look and see whether he can pick the other one out. At the very least he should know his name. Might even know where he lives today.'

Bob had been wading through a London telephone directory and had jotted down the addresses and telephone numbers of twenty-seven S. Elmses.

'Bloody twenty-seven.'

'Just be thankful his name isn't Smith,' I added.

'Yeah, could be worse, I suppose.'

My attention turned back to the display of faces looking proudly back at me on my desk. I thought about how ironic it seemed that Grainger, who loved to play golf, had died on a golf course and that Martin, once a rough little fighter, had ended up as a quiet and caring vicar. I wondered whether Louisa Grainger had any old photos where both of them were together and decided I would give her a quick call in the morning. Then, out of the blue, I realised that I had seen a photo of Martin Brookes before. It was sitting on the sideboard at Doreen Calderwood's house in Laurel's End. It wasn't too late in the day so I ferreted about in my diary for a phone number. Here she is ... Doreen Calderwood. I dialled the number, hoping she was at home.

'1-8-7-6,' she answered.

'Hello, Mrs Calderwood, this is Detective Inspector Calloway.'

'The dentist?' she said.

'No, the police officer who came to see you before, you remember?'

'The postman? Hold on I'll have to get my hearing aid thingy ... hold on, don't go away.' I could hear Doreen chatting away to herself as she went in search of her hearing aid. I couldn't help but smile; she always was a bit of a character and such a nice lady too.

'Hello, I'm back now ... who did you say it was, the dentist?'

'It's Detective Inspector Calloway.'

'Oh, hello, dear. How nice of you to call. You're lucky to get me at this time of the afternoon because when I'm watching *Countdown* I don't answer the phone but it finished a moment ago. I have it on loud and save the battery on my hearing thingy,' she said with a chuckle.

'Good idea. Mrs Calderwood, do you still have the photograph of Martin Brookes on your sideboard? The one you showed me?'

'Yes, I've still got it. I talk to him every day and tell him how much I miss our little cups of tea at the church,' she chuckled again.

'That's nice. Do you think I could come and have another look at it, maybe tomorrow?'

'If you like, yes. You'll have a piece of cake, won't you, dear?'

'Yes please, that would be lovely. I'll come about 10 o'clock if that's OK with you?'

'Any time. Come when you like, I'll be here,' she said cheerfully.

'Thank you, Mrs Calderwood. I'll see you in the morning then.' With that, she had already replaced the receiver and I realised that I may not get off so lightly tomorrow. A lovely lady, nonetheless.

Chapter Twenty-Seven

'So, what in hell have you been up to? For Christ's sake, John, you're no spring chicken any more,' said a shaky, yet irate, Debbie Fisher.

'Look, it's nothing, Deb. You don't need to worry about it.'

'John, look at yer. All bruised up ... tell me what happened ... was it in the pub? You should pack it in ... I don't wanna worry about you getting hurt as well as everything else.'

'It'll be alright. Don't keep on. I'm here, ain't I? Now tell me about this bloke you saw.'

Debbie let out a frustrated sigh at the stubbornness of her brother. She peeped up the stairs and briefly listened silently to check whether their conversation had disturbed Kim, but it was all quiet.

'Keep yer voice down, I don't want Kim to be woken up. She was tossing and turning all night. She needs her sleep and I don't want her seeing you in this state, it'd send her right off.'

'Yeah, I know. So ...?'

Debbie's eyes welled up again and she turned to John, reaching out to hold him tight. Fortunately for John Garron he saw the lunge coming and was able to take hold of Debbie's arms before she inflicted more pain to his rather delicate ribs.

'I thought he was gonna get in the house. I'd have got a knife if he'd come near my baby.'

Debbie's tears flooded down her cheeks and she trembled in John's arms.

'What'd he look like, Deb?'

'It was dark ... hard to say. I just went to close Kim's curtains a bit more and I saw him on the path. I stepped back, and then I looked again to see if he'd gone and I couldn't see him at first but he was over the road. He stared right through me, John. It was horrible. I just thought it was some drunk finding his way home but then …'

Debbie caught her breath; her eyes were glistening with tears and her hands were shaking in fright.

'Tell me,' John said as he gently cuddled his sister and tried all he could to coax more of the story from her.

'For a second I thought he had a gun … he raised his hand up and pointed his finger at me … and then he stood there, grinning. God, John, I was so scared.'

Now Garron was worried too.

Every tender rib tingled as his beating in the pub cellar flashed across his mind. If it was him he was going to have to do something about it, and soon. There was no way he could allow Debbie and Kim to be threatened.

'Tell me about his face, Deb. What'd he look like? Try 'n' remember,' he urged.

Debbie released her grip and John Garron couldn't pretend he wasn't pleased. She took a sip from her lukewarm tea and tried to compose herself. She tiptoed to the foot of the stairs and listened for Kim; again, all was quiet.

'Well, he was slim and he had a dark coat on and a beanie hat.'

'What about his face?'

'White … sort of … he didn't look English but I dunno really. You won't do nothing stupid will yer?'

John Garron leant forward against the kitchen worktop and took in what Debbie had described. His mind was whirring and he was trying to decide whether Debbie and Kim were really in any sort of danger or whether this was just for effect. Although he couldn't be a hundred per cent sure as to this bloke's identity, his suspicions were high.

'Mummy,' called Kim as she woke from a disturbed night's sleep, a little chilly due to the departure of the bed quilt during the night.

'Look, you'd better go. She can't see yer like this. Call me, yeah? In a bit.'

'Yeah, I will. Try not to worry now. He won't show up in the day and to be honest I don't think he'll be back at all. He's done what he wanted to do. Listen, that message was not for you, it was for me, and I will sort things out, right? You are not to let it get under yer skin, you've got

Kimmy to look after. Tell her Uncle John loves her very much and I'll give yer a bell a bit later. Now go see her.'

'Alright. Don't let the door bang or she'll be asking questions. Don't miss a trick that one,' Debbie said with a sigh.

She gave her brother a kiss and smiled for the first time that morning.

Chapter Twenty-Eight

I parked the car at the end of the street and took a slow walk up the gentle incline towards the church. Paul Archer would no doubt be inside busying himself with his daily tasks and fussing and tidying. He was a nice chap and if I'd time after seeing Doreen I'd pop in to see him. I stopped opposite the church and took a long hard look at it. St Dom's really was an impressive building and I wondered again what really happened that morning when Martin Brookes was murdered. My eyes scanned the building from top to bottom until they reached the entrance door and I recalled how it was difficult to open due to the lock turning the opposite way to what was expected. I wondered whether the killer knew that or whether Martin had left the door ajar.

Was he expecting someone to come to the church that morning? I couldn't ask him, that's for sure. I tried to imagine myself as the killer and thought about how I would approach the church, bearing in mind that no-one saw or heard anything. No-one noticed anyone suspicious in the vicinity or leaving the church. Perhaps it was very good timing and good planning, or just luck. First Daniel Grainger, then Martin Brookes. Hopefully Bob would have some luck with finding Stan Elms so he could fill in a few of the gaps.

Predictably, as I got within sight of Doreen's house I saw her at the window. I opened the front gate, which rattled with age and frailty, and immediately the front door opened and there was Doreen with a welcoming smile.

'Hello, dear. On time I see. Do come in.'

'Thank you, Mrs Calderwood. How are you today?'

Instantly, I wondered whether that was a wise question as I could find myself listening to Doreen's list of various ailments and it would be dark in eight hours.

'Mustn't grumble, dear. Are you alright?'

Got away with it.

'Yes, thank you,' I said and followed Doreen into the lounge, my gaze steering to the sideboard, but it was clear and Martin's photo was elsewhere. Insurance, perhaps, that I would stay long enough for tea and cake. Doreen's living room was just how I had remembered it to be, albeit the flowers had been renewed. The coffee table was host to a TV guide and a ball of wool as well as the TV remote and an old-fashioned magnifying glass. Perhaps the print was a bit small for her these days.

'How are things going, dear? Have you got him yet?'

'Not yet, I'm afraid, Mrs Calderwood, but were getting closer.'

'Dearie me. He won't come back, will he? I'm just worried about Paul.'

'No, we really don't think that will happen. You mustn't fret.'

'Hmm … makes you think though,' she said as she made her way into the kitchen to fetch the tea and place the slices of Victoria sponge onto a large plate.

'Where have you hidden Martin's picture?' I asked playfully.

'I've given it a wash.'

Panic filled me as I got an image of Martin Brookes' photo tumbling over in Doreen's washing machine.

'A wash?' I said.

'Well, more of a wipe really. It was so dusty and had all those little, tiny thunder flies in the frame. Do you know the sort I mean?'

'Yes, I do,' I said with a certain amount of relief.

'Right, here we are then,' said Doreen, as she carried in with her a tray of tea and delicious Victoria sponge.

As we supped our tea and enjoyed Doreen's tasty Victoria sponge, we chatted generally about all sorts of mundane things. I knew it was part of the deal to spend some time nattering if I wanted a look at that photo of Martin. I couldn't really expect to shoot in, grab the photo and disappear. By the time I had been brought up to date on the life and times of Doreen Calderwood, another hour had passed and, whilst I found her very pleasant to talk to, I had to a look at that photograph.

'Mrs Calderwood, do you think I might be able to have a look at the photo now?'

'Oh, I do chatter away don't I? You should have said before. I'll take these things into the kitchen and I'll get it for you.'

'Thank you.'

Doreen banged and crashed in the kitchen as the tray probably went down onto the worktop a little harder than she meant.

'He wanted it back, you know,' Doreen called from somewhere in the depths of her kitchen. Rather than shout I waited for her to surface again. 'Here it is, dear.'

'Why did he want it back?'

'Don't know but he mentioned it a couple of times and I kept forgetting. I was going to take it over to him on that day but what with the phone calls and getting no answer, I forgot again.'

I sat with Martin's photograph and studied him once more, although this time much more thoroughly. So, there he was. He stood posing for his picture in what looked like a fairly heavy coat, patterned with camouflage, and with his trousers tucked into long socks that came up just below his knees. He wore ankle length boots similar to walking boots. Doreen crowded beside me to get a better look.

'He told me that he had been walking somewhere in Epping Forest. High Beech, I think, and had his picture taken when he got back again.'

'Did he tell you who he was with?'

'I asked him that and he said he was with friends.'

'Friends, eh?'

'That's what he said. He had that stick because he had a bad knee. I remember he told me that. Something to do with a fight he said but I think he was having me on. Martin would never be in a fight.'

The photo wasn't crystal clear and so I asked Doreen if I could use her magnifying glass for a better look. I ran the glass over the photo to see whether anything stood out with regard to what he was wearing but nothing really did. I could see that he was standing in front of a building that looked like a public house.

'It's The Fallen Oak, by the way,' said Doreen.

'What is?' I asked.

'The pub that's behind him in the photo. You can't see the name in the photo but I know it is. My sisters took me a few times, years and years ago. I knew it as soon as I clapped eyes on it. We had a New Year's Eve do there one time; good it was.'

'So you're from the East End?'

'Oh yes. A very long time ago. I haven't been back there for years and years.'

I stared harder and I could see a part of the lettering on the front of the pub which read 'The Fal...' – nothing more was visible.

'Did Martin ever say that he went in that pub?' I asked hopefully.

'He told me once that he used to win a lot of games of darts and I guessed that was where he went when he played. They had a good darts team in my day, or so my mum used to say.'

'Mrs Calderwood, may I take this away with me? I promise I'll take care of it.'

'Well, you may as well, if it helps. He wanted it back after all so I would have lost it anyway, wouldn't I?'

'I guess so but now you can have it back when I'm done with it. How's that?'

'Smashing, dear,' she said.

* * *

I was so preoccupied with the latest find and had reached the outskirts of Chelmsford before I realised that I had completely forgotten to pop in to see Paul Archer, so it would have to wait until another time. The photo frame of Martin that lay on the passenger seat beside me potentially gave us another piece of information. The Fallen Oak, Doreen had said, might possibly be the pub where Martin played darts, and maybe Grainger and Elms used to go along too. With two of these guys having been found dead with matching playing cards on or near their bodies, I wondered if the pub might have more to offer than just a friendly barmaid. Pubs like that one in London's East End revolve around gossip so it had to be worth exploring. Our last trip down to the capital was quite fruitful and had got us this far, so I just felt it would be beneficial to pay a visit to The Fallen Oak and speak to the man in charge; the landlord.

Bob was just putting the phone down when I got back to the desk.

'So you're back, just when all the hard work is done.'

'What do you mean? I had to be served tea and eat two slices of Doreen Calderwood's Victoria sponge,' I replied.

'You're kidding me.'

'Yep, it was three slices.'

'Do you know what it's like to repeatedly make phone calls to people who tell you that you have the wrong Stan Elms?'

'So, are you barking up the wrong tree or the wrong Elm? Get it?'

'Oh, ha fucking ha,' said Bob, who had clearly not got on too well in his mission of finding the right Stan Elms.

'How many have you checked?' I asked cautiously.

'Twenty so far. Six were already dead but thankfully none of them were our boy as far as I could make out.'

'Good. Well, do you want to know how I got on?' I asked.

'Don't tell me, you asked her out on a date and she turned you down.'

'No.'

'She accepted?'

'No. Now listen for once. I took a look at that photo that she had on her sideboard and it seems that we may have another trip to the smoke to take.'

'Why?'

'It was what was in the background that was interesting. Listen. Martin Brookes played darts in a local pub. The photo had a pub in the background that was known for its darts teams, so maybe he and Grainger and maybe Elms used to drink in there. We have a link through the Repton Gym but maybe we can establish another connection with them at the pub. Perhaps we can find out some more about their past and try to work out exactly who wanted Brookes and Grainger dead. I'll find out who the landlord is and we'll go down and have a word or two. What'd you say?'

Bob just gave me a blank look and I wondered whether he had been listening at all. For a moment I thought he looked a little unwell.

'Hey, you OK?' I asked.

'Yeah. OK then, we'll have to go, I guess.'

'Sooner the better. Are you in court tomorrow?'

'Nope,' he said.

'Nor me, but I want you to agree to one thing.'

'Yeah, I know … keep my trap shut,' said Bob.

'That and … we take my car.'

Chapter Twenty-Nine

Bob and I cruised down the M11 and, for the second time in the last week or so, encroached into that old part of the East End once ruled by the organised crime gangs of the 1960s. Now we needed to venture a little deeper into the infamous territory. We passed along Mile End Road and managed to avoid getting into a confrontation with any removal lorries or portly bus drivers. The biggest concern on my mind was that this time I cared considerably more as to whether the car got scratched in the chaotic game of dodgems that was the daily turmoil in the East End traffic. We had left the comparative peace and tranquillity of the Essex countryside a long way behind us and now had to allow ourselves to be absorbed by the tension and claustrophobic atmosphere of East London. As we stopped and started, along with the buses and a variety of other vehicles, Bob piped up suddenly.

'Did you see the Royal London back there?'

'The hospital? Yeah, can't miss it. What about it?'

'Do you remember The Elephant Man, Joseph Merrick?' Bob asked.

'John Merrick, you mean?'

'No, his name was Joseph. They called him John in the film, that's all. Anyway, he was exhibited in a Penny Gaff shop opposite the hospital when he first came to London before a doctor took him in at the hospital, and that's where he stayed until he died.'

'How d'you know about that then?' I asked, flabbergasted.

'Read it, I s'pose. He was born in Leicester and died in Whitechapel.'

'What's a Penny Gaff shop?'

'There was a lot of 'em in them days. They were sort of entertainment houses in the 1880s. A penny to get in and "gaff" is Irish slang for house.'

'Blimey, I'm impressed.'

Dave Copson

'Not just a pretty face,' said Bob.
'Nor was Joseph Merrick.'
'Ha, ha,' grimaced Bob.

* * *

The Fallen Oak public house was situated near a market and the parking restrictions only applied on market days. Fortunately for us, today was not one of those days. The building was old and had a thick layer of grime on the brickwork. The window frames had not seen a paint brush for a good few years but then neither had Bob's flat. The net curtains appeared to be a grubby grey colour, albeit they were very likely white at some point in their life. I had established that the landlord was one John Garron. I followed Bob in through the front door. The pub was quiet with only an elderly couple sitting in the lounge, neither of whom took any notice of us. The walls were adorned with garish, flowery wallpaper and a number of small picture frames which showed an array of old photographs of the area during the war. A young girl was behind the bar, chatting to a man sitting on a bar stool nursing a pint.

'What're you having?' asked Bob

'I'd better have a coke,' I replied as Bob ordered himself a pint.

The young girl didn't hurry herself and finished her conversation with the man at the bar as she leisurely poured Bob's pint.

'Not seen you two before,' she said.

'That's cos we ain't been in 'ere before,' replied Bob in his own warm and gentle way.

'What brings you in here now then?' she asked.

Bob took a sip of his pint, looked around the pub and turned side-on to the bar, facing the man on the bar stool. He had a good look at him and then turned his head towards the girl.

'Can you tell us where we can find John Garron?'

She was slightly taken aback and gave Bob a hard stare before committing to an answer.

'Depends on why you want him.'

I was quietly interested in this little tête-à-tête and considered how I would have spoken to her in order to get the information I wanted, but was happy to leave it to Bob as he was certainly more familiar than I was with the folk from this neck of the woods.

120

'You're not his mother, are yer? Just like to talk to him, that's all.'

'Well, I ain't seen 'im and he's not here. Who are yer anyway? I'll tell him yer called by.'

'Not a very friendly welcome. No wonder the place is half empty. Is he upstairs?'

'No, he's out and he won't be back till late either.'

'How d'ya know when he'll be back if ya ain't seen 'im?'

An awkward look came on her face and she blushed ever so slightly, and that was all Bob needed to know that she was lying.

'Look, he just ain't 'ere, alright.'

She scurried away to the end of the bar and began to appear to be busy. Bob looked at me and gave a smirk. He was beginning to quite enjoy himself. We were in no particular rush so we waited patiently and sat nosing around the pub. I could see that the rear of the bar led to a corridor that went to the back of the pub. There was at least one room branching off to the right and a turn to the left further along. I couldn't see where the stairs were but they would obviously be close by. Our mysterious girl had stepped out from behind the bar and taken another two drinks to the table where the elderly regulars sat. I noticed that as she made her way back to the far end of the bar, she gave a nervous glance in our direction then looked away sharply. I, like Bob, wasn't entirely convinced that Garron wasn't on the premises and I thought it was interesting that she was trying so hard to cover for him. If that's what she was doing.

'You having another one?' Bob said as he turned to me.

'No, and nor are you, unless it's non-alcoholic,' I insisted.

Bob huffed and puffed but he knew I was right and didn't bother to argue. He was fiddling with his mobile phone when he turned to me and smiled. Bob winked and then called to the girl.

'Excuse me, excuse me, darlin'.'

'I'm not your darlin'. What d'ya want?' she snapped.

'I was just wondering, seeing as you're a nice-looking girl, has he ever said you're good-looking?'

'Why would I wanna tell you? Anyway, it's got nothin' to do with you.'

'No, I s'pose not. But tell me, do ya think he's a handsome-looking bloke?'

'He's alright.'

'Well, I'd say you're doing 'im an injustice, wouldn't you?'

'What you on about?' she said, getting a little bit more rattled.

'Look here, he's quite handsome, don't you reckon?'

Bob turned his phone towards the girl and she looked straight at it. Her eyes bulged and her face coloured up properly now.

'Don't s'pose he does much boxing these days do you? But he looks as though someone's been doing some practice on 'im, wouldn't you say?'

Bob turned to his right and stared straight at the bloke that had been sitting at the bar since we came in.

'What would you say, Mr Garron?'

John Garron sat motionless and looked down at his pint. After a few seconds he spoke.

'Where d'ya get the photo?'

'Repton Gym. Bet you were good in those days. Obviously, you're not much good now,' said Bob, now smugger than ever.

Garron turned towards Bob with a scowl and looked us over.

'What d'ya want?' he asked cautiously.

'I'm Detective Sergeant Hand and this is Detective Inspector Calloway and if it's not too much trouble, we would like to have a word please.'

Nice one, I thought. Obviously Garron had appeared on at least one of the photos Bob had taken at the gym and he must have felt that he had seen this man on the bar stool somewhere before, and whilst he was toying with the barmaid, he was putting it all together in his mind.

'Obviously I haven't changed that much,' said Garron.

'Bit slower, perhaps. What's the story with the battle scars?'

'I've got a big cat,' retorted Garron, determined to give Bob as little as possible.

'Well, I'd like to meet it. Shall we go through or would you like to stay in full view of your customers, not that you've got many?'

Garron got off his stool and walked around to a gap in the bar at the end where we sat. He didn't speak, he just led the way into a room down the corridor. The room was quite small but had a sofa and two other comfortable-looking chairs, a table and a TV. The old original fireplace had been bricked up and an electric fire stood on the hearth. The walls were painted a dirty magnolia. The whole place looked as though a handful of dirt had been stirred into the paint before any had been applied. Garron sat in one of the large armchairs and we perched on the sofa facing him.

'What's this? Good cop, bad cop?' he asked.

'No. No need for games, Mr Garron, we'd just like to ask you a few questions about a couple of men who we think may have frequented your pub a few years back,' I said.

'Really, why, have they done somethin' naughty?'

'No. Do you know Daniel Grainger and Martin Brookes?'

Garron sat and stared. His expression, unaltered. His face as hard as a diamond.

'I did,' he said.

'By that I take it that you are aware of what has happened to them since. Am I right?'

'Yeah. Nasty business.'

'Indeed it was, Mr Garron. Can you tell me whether they used to drink here?'

'They were in quite a lot back then. Brookes was in the darts team so he was forever chucking arrows across the room. Bloody nuisance. He used to stand right back and aim from further away so that the board felt a lot closer in the matches. Bloody lethal.'

'Do you recall Grainger too?'

'Yep.'

I was happy that we had established a connection for Grainger and Brookes at the gym and at the pub and now Garron too, for that matter, but I needed more.

'Mr Garron, what can you tell me about Daniel Grainger?'

'He was like a lot of people from round here, ordinary really. He went to school around here, he worked doing a bit of decorating and a bit of nicking stuff, normal thing in them days.'

'Was he in trouble with the police?'

'Him and all the others. Just how it was though. Nothing bad, just came with the territory, as they say.'

'Was he a violent man?'

'He went along with the flow. Did what he was told, that's all.'

'What about Brookes? Did he do what he was told too?' I asked.

'He wasn't so brave, really. Bit soft sometimes. Could still be a sod, that's for sure. They used to parade about pretending they were tough but they had their limits.'

Dave Copson

'Who would want to kill them, Mr Garron?' said Bob.

Garron looked at Bob as if he had a nasty taste in his mouth and shrugged.

'Out in the sticks, weren't it, where they got done? That's what was circulating around here, anyway,' he eventually said.

'Yes, it was. So, did they have any enemies that you know of?' I asked.

'A lot of blokes have had some of them in the past. In those days a lot of stuff went on. No-one used to talk though. The kids of today are amateurs compared to the sorts you had roaming around the manor once upon a time. Grainger and Brookes weren't what you'd call "big noises" in this patch but they tagged along for the ride.'

'Do you know whether they were involved in anything tasty in those days?' asked Bob.

Garron looked quizzically at Bob, staring hard again.

'Bits and pieces and rumours, that's all.'

'Give us some of the rumours.'

'Well, there was a big job here at the pub a long time ago but it's a bit sketchy really.'

Garron fidgeted in his comfy chair and I wasn't sure whether he was uncertain about what he was saying or uncertain as to whether he should be saying it. Bob pushed him a bit further.

'Go on then. Don't give us half a story.'

'Have you ever heard of a couple blokes that called themselves The Crew?'

Personally, I hadn't, but Bob recalled the name.

'Yeah, I remember. Two brothers, weren't they? Robberies, burglaries, threatening kids and old ladies. Right pair of wankers.'

'Sounds about right. Well, years ago they did a job in Hornchurch and from what I heard at the time it didn't quite go to plan. I think they hurt some people, but apart from that the story goes that they came away with a lot of stuff.'

'Stuff? How much?' said Bob.

'Diamonds, I heard. A good few bob's worth by all accounts. Don't know how much though 'cos, like I say, people knew to keep their gobs shut. Anyway, someone obviously had got wind of it and one night at the pub, here, they got a big surprise.'

'What sort?' I asked.

124

'I heard that some blokes caught 'em cold and took the stuff they had on 'em. Apparently, they were waiting to meet someone who was gonna pay 'em for the stuff and help 'em shift it. They weren't the sharpest tools, ya know, and probably didn't know what to do with it anyway.'

'So they were robbed of the goods? Was that it?'

'Not exactly. One of The Crew was killed and the other one hasn't been seen since. Got away somehow, they say. Point is, the rumour is that Grainger and Brookes were involved.'

I sat trying to take it all in.

As hard as I tried I couldn't see Martin Brookes as a villain. Did he put down his shotgun and pick up his Bible? If there was any truth in the rumour then both Grainger and Brookes would have gained an enemy overnight. Did the brother catch up with them both?

'What were the names of The Crew?' I asked.

'They were known as Bernie and Oscar but they had other names. They were from Eastern Europe. Don't know where. But if I was looking, I'd be looking for Oscar or whoever he is.'

'He certainly has a reason to be peeved, I guess. Providing all this is true,' said Bob.

'Well, they got stitched up that night, that bit is true. I should know, it's my pub. I had to go through all the questioning from the police at the time. I was only glad that I wasn't here when it happened. Place was shut for bloody ages after, right pain in the arse it was. They never found anyone for it either. No-one round here wanted to help the police. Everyone was just happy that the pair of 'em had got done over. No-one hardly spoke about it, even in here. Whoever did it had full protection from all the people on the manor. That's how it was.'

'Surely Grainger and Brookes had some help. You said they weren't really all that tough. Don't sound like they could have done it alone,' I said.

'S'pose not. But like I say, it was all hush-hush,' said Garron.

'Do you know Stan Elms?' said Bob, changing the subject.

'Yeah, that was a shame too,' said Garron.

'What do you mean, a shame?' I asked.

'Well, he's dead, ain't he? Not long ago, I heard. At his allotment, I think. Apparently, someone bashed 'im on the swede and left 'im for dead. He used to drink in here too.'

'Oh, fuck,' said Bob loudly.

'Do you know where it happened, where his allotment was?' I said, trying to be composed.

'Er …yeah … Ah, that's it … Plaistow. Elms lived there for years. Yeah, bloody shame.'

Bob and I looked at each other and let the enormity sink in for a moment. We were undoubtedly thinking the very same thing … ace of … what?

'Do you know the surname of the brothers? Can you remember?' I asked.

'I never did know. I don't even know where they were from. Could have been Albanians, Bosnians, Czechs … I don't know. Don't think they were Polish or Russian but I ain't sure … long time ago.'

'You said it happened in the pub. Whereabouts and what exactly did they do to 'im?' enquired Bob.

Another curious look came Bob's way.

'It was a right mess. Whoever did it certainly meant it. Took loads of cleaning up. They blew 'is guts right out the back of 'im. All over the wall.'

'Where did it happen?'

Garron looked at Bob and thought for a moment, as if he was trying to recreate the gruesome scene in his mind.

'Right where you're sitting,' he grinned.

* * *

I was keen to move and get ourselves over to the nick at Plaistow to see what we could find about Elms and whether all this was true. We wound things up with John Garron and followed him back along the corridor into the lounge area of the pub. The barmaid sneered at Bob as we wandered around to the right side of the bar. We both thanked John Garron and told him that we may well be back at some point for another chat. Again the barmaid gave us both a blank look and continued changing the empty bottles of spirits on the optics for full ones. We left and made our way to the car.

'What did they want?' she asked Garron.

'It was before your time, don't worry about it.'

'I knew they looked dodgy, especially that one with all the chat. Why we got the law coming round asking questions anyway?'

'I told yer, before your time. Now leave it, and Sandy, thanks for what you did earlier, you're a good girl.'

'Any time.' She nodded, smiled and carried on with changing the optics, ready for the evening rush.

Chapter Thirty

Plaistow Police Station was in Barking Road, back towards West Ham, so it didn't take us too long to get there. Once I had parked the car we made our way into the front of the building and up to the front desk. I made our introductions and tried my best to explain why we were there. The desk sergeant asked us to take a seat whilst he went off to find someone who could help us.

'What if he's lying, Dave?'

'About which bit?'

Bob sighed and looked down at the floor as we sat and wondered whether this wild goose chase was going to lead us anywhere. The street outside was busy with cars, buses and people scurrying in all directions. The doors at the front of the station opened and in walked a big guy who looked as though he was West Indian or maybe African. His clothes were dirty and he wore a colourful woollen hat that was far too big for his head, which caused it to flop about as he moved. He held a beer can in his right hand which he threw into a bin in the foyer.

'Good shot,' said Bob.

The big guy just glanced quickly in our direction and carried on walking in. He stopped at the front desk and banged on the bell to get attention.

'He'll be back in a minute, he's gone to get someone who can help us. Shouldn't be long,' said Bob.

'Hey,' shouted the big fella, who was getting ever more impatient.

We sat and watched him continue to bang the bell and briefly looked at each other, wondering what he was going to do next. After a couple of minutes of watching him go from banging the bell to leaning most of the way over the desk, to the point where it looked as though he was about to end up in a heap on the other side, he finally gave up and stormed back out again, mumbling to himself.

'What was all that about?' I said.

'Who knows?' answered Bob.

As we watched him standing outside on the pavement, the desk sergeant returned.

'Excuse me, sir. Would you both like to follow me, please?'

We rose and did as he had said. He held open a double door and beckoned us through into a corridor that led to a stairwell. We made our way up the stairs behind him to the first floor and were taken to an office.

'Please wait in here, someone will be along shortly.'

'Thank you,' we said simultaneously.

The office was well furnished and looked out along Barking Road. The late-afternoon traffic was relentless outside and we stood gazing down at it until the door behind us opened. We both turned around to see an officer enter.

'Good afternoon, gentlemen. My name is Inspector Trevor Eaden, how can I help you today?'

'Good afternoon, I'm DI Dave Calloway and this is DS Bob Hand. Thank you for seeing us.'

'Pleasure. Now, what brings you here?'

'We are from Essex HQ at Chelmsford where we're dealing with a double murder, and we've just gained some information that suggests that a recent murder on your patch may be connected to our investigation.'

Trevor Eaden sat at his desk and invited us to be seated too.

'So, who are we talking about today?' he asked.

Bob spoke first.

'Elms. Stan Elms.'

Trevor Eaden looked at Bob, then at me, before sitting back in his chair and reaching for a folder on his desk.

'Elms,' he said, opening the folder and taking a look at whatever was inside it.

'Is it true that he was murdered recently?' I asked.

'Yeah, it is.'

'On his allotment, we believe?' said Bob.

'That's right. Who's been giving you your information, may I ask?'

'Just someone who's been kind enough to help us out, that's all.'

Bob was reluctant to say too much straight away and obviously wanted to protect the information we had so far. What we needed to achieve was to gain a little bit more.

'Well, the murder of Stan Elms has been a dead end to us so far. He was found by some kids, lying on his allotment. Another man thought he had had a heart attack but when he got close enough he could see what had happened. I got there fairly quickly and within no time a murder weapon had been found. A spade had Elms' blood and hair on it but no sign of a print or anything pertaining to the killer. The ground was a boggy mess and the only footprints were from either Wellington boots or other typical gardening footwear. Nothing out of the ordinary. It wasn't until one of our PCs went to talk with his wife that we discovered something else, but even that hasn't developed into anything helpful up to now.'

Bob was busting to say it.

'Where did you find the ace of spades?'

Trevor Eaden stopped and froze for a moment. He looked at us both and appeared to be quite surprised, to say the least. Bob had timed that nicely. I decided to speak up and let Trevor Eaden in on the story.

'Trevor, we've been investigating two murders that both involved playing cards. Aces. A man named Martin Brookes was murdered at his church and a playing card was found at the scene by a lady that helps out there. It didn't mean very much to us until one of Bob's colleagues told us about an incident a couple of years ago that he had also drawn a blank with. The accident didn't raise suspicion until he told us about the playing card that was found at the scene, similar to our job. I examined the two cards – the ace of hearts from the death of Martin Brookes and the ace of clubs from the death of Daniel Grainger – and found that the back of the cards had not only the same pattern but both of them had a blue colouring around the edge. To cut a long story short, we visited a church in Mile End Road where Martin Brookes had previously worked and that led us to a boxing gymnasium in Bethnal Green, where we managed to make a positive connection between the two men. Another name cropped up there which was Stan Elms but we didn't have any idea where he was these days. When we followed up on something in the Martin Brookes case we stumbled upon the news of the death of Elms and thought we would come along here to establish whether another ace had shown itself. And now it's getting interesting because we believe there is a fourth member of this little cluster of unfortunates, but as yet we haven't found him. If at all possible we are rather hoping to find him alive.'

'Christ, you have been busy. Well, I'll do whatever I can to help you.'

Eaden began to move some papers around that he had taken out of the folder on Stan Elms. Photographs were laid out on his desk of the murder scene.

'Here's where we found Elms. You can see the obvious damage, and this one shows the spade that we took from the scene. Here's a photo of the card that had been posted through the letterbox of his house. His wife picked it up off the doormat and showed our officers.'

'Have you got the card? Would you mind if I take a look at it?' I asked.

'I can get it for you.'

Eaden picked up the telephone which was on his desk and asked for someone to bring the evidence to his office.

As Eaden switched a kettle on to boil and chatted with Bob about our journey down here, I began to feel a rather silly excitement building up inside, knowing that I was going to get my hands on what was seemingly the third part of our jigsaw. The desk sergeant that we met on our arrival soon stepped into the office and placed a clear, sealed bag on Trevor Eaden's desk.

'Cheers, Roger. Right, here we are then. The ace of spades.'

'May I have a closer look?' I asked.

He handed me the bag and I immediately turned it over to give myself a clear view of the back of the card. There was the blue shading around the edge. I sat nodding a sort of confirmation to myself and was warmed by the sense that we were now getting somewhere at last, and even though there were a lot more loose ends to tie up before we could find our killer, I felt that it was all chugging along nicely.

We had inherited the Grainger case from Andy Potter and been able to link it firmly to that of Martin Brooks, which gave us the upper hand in how this was to be investigated and in which direction we chose to take it. Trevor Eaden would, naturally, give us his full support and assist in any way that he and his team possibly could by continuing with the investigation into the death of Stan Elms, but ultimately it was our show and Bob and I were the ringmasters. The investigation would be led by myself, and Chelmsford HQ would be the base for the storage of all the information, including the precious ace of spades. Trevor ensured that all the relevant details were made available to Bob and me and wished us well.

My trusty Mondeo was now the collection point for the data we needed on Stan Elms until we could get back and store it all away safely. On our journey out of the East End and back towards the Essex countryside, we reflected on what had turned out to be quite a day.

One full of surprises and shocks.

We really must stop turning up dead people.

Chapter Thirty-One

The Fallen Oak was crowded tonight, more than usual, thanks to a karaoke machine and a flood of wannabe pop stars. One or two of them weren't bad but there were plenty that sounded more like the rag and bone man's horse having a coughing fit. At least that's what Sandy and her sister Jackie thought as they worked the bar and once again tolerated the poor attempts at chat-up lines from the local 'Chippendales'. More like something from Chipperfield's, as far as the girls were concerned.

Upstairs, John Garron had retreated from the noise in search of something to relieve his aching head. He never liked these themed nights but it was a surefire way of getting the punters packed in and significantly increasing the takings behind the bar. Garron would have preferred a stripper but that sort of entertainment was frowned upon these days. He found some aspirin and, although he wanted something stronger, he made do with them. He took a cup to the bathroom sink and half-filled it. Before he drank down the tablets he caught sight of himself in the mirror and inspected the scars on his face.

Better than they were.

Fading with time.

He looked down at the back of his hand where the postcard had been pinned to him and studied the ugly circular mark. It didn't look as bad as it had done but it was the one reminder that made his blood boil most of all. Back in the mirror, the 61-year-old returned his gaze. He thought about how he had aged and wondered whether things would have been different if he wasn't in the pub game. He downed the two tablets, wiped his mouth on his sleeve and headed back downstairs to the aggravating din of the karaoke. As he reached the bar, Sandy stepped into the corridor and collided with him.

'Whoa, steady on. I've told yer not to run around where there's glass and wet floors and yer still come charging …'

'Some bloke just poured his pint on the karaoke machine,' blurted Sandy.

Garron's senses tuned in to the welcome silence from the infernal machine and realised that all he could hear was the normal rumble of chatter in the pub. Much nicer, he thought.

'Say that again.'

'Some bloke just bought a beer and tipped it straight into the machine. Jackie served him and she said he just went straight over and turned his glass upside down over it and then walked straight out.'

'How long ago?' said Garron, immediately realising that the sudden silence from the commotion already answered his question.

'Just now,' said Sandy, stating the obvious.

Garron elbowed his way through the busy pub and headed for the front doors, impeded by a host of people trying to mop up the mess with beer towels and whatever else they could find suitable. He opened one of the double doors and peered out into the dark. Only one of the street lamps was working since an HGV flattened the one at the end of the street just thirty yards to the left. He could see a few people milling around but didn't see anyone who may have been to blame. To the right he could hear raised voices coming from a group of youths, about ten of them, nothing out of the ordinary. They were pushing and shoving a couple of others around. He stood and looked across the market square and decided to take a quick look before going back inside. The mob to his right wouldn't be a problem, they would know Garron and would also know better than to cause him any trouble. He wandered slowly across the road, aware of every shadow and every sound.

Was it him? Oscar?

Then he heard something just ahead of him. He side-stepped into a shop doorway and waited. An elderly man with his dog beside him came from the opposite direction and shuffled past. Garron stood for a minute and wondered whether this was another of Oscar's scare tactics.

Not gonna work.

He relaxed a little and became aware that he had been standing with his fists tightly clenched; ready.

No second chance.

His mind was starting to play out precisely how he would exact his revenge when Sandy called out across the square. Garron recognised a tremor in her voice and quickly headed back to the pub.

'John ... John ...'

He appeared out of the gloom.

'What is it now?'

'John. Your motor.'

'What about it?'

'It's on fucking fire.'

He stared at her for a few seconds without seeming to register what she had said.

'Oh Christ. Call the fire brigade then.'

'Jackie's done it already. Hurry up, it's right next to the sheds.'

'I know where it is. I fucking put it there.'

Garron ran down the alleyway which led to a piece of rough ground at the rear of The Fallen Oak. He always parked his car there, away from the street and the traffic wardens and out of sight from the local hoodlums. He scampered down the alleyway, the acrid smoke already in his nostrils, and was hit by the scorching heat as he turned the corner at the end. He took a half-step back and with his head lowered, he went around to the boot of the car to look at the other side. As he did so he could see the petrol cap on the floor beside the car. Trails of blazing fuel began to run in all directions as the engine components popped and hissed. The smoke was everywhere. The dry, toxic, super-heated intrusion of it hurt his lungs. Garron began to cough as he felt his chest cramping in its desire for oxygen. He braved the painful barrier again and slipped down the nearside of the car, peering inside, but all he saw through the carbon-crusted windows was the bright, glowing orange of the dashboard as it melted and dropped in charred lumps onto the flooring. A tyre exploded at the front of the vehicle and sent a shower of roasting-hot carbon particles and sparks into the air. The wind carried them like shooting stars over fences, onto roofs and into the guttering of The Fallen Oak.

Then he saw it. The petrol can.

A molten softened blob of hot plastic that was just within reach. Maybe it would be evidence, maybe there would be fingerprints. Something in his mind told him that this was a waste of time but it was right there.

He could reach it.

No guts, no glory.

The flames changed direction in the wind and singed his hair and eyebrows. He yelped from the soreness. His face felt as though it was on fire. Get it … Get it. His outstretched hand brushed against it and he dropped it instinctively, as his nerves sent the warning message to his brain and back to his hand in a split second of panic when the searing pain shot into him. Suddenly he felt himself falling backwards as someone from the pub pulled at his arm and led him away to a safer distance. The heat intensified rapidly as his car became fully engulfed in a raging fire. No-one was going to get near it now. The crowd from the pub stood well back and Garron reluctantly joined them. His hand was red-raw and was very sore. Every onlooker seemed to jump at the same time as a ten-foot flame belched out from the exposed fuel tank, scorching the adjacent fencing. Garron inspected the damage to his fingers to reveal two huge, hanging, plasma-drenched blisters.

Nothing could be salvaged.

Nothing left.

Message received, he thought.

Chapter Thirty-Two

The email displayed the instructions quite clearly ... *10 o'clock in my office.* I had half an hour to gather all the information together that I assumed I would need. The lower drawer in my office desk secured the files that related to Martin Brookes and Daniel Grainger. The file on Stan Elms that I had collected on our visit to Plaistow was in a securely locked, free-standing cabinet to the rear of my desk.

Bob was fussing about with pieces of paper and mumbling away as he tried to locate the notebook that he had used when we met Chris Fragakis at the church and GD, 'the bear in a tracksuit', at the gym.

'Right, I need a coffee and a fag,' said Bob.

'Don't hang around outside for too long, we don't want to be late,' I advised.

'Yeah, yeah.'

DCI Corrigan had certainly mellowed somewhat towards us since the investigation started to unlock one or two more relevant pieces of information. Initially, all I could report on was just how scrumptious Doreen's cake was, but thankfully things had developed a bit more since then.

More dead bodies and dead ends.

But maybe there was light at the end of the tunnel.

I knew that we didn't have a huge amount of evidence from the crime scenes but I felt it was important that the bodies were linking together. The motive was unsubstantiated as yet but it certainly appeared that Oscar had a reason to be aggrieved, seeing as his brother was blown away all those years ago, providing, of course, that our trio had been involved at the time. Garron didn't quite spell it out but his story did make some sense. I smirked as I recalled how Garron had told

Bob that he was sitting in the exact spot where Bernie got murdered. The coy grin on Garron's face said that he enjoyed it too.

It was 9:45. I sat and stared blankly at the clock.

Waiting for the other boot to drop.

It was a story that my dad used to tell of an old soldier returning on leave from his spell on the front line. He told of how the soldier roomed upstairs and would sit on the bed to remove his boot from his swollen foot and how after the ensuing struggle the boot would drop to the floor with a thump, startling those in the room below who would then, in anticipation, look up and 'wait for the other boot to drop'.

The anticipation of something about to happen.

And then it happened; ten minutes early.

'Come along then, gentlemen, into the lion's den.'

'We're on the way, sir.'

Except *we* weren't, were *we?*

As I tried to be composed and gather the folders into some order I looked towards the far end of the office in expectation of seeing Bob returning from his contribution to polluting the atmosphere outside.

No chance.

I knew this would happen.

I ambled slowly towards Corrigan's office with one eye straining to look behind me to see if he was in sight yet but he wasn't, so I decided that I would have to go in. What else could I do? Corrigan's door was closed which bought me, or rather Bob, an extra few seconds, which as it turned out, were all that he needed.

'C'mon,' I urged as he wandered in, oblivious as to why I was standing at Corrigan's door with an armful of folders and files. Then the penny dropped, and Bob swept up the items on his desk in a rather nifty movement and joined me at the office door. I knocked and waited.

'Come,' Corrigan decreed in his usual authoritative style.

Corrigan's desk was always in perfect order. Pens and pencils stood to attention in holders, paperwork neatly stacked, his telephone in its place on the right side of the desk.

Not the left.

Never askew, always pointing straight at the office door.

The studded, dark-blue leather chair that he sat so majestically in oozed superiority. Every item of stationery seemed to be purposely laid out, almost symmetrically, as if it was never intended for use but only

Syrup and Cyanide

to be admired. I often wondered whether he had another desk hidden away somewhere that looked more like mine but I doubted he could ever have been any different to how he was today.

Bob and I sat opposite him and waited for him to speak. We knew the order of play and it was pointless talking to him until he was absolutely ready to engage with you, otherwise you would spend a few minutes explaining something to him and then he would look up and ask a question about some other subject that he wanted to discuss, ignoring whatever you had just said. The room was silent, just the way he liked it. That way he could collect his thoughts and prepare his onslaught. I had sat looking at my notes and reports whilst Bob was downstairs and prepared myself as much as possible for the first question. I knew the explanation of where we had been and who we had spoken to and what we had discovered would, predictably, be top of his agenda. I hoped that the reports that Bob and I had composed as we went along would answer all of his questions. Finally, he stopped reading whatever it was that he had in front of him, let out a sigh, adjusted his reading glasses onto the end of his nose and peered at us both in turn.

'Righty-o then, what are you going to impress me with this morning? And please do stick to the point.'

I spoke first, which suited Bob anyway.

'Sir, we have managed to establish a direct link between Martin Brookes, Daniel Grainger and Stan Elms. It appears that they all heralded from the same part of East London and attended a boxing gymnasium during the same period of time. They were known, locally, to be friends. It also appears that they may have been part of a gang that carried out a killing at The Fallen Oak public house in Whitechapel approximately seventeen years ago, but this isn't confirmed as no-one has ever been charged with the crime. The only connection we have with that event comes from the landlord; a John Garron, who still works there today and was around at that time. Although, he isn't sure or isn't saying for certain that they were involved. Our only suspect for the deaths of Brookes, Grainger and Elms up to now is the brother of the dead man, who may have resurfaced and be conducting his own revenge for the murder of his brother, which would suggest that they were involved. He was known as Oscar, which is not his real name. What we do have is a positive connection between the playing cards that have

139

been found at each murder scene. All aces. The cards all have a blue colour on the back of them and have been coloured in by hand at some point in time. This ties them to the same pack, we feel, and indicates that the same person is carrying out the killings.'

I paused, hoping that that initial statement would appease him somewhat. Corrigan looked down at his own copy of my report that I had provided for him to follow and was deep in thought.

More silence.

The ritual carried on in this way with me doing the bulk of the talking and Bob doing the bulk of avoiding Corrigan's eye. I was able to recount everything that we knew up to date about the murders and the crime scenes, not that they helped a lot. Corrigan seemed to accept my reasoning for where we had travelled to and who we had spoken with along the way, from our initial meeting with Chris Fragakis at the church where Martin Brookes worked to our recent chat with John Garron. I had explained how we had met with Andy Potter and how he had alerted us to the fact that he too had discovered a playing card at his crime scene two years earlier, and how it was not considered to be a significant find in the absence of any other information.

Just a good luck charm in Grainger's golf shoe.

Once I got in my stride and found that I could give an answer to everything Corrigan asked, Bob decided that he would finally contribute, and between us we seemed to have convinced the DCI that we had come a lot further in the past few weeks than just the tale of Doreen Calderwood's mop bucket. Whilst we felt that we had got on well of late, Corrigan pointed out that there were a number of pieces missing, which we also knew to be true. Bob and I were aware that working backwards was one thing but we were trying to dig up information from seventeen years ago. Information that had been firmly buried by the people around at the time. We both suspected that Garron had more to offer and that we would be talking with him again. Our friendly 'bear in a tracksuit', Gerry Dawson, might also be very useful if he could identify the fourth member of the cluster of friends. It would be a bonus to find him before he became murder victim number 4, unless he already had.

Our meeting with Corrigan lasted two hours. We went over everything that we knew and discussed what we would do about getting the answers to the pieces we didn't know about. By the time we left his office, I had mixed feelings. Part of me wanted to collapse into a chair and recover my thoughts and the other part wanted to get out there and get working straightaway on the case.

The chair won.

Chapter Thirty-Three

The wind had calmed gradually over the past couple of days and the clouds were finally breaking, kindly permitting a stream of sunshine to create a blinding glare on the wet road. He reached for the sun-visor and flicked it down just enough to protect his eyes and continued towards Writtle. The effects from the high winds were apparent as he drove over the twigs and broken pieces of thin branches that had landed on the road and been crushed by the traffic on the previous day.

Six miles to go.

The Visitor didn't have an elevated heart rate or any need to feel the rush of adrenaline that preceded his other conquests.

Today wasn't the day.

As he drove ever closer he every so often caught sight of his face in the rear-view mirror. He liked what he saw. Another masterful disguise, at least as far as he was concerned. The greying wig that showed just enough hair beneath his flat cap, the 1970s Magnum-style moustache and the cheap sunglasses. Anyone else would have said he looked an idiot but he didn't care. He knew it would do what it was intended to do; stop him being recognised and nothing more. He didn't care how he looked as long as he didn't look like himself. The car radio was getting on his nerves as he fiddled with the controls to find something else to listen to. He hated local radio. He hated the inane, stupid competitions and ridiculous phone-ins. At least that was his opinion. He had been driving almost unaware of the background noise and now wondered why he hadn't changed the station ages ago. Still, it didn't matter now, he was almost there.

The lime trees that lined the road had also been blown about quite furiously yesterday and had contributed to the debris on the paths and in the front gardens. Some of the locals' dustbins were still lying over on their sides and small pieces of twig were resting at the bottom of car windscreens, trapped in amongst the mechanism of the windscreen wipers. The rain that had lashed against everything in its path was now reduced to an occasional fine shower either side of the welcome spells of sunshine, which created a rainbow over the village. He had never been to Derek Bladen's house and had never really wanted to, although he had done his homework on him, but it was different now. It was time to plan the finale to the job that he had started a couple of years ago.

Own back.

Retribution.

Call it whatever you want.

* * *

The Visitor had parked his car and walked calmly along the road for about 150 yards to Bladen's house. His walking stick aided the very slight limp that he had acquired especially for today. He was pleased with himself and enjoyed the illusion that he felt he had created. Whether anyone would actually know him or not, he still felt the necessity for the disguise.

No need to take any risks now that the job was almost complete. As he ambled along on the other side of the road he glanced across in the direction of Bladen's house. Nothing special or out of the ordinary about it. It was a semi and had a path that seemed to lead around to the back, which The Visitor logged in his brain, just in case it provided a way in or maybe a way out, should he need it. The roof tiles were almost completely covered by moss, a little of the original red colour showing through in glimpses. The upstairs windows had garish curtains on show. Those on the left side were pulled half closed, displaying what The Visitor thought was an awful choice of colours. The right-hand side were drawn fully open. A large hydrangea bush sat in the front garden, partly blue, partly pink, due to the different levels of acid in the soil. A doctor's surgery was nearby which caused him a problem. There would be cars going in and out and too many people around for his liking, which made up his mind that he would have to do this on a Sunday.

That would be just fine.

Quiet roads for a quick getaway too.

143

He would prefer to lure Bladen out of his retreat but the old bastard hardly ever went out these days, he knew that much. Then there was the added issue of Bladen's wife. She would be there, somewhere.

Kill her too?

No, it was never in the equation and it wasn't her he wanted.

Maybe he could prise Bladen away from his house but then he remembered the oxygen bottle that Bladen relied upon. He gave a sort of half smirk and wondered if he could have a bit of fun with that. As he wandered on to the end of the road he allowed his mind to set the scene. Just him and Bladen. He considered the sort of thing that he would be saying to him and saw the pain and terror in his face.

Yeah, it was all gonna work out just right.

The Visitor turned back again and decided to take one more wander by just to get a feel for the road and make himself acquainted with the neighbourhood, to feel as though he belonged and had the right to be there and, on the day, the right to carry out Bladen's punishment. This was not intended to be a long visit, just enough time to learn a few pointers that might be important.

Grainger's golf club was easy. There had been lots of opportunities to walk amongst the countryside and work out exactly how he wanted to deal with him. The binoculars allowed him to scan the course and decide whereabouts to strike. The shed at the rear of the first green was perfect. He knew he could draw Grainger out to him and slip away unnoticed immediately.

The church, too, made easy pickings. He had watched the routine for a couple of weeks on different days and at different times. He had even been inside when Brookes had popped home and left the front door unlocked. He was, once again, pleased with his plan and felt it had been executed beautifully. Then came Elms and the advert on the fence for people who wanted to 'grow their own' to come along and be a part of the community. It was all just a phone call away. An arranged meeting late into the afternoon sorted that little job out nicely.

Easy in, easy out and not a trace.

The card delivery was a bit chancy, maybe, but it was OK, and as ever he was in absolute control. As far as anyone was concerned this bloke in the flat cap who walked slowly with his stick was just another resident who had popped out to the local village store and was making his way back again. As The Visitor approached Bladen's house again he noticed a woman walking up to the front door and he stopped to see whether he would see Bladen. He was forty yards down the road but he had a good view of the door and would be able to see whoever answered the caller's knock. The woman looked at the bay window and leaned slightly towards it as if to peer inside, but as she did the front door began to open. She spoke to someone but, disappointingly, The Visitor's view wasn't as good as he thought it was going to be as the door only opened a few inches. He thought his chance had gone when the front door closed again but it was only brief, until it opened wide and there stood Derek Bladen.

A door chain.

More information.

Bladen looked even older than he expected him to. Slowly, The Visitor walked on, closer and closer, protected by his cunning disguise. Bladen took no notice of him and spoke to the woman but The Visitor couldn't hear what they were saying and decided that he didn't care. By the time that he had passed Bladen's house, the woman was already heading out of the gate and turning back in the direction from whence she had come. Bladen stood by his front door watching her go and then he finally noticed The Visitor across the road. He nodded in his direction and closed the door.

'Don't you fucking nod at me,' he mumbled under his breath, and continued on to get back to his car. He waited until he was on an empty country road before he pulled off the wig and threw it onto the passenger seat beside him. The glasses and the moustache got the same treatment.

'I'm gonna get you, Bladen,' he said. 'The next time you nod at me your fucking head'll fall off.'

Chapter Thirty-Four

I knew my kitchen needed a bit of redecoration, as did most of the rooms if I'm honest, but when you live amongst it, it tends to become normal, and these kinds of jobs get relegated down the 'to do' list. The old shed outside played host to so many half-filled pots of paint of all different colours from bygone days, most of which had probably gone solid. I really should have a good clear out and get rid of them. But with no-one else to generate the enthusiasm but me, things stayed just as they were.

No hurry. There were more important issues to worry about.

I had made myself a cup of coffee and sat looking out through the kitchen window that faced directly into the garden. A green woodpecker was on the lawn. Prodding and digging away. I watched it for about five minutes before it took off like a dart into the sky and came to rest on a neighbour's beech tree three gardens down. I have always enjoyed the garden birdlife and made an effort to put food out for them each morning. The bird table had the general bird seed, the hanging feeders had peanuts for the tits and niger seed that the goldfinches love, and another feeder had the balls of fat that held a variety of different seed, a bit like a selection box for birds.

My peaceful moment of daydreaming was broken by a strange buzzing noise coming from the living room. I listened to it for a moment before realising what it was. I sighed as I got up and made my way into the living room, following the sound. Something moving on the coffee table caught my eye. My mobile phone; rhythmically buzzing and twisting like a stranded bluebottle on a window sill. I picked it up to see that it was a call from Trevor Eaden, the inspector from

Plaistow whose team had been alerted to the allotments where Elms was discovered.

'Good morning, Trevor.'

'Morning, Dave, I hope I'm not tearing you away from anything important.'

'You are actually. Bird watching. I'm in that place called home for a change and enjoying the wonders of nature.'

'Sounds delightful, mate. Wish I could say the same, but I'm enjoying the wonders of policing instead.'

'Poor old you. What can I do for you today?'

'It's more a matter of what I can do for you, hopefully. I've read your latest email about the progress you and Bob have made in the case.'

I had been updating Trevor and Andy Potter quite regularly as to how we had been getting along, and letting them know what discoveries we had made in case they could help at all.

He continued, 'An elderly gentleman who lives opposite the Elms' house came into the station yesterday evening and spoke to the desk sergeant about seeing someone at the door of the house on the afternoon that Stan Elms was murdered. We had gone through the usual procedural door knocking along the road, both sides, but hadn't managed to get answers at all of them. Letters were posted in the letterboxes asking people to contact the station if they had seen anyone or anything and felt they may be able to assist us. Until now we'd had no responses and thought that it was leading nowhere, but then Mr Haroldson popped up and it seems he had a reasonable look at our ace of spades delivery guy.'

This was good news indeed.

I put my coffee mug down next to Ana's picture and sat on the sofa, reaching at the same time for a notepad and pen.

'How come it took him so long to come forward?' I asked.

'Apparently he went to stay with his brother that evening and was gone by the time we came-a-knocking. He was looking out for his car at the time and noticed someone across the road at the front door. He had been with his brother ever since and just returned, which is when he found our letter on his doormat.'

'How much did Mr Haroldson have to say about it? Did he get a look at his face?'

'He said that a man came from the direction of the allotments and wandered up to the front door, paused for a moment, and came away again back towards Barking Road. When he was pushed for a bit more, he said that the man was about six foot tall, wearing some sort of hooded coat or jacket, and that he could see as the man turned out of the gate that he had a beard. Also, he wore some dark glasses.'

'Dark glasses in the fading light. Whoever he was, he certainly wasn't showing any features unless, of course, the beard was real. What about his footwear? Could Mr Haroldson see what he had on his feet?'

'He said that it looked like he had Wellington boots on, which didn't help a great deal as the allotment was down-trodden by exactly that. Expect our man had come prepared in his choice of footwear too.'

'Sounds like it. What is important is that he was seen, as opposed to the other killings when he ghosted in and out unnoticed. It isn't much but it might mean that he is gaining in confidence and might be likely to slip up.'

'Yeah, Dave, that thought crossed my mind too. The allotments are around the back of Mulberry Towers but anyone could have wandered by and seen him with Elms. He was completely secluded when he done for Grainger and Brookes.'

'Well, thanks for that, Trevor, hopefully we're closing in slowly.'

'That's true, mate. Listen, I'm sorry but that's all I have for now. We'll keep digging and if I can come up with anything I shall be straight on the phone.'

'Great, thanks, Trevor. Speak soon.'

I sat back on the sofa and held Ana's picture, studying the fine lines of the pencil and wondering how she did what she did. I placed the picture back on the coffee table and dialled Bob's mobile number. I found him at his desk.

He answered.

'What the fuck do you want?'

'Good morning to you too. Having fun?'

'Huh, you could say that. You picked the right day to have off. Bloody Corrigan has been having one of his mornings, you know; "why aren't you out there finding criminals etc. etc. etc."'

'Then it's a good job I'm here, by the sounds of it. Listen, I had a call from Trevor Eaden at Plaistow and it turns out that a neighbour who lives opposite the Elms' house saw our man deliver his calling card on the afternoon that Stan Elms was killed. The sighting wasn't brilliant but it all seems to fit with the time of day, and he was wearing a hooded coat of some sort and the neighbour said that he noticed that our man had a beard, which as you are about to tell me, might have been false, but that's all we have.'

'Oh well, that's something I suppose. Listen, I don't think we're gonna learn anything new from that Garron bloke, he's probably told us all he knows. What d'ya reckon?'

'I disagree with you and I think we ought to do it sooner rather than later. I'm back in tomorrow, we'll make some arrangements then.'

'OK, mate, see you soon.'

Chapter Thirty-Five

Moving the beer barrels around the cellar was beginning to become a bit of a strain for Garron on his own. He was strong but his muscles weren't as finely tuned as in the old days at the Repton Gym. Twenty more barrels of different lagers and bitters, Guinness and cider had arrived this morning and almost forty empties had been taken away. Red, white and rosé wine, vodka, whiskey, brandy and martini in a variety of bottle sizes also plagued Garron as he wrestled to manage the invasion of alcohol. The draymen, as they were still known, would help out with the full barrels as far as rolling them down the narrow alleyway and turning them so that they would roll freely over the planks which led them to a gentle drop onto a pile of sandbags at the bottom of a slope into the cellar. One of the draymen would be down in the cellar with Garron to aid the shifting around. From there, they would be manhandled across the cellar floor and into place, where they would be ready for connecting into the system or just stacked as reserve stock. Delivery day was becoming a nightmare for Garron. He could do it all by himself once upon a time and still feel fighting fit, but the last few years had been less of a breeze and more of an uphill struggle.

He could feel his ribs aching. Still, the bruises were evident.

He mopped the sweat from his face with his handkerchief and stuffed it back into his pocket.

'Alright, chief, that's your lot for now.'

'Thank you, mate, see you next time,' replied Garron.

The second drayman clambered out into the relative light and said his goodbyes. Garron reached up and shut the trap door to the outside world, rendering the cellar into a dark and dank space. He didn't relish another challenge with the barrels but knew it would come around soon enough. He ordered twice each week and received the deliveries twice too. He made his way up the creaking steps that led into the rear of the pub, each step groaning as he climbed. He reached for his handkerchief again.

'Yer should get some 'elp, yer silly sod.'

It was Janice, the girl who helped out at the bar when times were busy. She had been in to collect her wages and was just going down to the cellar steps to let him know she would be on her way.

'For once, young Janice, I think yer might be right,' Garron conceded.

'Why don't yer let me ask around for yer? Yer not getting any younger, are yer?'

'Cheeky mare,' said Garron but something inside told him she was probably right.

But he was stubborn.

No guts, no glory.

When Janice had finished whining at him he went upstairs to get cleaned up a bit. He dropped his shirt off his back and kicked it towards a pile of clothes that was building up in the corner of the room. The bathroom was small but enough for what he wanted. As he lowered his arms into the water it stung the insides of his forearms, which had become sore from grasping the barrels in a sort of bear hug as they slipped slowly towards the floor, causing a rub on his skin. Tiny little scratches felt like razor cuts and left redness as a reminder. He thought again about what Janice had said and dismissed it almost straightaway, knowing he probably shouldn't do.

The wash and brush-up felt good. He stood and stared for a moment at the man looking back at him in the mirror and wondered how much longer he would be the landlord of The Fallen Oak. On some days he felt that he could be persuaded to leave it all behind, but he had been there for a lot of years.

What else did he have?

He stood looking into the wardrobe and selected a shirt that would be presentable enough to wear for tonight. White always looked good on him. Maybe a tie too. The jeans he had laid on the bed had been ironed and his shoes had been polished. But not for the pub audience.

For his special girl. His world.

Kim was thirty-five today.

He heard the phone ring and instinctively looked at the bedside table where the handset sat, but it wasn't there. He had had it in his hand when the draymen called and had walked downstairs with it and left it down there somewhere. He cursed and started to make his way down the stairs. He knew Janice had gone and that the place was empty, so the fact that he was wearing only boxers and socks didn't really matter. As he got to the foot of the stairs the ringing stopped but he carried on to the bar area where the main telephone was, at the back of the bar next to all the crisp boxes and packets of peanuts. Immediately he spotted the handset from upstairs on the top of the bar. It had been left there when he peered out the front windows to see whether the hiss of brakes he had heard was indeed the beer lorry.

A full minute passed and Garron realised he didn't need to stand beside the main phone with the other handset in his hand. As he dragged himself back along the corridor towards the stairs the phone began to ring.

'The Fallen Oak pub,' he answered, as he leaned against the wall at the foot of the stairs.

At first there was no sound, no-one spoke to him.

'Hello?' he tried again.

All he could hear was noise that sounded like it was coming from the inside of a moving car. He could hear vehicles passing by but nothing else. No-one spoke.

And then.

'She has been busy, your sister, not stopped in that kitchen of hers. There's a big cake and she's got balloons and ...'

'Who is this?' Garron asked, but he knew who it was. He was certain.

'She's a big girl now, ain't she, that Kim? Have yer bought her something nice, eh? Something she can do that's not too difficult?'

'You keep away from her, yer bastard.'

'Long time ago, ain't it, what is it seventeen, eighteen years? Do you think she's remembered yet or is she still sitting there wondering what hit her?'

'You keep away from her, you hear me, you fucker?' he shouted, gripping the handset so hard that it was a wonder it didn't flatten in his hand. He shook with temper; his heart rate bounding away in his chest.

The phone went dead.

He threw the handset hard against the wall, smashing it into several pieces.

Garron realised that he was sweating again, only this time it was with anger. He went straight to the windows to see if there was a car nearby but he knew it wasn't going to be sitting there waiting for him. The car was travelling on a busy road, maybe a motorway, too far away to worry about. Nowhere near the pub in Whitechapel but how near was it to Debbie's house and how near to Kim?

The clock in the bar told him that he had another hour and a half before he had to be at Debbie's. It would take him a good part of that to get there, what with the traffic filing out of London at this time of day. He was shaking as he went upstairs to finish getting dressed. Sitting on the bed, he pulled on his jeans and fiddled with the button front. He didn't like buttons, preferring a zip, but they looked smart. As he posted a belt through the loops around the waist his hands trembled. In front of the mirror he put on a clean, crisp white shirt and a claret-and-blue tie. Nothing ever really got through to him like this, even the bare-knuckle fights he had had at the pub; in the back yard, all bets placed. They never bothered him, probably because almost all of the bets were safely on him to win.

The phone call played again in his head.

The voice.

He wondered whether he should phone Debbie, just to see if everything was alright, but it would probably worry her as he never called before he was coming over and if he was supposed to, he usually forgot. No, he would just get ready and go. As luck would have it, he had done a deal or rather called in a favour from a mate who, let's say, managed to acquire motors. Bobby Lee was the man to turn to if you needed some wheels, and was prepared to ask no questions. The business he ran had no premises to work from, no dodgy shop front, just word of mouth and a number of contacts that he had built up over the years. Not necessarily the years he had spent on the outside either. Garron had needed something to get around in after the episode with his own car at the rear of the pub. He wasn't one for using buses and couldn't afford to keep jumping in a taxi. He grabbed a jacket and sauntered down to the bar and had another peep out of the front windows; just checking. The street noise invaded the quiet of the bar as he unlocked and opened the doors and ventured out into the market square. The sun was still managing to shine across the top of the canopy that covered the majority of the market stalls, but would soon be fading away. Plenty of the locals were still knocking about. As he strolled away from the pub a number of people shouted, nodded or waved in his direction. He had left the car nearby at the rear of a factory unit. The manager had used The Fallen Oak for years and had no problem with the landlord leaving it there until he got rid of the burnt-out motor at the rear of the pub. Garron walked down the side of the factory unit and around to the rear, where he found his temporary car just as he had left it earlier. He wouldn't want to keep it for too long, not with its likely history. He had bought some cheap seat covers from an indoor market and put those over the front two seats in an attempt to stifle the odour within.

At least that made it feel a little less sleazy.

He fired it up and got going.

Chapter Thirty-Six

Kim referred to a number of the neighbours as uncle or auntie but they were not really relatives. Just neighbours. People that were kind enough to respond in any way that pleased Kim. Debbie had relied on many of these people over the years since Kim was injured. They had visited when they could and had sat with Kim when Debbie needed to work, or just to go to the shops. Debbie was lucky to have them near. So too was Kim. Kim's condition had slowly improved during the first five years after the initial treatment had run its course. The doctors had told Debbie that it would be slow and that there would be good days and bad.

They were right.

But the worst seemed to be behind them now and Kim enjoyed her fairly simple existence most of the time. The difficult times were usually reduced to her feeling frightened by sudden noises, like a door banging, or if Debbie were to drop a glass in the kitchen it would sometimes cause Kim to tremble for about ten minutes. Debbie spent lengthy periods sitting with Kim or perched on her bed during her more anxious moments, which had thankfully become a lot less frequent. She was someone that even Debbie sometimes found hard to remember as she once was.

So much water had flowed under so many bridges.

Today, Debbie was trying to put it all behind her.

She had been awake since 4 a.m. thinking about the arrangements for Kim's birthday. The cake had been made yesterday and had been taken next door for the intricate task of the icing of Kim's name and 'Happy Birthday'. Debbie, as hard as she tried, was not a natural when it came to icing cakes. The composition was easy. Marzipan was the key.

Kim loved it and Debbie didn't mind her devouring as much as she liked today, within reason. Although Kim's rather hopeful request for marzipan at breakfast was turned down, it did raise a smile for Debbie and a much cheekier one from Kim. The opening of her presents was mostly dealt with just after breakfast except for one; Uncle John's. Kim would wait until he arrived and would be on full alert, listening out for him. She had asked her mother numerous times during the day what time Uncle John was coming and Debbie, with her angelic patience, had quietly told her that he would be there when he got there.

* * *

The Peugeot was running low on fuel as Garron trundled off towards Hornchurch. His mind was still straining with the torment of the call. He was so preoccupied by it that he hadn't given any thought to how much fuel was in the tank.

Now he knew. Not a lot.

The petrol station was within reach, much to Garron's relief. He was agitated enough without the bother of hunting for a petrol station. Glancing repeatedly at the fuel gauge, he approached the forecourt. One pump was free so he guided the Peugeot alongside the pump and parked up. Half a tank would do for now and give him enough juice for the rest of the week. There was enough time to pay and get going. Soon he would be giving Kim a cuddle and making small talk with people he didn't really know that well. After the way today had played out, he was keen to get to Debbie's and make sure everything was OK. Having paid, he hurried out onto the forecourt and got into the car. As he waited to rejoin the traffic and eyed the vehicles blocking his exit, he froze momentarily.

Was he being watched?

A chill ran through his veins.

Garron was no soft touch and he didn't like the feeling that anyone might be getting one over on him, especially Oscar. He shrugged the thought off as quickly as it came and got moving towards Debbie's. The weight of traffic was in his favour and he got himself to Debbie's a lot quicker than he thought he would, which pleased him. He found a gap to park not far from her house and began to walk over the road. As he did so he couldn't stop himself looking at every car parked along the road with some suspicion.

No; silly.

Debbie opened the door and gave him a hug and he went inside. The chatter from the living room was immediately evident and he felt a slight doubt as to how long he could keep up the small talk. But that didn't matter, it was all about Kim. He had ordered Kim's present online, as usual, and once it arrived at Debbie's she had done the wrapping. It had been that way for years. Kim never questioned the handwriting on the label. Sometimes Debbie wished she would.

When Garron walked into the room Kim smiled the biggest smile of the day. She let out a squeal and anyone that knew her also knew that Uncle John had arrived. Kim was in a big armchair surrounded by the attention of her friends and neighbours. She made it clear to everyone within earshot that her excitement could not be contained.

'Uncle John,' Kim cried out.

Garron wrestled his way through to Kim and held her in his arms. Kim squeezed as tightly as she could and laughed with joy.

'Hello, birthday girl, you look beautiful.'

'You … look … beautiful … too,' she said, which raised a smile on the many faces in the room.

Garron was looking around at the open presents that were spread around the room, wondering what Debbie had done with the one he had ordered for Kim's special day, when she appeared at the living-room door with a well-wrapped box.

'Kim, I've found another present. I don't know who it's from,' she teased.

'Uncle John,' she said with a great big smile.

Seeing Kim so happy filled Garron with emotion. She had been his shining star since the day she was born. Debbie sat beside Kim and rested the box on her lap. Kim started to pull at a corner of the wrapping paper that Debbie had left available for her to get a start at unwrapping the present. As the box began to reveal itself, Kim became more and more excited. Debbie frantically tried to keep pace with Kim, gathering pieces of torn paper and screwing them into a ball, as she ripped and tore at Debbie's hard work. Everyone was attentive, anticipating the eventual sight of Uncle John's present to his favourite girl. Garron had done his homework and been chatting with Debbie, who would always be on hand to give him some advice on what to get for Kim. Over the years, he had bought her a huge variety of different gifts; music, clothes, vouchers for fashion shops, books that she used to enjoy reading … before. It had been more difficult to choose for her since Kim's life changed but Debbie was there to come to his rescue.

Finally, the box was open.

Kim was beside herself.

With a little assistance from Debbie, Kim slowly drew the final present of the day from its packaging. She glanced up at her friends who were all waiting to see what she had been bought. An air of expectation hovered in the room. Garron hoped she was going to like it but there was no need to worry; evidently she was delighted. Kim let out another cry as she pulled the garment out of its box and onto her lap. Kim's friends, too, showed their approval by letting out a simultaneous gasp.

One girl started to cry.

Debbie wasn't far behind.

Kim held the dress against herself and with shimmering eyes, looked all around the room. It was the exact one she had seen in a fashion magazine. Kim had not stopped mentioning the dress for weeks after. Debbie had to bite her lip and not give anything away but she had already had a quiet word with her brother about the prospect of him buying it for Kim's birthday. The style of the dress was quite formal with the top part being décolleté. It was a deep crimson and Kim could not wait to try it on. What neither Debbie nor Kim knew was that Garron had another surprise for Kim. In his pocket was an envelope which contained two tickets to a London musical. Somewhere for Debbie to take Kim where she could look beautiful in her new dress. Kim loved musicals and had watched a number of them on the television but had not been able to go. She would sing along to the songs and cry at the romance of them. She had DVDs of all her favourites, which was most of them, and sat through them time and time again. A few months ago, Garron had checked with Debbie that Kim would be OK to go to see something nice in London one day and Debbie had said it would be fine, unless she was having a bad day. The subject had not been mentioned again and Garron planned his special surprise for Kim.

There was a lot of attention given to Kim's new dress and all her friends wanted to see her in it, so they helped Kim upstairs to her bedroom and the sound of excited chatter slowly diminished to a distant mumble with the occasional squeal of joy.

'John, that was really lovely, thank you,' said Debbie.

'Anything for that girl, Deb,' he replied.

'Don't think I've ever seen you look so smart either,' Debbie laughed.

'Must admit, it's not too often. Listen I've got something else to give her.' He reached into his trouser pocket and brought out the envelope. 'It's for Kim but it's for you too, really.'

'What d'ya mean, for me?'

'Well, I thought it'd be nice if you both got to go out, together, to do something nice. A bit of a treat.'

'What you on about?'

'Look, ya know how much she loves her musicals? Well. I've got yer both some tickets to one of those shows up town,' he explained.

'You ain't. Oh, John.' Debbie hugged him and planted a big kiss on his cheek. Her eyes were filling with tears again.

Kim's entrance into the living room was preceded by a fanfare, or the best impression her friends could muster. All the heads turned towards the door and in she came. One of her friends held her arm for a little support as she walked up to her mother and her uncle with more tears of joy in her eyes.

'Oh, darling, you look amazing,' Debbie said.

'You're beautiful. Just like a princess,' echoed her proud Uncle John.

He held the envelope out to Kim and she took it in her hand.

'What is it?' she asked.

'Take a look, darling,' encouraged Debbie.

Kim opened the envelope and held the two tickets in her hand. She gasped as she realised what they were and put her hand over her mouth. More happy tears ran down her cheeks. Kim gave him a kiss and hugged her mum before retreating back upstairs with the girls to get changed back into her other clothes.

'She'll love yer forever, ya know.'

'Wouldn't have it any other way, Deb … Oh, nearly forgot her card,' he said.

'What card?' said Debbie.

'Her birthday card.'

'What are yer on about? She's got her card. You put it in the door yesterday.'

Debbie stepped across the room to fetch the card from the fireplace.
'Here, yer daft sod. I thought yer writing looked a bit drunk.'

Debbie laughed at him and went into the kitchen, shaking her head in disbelief at how silly he had been.

He looked at the card and opened it.

The card he had written for Kim was still in his pocket.

Chapter Thirty-Seven

The motorway was running freely without any sort of delay in sight and the roadworks that had recently caused me a headache had been finished, allowing the lane restrictions to be removed. Glancing to my left, I could see a cloud of dust rising into the air behind a tractor that was chugging along the furrows some 500 yards away. I was glad that I didn't have to rise for work that early. It dawned on me, as it had done a number of times since my move to Essex, that it was a much more pleasant journey to work these days as I was heading away from the London chaos and not towards it. The traffic on the opposite carriageway was comparatively heavier with vehicles charging towards the busy end of the motorway, all hoping to get to the end before it all came to a grinding halt. I was in good time this morning and felt remarkably relaxed as I drove through the gates that marked my destination. I parked the car in the station yard and reached across to grab my mobile from the hands-free holder. The screen was blank, which was not unlike my memory this morning as I had forgotten to switch it on before I got in the car. It would usually chirp soon after it is switched on with all sorts of messages relating to work or meetings that may have been cancelled or postponed, but this morning it was quiet and now I knew why.

It wasn't awake.

And nor was I, very much.

I entered the building at the rear and began to trudge up the stairs. I could go to the front and use the lift but I thought the little bit of exercise was preferable, albeit only a token effort. As I got halfway up the first flight my phone duly began to register the incoming text messages and emails, as well as six missed calls and a voicemail message, which I thought was a bit excessive, even for me. I glanced down at the screen and decided that I would be able to pay better attention to it once I was sitting down at my desk with a very welcome cup of coffee to inspire my sluggish brain. The corridor at the top of the rear stairs was badly in need of some tender loving care. The painted plaster was grubby from people putting their hands on the wall and had scuff marks along by the skirting board. A mustard-coloured carpet had been well used over the years and wasn't mustard-coloured any more. I wondered how far the station budget would stretch this year and whether the whole station would get a face-lift before the money ran out yet again. As I got further along the dingy corridor towards a set of double doors that would lead me into the floor where my desk was situated, my phone began to ring in my pocket.

It was DCI Corrigan.

I decided that he could wait a few more seconds.

The half-glazing in the doors allowed me a view into the office. I could see a cluster of people ahead of me standing in a half-circle with the DCI at the helm. It was probably another briefing that I was late for, no doubt. Although, glancing at my watch, I knew I wasn't late. Maybe one of the messages on my phone was there to tell me to be in early for some reason or other. As I pushed one side of the double doors open the whole gathering turned to look at me.

Their faces were ghostly.

The silence was deafening.

In an instant I must have looked as pale and withdrawn as they did. A few of them looked down to the floor to avoid eye contact, the rest stood motionless, and then Corrigan spoke.

'Dave, can you come into my office please?'

Again, a drained feeling washed through my veins and left my legs a little wobbly. As I followed the DCI into his office I swear that I couldn't feel the floor beneath me. Almost as if I had lost the feeling in my feet.

Floating.

An 'out of body' experience.

The onlookers were all silent except Terry Brush, who simply said he was sorry.

But for what?

I entered Corrigan's office and instinctively closed the door behind me. Whatever he was going to say was clearly important.

'Sit down, Dave. I'm afraid I've got some bad news,' he said with a serious, sombre expression.

'I take it this is why my phone has been full of messages and missed calls,' I said, more for the sake of something to say than anything else.

He simply nodded and then paused for a few seconds, clearly trying to find the right words.

'One of our cars was despatched to an RTC earlier this morning and when they arrived, they discovered that a pedestrian had been run down as he crossed the road. It seems to be a hit-and-run accident.' The DCI took in a breath and looked me squarely in the eyes, and uttered the words that I had been trying not to pre-empt.

'Dave, it was Bob. He's in a bad way. The air ambulance took him to Queen's Hospital in Romford. They have a trauma centre there.'

I leant back into the chair and felt completely limp. I couldn't have stood up if the building was on fire.

'How bad?' I asked, although part of me didn't want to know.

'I managed to get through to the hospital about twenty minutes ago, which is why I was calling you, but your phone was off. The doctor that I spoke to didn't give me a good feeling about this, I'm sorry. Bob is still being assessed by the doctors so I'm afraid I don't have the full story right now, but I'm very concerned.'

My mind wouldn't allow me to concentrate on anything the DCI had just said, although I heard every word. I had seen people refuse to accept the obvious truth that sat right in front of them on many occasions and now I was doing it. I wanted to ask questions but I couldn't compose myself immediately. Finally, after a period of silence I spoke.

'Is he going to die?' It just came out, awkwardly.

'I honestly don't know, Dave. I wish I could say he was going to be fine but I just don't know. The doctor said that he had received a head injury and that there was some degree of swelling on his brain. He had been hit pretty hard, Dave. They had not long got the scan results back and were still studying them. I wish I knew more.'

'Where did you say they took him?'

'Queen's Hospital in Romford.'

'I'm going down there,' I said, without suggesting that I was going to ask permission. Bob was my partner and I was going, and that was that.

'I want you to go with Terry, not on your own. We don't know how bad things are, after all.'

Dave Copson

'I'm fine on my own, I'll go now.'

'No, you will go with Terry and he will be driving. Is that clear, Dave? I insist upon this. Bob may be in a serious condition for all we know and I don't want you there alone.'

He was right, of course, so I had to agree that his request was the sensible one.

'When you both get there, I want to know what is going on, understand?'

I was left in no doubt about that and, of course, he was right again. He should be informed at all times. I got up slowly from the chair and made my way slowly back out into the office. It was like walking through a cloud of uncertainty. As I appeared into view there was an obvious uncomfortable atmosphere waiting for me. Faces lifted from their laptops and studied me for some sort of reaction to the news. I scanned the office for Terry Brush and saw him walking towards me.

'Terry, we ...'

'I'm ready, guv,' he responded.

It occurred to me then that Corrigan must have been briefing him when I wandered in earlier. I nodded and followed him towards the front stairs. Terry was a good copper as well as a nice guy and I was glad to make the journey to the hospital with him. He was one of the first people to make me feel welcome when I arrived at Chelmsford. Sometimes the rank markings will deter people from approaching you. He didn't know me, after all, and I was to be his boss, but he was very relaxed about it all. I never got the impression that he was creeping around the new detective inspector, he always came across very well; genuine. We chatted about what had happened, at least as much as we knew, which wasn't a great deal really. As Terry was driving, it allowed my mind to begin to question why the driver didn't stop. Maybe it was a stupid question, in some ways. Maybe he or she would turn up at a police station in a day or so and admit to what had happened. That was fairly common.

What did happen?

Terry parked the car and we made our way across the parking area towards the hospital. I was in such a strange trance that I hardly had any appreciation of how cold the rain was as it lashed onto the cars and bounced off the roofs. Minute pieces of hail felt like needles as they spiked against my cheek. I squinted and tried my best to peer through

164

the rain at the signpost ahead of me. Terry was already huddled in a smoking shelter having made a dash for cover. I decided to join him and wait out the worst of what I hoped was just a sporadic heavy shower.

'My umbrella's in the boot of the car,' he said helpfully.

'Not much good there.'

'I know. Which way do we go to get into the reception?' he asked.

'That sign said the reception was around to the left. Fancy making a dash for it? We're wet anyway.'

Terry nodded and we both abandoned our retreat, sloshing in and out of the puddles that had appeared so quickly. The rain had calmed just a little and was slowing down as we got ourselves to the double doors that were protecting a number of people standing inside, all looking up anxiously at the dark skies. A man had seen us approaching in a hurry and was holding one of the doors open for us. We both thanked him as we hustled our way inside and into the dry.

'Could have really done without that,' Terry said as he shook some of the raindrops from his trousers and waggled a sodden shoe in the air. 'That last puddle was like a bloody lake.'

The reception desk was to our right and had a queue of people standing in line waiting their turn to report for appointments or, like us, get directions for where to find friends and loved ones. The lady at the desk was tall and slim and spoke with an accent that I couldn't place. Thankfully, the queue moved along quite well and we were fairly soon at the desk waiting to be helped. I told her that we were here to see Mr Hand who had been admitted this morning following a road accident.

'Are you relatives or friends?' she asked with that eastern sounding twang to her voice. Maybe Hungarian.

'We work with him, we're police officers,' I said automatically.

She looked us both up and down and tapped at her computer. She was certainly in no particular hurry and told us to wait in a seating area nearby, and that a doctor would come along and speak with us soon. She pointed out that we could get a hot drink from the W.I. canteen a little further along the corridor towards the lifts. We passed on the refreshments and waited. A newspaper had been discarded on one of the seats so I picked it up, but before I had attempted to read a word I lobbed it back onto the seat opposite. I wasn't in the mood for reading, or anything else really. We hadn't said very much since we got into the hospital. I think both Terry and I were dreading some kind of terrible news from the doc. We sat watching people come and go through the main doors: visitors, hospital porters, taxi drivers looking for their fare.

I didn't like hospitals.

Poor Bob didn't have a choice.

'Sorry about the scene you walked into this morning, guv. No-one knew what to say, really. Corrigan called us all together and asked if we'd seen you but no-one had. I thought it was you he was gonna tell us had got some trouble but when he said Bob had been hit by a motor, bloody hell. Corrigan said he had been trying your phone and that it was off and I kept thinking how you were gonna feel when you found out. Nightmare.'

'Don't worry Terry, one of those things,' I said, almost nonchalantly.

We sat in silence, watching doctors and nurses mill about with clipboards under their arms and patients being wheelchaired to and fro. A minute feels like an hour when you are just sitting, not knowing what sort of news you are going to hear. A police officer walked by us with a prisoner handcuffed to him. The prisoner scowled at us as he wandered by, sporting his new dressings that were covering some sort of wound to his head and a nice new sling on his arm. I realised then that Terry was in uniform, I was suited. Anyway, that would be the end of his day out.

'Might get a coffee, guv. D'ya want one?'

Before I could answer a doctor appeared at my shoulder. I stood. as did Terry. He was about twenty-five and looked like he had been awake for days on end. I expect he felt like he had. He introduced himself as Doctor Aziz and asked us who we were again, by way of confirmation. I suppose they must see quite a few police officers in the hospital and he wanted to be sure he was addressing the right ones.

Fair enough.

He looked beyond me and suggested that we sat at a table at the W.I canteen. He asked us if we wanted any tea or coffee but we declined. Even Terry declined, having just said that he was going to get a coffee. Doctor Aziz spoke very clearly and with a diction that I wish I had mastered. He took his stethoscope from around his neck and put it on the table in front of him, holding it tightly as if it were going to wriggle away at any moment.

'Let me see what I can tell you about your colleague. Fortunately, I have been with him the whole way through this morning apart from when he was taken for a CT scan. When he arrived he wasn't conscious. This was because he had been sedated by the ambulance crew so that they could manage his airway better. The paramedic who came in with him described to me that he had been struck by a motor car from behind. This was confirmed by a witness to the accident at the scene who spoke to the paramedic. We quickly surveyed your friend for injuries that were apparent and any that may still have been hidden, and found that he had an injury on the back of his head. He had lost a significant amount of blood but wasn't directly in any great danger because of it. He was, however, what we call "time critical". That is to say that his condition was at a level that required us to be urgent with his care from the start. He was taken for x-rays and a CT scan was organised. Both of these things would show us a lot more with regard to his condition. Now, what we have learnt is that the head injury has caused significant swelling to his brain, and the x-rays also showed us that he has a broken pelvis and some damage to his lower spine. His arms and legs appear to be fine and uninjured with the exception of a few minor grazes.'

'Glad something is uninjured,' said Terry.

'Yes, quite,' said Doctor Aziz.

'What will happen now?' I asked.

'What will happen now is that we will continue to closely monitor his head injury and if the consultant deems it necessary, he may decide to operate to relieve the swelling on his brain. The pelvic injury is being managed for now and we are still looking closely at the x-rays with regard to his lower spine; it's the lumbar region.'

'Is there any chance we could see him? Can we speak with him?' I said.

'Not currently I'm afraid. He is in intensive care and the staff there are paying very close attention to him, and anyway he is asleep, which, as I said, is as a result of the drugs we have administered to him for his own welfare. I'm sorry that the news is not better but do remember it is early days and he has a long journey ahead of him that we shall be assisting him with. I suggest you give me a call this afternoon and I will, hopefully, have some more up-to-date news of how he is then.'

Doctor Aziz left me with a number that I could use to talk to him about Bob's condition and made his excuses for now, leaving us to sit in silence once again. We didn't speak; we just sat and stared at the table in front of us, where a large man sat devouring a huge piece of cake. Terry reminded me eventually that we should call the DCI and let him know the score. I agreed and suggested we go to the front doors and check the weather. If it was dry we could wander outside while we took it all in and give Corrigan a call at the same time. I felt as though I had already done a day's work and yet it was only 11 o'clock. The rain had stopped a while ago and the ground had dried almost completely, so we stepped outside and that alone made me feel better straightaway. The flowers that surrounded the front face of the building were still glistening with tiny raindrops that had yet to drip to the earth below. The air smelt really fresh and clean and was helping to enable me to think straight at last. Terry had found a dry bench that had been protected somehow by an overhang above and sat down, obviously moved by the whole experience this morning. I pressed the button on my phone that would take me directly through to Corrigan's telephone in his office.

Chapter Thirty-Eight

Having spoken to the DCI and explained exactly what Doctor Aziz had said about Bob's condition, Terry and I began a sedate drive back to Chelmsford. The threat of the rain clouds had all but dispersed and the day was brightening up. At least the weather was.

'You gonna call him later; that Doctor Aziz?'

'I will do, Terry. Better leave it till about four, eh? Give him and his team a chance to see how it goes. He said they were watching him, so he'll be alright.'

'Hope he is, guv.'

So did I.

It wasn't until I got back to the station that I gave the case Bob and I were working on a single thought. Not surprisingly, Corrigan was way ahead of me on that one. He was going to be a man down for however long it was going to be and he knew he needed to get me coupled up with someone else in order to continue with the business that Bob and I currently had in hand. He asked Terry and me to go into his office and go over what Doctor Aziz had told us once again, and it was during that chat that he told Terry that he would be joining me on the case. I had a strange, mixed feeling about it. Whilst I knew Terry would be good to work with, I was still sore at losing Bob. I knew that the job had to go on and that I couldn't really do anything about what had happened, so I tried to let it go. Besides, Terry was a good guy and I was sure that we would get on just fine. All I had to do now was make sure that he became completely familiar with the case so far. I decided that the best thing to do was get all the information together and send Terry home with his newfound homework. He said that he was aware of quite a lot of what had gone on because he had taken an interest in it and listened to bits and pieces that Bob and I had discussed in the office.

He insisted that he wasn't entirely in the dark about it. This gave me some hope that Terry would be OK. He promised to give it his full attention tonight and I didn't doubt him for a moment. He would be reading all night and taking it all in. He was that sort. I felt I could trust him to do a thorough job and I knew that he was very keen to get involved in this case, so with a bit of luck things might work out for the best after all. I told Terry that we would get our heads together in the morning and get to work as soon as he was up to speed. I had a feeling that he would be ready and raring to go as soon as he got to work tomorrow. With Terry off home with a full copy of all the details he would need, I began to give thought to where Bob and I were up to.

Another visit to see Garron.

That was it.

I spent some time revisiting some of the events of the case and going over what Garron had said the last time we met. I made brief notes regarding the questions I might have for him this time. This was all done with one eye on the clock, ensuring that I didn't forget to call Doctor Aziz. At the appropriate time I made the call, only to find that the doctor had nothing more to add to what he had already related to Terry and me earlier. They were still monitoring Bob's condition and continually checking his vital signs. Bob was still unconscious, which he said was no bad thing at the moment, and it was suggested that I call in the morning to see whether there would be any new information.

* * *

Gary Walden and Stuart Cunningham were the two officers that attended the RTC this morning that involved Bob. They had spoken with a witness at the scene and had got a certain amount of information about the car and what actually happened, apart from the obvious. It took me a bit of time but by the end of the day I caught up with both of them in the yard before they got to their cars and left for home. They told me how sorry they were to find out that it was Bob and how much of a shock it was once they realised that the man on the ground was someone they both knew as a friend and colleague. They described what they saw and talked about how they found him lying in a puddle of blood. A passer-by had managed to secure a scarf around his head which, in the end, was simply held in place because it kept slipping off. He was lying in the road, shoved hard up against the wheel of a parked car with his legs crossed almost under the car. Blood spatter was on the wing and door of the car, adding to the horrific scene. Whilst Stuart helped as best he could with Bob, Gary spoke to the person who had seen the collision but he didn't have a lot to add that would be very helpful. The account he gave was fairly brief and, of course, it all happened very quickly. The witness was a gentleman who was out walking to the shops and turned when he heard a screech of tyres and a dull thud. He said that he saw a man hurtling towards the path, his arms flailing in the air as if to grab onto something that would save him from falling, and then he disappeared out of sight behind a parked car. I asked Gary what the man had said about the car that was involved.

'That's the thing that I don't get,' he said.

'What do you mean?'

'Well, according to our witness the car stopped and crunched the gears into reverse as if to try to hit Bob again. The driver was probably in a panic and got the gears mixed up but he said it looked like it was deliberate. Then the car zoomed away and out of sight.'

'Did he see the driver?'

'He said he got a decent look at him but nothing was registering at the time. When I asked him to describe the driver he just said he couldn't. I asked him why not and he said because he had a big beard and a hood on his head. All he could see was his nose. Lot of good, eh?'

I stared at Gary and allowed the details he had recounted to sink in. A hood and a beard; just like the man that Mr Haroldson in Plaistow had seen at the door of Stan Elms' house.

Christ.

Could it be?

I thanked Gary and Stuart and asked them to keep me posted with anything else they should find out, and told them that I would reciprocate with the details about how Bob was doing.

Chapter Thirty-Nine

Kay Cullen's flight from Belfast International Airport parted the rain-soaked clouds and landed on time, creeping gently along the tarmac towards its chosen gate. She travelled light and only had one bag with her in the cabin, which was placed down by her feet in accordance with the stewardess's instructions. Her shoes were still off. One suitcase was in the hold. Kay had worn her seatbelt throughout the short flight and remained fastened into her seat. She always selected an aisle seat if at all possible, as looking out of the window and learning precisely how far she could fall to a very sudden end was not something she wanted to contemplate. She had never been a fan of flying and chose to use alternative forms of travel whenever possible.

Kay was born in Lisburn, just outside of Belfast. From the time she first entered her junior-high school she was already well known locally as an established athlete. Her father used to call her Leggy, which became a bit of a nickname that followed her through school and into her athletics career. Some people actually thought that her name was Leggy Cullen. Her particular field of expertise was the 400m hurdles. Her parents' house in Lisburn was adorned with Kay's triumphs. Medals, trophies, shields and many photographs of her holding her awards and certificates could be found in every corner of the house. Her parents, Des and Maggie Cullen, were incredibly proud of their daughter. Twenty-five minutes after landing at Stansted Airport and jostling for position to retrieve her suitcase, Kay wandered along the corridor that led her and her fellow passengers towards the arrivals lounge. The straps of her bag were draped over her left shoulder and her fist grasped a bundle of the strap tightly. Her right hand pulled the suitcase along behind her as she tried her best not to allow the small wheels to hit anyone's feet as they shuffled along close behind. She wore jeans and a T-shirt that had her athletics club motto emblazoned across the chest, with a bulky woollen jumper on top. Her straight blonde hair reached almost to the middle of her back but when she competed it was always in a fishtail braid. Her flat-soled pumps were designed with a leopard pattern and thick white laces. She wore pumps for two reasons: comfort and the fact that at 5'11" she didn't need to appear any taller. The beige jumper had a large neck that allowed it to fall almost completely off of one shoulder. Her T-shirt was dark blue which matched the jeans that clung to her perfect figure.

Kay Cullen was easy on the eye and often mistaken for a model.

At twenty-nine she was enjoying some of the best form of her athletics career. Her 400m hurdle times were at a season's best and getting ever closer to the personal best that she ran at a meeting in Belfast two years ago. She called that run 'the miracle run' and vowed, one day, to match it. Her dad said it was just the beginning, but she had yet to repeat the time. After her most recent event four days ago in Scotland, she had returned home to see her parents before flying across the Irish Sea to Essex. She had been competing in the grounds of the Stirling University campus and had spent some of her precious spare time meeting a friend in Glasgow. Suzie Li had been a member of Kay's athletics club at the time when she first started to take the sport seriously but had to retire from it when she became plagued by repetitive injuries.

Kay's mobile phone finally resumed business as she wandered into the arrivals lounge, her eyes scanning the foyer for a familiar face. She sat close to a window that reached the full width of the lounge, enabling her to see if her lift was anywhere in sight. It wasn't. She turned her concentration to the text message that had just landed on her phone.

Gonna be 20 mins ... traffic x

She shook her head at the message but was calm. Twenty minutes isn't so bad, she decided. A group of men dressed in a variety of football shirts were paying close attention to her and making their thoughts rather obvious. They were speaking louder than their alcohol-drenched systems realised. It was one thing having blokes look you up and down but these were becoming obnoxious very quickly. Kay looked out of the window, the reflection of which allowed her to see what they were up to without them being fully aware. It was nothing new to her and she was quite used to that sort of attention. It went with the territory, as they say. As their decibel level rose they, in turn, gained the attention of the airport security. Three security men made their way towards the group, as Kay watched in the reflection, and began to speak to the men. They gesticulated in every direction except Kay's and after just a couple of minutes began to wander away with the security men close behind. She checked her watch and reckoned that the twenty minutes must be up by now, or at least hoped it was. She scanned the lounge area again and just as she was about to give up, she saw him at the far end of the building walking towards her, but without a clue where she was. He was looking straight ahead and as hard as she tried to catch his eye, she couldn't seem to do it. Kay decided to head him off by walking diagonally across the lounge, dragging her suitcase behind her. Finally, their eyes met, and they were all smiles.

'Hello, darling,' said Kay.

'There you are. I'm sorry I'm a bit behind but I left home a little late and then found a tailback of cars on the approach to the airport.'

Kay hugged him and he held her close, both exchanging a kiss. They walked hand in hand to where he had parked the car in the short-stay car park just a couple of hundred metres from the building, and very shortly they were on their way.

'How was your flight?'

'Yeah, it was OK. As soon as you're up, you're coming down again. How has your day been?'

'Really weird. One of our guys was knocked down by a car on his way to work and then I was told I was gonna be taking over from him on the case. It's a shame for him, of course, but exciting for me.'

Terry Brush and Kay Cullen had met when he took a holiday in Ireland three years ago and had been hopping across the Irish Sea ever since. It created a challenge. Fortunately, they were a strong team.

Chapter Forty

Bob Hand had no family to speak of. A brother had moved to Canada eighteen years ago and had not been in touch for the majority of that time. Both of his parents had passed away and what remained of the rest of his extended family was spread all over the country; most of them were untraceable. I wouldn't know where to begin.

Bob had never cared.

He was one of life's loners.

Although I had known him as a work colleague, I never truly felt that I knew him as a close friend. When we were at work, whether it be the days in the past or the more recent times, I could never quite crack the outer coating of the life that Bob secretly absorbed himself in. He'd always been a great bloke to work with but he was just one of those guys that relished his private time. I felt a responsibility for him now that he was all alone and probably unaware of the state he was in.

The Intensive Care Unit on the second-floor level was not too difficult to find. Dressed for work in a dark charcoal suit, white shirt and light blue tie, I stood in the lift and as it began to ascend the shaft once more, looked at my reflection. I counted myself lucky not to be where Bob was right now. When I got to the main desk I would have to ask for Doctor Aziz, as he had suggested that I talk to him first in order to find out the exact state of play regarding Bob's condition this morning. I considered that Bob may not be in this unit now and hoped that he had been moved, which could suggest that he had had some degree of improvement. The lift doors opened, and I came face to face with an elderly patient in a wheelchair who was being assisted by a young man in a porter's uniform.

'One in, one out,' he said cheerfully, as his chair was wheeled slightly to one side, allowing my egress from the lift car.

I smiled but didn't really know what to say. Stepping out into level 2, I could see the main desk to my right and headed towards it. Doctor Aziz was standing at the desk looking at what looked like a set of patient notes and twiddling his pen around his fingers, seemingly in deep thought. It was 9.15 and the Intensive Care Unit was a hive of activity. He glanced to his left as I came into his peripheral vision, and closed the folder that had been holding his attention and turned to speak to me.

'Good morning, sir,' he said.

'Good morning, doctor.'

'Let's go in here,' he said, gesturing towards a side room that turned out to be an office that the Duty Doctor used.

'Is that you today? Duty doctor?'

'No, but he won't mind if we step in here for a few minutes. It's a little more private.'

Doctor Aziz pulled a chair out from under a desk for me to sit on and perched himself on the corner of a low-level unit by the window.

'Have you managed to slip away from the police station this morning?'

'No, I haven't been in yet, I'm going in straight from here. That way, I can take the latest news in with me. I'm sure I'll be swamped with questions from everyone.'

'Of course,' he said.

The Duty Doctor's office was fairly small. A cabinet reached from floor to ceiling, heavily stacked with folders of all colours and sizes. The desk at which I sat had seen better days but no doubt was still serviceable. The blinds at the window were of the horizontal type, the ones that gathered dust unless they were regularly wiped. They weren't. There was a large chart on the biggest wall that looked very much like a rota for the staff, with numerous entries and crossings out on it. It had different colours for each of the names on the left of the chart and areas blocked out in black at various intervals through the year. In truth I didn't expect to find Bob would be taking guests and imagined that he would still be in need of lots of rest.

'Well, what I can say is that your friend, Mr Hand, has had a fairly stable night's sleep. He has had someone paying close attention to him throughout the night and up to now he has responded about as much as we would expect, given his injuries. Specifically, we are concerned with the swelling in his head and that remains our top priority for now. His pelvic fracture is stable and the fact that he has not been able to move around has helped that. The base of his spine appears to be severely bruised and further x-rays that we will take this morning will hopefully show nothing more alarming. It seems likely that the impact he received to the back of his head may have been worse than we initially thought but again, that is something that will show itself in the course of the next few days. Currently, I am not allowing any visitors until we have a clearer view of everything, and then I will decide again.'

'All of that doesn't sound very encouraging,' I said.

'With this level of trauma it is pretty much commonplace. We have to understand that he has received a big, heavy blow to his head and his brain has been severely rattled in its casing. That is what the swelling is all about, and until we either see some signs of improvement or, maybe, one of the x-rays or scans shows us something, we have to be patient.'

'How long will it be before the swelling starts to subside?'

'I can't say for sure but let's just say it is something we are watching closely.'

I suppose as a doctor it must be difficult in certain cases to try to be too accurate. Some people would hold them to it and as he implied, everyone is different. I felt a little let down but perhaps I had subconsciously promised myself some good news. It quickly became apparent that I need not take up any more of the doctor's time. I had his number and he had been very generous in allowing me to have it. If he was unobtainable I could always call directly to the I.C.U desk. I made my way back down to the ground floor without seeing Bob but I appreciated that it was the doctor's call and, after all, he couldn't have spoken to me. I didn't want to see him until he was ready and able.

* * *

When I walked into the station it didn't take long before the onslaught of questions from well-meaning people began. It was to be expected and it would not have been right otherwise. I fended it off a little because there wasn't any significant news to give to anyone. Things were pretty much the same and we would have to wait. Everyone accepted that it was a matter of time and that with any luck there would be some more encouraging news to pass on soon. I knocked at DCI Corrigan's door and was called in. As I stepped inside, Terry turned to look at me.

He was sitting at the desk with Corrigan, both of whom asked the most popular question of the day.

'The doctor says he needs more time to establish the exact situation. Bob is comfortable but not conscious yet. He's having some more x-rays and scans today at some point; hopefully we'll know a bit more later on.'

'Did you manage to see him? How does he look?' Terry enquired.

'No, I didn't see him. It's too early but he's in good hands, as they say. There's nothing much we can do but wait until he starts to show some signs of improvement, hopefully soon.'

'Well, thank you for passing that on, Dave,' said Corrigan.

Noticeably, he had been calling me 'Dave' ever since Bob's accident. Maybe he was going soft. Corrigan pushed his glasses higher up onto his nose and sat back in his chair.

'Terry, here, has been impressing me with his knowledge of the case that you and Bob have been following. I suspect he knows it better than you, Detective Inspector.' That was more like it. 'I understand that you've had a shock, both of you, but we must push on with this. I want to see some progress in the coming weeks and I do expect that you will be able to deliver that progress. In other words, get a move on. Let's see if some of these loose ends can't be tied up now that Terry is going to bring a spurt of enthusiasm to it, eh?' He looked up at me over his frames and pierced into my mind with his beady eyes.

'Yes, sir. We'll get on just fine.'

'I know you will,' he said in a manner that said, 'you had better'.

I caught a sideways look from Terry that I had seen come from Bob many times. One of desperation to get out of the office and get a coffee. Fortunately, Corrigan had had enough for now and our escape was made relatively easy on this occasion.

Chapter Forty-One

Kim's birthday card sat by his bed, next to a clock and a bedside lamp; on show, just as it was intended. He didn't want to throw it out, that would be unthinkable. Instead of bringing pleasure it had brought anger and a tension that was just too much to bear. He lay on the bed, staring up at the cracks in the poorly plastered ceiling, counting them, thoughts drifting in and out without permission. However much he allowed his mind to wander, there was no escaping the place it returned to.

John Garron was sure it was him who terrified Debbie that night outside her house, and sure, also, that he had poured beer into the karaoke machine and then torched his motor at the back of the pub. Now this shit. Did he post a birthday card for Kim into Debbie's door?

'Course he did.

Garron didn't need to delve too deeply to come up with a reason for all this. He had wondered if it might come back to bite him one day. Seventeen years is a long time but he understood the rules better than most in this neck of the woods. He knew Oscar was pissing him off purposely and biding his time. He was pretty sure that Debbie and Kim were safe and that all the silly tricks were just attempts at worrying his prey before he went in for the kill; got his revenge. Revenge for something that Garron believed to this day Oscar was just guessing about.

He wasn't sure.

Oscar was flailing in the dark.

Garron got up off the bed and went down to the bar. As he got down to the ground floor the odour infiltrated his nostrils, revolting him at the thought of how much beer had gone on the floor and soaked away night after night. He stood behind the bar, reached for a short glass and poured himself a whiskey, a large one. He looked at his reflection in a section of mirrored wall and wondered how, after all these years in the pub game, he had not become an alcoholic. He had seen it many times. Discipline was his answer and the self-respect he had for his physique, which was not doing too bad for a bloke over sixty. He stared harder at the face that carried numerous notches, like an old piece of chiselled wood, and saw the most recent marks that 'someone' had left him with in the cellar. He raised the glass and took a swig, holding it there by his lips, seeing his hand, which showed a scar that held another memory of the same event. He never believed that anyone actually needed a drink, but at times like these he questioned his judgement. It went down easy and he knew that that was the danger.

Too easy to pour another and another.

Discipline.

Control.

He put the glass into the glass washer and did what he had done for so long; he walked away from temptation, as hard as he felt it was, right now. As he made his way back to the stairs he could feel the ghosts of that night in the corridor. He stopped by the doorway to the back room, the room where Bernie got blown away just when he thought he was the big man. Garron sneered subconsciously and stared inside at the wall that had been running with blood and bodily matter. He could hear the police questioning him all over again and could hear his stock answers …

I wasn't here. I didn't see anything.

That part was true at least. But Garron didn't need to have been there to know all about what went on. He knew the plan for the night, the diamonds, the fence who didn't turn up and the mob that did. Most of all, he knew the purpose for the whole evening's entertainment and that was what he was sure that Oscar didn't know. The fact that it turned out bad wasn't entirely a surprise to Garron. He expected it. What he didn't expect was for Oscar to squirm out of his meeting with death or to see him return to exact his revenge.

Garron would never yield.

No guts, no glory.

Chapter Forty-Two

Doctor Aziz was very clear that although there had been a distinct change in Bob's condition this morning, we were not to let our hopes for a quick recovery get the better of us. I had telephoned early, about 6 o'clock, and as luck would have it, Doctor Aziz was on duty; lucky for me but not necessarily so lucky for him. He had told me that during the night Bob had started to respond. 'Slightly,' he said. He explained that Bob's brain still had to deal with a lot of pressure, which was caused by the swelling inside that had been a consequence of the trauma he had received when the car propelled him down the road and into a parked car. The car had hit Bob from behind and struck his legs and pelvis, which brought his head down hard onto the top of the windscreen and the structural support that runs along the front edge of the roof. He was certainly lucky to have survived at all. As the doctor began to describe the symptoms that Bob might present with in the coming weeks, I realised that nothing should be taken for granted. Bob had merely flickered his eyes and opened them momentarily but had not responded to any voice commands. Apparently, he might drift in and out of sleep, and sleep for long periods. Until he began to respond a little more they would not know how difficult it might be for him to carry out fairly routine tasks. They would have to listen to his speech to establish whether it was slurred and check whether he was able to focus properly. There were a number of issues that Doctor Aziz said would need to be considered but for now it was a matter of time and rest. At least it was a positive step.

I had poached a couple of eggs and was just placing them onto two rounds of toast when my mobile interrupted with a horrendous high-pitched squeal from the other room. I thought there was a cat fight going on in the living room but soon appreciated that I had, once again, been the victim of whoever was changing my ring tone at work. I had vowed to be more diligent with regard to leaving the blessed thing lying around on my desk but clearly someone had seized the opportunity and struck again. I gently put the eggs on the toast, trying not to rush and drop them on the kitchen floor, and cursed the timing of the call. Carrying my breakfast into the living room I could see the phone buzzing, squealing and spinning stupidly on the coffee table. I lowered my plate down and reached to pick up the phone and end the ear-bursting torment. It was Terry.

'Morning, Terry.'

'Morning, guv. Have I got you out of bed?' Terry knew damned well that I would be 'up with the lark'.

'Not much chance of that. You've interrupted my breakfast instead and that's worse.'

'Sorry, guv. I've been thinking about the case.'

'Good, can I have my breakfast now?' There was a silence on the other end of the phone that meant Terry wasn't sure whether I was joking or not. I was, of course.

'Guv, it's about this Oscar fella. I know we can't actually confirm it was him but there have been two sightings up to now. One by Mr Haroldson in Plaistow, which wasn't a lot of use, and then the bloke who saw Bob get bowled over.'

'We don't know that was him, Terry. The so-called sighting in the car was even less fruitful than the one in Plaistow at Stan Elms' front door. It's not a lot to go on.'

'I know, guv, but if it was him then why was he targeting Bob?'

'Well, if it was him then I've no idea, but we don't know it was, Terry. The Plaistow sighting, albeit inconclusive, did at least tie in to the timing of the incident on the allotment but Bob's accident could've been a random hit-and-run. We don't know. That's the problem. What we do know is there have been three murders that can be linked to the killing of Bernie at The Fallen Oak, assuming that these people were part of the original gang that night. As far as we can tell there is another possible member of that little group still out there somewhere and the way things are going, he'd better hope that we get to the bottom of this before the killer catches up with him too. I agree it sounds like Oscar is exacting his revenge on these blokes for his brother's murder and there is some link to the playing cards that keep turning up, but even that's still a mystery. Look, Terry, I think we should pay another visit to Mr Garron at the pub in Whitechapel and see if we can dig a bit deeper into this. I think he knows who Oscar is and he could even know where to find him, but for some reason he isn't giving us the full story. We'll get down there in a day or two and see how we get on, okay?'

'Yeah, guv, of course. I'll see you. Enjoy your breakfast.'

Enjoy my breakfast … That's a joke.

Not-very-warm poached eggs on not-very-warm toast. Yeah, right.

I sat and gazed at Ana's excellent pencil drawing on the coffee table and let my brain replay my conversation with Terry. The comment he made about the possibility of Bob being targeted by Oscar started all sorts of cogs whirring in my head. My eyes wandered around the room and settled on the fireplace. I never liked that clock. I was out with Ana one day and we passed an antique shop, almost passed it, anyhow. I did my best to pass it but I was too late as Ana had stopped abruptly, tugging on my arm and saying that we should go in for a look around. The problem with 'a look around' is that it never was just that where Ana was concerned. I felt my wallet groan as she hurried me in through the door, causing the doorbell to ring and alert the old gentleman at the rear of the shop that some gullible fool had been dragged in off the street and no longer could expect to get away without parting from some of his hard-earned cash. Half an hour and £25 later we emerged with said clock. If it wasn't for the fact that it brought back another treasured memory of Ana I would have got rid of it long ago.

But I couldn't.

Not yet anyway.

I cleared away the breakfast things, washed up and began to think about Bob again. I wondered whether he had shown any more signs of improvement. I would call the hospital again later, after lunch, and decide whether to go in around tea-time, but only if there was any real point to it. It might sound a little hard but if Bob was still flat out I may as well wait until he could engage with me. I stood and watched the blackbirds lining up on the fence, ruffling their feathers and patiently waiting their turn to get to the bird table. A knock on the kitchen window scared the big, greedy woodpigeon off and vacated the table for others to have a turn. The sun was poking its way around the edge of an obstinate black cloud, the first glimmer of it so far this morning after I awakened to a blanket of gloom. A text message landed on my mobile so I went to investigate, only to find it was Terry once again.

Did you know he was known as Napoleon?

What? Who? I decided I could just about bear to wait until tomorrow to find out the answer. I grabbed my coat and went out in the direction of the newsagents to get myself a morning paper, passing people that had normal jobs and normal lives with routine and order rather than chaos and dead bodies.

Napoleon?

One thing that I did know was that it wasn't Bob who was messing with my phone; he had a solid alibi now, unfortunately. As I made my way along the road I started to scroll through some names in my head of possible contenders who might just be the Phantom Phone Fiddler.

Chapter Forty-Three

The Visitor was eager to finish the job. He knew inside of him that it would be silly to rush things but he wanted it behind him at last. He had waited a long time, given it a lot of thought and spent a lot of sleep-deprived nights considering every little detail. Nature had not assisted him in getting rid of any of them so he felt it was up to him.

They deserved it.

Had it coming.

He loved the sound of the old saying … '*Revenge is a dish best served cold*' … loved it.

He wanted to go out with a flurry this time, to do something a little more dramatic and to deliver the message more strongly than before. He sat in a café, towards the rear, away from the window but maintaining a good view of the street. It was 3 p.m. Why he was there he couldn't really be sure. Maybe it was the anger that was brewing up inside him as it did before a hit. Maybe he just needed to be somewhere other than cooped up inside, surrounded by his thoughts and worrying about whether it would go right. Why shouldn't it? He thought back to how he had drawn Daniel Grainger from the clubhouse and watched the little shit scamper up the fairway towards his punishment. How he had coaxed Martin Brookes up to the church on that wet and windy day. Pathetic Martin Brookes; never had what it really took to be a tough guy. He followed the others and limped along behind them … pathetic. He was more than happy to waste him; Brookes had got on his tits for years. Then, Stan Elms. How nice of him to invite another keen gardener down to the allotments for a look around. That had to be over quickly, he didn't like being so exposed and had made sure that he was in and out fast. He brought the spade down hard and another one for luck. Then he was gone. It was the idea of posting the card through

185

Elms' front door that he liked, even though there was a little risk to it. He wondered whether Elms had recognised him just before he struck him with the first blow, but probably not. The other two did though, especially Brookes. The Visitor smirked to himself and sat nursing a cup of tea as he relived Brookes' pleas for him not to kill him.

No chance.

* * *

Andrew Carver was last out of school again. He didn't understand how he managed to be so slow at getting out when his mates had already got themselves down to the bus stop and were ready to jostle for position in the queue in order to get a seat for the journey home. Some days the bus looked a bit like it could be on one of those Indian railway programmes, albeit without the hordes of desperate people balancing on the roof. As Andrew hurried along towards the stop he could see the bus had just arrived and was being invaded by the mob of schoolchildren, all barging each other and pulling at school bags to get ahead of the person in front. If they battled for long enough and managed to delay the bus he might just get there and be able to jump aboard. The last of the schoolkids were virtually on the bus and he still had 200 metres to run. By now he had slowed to a jog as he was being hampered by the weight of his games kit, and the fact that it was laden with mud for his mum to wash off only added to the weight. Finally, he gave up the chase and walked. He swapped his bag onto the other shoulder and returned the V-signs that were being shown to him from the back window of the departing bus. It was not exactly crucial that he rode home on the bus as he didn't live too far away from the school, but he liked to enjoy the banter and the laughs with the others on the way back. But not today.

His mum checked the time on the living-room clock and muttered that Andrew was late again. She didn't worry because she was used to him being last out of school. She would fall over with shock if he came in early. Besides, it gave her an opportunity to see a bit more TV before he got in. Right on cue, about thirty minutes later than most people got home from school, Andrew walked in and launched his games bag, skidding it across the tiled floor towards the washing machine for his poor old mum to sort out. He sat down next to her on the sofa.

'And good afternoon to you too,' she said.

'Hello,' he replied, fairly uninterested in whatever it was she had on the TV.

'I suppose now that you've finally got here you want me to sort out your dirty sports kit and get you some dinner, do you?'

'Yes please,' said Andrew politely and without any appreciation of his mum's sarcasm.

'And what have you got there? It's dirty, Andrew.'

'Found it outside in the kerb.'

'What is it? Honestly, you'll pick anything up.'

'It's a card,' he said.

'What sort of card?' she asked with a disapproving grimace.

'A card; like one you do card tricks with or play card games.'

'Well give it here, it's filthy. It'll have to go in the bin and you will have to wash your hands, young man.'

'Oh Mum, can't I keep it? It's the Joker.'

'I'll give you Joker; now get washed for dinner please. Honestly, you're the Joker round here. Where did you say you found it?'

'Down in the kerb. You know, where all that blood was. Where that bloke got killed.'

'Oh, Andrew, how disgusting. Now you scrub your hands properly. And I've told you before, he didn't get killed.'

'Mr Goff said he was gonna die when they got him to hospital.'

'Andrew Carver, that is quite enough and you shouldn't go listening to what Mr Goff says either, it's not true. Silly old duffer makes it all up.'

Andrew shuffled towards the bathroom to give his hands a scrub before dinner but not before he had a quick, cheeky glance at the card that his mum had put on the worktop next to the bin. He would get washed and rescue it if it was still there when he came back to have his dinner.

Chapter Forty-Four

I called Terry at home, hoping to catch him before he left for the station, but it was his girlfriend, Kay, who answered the phone.

'Hello,' she said with the softest of Irish accents.

'Hello, this is Dave Calloway. Is Terry there please?'

'Oh, hold on, he's just getting in the car. Let me see if I can catch him for you. Did you say Dave?'

'Yes, Dave Calloway.'

I understood from what Terry had been saying that Kay was a very good athlete so I imagined that if anyone could catch him, she could.

However, it wasn't to be.

'Hello, Dave, I'm sorry, you have just missed the Wee Fella,' she said in that deliciously smooth tone of hers.

'OK then, never mind, I'll text him,' I said.

'If you don't mind me asking, are you the guy who's working on this murder case with him?' said Kay.

'I am, yes. I hope he hasn't been giving away too much.'

'No honest. It's just that he hasn't stopped reading and making notes. He's so excited to be working on this case. I've seen him occupied with a lot of different ones but this one seems to be very important to him. I'm sorry to hear about the other guy who was hit by the car, must've been awful.'

'Yes, it was. That's what I was going to talk to Terry about. I'm going to the hospital before I come into the station so I just wanted to let him know in case he thinks I've disappeared somewhere.'

'I see. Well I'm sure he'll want to know all about your friend when you get to work. As for me, I've got to get these long, lanky legs stretched out. I'm going for a run now that the Wee Fella has gone for the day.'

'Right, well I hope you enjoy it. Nice to talk to you,'

'Yes, I will. It was nice to talk to you too. Perhaps we'll meet before I go back across to Belfast. You must come round for dinner or something.'

'Maybe I will. I'll text him. Bye for now.'

Good morning Wee Fella!!
Just shooting off to see Bob before I come in.
Catch you soon, Wee Fella ... Ha ha.

I thought that I was fully prepared to set eyes on Bob in his hospital bed, wires and tubes and machinery all around him, but I was still quite shocked. His face was covered with cuts, grazes and awful bruises where he had been propelled into the parked car. A huge bandage covered his head and his eyes were swollen and blackened, and to be truthful I had to look twice to confirm that I was looking at the same man. His nose was swollen too and decorated with blue, purple and green. The news from the nurses at the desk was certainly positive. They spoke about twitching of his eyes and movement in his facial muscles. They felt sure that Bob could hear most of the time, when he wasn't asleep, although that wasn't always obvious. The swelling, I think they called it 'oedema', had reduced in his head and he was starting to return to normal. They would be monitoring his awareness of what was going on around him and encouraging him to try to speak. Sometimes, apparently, a person that has suffered a traumatic head injury may lose their speech initially or may slur their words. We would have to wait and see and hope for the best. I soon became quite glad that I had not seen Bob at the scene of the accident, if it was technically an accident, as he would have looked even worse than he did now. Less swollen, I guess, but covered in blood.

Blood on his clothes.

Blood on the car.

The last memory Bob would have had would be that he was struck from behind, but actually there was no guarantee that he would remember anything from that time. It was all just another puzzle waiting to unravel. I sat beside his bed and looked on as if I was expecting something to happen. I felt like a fisherman staring at his float in anticipation as it bobbed on the water in front of him, waiting for it to dip below the surface, indicating a bite. I studied Bob's arm; pale, bruised where the nurses had cannulated in order to administer whatever drugs were necessary intravenously. My gaze drifted across his face again. I felt sadness and a kind of pity for him.

C'mon, Bob, we've got work to do.

Sarah Goodman was a ward sister according to the badge that was pinned to her breast pocket. Her uniform was crisp; dark blue with white piping. She had one of those upside-down watches hanging from her top pocket and a stethoscope poking out of a larger, lower pocket at thigh level. She was thin and quite tall with short blonde hair, very attractive, and she had that inherent kindness about her that so many nurses seem to naturally possess.

'How is Mr Hand this morning?' she asked, as if I knew.

'Battered and bruised by the looks of it,' I replied.

She began to press buttons on the nearby monitor that made it bleep and buzz. She scrolled the information and studied the readings on the screen. I sat watching her at work, wondering what she was gleaning from the technology. Next, she shone a little pencil torch across each of Bob's eyes, checking the reaction to light in his pupils. That bit I understood.

'I'm going to take a spot of Mr Hand's blood. Are you stopping? I don't want you fainting on me.'

'I'm OK, as long as I'm not in your way.'

'You would have known by now if you were,' she said with the ward sister's authority.

Her blue eyes glinted, allowing a suggestion of half a smile. She cleaned an area of Bob's finger. Clearly a spot is precisely what she intended to take. I looked at Bob as she pricked his finger, hoping that he would wince or react in some way, but he didn't alter.

'Right then, can I get someone to get you a cup of tea?' she politely asked.

'No, I can't stay for long, thanks. Sister, how long will it be before things start to improve?'

'That's an open-ended question I'm afraid although I would be much happier if it was sooner rather than later. He's essentially stable; it's just a matter of him stirring really and seeing as you've mentioned it, I think it's a perfectly good time to have another little go.'

She began to move Bob's arms, bending them slowly, and his wrist too. She squeezed his hands one at a time and pinched the ends of his fingers. I assumed that this was a daily ritual.

'Mr Hand, can you open your eyes for me?' she said quite loudly, 'Open your eyes now, Mr Hand. Hello, Mr Hand. Your friend is here to see you. Open your eyes,' she persisted.

A flicker.

A slow determined blink.

Then they opened. A gaze into a black hole. Blank and yet twitching with life.

'Hello, do you know where you are? My name is Sarah; do you know where you are?'

I was mesmerised and didn't know whether I should celebrate or not.

Inside I was celebrating.

Bob still didn't look like Bob to me but then I guess he had been through a lot and probably had some more to go too.

'Mr Hand, you're in the hospital. My name is Sarah. Can you squeeze my hands? Both hands.'

She oozed empathy but her manner also expressed that everything was carried out through an obvious hard outer shell. Nurses had that ability to be hard and soft all at once.

'Bob, can you hear me?' I said.

He turned his head slightly; the cervical spine collar having been removed a day or two ago once the consultant was happy that the 'C' spine could be cleared and was no longer considered to be in danger from any injury or movement. His eyes seemed to be trying to focus and he opened his mouth as if to speak, but all he did was smack his lips together and stare.

But he was back. Up to a point anyhow.

* * *

When I got to work the office floor was empty. It was almost as if everyone had got up and left all at once, leaving their desks cluttered with paperwork. Similar to the scene of a disaster movie where the staff had run from some impending doom. With any luck it was due to another meeting that I had managed to miss. I made my way towards the DCI's office and found that the door was open. He was inside at his desk, as ever. I entered and immediately passed on the good news about Bob. Corrigan was pleased and remarkably human towards me for a change. It seems that where Bob was concerned he showed sympathy and mentally pushed the daily stresses of work to one side. Good for him. Our chat about Bob lasted twenty minutes, which was a new personal-best time for me. I don't think I had ever spoken to him in quite such a relaxed manner since I arrived at Chelmsford. When I left his office, I walked straight over to Terry, who was now sitting amongst a crowded and bustling office scene. The one I was used to. I didn't ask where everyone had gone to as I was just glad that I hadn't had to endure any of it.

'You ready, Wee Fella?' I teased.

'She's gonna pay for that when I get home,' joked Terry with a big grin.

We made our way down to my car and laughed about his new name, which I promised to keep a secret.

Well, probably.

Terry proudly told me all about Kay's athletic achievements as we travelled down towards East London on our way to Whitechapel. She had done a bit of modelling, and had worked in an estate agent's in Belfast city centre. Everything she did revolved around her athletic meetings and the constant training routines that went hand in hand with being so dedicated to her sport. Originally, she concentrated on the shorter 100m hurdles event and with that success came a step up to the 400m hurdles, where she found her own particular niche. Kay was not able to support herself without some sort of work and she had to hope her boss would be kind enough to allow her to maintain her athletics career, which included some travelling every now and then. Terry spoke of her success in Stockholm and Helsinki as well as the inevitable events in and around Belfast. Fortunately, she was popular with those who followed her career and generally didn't have too much bother getting time off to attend competitions. Although Kay had not made it big, she was still known locally, around Belfast, as the 'Golden Girl'.

By the time we had wrestled our way into Whitechapel it was approaching lunchtime and the traffic was thick. Roadworks seemed to be everywhere, no matter which direction we turned. Diversions that took us away from our intended destination added to the test of our tolerance levels but I suppose we shouldn't really have expected anything else. It was the East End after all. The rear of The Fallen Oak came into view as we drove in from an entirely unanticipated direction.

A rough piece of ground between two low-level buildings led us nicely to an area at the back of the pub. If I had known about it before I would have come this way in on purpose, but I hadn't. However, I guess it worked out quite well in the end.

The rear aspect of the pub didn't leave a lot to enthuse about, but then nor did the front really, except that the rear looked even scruffier. An old, battered skip sat half-filled with debris that some of the locals must have learnt about and gradually taken advantage of. The rusted shell of a burnt-out car sat on its rubberless wheels, with some of the wiring hanging out from where a door once was. The driver's seat was missing; someone's treasure trove perhaps. The battle-scarred fence, or what remained of it, stood feebly, blackened and charred, beside the remains of the car. An area of ground that surrounded the scene of the blaze was stained black and still had the remnants of the exhaust pipe and hundreds of pieces of broken glass strewn across it. Three big paladins lined up beside some kind of out-building with more broken windows than intact ones. I was beginning to think twice about leaving the Mondeo here unattended, but I knew that around here there was little choice of where to park so I decided to take the chance. I wouldn't have been so keen at night.

I tried to open a couple of doors but they were locked, so we made our way down the side alley towards the market square at the front of the building where I knew we would find the main front door. The alley was littered with cans and bottles, old newspapers and general rubbish. The doors to the pub cellar jutted out; the wood dry and cracked. It was a wonder they didn't simply fall apart the next time they were lifted. They looked original and must have seen some action after all these years. There were probably thirty to forty people inside the pub, many of whom gave us no more than a cursory glance as we entered. The girl behind the bar wasn't the one I saw before, not the one Bob made such an impression on, although she did give a smile to Terry as we approached the bar. Little did she know that Terry was already taken and the beautiful Kay was never going to come second in this race.

'What would you like?' she said to Terry with a naughty glint in her eye.

'Two cokes, please,' he said.

'Coke? Don't you want a beer?'

'No, better not, thanks.'

Better not?

You could almost hear the cogs whirring inside her head. Her expression altered and she became much more defensive. As she poured the drinks she kept glancing up at Terry as if she were trying to work him out. Coke? Terry handed over the cash and she turned to drop it into the till, which was already open. The coins in the drawer rattled as she firmly pushed it closed and headed straight to the passage that led to the rear rooms of the pub. I fully expected her to go straight to Garron and report that two strangers wearing suits had ordered coke to drink. Police.

Never seen 'em before.

Not from round here.

'You gonna ask if he's here, guv?'

'He's here, Terry. Did you notice how she disappeared through to the back while other people were waiting to be served?'

Terry nodded and sipped his coke.

'D'ya reckon he'll do a runner, guv?'

'He might not like us being here but he's got no reason to run off. He'll show in a minute. If he doesn't, we'll ask for him. But I think that his curiosity will get the better of him. Sit tight.'

I felt that every suspicion I had of her intent was confirmed when she appeared from the rear passage and looked straight at us. Not exactly what I would call a poker face. I was prepared to give him five minutes to show up before I asked for him but before I could take another sip of coke John Garron came out and took centre stage. He was dressed in a claret sweatshirt that displayed a single word in light blue: 'IRONS'. It was one of the nicknames given to West Ham United, although some people thought 'the Irons' were Scunthorpe United, but they were The Iron. I got that little gem from a quiz question that had been asked at a police dinner one droll evening. Garron looked across and clearly recognised me from our previous little chat. He made his way over to the table we sat at. He pulled a chair across from the nearest table and sat down without a word.

'Hello again, Mr Garron. This is Detective Sergeant Brush,' I said introducing Terry.

Terry nodded politely but Garron remained unmoved, unresponsive so far. His eyes were a steely colour that I had not noticed before and his expression was completely non-committal. I wondered whether he was trying to work out why we had shown up in his manor again. He certainly had nothing to worry about; he was here to help, as far as I was concerned, and that was what I was intent on getting him to do. Terry glanced at me and I could tell that he was itching to get going but I also knew that Garron was far too wise to be drawn into talking about anything until he was ready to, depending upon his mood.

'Mr Garron, I hope you don't mind us turning up uninvited,' I said, finally. Garron looked towards the bar, monitoring what was going on. He sighed and turned his attention to me.

'You mean I had a choice?' he said cynically.

I decided to let the awkwardness of his comment drift away unchallenged. I wasn't about to enter into a battle of wits with him. He was quite approachable before, even with Bob winding him up about his age and managing to aggravate the barmaid.

'A different girl today, I notice,' I pointed out.

'Yeah.'

It was clear there was going to be no point pussy-footing around with him today so perhaps it was time to get straight to the point and see what he had to say.

'What else can you tell me about Oscar, Mr Garron?'

He immediately looked quickly around the pub as if to check whether anyone had heard me mention the unmentionable. Garron stood up and pushed his chair back to where he got it from and said no more than 'In the back', suggesting that it would be more sensible to talk in private than out here where people could hear. He looked across at the girl behind the bar and she gave a silent little nod in response to whatever it was he had mouthed to her, acknowledging that she had understood. She watched us walk by the end of the bar and gave us her deadpan face, which wasn't too dissimilar from her happy face. I smiled at her, more to be a little condescending than anything. A bit of Bob's technique was rubbing off on me. Heaven knows how much fun Bob would have had with this one. We followed Garron into the same room that I had been in previously. It was easy to envisage the blood-spattered wall where Bernie had met his end.

'OK, Inspector. What is it you think I can tell you? He turns up after all this time and people start getting murdered. What else?'

That was the most we had heard from Garron so far and it seemed that he was pretty relaxed all of a sudden. Terry sat with a notepad poised to make the notes that we might need at some later stage.

So, Garron does think it's Oscar who is doing the damage.

'Why do you think it's him?' I asked.

'Gotta be, ain't it? He's come back to get his revenge for his brother getting wasted.'

'Have you seen him around then? Have you heard any whispers?'

'No, not seen him. Have you?'

I ignored his question. For one thing I wasn't sure whether the answer was yes or no. Someone had been seen outside Stan Elms' house and someone dressed in a similar fashion had been seen driving the car that hit Bob, but I didn't know whether it was Oscar or not.

'Mr Garron, if Oscar was responsible for these murders, how would he know who to target?'

'He's had a long time to work it out, Inspector. He's had all this time to get it right and plan his attack. He must've found out who was responsible for killing Bernie. He knew the territory and he knew who came to the pub and who the little cliques were. He just worked it out.'

'Little cliques like Grainger, Brookes and Elms, Mr Garron?'

'Yeah, exactly.'

'So, who's next, Mr Garron, who's the next target? Are we missing anyone from the "little clique"?'

Garron was sitting in an armchair with a soft corded pattern on the arms. It had seen better days, similar to most things associated with The Fallen Oak. He studied Terry again and looked him up and down.

'Where's the other one?' he said.

'The "other one" can't be with us today, Mr Garron.'

'Why's that, Inspector? I thought he would be only too pleased to frequent this pleasant little drinking den of mine.'

'I'm afraid he isn't feeling well enough to come along; maybe another time, Mr Garron,' I explained.

'Oh dear, what a shame. Nothing trivial I hope.'

Garron's obvious lack of sincerity in his voice was clear for all to hear.

Terry gave me look of disapproval but I just smiled as if to say 'leave it'.

'It's nothing for you to get all upset about. Now, shall we continue? You were about to enlighten me as to who was next on Oscar's list of victims, I believe.'

The girl from behind the bar appeared at my shoulder and asked Garron if anyone wanted any more drinks. We didn't and she turned away as quickly as she had appeared, back towards the bar. I wondered how long she had been standing just outside the door and whether she was listening to our conversation. Not that she was a problem, just nosy.

'Have you had any contact from Oscar lately?' I said, changing tack.

'I said I ain't seen him.'

'That's not what I asked, Mr Garron.'

Another stony silence.

Another shifty look.

'Well, I don't know but someone torched my motor. It's out the back,' Garron said.

'Ah, so that's yours. We saw it on the way in. Doesn't look at all well, does it? So, what makes you think it was down to Oscar?' Garron shrugged and said nothing, 'Do you reckon he thinks you were party to his brother's murder?' I asked.

'I'm the landlord and it happened in my pub, so maybe. There was another thing too. Just before the fire some git poured a pint of lager into the karaoke machine. I went outside looking for him, across the square, but couldn't find anyone. Next thing I knew there was smoke billowing up from behind the pub.'

'So, do you think that the idea was to get you distracted and then do your motor as well?'

'I reckon. But like I said, I didn't see anyone. Fortunately for him.'

'So who else is on his list?' I asked again.

Garron shifted in his seat and looked out into the empty hallway.

'I'll see what I can find out. Can't say fairer than that, can I?'

'That would be handy. Thanks. There's one more thing. What were they doing in here; Oscar and Bernie? Late at night, wasn't it?'

'Yeah, so I believe. Like I said, I wasn't here.'

'But you must have let them in ... like you said, you're the landlord.'

Garron let that comment roll around in his head for a moment. It seemed that he was reaching for the best way to answer it. Then he sighed and began to speak, somewhat reluctantly.

'They wanted to use the back room and I couldn't see any harm in it. The till was empty and they weren't big drinkers so I couldn't see 'em draining the stock either. They were the big noise at the time and people didn't generally say no to 'em. So, I let 'em use it. I left the side door unlocked and told 'em to make sure it was shut when they left. I wasn't happy about it being unlocked at night but it was only one night so I went along with it. Then I got the 3 o'clock phone call asking me to get down here pronto. The police officer didn't even say please.'

'What were they doing at that time of night?'

'They said they were meeting some bloke, I didn't ask why. That was how it was. It seems they got a bit more than they bargained for,' he said.

'So how did anyone else know they were going to be in there, Mr Garron? Who did you tell?'

Garron grinned to himself and looked at both Terry and me in turn.

'I'm clean, Inspector. I've been through all this shit all those years ago and I'm not going through it again for you and your little boy.'

I half raised a hand to Terry and he stayed quiet. Garron was talking and I didn't want him to clam up now.

'Someone let the cat out of the bag though, didn't they? Someone wanted them dead. How come Oscar got away with it?'

'He was just a lucky boy,' Garron said with a stern look.

I still thought that he knew more about all this than he was letting on and I hadn't finished quite yet.

'Tell me, Mr Garron. If there were four men, for example, all tooled up and ready to kill, and Bernie and Oscar were in the back room, this room, how could Oscar have got out and what happened to the bloke they were going to meet? Why didn't he find the body, or did he know that there was no need to turn up? Answer me that if you would. Just for old times' sake.'

John Garron stretched his back in the chair and lifted his feet onto a rickety old coffee table that sat just to one side of his chair, and bore his steely eyes into mine.

'When you find Oscar, why don't you ask him? In the meantime, I'll find your missing link if he's still alive and, Inspector, why don't you tell your poorly friend that I hope he's back on his feet soon. I expect he'd like that. Send him some flowers from me.'

'I didn't say that he wasn't "on his feet".'
'No, and I didn't say that I meant it.'

* * *

Terry and I sat in the Mondeo and looked at Garron's burnt-out car, and wondered whether it was a piece of Oscar's handiwork or had just been no more than a pastime activity for some of the local hoodlums. If so, why was he playing games? Why mess around scoring points when he so callously murdered the others? There were still too many questions to be sure of the facts. The motive was plain enough though. Oscar was finally getting his revenge. Now we had to find him before he found the fourth member of the gang that killed Bernie, and we had better do it quick.

We didn't talk a lot on the way back to Chelmsford. Terry chatted for a while about his plans for the evening; Kay was doing a fish supper, his favourite, by all accounts. I was driving on autopilot and churning the things Garron had said over in my mind.

Cerys Matthews was singing her heart out on a CD and providing a bit of easy listening background music. On more than one occasion Terry asked me whether I had heard what he said but soon gave up asking. The M11 motorway was flowing smoothly and it seemed that we got back quite quickly. I turned into the station yard and parked up in my usual spot. Most of the admin staff had already gone home for the day and so too had DCI Corrigan, if the empty parking space was anything to go by. I told Terry that there wasn't much more we could do today and suggested that he got himself off home to Kay. I went up to the office, pulled my chair from its position tucked under the desk and slumped into it. There was something that was niggling away at me and I couldn't place what it was. The office was virtually deserted but for someone making an infernal noise with a vacuum cleaner at the far end. I think they were trying to vacuum up the furniture as well as the carpet dust. I sat and stared into space for a few seconds and decided it was high time I was on my way too. I checked that my desk was locked and that I had got everything that I needed to take with me, and began to amble out, when it hit me: Napoleon.

What did Terry mean about Napoleon?

Chapter Forty-Five

It was always the same when I first entered the house; empty. Not literally empty but a kind of 'Ana empty'. I wondered when I was going to get used to it but strangely I just didn't seem to. I let out a tired groan as I bent to pick up the post that had arrived earlier in the day and had sat, lonely, on the hall carpet, awaiting my return. A couple of the envelopes were instantly recognisable as items that were no good for anything other than recycling, and another looked like a gas bill. I was feeling pretty weary and the fact that my brain had refused to switch off on the journey home had given me a headache. I strolled through to the kitchen and dumped the post onto the kitchen table as I had no interest in looking at it right now. A cup of tea was well overdue so I half-filled the kettle and flicked the switch for it to boil. I put my jacket over the back of one of the dining chairs, removed my tie and undid the top button of my shirt. As I reached into the cupboard and took out the old-fashioned tea caddy that I bought from a car boot sale ten years ago, I wondered whether there were any tea bags left in it. I knew I was running low and couldn't remember how many had been there that morning. I peered in and saw that the answer was two. Enough … thank goodness, and one for the morning.

As I waited for the kettle to boil I stood and watched the blackbirds and starlings seemingly argue over the right to the remains of the seed that I had put out after breakfast. A black cat sat right on the edge of the flower border, fascinated by the birdlife, perhaps wondering which of these noisy creatures might be on tonight's menu.

Mentally, I named him Oscar.

Dark and dangerous.

There were some very dark clouds moving in and it had just begun to rain lightly. I wondered whether Oscar the cat's dinner plans might be scuppered for now. Predictably, Oscar slunk off as soon as the drizzle touched him. I thought about going to the hospital this evening and checking on Bob, which seemed like the right thing to do. I would go as soon as I had eaten. I dialled Terry's mobile and hoped that I wasn't about to interrupt dinner or anything else. The Wee Fella answered straight away.

'Hi, guv, what can I do for you?' he said promptly.

'There was something you said that I meant to ask you about. What was it you meant about Bob being referred to as Napoleon?'

'Ah that, it was just a nickname he got when he first got to Chelmsford, that's all.'

'What did it mean?' I asked.

'I didn't get it myself but one of the older blokes called him it … something to do with an old TV show, I think.'

'Why did he call him it?'

'When Bob first got to Chelmsford he used to like to work alone; he was quite secretive about things, kept his findings all to himself. He didn't like anyone looking over his shoulder when he was working at his desk on his laptop; that sort of thing. I think it was something about "uncle" but I didn't get it,' he explained.

'Thanks, Terry. Sorry to disturb you. I'll see you tomorrow, have a nice evening. Bye.'

It didn't take me long to put the pieces together.

That was my era.

Old 60s TV shows.

It was easy in the end. What Terry was alluding to had to be *The Man from U.N.C.L.E.* It started to come back to me. I could almost see the old black-and-white pictures on Mum and Dad's TV in the corner of the lounge. I would be glued to my TV heroes, sitting holding anything that I could use to resemble my 'gun', ready to fight off the baddies as part of the *U.N.C.L.E.* team. An old-fashioned fireplace was all we had for heat and every so often the wind would blow the smoke back down the chimney and out into the lounge where Dad would waft his newspaper at it.

Yeah, that was it.

I could almost smell it.

David McCallum played Illya Kuryakin and Robert Vaughn was Napoleon Solo. So that's where it came from. Bob used to like to work solo. What bothered me now was whether Bob still preferred to work solo. Had he been doing some digging of his own? Did that have any reflection on why he had ended up in hospital in this way? Those considerations were certainly food for thought.

* * *

The trusty microwave had come to the rescue once again as I devoured another ready-meal and washed it down with another cup of tea which, consequently, meant that I had no tea for the morning unless I found somewhere on the way back from the hospital. I grabbed my jacket from the back of the chair and got on my way. I trudged into the reception, unsure of what I would see when I got to Bob's bedside. The last time I saw him he was on the verge of responding to that nice Sarah Goodman, the ward sister. Couldn't say I blamed him.

I would certainly relish the opportunity to talk to him now. As I ambled along, it crossed my mind that I would relish the opportunity to respond to that nice Sarah Goodman too.

Dream on, old man.

Bob's bed was empty. I was completely taken by surprise and an instant chill ran through me. I did a double-take and wondered for a brief moment whether I had, dozily, managed to wander into the wrong ward, but I recognised the items that sat on the cabinet next to his bed and knew that I was in the right place. I stood for a moment and thought about sitting by his bed and waiting but I might have sat there for ages, so I approached the nurse at the nurse's station to see if she could tell me where he had gone to. A young Chinese nurse with jet-black hair was on the telephone. She broke her conversation and told me that she wouldn't be long. The ward was fairly busy; visiting time was probably at its most frantic. People that had been at work all day were trolling in and out and wishing that they didn't have this extra stress to deal with. Porters ferried the non-ambulant around in wheelchairs to and from a variety of different destinations. Doctors and nurses hustled passed each other without a word, almost unaware that the others existed.

'Can I help you?' said the nurse.

'Yes, I was looking for Mr Hand. I wonder if you might know where he's been taken or how long he might be?'

She flicked through some paperwork in front of her and excused the fact that she didn't have an immediate answer for me by explaining that she had only just come on duty and was still in the process of updating herself on what had gone on during the day.

'Here we are,' she said pulling the relevant paperwork from the pile, 'let me see if one of the doctors can have a word with you. I won't be a moment.' She smiled and went straight off to find someone, leaving me by the nurse's station with a rather apprehensive feeling as to what might have been happening today. My eyes followed her along the ward until she disappeared out of view into a room quite close by. It was the same room that I had stepped into when I first came to see Bob, where I had ended up having a chat with Dr Aziz. Within a few moments the nurse came back out of the room followed by a tall young doctor carrying a mug of something hot and steamy, although they all seemed young to me. He introduced himself as one of the trauma doctors and although he did tell me his name it was one that I couldn't repeat. The name badge that he wore only confirmed that I would stand no chance of pronouncing it correctly.

Far too many letters.

Aziz was far easier.

He invited me back into the room, where we could chat without raising our voices in competition with the noise from the ward. Once I was able to pay attention to him I realised that he was very likely a little older than my first impression had led me to believe. His accent suggested to me that he was probably Polish or of Polish descent. Either way, I was glued to his every word. We exchanged pleasantries and he got straight on with explaining why Bob wasn't at his bed tonight. Apparently, he had been moved to a room on his own temporarily and was sedated.

'I believe you were present when Mr Hand showed the first positive signs of recovery, albeit at a very early stage, and we have been watching him closely ever since in the hope that things would slowly continue to improve. Now they did for a while, but he started to respond less and it seemed to me that things were going backwards instead of forwards, so I arranged for another scan so that we could have a look at his head and see what was going on. What the scan showed was that there were signs of a bleed that had caused a build-up of intracranial pressure; pressure within his skull that was pushing directly onto his brain. This can also be caused by the cerebrospinal fluid that we have surrounding our brains. Please stop me if there is anything that you don't understand. I'm afraid "talking doctor" is something many of us are guilty of.'

I smiled and assured him that I was keeping up so far. He continued. 'It is worth acknowledging that, in some respects, Mr Hand has been quite lucky up to now. The injuries that he has sustained to his head could have killed him outright.'

Was that the idea? I wondered.

'Has anyone made you aware of the consequences of an injury such as Mr Hand has?' he asked.

'Not specifically, Doctor.'

'Then let me enlighten you, it will help you to understand,' he said with a sombre and sympathetic expression. 'With the exception of the first few days Mr Hand has been in what we call a minimally conscious state. This really says that he has had some degree of self-awareness, which is what you would have witnessed recently. There are also things like infection, which may occur following a fracture of the skull, and the possibility of damage to blood vessels in the brain which can lead to blood clots; those in turn are potentially dangerous and can also lead to strokes. We have to consider nerve damage too. I don't wish to alarm you but Mr Hand has had a serious traumatic experience.'

'I understand,' I said … and I actually think I did.

'As time goes on we will learn precisely how this injury has affected your friend and to what degree, but that doesn't mean we have any reason at the moment to look on the black side. His memory, reasoning and concentration levels will tell us how he is doing, as well as how he responds emotionally and behaviourally. So, for now, please try not to worry, and be assured that he is being watched closely.'

'Thank you, Doctor, I shall do my best to relay what you've said to the guys back at the station. Thank you for your time.'

'Not at all. You can call the nurse's station any time for an update.'

'Thank you, I will. Goodbye.'

I left the room feeling a lot more informed but in a greater degree of shock and surprise as to Bob's condition. As I walked out of the reception area and into a very fine shower, I tried frantically to recall something else. I was eager to get away from the hospital and get myself home to find some peace and quiet where I could chill out for a bit. Even before I had reached the main gates, I was thinking about the fact that I had lost Bob from the investigation for good and that it was a good job I hadn't lost Bob entirely. Christ, Bob, what a state. As I turned out into the traffic I remembered that I needed to get tea.

Chapter Forty-Six

'I swear I only left her for twenty minutes,' cried Debbie, shaking like a leaf, as John Garron pushed his way past her and into the living room, his heart racing, his face flushed with anxiety. Debbie had called as soon as she found Kim. Garron was at The Fallen Oak and left without a word. He drove hard down the Whitechapel Road until he met with the A12, braking hard for the speed cameras and causing the brake pads to emit an acrid smell. He shot around the A12 past Stratford and on towards the Green Man roundabout at Leytonstone. Onwards, he flew, as the A12 took him beyond Wanstead and Redbridge, reaching 70 mph as he burned rubber past Newbury Park, turning next when he reached the A125 for Romford, which took him past the Queen's Hospital where Bob Hand lay, and led him, finally, into Hornchurch. His thirty-five-minute journey had been achieved a full ten minutes faster than usual.

Two female paramedics were caring for Kim as she sat motionless. The TV was still on, showing the final few moments of a tennis match from Eastbourne. An oxygen cylinder was on the floor and the thin tubing that reached up to the therapy mask on Kim's face hung limply across the arm of the chair in which she sat. Her hair was ruffled and strands of it were stuck to her face with sweat. Vomit stained her blouse, the rank odour from which was hanging in the air throughout the living room. Kim's index finger on her left hand had some sort of a probe attached to it. The pulse oximeter was providing the medics with information about Kim's heart rate and the percentage of oxygenated haemoglobin in her blood. Kim's breathing was noisy and shallow; a sort of high-pitched wheeze. She coughed loudly and gasped in another breath. One of the paramedics, the red-haired one, was on her mobile, talking to the ambulance control about the ETA for the ambulance. The estimated time of arrival was reportedly 10–15 minutes. The dark-haired paramedic had already stuck some stickers onto Kim's chest which had other leads going to a monitor on the floor beside her, registering information about the proficiency of Kim's heart. Kim's left arm had a cannula taped in place in case the administration of other drugs was necessary.

Garron narrowly avoided stepping onto the open trauma bag as he bustled his way past the dark-haired one and held on to Kim's hand. Her face was pale, her skin clammy. She looked straight through him as if he wasn't there. The pupils in her eyes were larger than expected, like two black saucers.

'Kim, you're gonna be alright. Uncle John's here.'

The red-haired one had spoken to Debbie initially, when they first turned up, and established that Kim had had these events before, but only if she got highly stressed.

Debbie couldn't understand it.

She had been fine watching the tennis when Debbie popped next door, just for a quick chat, nothing too long. Debbie had stood in the kitchen, out of earshot, and explained what had happened to Kim all those years ago when she worked at the jeweller's shop in Hornchurch. The dark-haired one was upset by Debbie's story but fortunately had seen PTSD before and was very familiar with the symptoms that Kim presented with. She told Debbie that she had studied the effects of Post-Traumatic Stress Disorder in university.

'It's also known as Acute Stress Disorder and this is what seems to be happening here. What I don't understand is exactly what has triggered it today. Can you tell me whether Kim suffers nightmares and dreams about the incident at the shop?'

'She does dream quite often. I have the bedroom doors open at night so I can hear her and I often have to reassure her that everything is alright. She's been like it for years but has been getting better lately. I thought she had finished with all that stuff.'

'I see. Try not to worry in front of her; we need to get her calm now. One more thing; is there anything that you can think of that might have reminded Kim of that time. Does she react badly if she remembers things about it?'

'She doesn't remember much. I can't think of anything that would have reminded her at all. It's not something we talk about, not around her, anyway.'

Debbie sat and wiped her eyes.

Kim hardly noticed.

The dark-haired one asked Debbie again about how Kim was just before she left to pop next door, and Debbie repeated that Kim was absolutely fine. She knew where Debbie was going and she knew she wouldn't be long. There was no problem. Kim was perfectly happy, clapping every point at Eastbourne. Garron and the red-haired one had been talking softly to Kim and had managed to calm her considerably by the time the ambulance arrived. Despite Debbie's reluctance, her brother managed to convince her that it would be sensible for Kim to go in the ambulance and get checked at the hospital. Debbie would go along with her, of course. She told the paramedics that she was concerned that it would make Kim worse still but finally she agreed. Both paramedics reassured Debbie that Kim would not stay any longer than was necessary for that very reason. They understood that Kim would be better off at home as soon as she was stable again. Garron would wait for a call from Debbie and come along to collect them both and return them home.

John Garron watched the ambulance carry his angel off to the hospital and stepped back inside the house to tidy up. The paramedics had left some small patches on the floor that had been affixed to the rear of the stickers placed on Kim's chest. Another piece of plastic had held the cannula. Otherwise the room looked normal. As he turned the TV off, he saw that the tennis had been replaced by some crap quiz show. He had no time for that shit and wasn't in the mood anyway. He straightened the cushions where Kim had sat and immediately missed her terribly. It was an emotion that he didn't expect. It caught him cold and he breathed deeply, shaking his head. He realised just how much he had been sweating; nervous tension. As he stood upright he caught sight of himself in the ugly, garish mirror on the wall behind the TV and startled himself a little. A big, hard-faced sweaty man looked back at him with a face that could turn milk sour.

The scars were fainter.

But not the memory.

There was a knock at the door and as Garron walked through the kitchen he could see a shadow waiting patiently outside; one of the neighbours. Mrs Phillips announced herself and wondered if everything was alright; she had seen an ambulance leaving a few moments ago. He never liked idle gossip and wanted to make this little exchange as brief as possible, but he couldn't be rude to her or Debbie would be on to him later and she was upset enough. Mrs Phillips was taken aback when Garron answered the door, as if she didn't expect him to be there. Why would she? He briefly explained that Kim had been taken ill but would be back before too long. Just a precaution, he had said.

'Sorry I was a bit funny then, but I didn't think you were still here. I thought I saw you leave before the ambulance turned up,' she said, a little confused.

'No, I just …' Garron began but stopped suddenly. His blood ran cold.

'I'll leave you in peace. Do tell Debbie I called, won't you? I hope she's better soon. Bye for now.'

Garron stepped back from the door and closed it. Now he was worried. He slowly walked back towards the living room. The cogs were whirring in his head. He put his hand against the doorframe and stood motionless for a moment; his head was spinning and then it hit him.

The reality.

Kim's terror.

He stared at himself in the mirror above the TV and knew what had terrified Kim so badly. Mrs Phillips had not seen him leave because he wasn't here … but Oscar was. He had seen Debbie leave and somehow got into the front door. Had Debbie failed to shut it properly? He could have walked in as Garron had just done and stood at the doorway. Kim's gaze would have lifted from the TV, expecting to see Debbie's reflection but instead … it was him.

Oscar.

Maybe Kim did remember.

Garron didn't know whether Oscar had spoken or just stood there but either way it would have been enough and he knew exactly what he was doing … just enough to bring on this huge anxiety attack. Hurting Kim was the route to hurting Garron. Garron had worked it out and now he had to think hard. He knew immediately that the mirror had to go or it would petrify Kim every time Debbie appeared in it behind her. She would relive the fear and dread of the attack over and over like a mental torture. She would see Oscar standing there looking back at her.

Think … think.

He sat down on the sofa and held his head in his hands, sweating again. He loved Kim so much and the pain of what she had been through ripped into him like caustic poison pouring through his veins. Burning and destroying him from the inside. He breathed heavily as he stood to move the mirror from the wall but stopped and stood, perplexed. How could he just take it? What would he say to Debbie?

She couldn't know. He had to come up with a story that would be believable. He looked around the room and struggled to think of something. Maybe the simple version would do. What if he had stumbled and put his arm out to balance against the wall and avoid hitting the TV and when he hit the wall his elbow shattered the glass in the mirror. God knows he had wanted to do it in the past.

What if …?

Garron decided to go along with it and hope that Debbie would accept that he could have done that. She would tell him he was a clumsy git.

Yeah, it'll do.

It'll have to.

He lifted the mirror from the fixing that he had screwed into the wall years earlier and carried it outside with the glass close to his body in case any of the nosy neighbours were spying, and placed it into the boot of his car. Back in Debbie's house he pondered his thready plan, his mind coming up with all sorts of scenarios regarding what Debbie might do or say, and then a wave of panic flushed through him again. What if she gets another one? Shit. He looked around the room and considered a suitable replacement; a picture would be fine. Nothing close to hand was going to fit the space. He looked into the kitchen, seeing only a clock, a calendar with a picture of a half-stripped fireman on it and some kind of slate or tile with one of those silly poems about a woman's work and all that nonsense. He studied some other pictures that were diagonally placed up the stairs and saw one that would do the job. It was one that he hated equally as much as the ugly old mirror and quickly decided that he didn't hate it any more. He took it into the living room and hung it in place of the mirror. It looked OK and he knew Debbie liked it, so hopefully that would do in an emergency. Garron had a look around the house for any evidence that someone uninvited had been sniffing around but nothing else was out of place or suspicious. The bastard knew exactly which buttons to press as far as Garron was concerned.

It was typical of him.

Gutless and sinister.

Garron had been beaten up in the cellar, had his car torched and his karaoke machine wrecked, and the fucker had even sent Kim a birthday card posing as him. Now this. He was pushing buttons alright and all because he suspected Garron had something to do with Bernie's death that night at the pub all those years ago. But Garron knew that Oscar couldn't quite work out in his mind how it all tied together. If Oscar hadn't had a stroke of luck that night he wouldn't be working anything out. Garron knew that all he did was let Bernie and Oscar use the back room after hours. When the police called at 3 a.m. the next morning, the situation had changed significantly.

When Debbie sent a text instead of calling her brother he was already sitting in the car with the engine running, waiting, and eager to get to the hospital to see that Kim was alright and bring them both back home. As he rolled the car away from the house he remembered that the mirror was in the boot, unbroken. He would deal with that later. Garron was feeling almost as bad as he did when he got the call from Debbie a couple of hours ago, shaken and tired, but with a new level of hatred consuming him. It was time to stand up to Oscar now before he harmed Kim all over again.

It was time.

No guts, no glory.

Chapter Forty-Seven

As the late-afternoon sunshine began to diminish in favour of an advancing weather front that was promised to bring a wet conclusion to an otherwise pleasant day, Oscar was watching every move. His eyes were fixed on his target as he silently closed in, concentrating hard on his unsuspecting prey. There were no people close enough to disturb him as he remained out of sight, the way he had done for the last few hours, waiting and scheming. The timing had to be perfect, just as before, and the execution clinical. The kill would be fast and there would be no second chances today.

It was time.

No guts, no glory.

I sat quietly, watching him. He had no idea that I was there. If I was to save a life then I would have to move quickly and hope that I could create enough of a diversion to disturb his concentration and give his target enough time to get away unharmed. My brow was beading with sweat and my shirt was sticking uncomfortably to my back. There was a lot of humidity this afternoon with rain expected. He wasn't breaking cover and nor was I and I was sure he still hadn't spotted me, otherwise he might flee and I would have lost my advantage. I felt my phone in my pocket and realised that it was not on silent. If it received a call or a message now it would give away my position and could ruin everything. I carefully slipped my hand into the pocket and fumbled around to establish where the off switch was. I imagined the shape and tried to work out which was front and which was back until I eventually felt the button I was looking for. It was off now. There was no chance of me stealthily creeping around behind him or moving any closer. Any noise would certainly spook him. Then I noticed some movement behind a huge water butt. He was taking up a better position but I couldn't move because I would be seen. I had to wait until just the right time and catch him by surprise. He had a direct line of sight to his target whereas I was just off to one side and wouldn't be able to get ahead of him from here. I knew he would get there first but I just had to make sure that I moved as soon as he did to prevent his exposure time with his intended victim. Maybe I could still prevent any carnage.

I took my eyes off him for a second and he was off like a shot, keeping low and out of sight until the very last moment. He was exceptionally quick and deadly, using surprise as his weapon. I began to run, which compared to him was laughable, to get there as soon as I possibly could. I saw him prepare to strike, his eyes fixed, his approach remarkably silent. I raised my arms and yelled as I blundered along, looking more like the Wild Man of Borneo than anything else. I was still too late; he had got to his target and pounced. Sparrows and finches took off in all directions in a state of arrant chaos. Bird food scattered everywhere and the whole bird table tilted sideways towards me. I almost fell on top of it as I skidded to a halt surrounded by panic and feathers. Oscar the cat nearly shit himself but had still managed to win the day. I caught sight of him careering over a fence with something small and brown wriggling in his mouth. The sly bugger had beaten me again.

Chapter Forty-Eight

'Guv'nor, do you know the password to Bob's laptop?' Terry asked as soon as I got into the office.

'I used to, mate. Why?' I said, plonking myself down at my desk.

'Well, I was thinking that seeing as we can't ask Bob anything, maybe we could take a peek and see whether he has stored any info about the case that might be useful.'

'Not a bad idea, Terry. I don't know whether he'd be open to that though but then, as you say, we can't ask him either.'

I knew better than most that Bob would be anything but compliant but it wasn't a bad thought. Bob wasn't going to be taking any further part in the case and he was bound to have something that we could use. I told Terry that I would have a think and see if I could remember it. I knew it once upon a time. Or at least I knew the one he used then.

'Anything from Garron?' Terry asked.

'Not yet, but he knows how to get in touch. Here, pass Bob's laptop over, I'll have a go and see if I strike lucky.'

Terry reached onto Bob's desk and passed the laptop across to me.

'Do you want me to get you a coffee, guv?'

'Oh yeah, Terry, that'd be great, cheers.'

I opened the laptop and switched it on. The black screen looked back at me as I waited for it to come to life. I remembered the time when Bob refused point blank to use a laptop. He would always say that what he wanted to remember could be put onto paper. Maybe it could once but probably not any more. I couldn't do without mine these days. I chuckled to myself as I recalled the time that Bob kept sending me emails even though he was in the same office. 'Getting the hang of it,' he'd say.

It was quite amusing to watch him facing the fact that he needed the laptop after all, even though he still, occasionally, in his own stubborn way, insisted on calling it a toy. I've never been a whiz with computers but I got on with it a bit better than Bob did.

The screen colour altered to a marine-blue shade and a small box appeared with the word 'Password'. Now the fun began. I sat back in my chair and gazed at the poser. He had told me some time ago what his password was; why he told me I don't remember but I had a picture in my mind of us talking and Bob suggesting that he should select a password that wasn't going to be easy for someone to guess, and me telling him that that was generally the idea of a password. Then he did it, and he said it ... and what the hell was it? I started to try to think logically and jotted down some words that I might associate with Bob. But it was hard working on a blank canvas with no real direction. He hadn't got any children so their names were out, and he didn't follow a football team so that was no good. It was something daft, I think. I recalled the time he told me again and sat with my eyes closed, allowing that picture to appear in my mind, listening to the conversation and trying to recreate the moment.

'You gone to sleep?' said Terry, placing a coffee on my desk beside me.

'No, mate. I was just trying to get into deep thought. Trying to conjure up the moment that he told me what it was.'

'Difficult to know where to start, ain't it?'

'Yeah, you're right there, Terry.'

That was the extent of Terry's contribution but I couldn't blame him, Bob was a dark horse. He liked to play his cards very close to his chest.

'I'll tell you what I could have a bash at, Terry. Let's put in Napoleon.'

'Why would he use that? It was a name the blokes gave him, but I don't think he was privy to it. Still worth a go.'

Terry was probably right. I guessed that Bob would have been the last to know about his new nickname. Still, he we go.

n a p o l e o n

The screen swiftly confirmed what I had expected.

* * *

Sister Goodman answered my afternoon call to the nurse's station at the Queen's Hospital and I introduced myself. She said that she remembered me from my visit and promptly began to tell me the latest about Bob's condition. He had been moved back to his original bed, which was good news as it implied that he was no longer being watched so intensively. He had been awake more than asleep and was responding well to tests and treatments.

'Is he speaking?' I asked, hoping that I might be able to speak with him.

'He is very confused at the moment; sometimes he knows where he is and sometimes not. He seems to be focussing well and is responding to the nurses when they give him tasks like raising arms or pointing to objects. It may sound disconcerting but it isn't, so don't worry, it's pretty much how it goes a lot of the time. What is good is that the swelling seems to be reducing daily and this can be seen in his behaviour. As for speaking, he does try and occasionally says a word or two but not always in context to the questions asked. He's getting there though.'

'That's good. I would like to ask him one or two things as soon as he is up to it.'

'I shouldn't be quite so keen for now, we don't know for sure yet how this has affected his long-term memory. He hasn't responded very positively to having any recollection of how he got here or what happened. You are welcome to visit him, of course, but you have to understand that things are being taken slowly.'

'OK, thanks, Sister. I'll be along in the next day or so.'

* * *

I put Bob's laptop on the coffee table next to Ana's picture and went into the kitchen; a cuppa was high on my list of priorities. The garden was peaceful and Oscar the cat was nowhere to be seen, but then that was precisely how he played the game, after all. I went into a bit of a trance, gazing at the borders and wondering where the real Oscar was right now. I needed Garron to come up with a name before Oscar extinguished 'whoever he was'. There had been no more sightings or even rumours of sightings but then I didn't really know who we were looking for; a hood and a beard were not much good to me. I desperately wanted to be one step ahead of Oscar the next time he decided to strike but I needed to know his target first, and right now John Garron was still my best bet.

Chapter Forty-Nine

Kim slept peacefully as Debbie watched her from the bedroom door, the silence of the night barely disturbed by her gentle breathing sounds. At times like this Debbie felt terribly alone in the house, her eyes wet once more with tears and her body tired, as always. Leaning against the doorframe she looked lovingly at Kim, at the girl she existed for; Debbie's only true reason to keep going, to push on daily.

It was 02:30.

It was hell reborn.

Since returning from the hospital a couple of days ago, Kim had not been quite the same. Debbie could tell the difference. Only she would see the subtle changes, the backward steps. The nervous disposition that Kim had overcome was haunting her once more, as though some closeted ghost had escaped. She behaved startled and edgy when Debbie walked into the room, as if she was some naughty child trying to hide something from her mother. Her appetite had diminished considerably; no longer 'the dustbin of the dinner table'. John had always said that one day Kim would eat the plate as well. Not that Kim ever put a pound of fat on; she was still as beautiful and slender as … before. Fully awake now, Debbie resisted the urge to go back to bed, knowing only too well that sleep was out of the question. Her angelic vigil had become a regular nightly routine. Just like the old days. Whether Debbie got out of bed or whether she simply lay staring at the ceiling, through the cheerless half-light, she was awake and listening intently to Kim. It was what had caused the return of the extreme anxiety that puzzled Debbie mostly. She still had no idea what had set her off like that. She had been doing so well lately too. Routines were established and had been for years but all of a sudden it was like she and Kim had revisited those early days, when Kim was showing all the effects of having been through the mental trauma of her head injury and all it brought with it. She was so jumpy and would become tearful for no apparent reason, although Debbie knew there must be an explanation. To pressurise Kim for answers was not the way Debbie dealt with these things. She had an abundance of kindness and patience and would simply be Kim's best friend.

It would come out.

It always did.

She quietly walked downstairs, the carpet fibres caressing the spaces between her toes. There didn't seem much point in trying to sleep at the moment. The obligatory cup of tea was out of the question as the kettle would make too much noise in the dead of night, and as Kim had been sleeping very lightly it was bound to wake her. The silent flow of something stronger was a non-starter; she knew where that could end up. Debbie went into the living room and sat down. A TV magazine was on the arm of the sofa which she picked up and began to flick through, not concentrating on any of the articles or programme lists at all. Just flicking through until she threw it down beside her.

Pointless even trying. Escape, not possible.

The house was so beautifully quiet, so serene in the dead of night, and Debbie felt a huge sense of relief knowing that whilst there were no cars on the road and no sudden noises from outside, Kim could rest undisturbed. Right in front of her on the floor she could picture the paramedics, kneeling down, ferreting around in their medic bag with a frightening urgency whilst Kim lay slumped in her chair.

Her face was so pale.

Her hair, lifeless.

Debbie put her hand to her mouth to hold back any sound as she cried at the memory that she actually thought Kim was dead. When she opened her eyes the ghostly paramedics had gone. Just another damned image to store away for a rainy day. The doctors at the hospital had tested and checked Kim for any evidence of a stroke or a seizure but the results were all negative.

What then?

Why now, Kim?

If Debbie had a pound for every unanswered question, every puzzled look from a doctor or a consultant regarding Kim and her recovery, she would be a rich lady. It had been a long and cruel seventeen years.

Sometimes Debbie had to screw up her face and try desperately hard to remember how things were before the accident.

Accident, injury, attack; it all amounts to the same outcome.

One big, torturous life of hell for both of them.

Debbie's head nodded forwards as she willed herself not to fall asleep down here. She knew she should be in bed and get as much rest as possible. There was no time to doze during the day unless, of course, Kim did too. Quietly she pulled herself to her feet, sighing and shaking her head. A small chink of light from a streetlamp intruded through the kitchen blinds, shining its guiding torchlight onto the carpet in the hallway, inviting her to find the foot of the stairs in the murky darkness. Pausing at the doorway she turned and glanced into the living room and looked directly at the picture that was now on the wall above the TV. Instinctively she expected to see the chair where Kim sat reflected in the mirror and was reminded that her big lummox of a brother had unbelievably managed to break it. How, was anybody's guess, despite his ludicrous explanation. As Debbie began to gently tiptoe up the stairs a wave of uncontrollable emotion swept over her, as it had repeatedly done across the years with an errant unpredictability and no sense of timing whatsoever. She lowered herself silently onto the stair-treads and felt the tears run helplessly down her cheeks. At these times of exacerbated stress, she missed her husband so dreadfully.

Chapter Fifty

I had spent another fruitless hour and a half trying to remember the password to Bob's laptop and, surrounded by pieces of paper, some discarded in the direction of the fireplace and others slowly piling up beside me, I had finally given up. Not forever, but for now I needed a break. Why I wanted to enter iguana as an option I will never know. The stupid word kept repeating in my head and trying its best to convince me that it was the answer. But it wasn't.

I knew that I could ask the Technical Support Team to assist but at this time I was determined to recall the password by myself.

The pub that had opened recently just down the road, in the heart of the main street, was one of those yuppie-looking places that served strangely colourful drinks. The car park was strewn with a variety of 'boys' toys'. Smart BMWs and the seemingly obligatory brand-new Jaguar sat in full view of the punters in the cocktail lounge. The beautiful and the glamorous flaunted their perfect legs and shapely figures at anyone who might want to look on with a hopeless admiration and an aspiration of what might have been, had they had the financial backing to follow up the empty, although painstakingly well-rehearsed, chat-up lines.

The walk helped to clear my head and ease the tension that had built up at home. I was glad to leave the laptop charging away quietly on the coffee table; it would be there waiting to tease me further when I returned, that's for sure. It was unusual for me to make the effort to go to the pub; maybe at lunchtime but hardly ever in the evening. I pushed the large, glass double doors open and was engulfed by the mumble of voices inside. Inquisitive people were queuing at the bar, all wondering what the atmosphere would be like at this new venue. As I got further into the pub the noise level increased considerably and the glare from perfect lipstick-framed teeth was ubiquitous.

I was in the mood for an ale of some sort and played it safe by ordering myself one that I had enjoyed before. The girl who served me was noticeably more cheerful than either of the girls at The Fallen Oak. Her make-up was exact and her pleasing smile welcoming. I stood with my back to the bar and absorbed the scene around me, allowing myself to relax as much as possible. Highly polished wooden-topped railings separated the areas that were designated specifically for those who wished to enjoy an evening meal, heavy looking armchairs offered a sense of being swallowed up into a world of incomparable comfort for those wishing to sit and natter in their groups. Chest-high tables, some free-standing, others affixed to the walls, were accompanied by high-legged stools. Photographs of old movie stars featured amongst the décor: Bogart, Bacall, Bardot … Rita Hayworth with her irrepressible curls of thick, red hair, and that smile.

I could see out into the car park where the boys' toys gleamed and spotted a white stretch limo rolling slowly down towards the front doors of the pub. As it drew alongside the entrance one of the passenger windows lowered and out popped a blonde head, followed by an over-exaggerated squeal of excitement. Doors opened on both sides of the car and an array of fashion-inspired women disembarked into the foyer. Her pink vest suggested her name was Diane as she bowled in towards the bar, her breasts clearly and unmistakably leading the way. Shona, Marie and Taylor followed closely behind as their own breasts endeavoured to claim centre stage. Diane pushed her way up beside me and stuck an elbow into my ribs in her need to get more alcohol inside her already well-fuelled system.

'Sorry darlin',' she said, as her perfume invaded my head.

'That's OK,' I replied politely.

Another four girls had squeezed out of the limo, all adorned in the same style of pink vest, names emblazoned across the front. They reminded me of a crowd of girls on their holidays in Malia rather than a group from around here. Diane seemed to be the one that was organising who wanted to drink what and in which quantities. Some of the other girls had already established a fan club of smartly dressed blokes who wasted no time in making their move. It was quite amusing to watch, really.

The use of trusted tactics.

The use of blatant lies.

I was thinking about ordering another drink when Diane muscled in again. She was ordering cocktails, I knew that much, but what all the fancy names meant was beyond me. Expensive is probably what they meant. The barmaid that served me before was now fully employed jotting down the list of Diane's cocktails and the others on duty were at the far end of the bar attending to customers, so I waited. The wait was certainly entertaining and became more so when the drinks list was repeated back to Diane.

'Let me just get this right. You want a Good Fuck, a Sexy Lady, a Bambi Boo Boo, a Party in My Pants, a Frozen Mudslide, a Caprioska and a Swimming Pool. Is that right?'

Amazingly, it was.

Didn't ladies drink sherry any more?

The screams and squeals of over-exaggerated excitement intensified as the ever-hopefuls at the end of the bar jostled for position; testosterone spilling in all directions. The chase was well and truly on but as my dad always said, 'You can chase as much as you want but if the girl doesn't want to be caught you may as well save your shoe leather.'

The cheers rang around amongst the pink-vested girls as the cocktails arrived and were placed on the bar in front of Diane. Straws, umbrellas and other fancy items stuck out in all directions as she passed them along the bar, calling out the names to whom the drinks belonged. Naturally enough, she couldn't resist bellowing 'Who wants a Good Fuck?', predictably getting the reply from the one called Mona which was immediately followed by a big cheer from the BMW brigade. I felt as though I could taste the drinks myself as the odour of alcohol venting the air reached a new level. Diane continued to call the names of the girls and those of the drinks, especially if it raised a laugh.

'Who wants a party in their pants tonight then?'

When the girls were busy refuelling and the boys were getting into their patter again, Diane turned to me and raised her colourful mixture, saying cheers to everyone around her no matter who they were. As she shoved her lavishly decorated glass my way, I stepped back half a step to avoid getting a soaking. I put my arm out to stop her falling onto me and grabbing my hand, she asked, in reference to the cocktail, if I wanted one. She would pay, she said. I didn't doubt that she had money to burn, maybe she paid for the limo; maybe Daddy paid for the limo.

'No thanks. They must cost a bit,' I clumsily remarked.

'A fucking fortune ... and most of it is crushed ice.'

I laughed and suggested that there was enough crushed ice in the glass to build ...

I froze.

That was it.

I put my glass on the bar and walked straight through the crowd in front of me, dissecting the BMW boys and the pink vests. One of the voluptuously breasted vests grabbed my hand and rubbed herself against me, or at least tried to, but I was in full flight already.

'Please yourself,' she shouted.

I was pushing the glass double doors within a few seconds and before the apparent offer really registered, venturing out into the evening air. It was windy but dry and I was immediately into my stride. I could be home in about ten minutes if I got a move on. All I had to do was to retain the thought that had crash-landed into my head, spreading debris far and wide like some meteor that had exploded through the earth's atmosphere and scattered millions of tons of sand at the site of a newly created desert crater. The traffic had quietened significantly and the streets were only sparsely occupied by a few cars. I strode on purposefully towards home, always aware of who was about; strangers could be strange.

Putting my key into the door, I glanced behind me once more, it just made me feel better. It was undoubtedly nothing more than a silly reaction to an event many years ago when I was followed home by an unsavoury sort that I had nicked earlier that day. He never actually approached me and nothing ever came of it there and then, but two days later a note was passed through the letterbox containing a number of threats, none of which were ever carried out. Played on my mind for a while, that's all.

The laptop fired up and my anticipation grew when something caught my eye. My arm had glitter on it ... Diane, no doubt. The marine-blue screen showed itself once again and I waited for what seemed an age for the blessed contraption to ask for my password. I thought momentarily of Bob, still in the hospital. It seemed like he had been there for far longer than he actually had. I wondered whether he really knew what had happened to him yet.

The box requesting a password came into view and I thought hard, fighting the ridiculous urge to type iguana and see it fail again.

No, this time I've got you where I want you, you bloody nuisance.

Recalling the moment at the bar with Diane, I said out loud to myself:

'... enough crushed ice in the glass to build an ... igloo.'

I typed it in.

i g l o o

My heart was stupidly skipping a beat like I was some kind of love-struck teenager plucking up the courage to talk to the girl that I had been passing in the school corridor; meaningful glances colliding in the chaotic rush from one classroom to another.

Janice.

Pretty ... dark hair.

Her name shot into my head.

How come I could remember her name and struggle so much with Bob's password. I guess Bob was a lot less appealing than Janice. I wondered where she was nowadays. I pressed the Enter button and in an instant, I was staring at a screensaver. The picture that Bob had saved was pretty standard, as I would have expected, I suppose. It was just some sort of mountain scene; huge conifers and a glistening, calm river. Probably something he picked for no apparent reason. It intrigued me for a few moments, as did most things that related to Bob Hand.

On the left-hand side of the screen there were several icons, the normal stuff. One allowed access to the internet, another to emails. My finger stalled in midclick as I pondered whether I should be looking at Bob's emails. They would no doubt be very similar to mine as far as work was concerned and I couldn't imagine him using it for much else. A guilty click opened the folder and I immediately saw messages from DCI Corrigan; the same as those copied to me. There was an array of notices relating to procedural stuff and jargon about this policy and that. There were two from the pensions department. It seemed he had been trying to work out what his pension would be worth if he was to retire early. That was rather ironic to say the least. The rest amounted to nothing very interesting and nothing that was new to me, so I returned to the original screen. My Documents, My Computer, a shortcut to

Word, all the usual stuff. Nothing that inspired me to have a peek into it really. Nothing that looked as though there would be anything about the case at all. Maybe the silly old sod did keep it all in his head after all. I wondered if the info was still in his head now after what had happened to him. I floated the curser over the My Documents folder and decided to have a look anyway. Once open, the folder displayed about thirty different items. He clearly didn't keep things for the sake of it. Some were instantly recognisable as some of the video clips that had circulated the office; jokes and the like. Many of the folders were self-explanatory; emails to the clerk of the court, emails to solicitors. At the bottom of the screen I spotted a folder marked 'Photos'. I sat up straight as my back cracked and creaked, having sat hunched over the laptop without moving. I opened it. It revealed four other folders, all of which were unnamed. Another guilty heartbeat skipped by as I opened the first of them.

Chapter Fifty-One

At 6 a.m. Terry Brush's bedroom had never smelt so good. The air was heavenly and he felt as though he was floating softly above the sheets as he lay on the ruffled bed. He could only just hear the sound of running water from the en suite shower room above his own content purring. The last night with Kay before she returned to Ireland had been amazing.

Kay was always amazing. She made love like an angel; he always felt like a devil. The shower stopped. He turned his head towards the mirror and could see her in the reflection. Her perfect soft skin, her wonderfully sexy figure and her golden blonde hair that lay loose against her breasts. She looked into the mirror and smiled.

'Are you spying on me, Terry Brush?' she said playfully.

'Might be,' he laughed.

'What is it coming to when a girl can't take an innocent shower without some dirty old man watching her, eh?'

'I like watching you … and not so much of the "old man", cheeky.'

Kay laughed and came back into the bedroom, a towel around her waist covering just her bottom half. She reached for her hairbrush which was next to the bed and Terry grabbed her hand, pulling her on top of him and holding her tightly. Kay squealed and rolled beside him, her hair lying damp on the pillow.

'I think I'll hide your flight tickets and keep you here all to myself,' he said.

'Oh, will you now?' Kay said in the sexiest of soft Irish accents. 'How would I explain that to my coach when I didn't turn up for training tomorrow and the team are short of one of their members?' she teased.

'Maybe I could persuade you to stay,' he said suggestively, as his eyes did all the talking.

'How exactly do you suppose you're going to do that then, mister?'
'Well. Actions speak louder than words, miss.'

Terry simply couldn't get enough of Kay, nor she of him. An hour later they were both scurrying downstairs; Terry dragging Kay's suitcase behind him. Kay was complaining that her hair was never going to dry before she got on the plane and that she was going to miss it. Terry insisted that there was plenty of time and that with her sense of direction she had no idea how far away the airport was anyhow.

'I don't want to miss it, OK? That's all I'm saying.'
'You won't miss it, I promise,' he assured her.

It had been several months since Kay had last stayed with Terry and she could feel the pain of leaving again. They both could. They loaded Kay's things into the car and set off towards Stansted Airport. A heavy and sudden shower pounded onto the windscreen as they journeyed north on the M11 amongst the Monday morning traffic.

'Oh God, I hate it when it rains,' she said.
'You run in the rain, don't you?'
'Yeah, but I don't like flying in the rain … I don't like flying at all. Can't they wait till it stops?'
'Don't think it works quite like that, honey.'

The airport was moderately busy; a huge group of around one hundred Japanese tourists seemed to fill the entrance to the arrivals lounge. Kay and Terry bustled through in search of a monitor that would be able to direct them to the correct desk where Kay could check her case in. She always had a fear that it would not be loaded onto the plane. Her running shoes were amongst the most expensive things she had ever bought and she would be lost without those. Many women would be worried about clothing or jewellery or expensive perfumes or other items, but not Kay; it was all about the athletics.

Terry relayed the desk number to Kay and she hurried off towards it with Terry strolling calmly behind her. Kay stood at the back of a short queue with her hand luggage and turned anxiously around to see him ambling along. C'mon she gestured. When he joined her, she was already building herself up for the flight.

'I hope the rain stops before we take off.'
'Someone over there was saying something about a thunderstorm.'
'Jesus, they weren't.'
'No, they weren't. It'll be fine, silly.'

Kay held Terry close and kissed him hard. The look in her eyes said she didn't want to go, or was it saying she didn't want to fly? Either way, he dreamt and wished for the day when she didn't go.

Once Kay's case was checked in, they went off in search of somewhere to get a drink. There was a coffee shop that would fit the bill nicely and they settled themselves into one of the snug tables. The flight to Belfast International should only take about an hour and a half, maybe a little less, but it was an age as far as Kay was concerned. As they sat quietly, sipping coffee and people-watching, she began to think about what she had to do when she got home. She had every intention of going for a run to get the tension of the flight out of her system. She knew that she might be a little weary but it was like a therapy to her. Eight or ten miles would do, at a good steady pace, and then a nice long hot, soapy bath followed by an easy evening and a novel, the one she brought with her and didn't even start.

'When's your next competition?' he asked.

'It's on Saturday at the track. I've already qualified for the UK National competition but I want to do a good time. I need to prove to myself that I can run it fast and not hit the wall before the last fifty. So far, I've been posting good times, not far off my PB and certainly close to a season's best. Trying to stay injury-free is most of it. I'll be OK.'

'You'll be a star. Anyone called Leggy has gotta be good,' he joked.

'That's a label that I can't shake off, for sure. Still, could be worse, eh, Wee Fella?'

'Yeah, thanks for that. The guys will make the most of it, I'm sure.'

Kay pulled him close, kissed his cheek and rested her head on his shoulder. Her grip on his arm became much tighter and she pressed her head hard onto him. Terry held her hand, concerned for her.

'Hey, are you OK?'

'Yeah.' Her reply was anything but OK.

He turned to face her and she tried to keep her face down, out of sight. He gently placed one finger under her chin and lifted her head up into view. The tears had already reached her cheeks and were steadily making their way down. She nestled her face back into his neck and kissed him again.

'I don't want you to go any more than you wanna go, believe me. I love you very much, Kay, and one day we won't have to do this.'

'What do ya mean?'

'Well, they have policemen in Ireland, don't they?'

Kay allowed the penny to drop, a little taken aback by the consequences of what Terry had suggested.

'No, you can't just give up all you have here, that's not fair.'

'I'd give it all up for you, Kay Cullen … Leggy.'

Finally, she had to snigger and cursed him for making her giggle when she was doing her very best to feel glum. She knew she had to find a way to stop the pain that burned so deeply every single time.

Fifty minutes later she was climbing the steps and boarding her flight.

The tears were still falling as she turned and waved towards the windows of the building, hoping that he might be able to see her.

As soon as she had strolled through the departure gate and out of sight, Terry had turned and wandered out, making his way back to the car. He found it easily enough amongst the hordes of vehicles and sat for a moment and contemplated the torment of Kay leaving again. He started the car, wiped the windows once and began to creep slowly out of the short-stay car park and towards the M11.

Her aisle seat was near to the front of the aeroplane, near the driver, she always said. At least she would get there before all of those behind her. One of the cabin crew closed the outer door and began to take up his position to remind the passengers what they needed to do in case of an emergency. That was the last thing Kay wanted to listen to right now. She smiled politely in his general direction and never heard a word of what he advised. She checked her seatbelt for the umpteenth time and put her head back against the headrest, and waited for the rumble of the engines to signify the inevitable.

The roundabout sign directed Terry south towards London as he pulled the car into a lay-by and waited patiently, watching the sky above the airport. Kay didn't know but he always did this, just in case it was her flight that he could see rising into the sky over Essex. He could tell the branding on the aeroplane wing and knew the time of departure; the rest was a guess. He was sure that her flight should be on its way very soon, providing it got off the ground as expected and without delay. The car radio played 'Rainy days and Mondays' by The Carpenters as he peered up above the trees that ran alongside the motorway at the ever-growing threat of rain and thought of her worrying about it.

The small window to Kay's left was running with water; rain. She closed her eyes as the aircraft hurtled at speed along the runway and could feel the power pressing her back against her seat. She gasped ever so slightly as the aeroplane's nose began to tilt up into the sky, holding her breath and gripping at the armrests. She didn't need a mirror to know that her face was a little pale but that would return to normal once they levelled out.

I wish the bloody thing wouldn't bump around as well.

There it was, or might have been.

Hard to tell really.

Terry's view of the aeroplane's colours and motif was distorted by the rain, and the appearance and disappearance of the aircraft in and out of the low rain clouds certainly didn't help. He was pretty sure that was Kay's plane. He watched for as long as he could see something and then once the last sight of it had vanished into the misty, grey backdrop, he headed for the motorway entrance at Junction 8.

He would never see her again.

The BBC news at 6 o'clock that evening announced the disaster in the Irish Sea. Not a single person was expected to be found alive. She was gone.

Chapter Fifty-Two

My whole body was numb.

Sickened by the news.

I sat semi-recumbent with my pillows propped up in bed. The call during the night from DCI Corrigan didn't bode well. When the phone disturbed me at 01:35 I immediately thought of Bob in the hospital. Corrigan's voice told its own story and filled me with dread before he had even begun to relay the terrible news. Neither he nor I had watched the TV that evening at all. He had remained oblivious to the fateful event until after midnight when Sam Barber, a close friend of Terry, had telephoned the control room to explain that Terry would not be turning up for work. They in turn had informed the Detective Chief Inspector.

I had spent most of my time looking at Bob's photos and working out what they meant. The things I appeared to have discovered were, quite possibly, damning and I went to bed quite early, uncertain of how to react to them. I was going to call Terry for a chat but didn't want to disturb him. Thank goodness I didn't.

Corrigan could wait too.

I sat up until 3 o'clock, just gazing ahead and thinking about everything and nothing. The emotional mixture of sadness and disbelief drifted from sympathy for Terry to despair for Kay. The silence in the house deafened me: blackness all around. My mind whirred in a confused state and was beyond my control, I tried to imagine what Terry must be going through, but I knew I would never get even close to how he felt right now. The constant reminder of it all being true hit me over and over.

I felt sick again.

* * *

My journey to the station was all going to be done on autopilot, I felt sure. If I had been dishing out the advice I would have told myself not to drive this morning until my head was right. In many respects I didn't want to get to work and face the sadness all over again, but knew it had to be done at some point so it may as well be today. I had eaten as much breakfast as I could but really wasn't in the mood. I stood by the sink and looked out at the garden. There were no birds feeding and none flying under the dreary sky. The flowers bowed their heads in sadness, heavy with tears. Oscar the cat had turned up this morning to give his support, or so it seemed. He looked back at me with a stare that appeared to say 'I know'. Before I finally left the house, I paused to pick up Ana's drawing that sat on the coffee table. Looking at it, I felt my eyes fill with tears at the thought that something so awful could ever happen to her. Banishing the thought from my mind, I carefully replaced the frame and walked out to the car. My legs were like jelly. The radio purposely stayed off. I had considered something soft and classical but decided to drive along in silence instead. I found myself driving on the motorway before I really knew where I was or how I got there; autopilot. The rain that had soaked everywhere last night had completely subsided and moved further north, leaving many huge puddles behind as evidence of its visit. There was a break in the clouds to the east that permitted the morning sunshine to pierce through the drabness and horror of the beginning of the day, causing me to shield my eyes as it reflected brightly on the wet road. The motorway spray continued to pepper the car as I got within sight of my junction and signalled my intention.

Bob's laptop sat on the seat beside me, quietly holding on to its secrets. It felt as though I was harbouring a time bomb that was waiting to be disarmed; one false move would see it devastate everything in the vicinity. I was the only person, as far as I knew, that had seen the photos for a long time, maybe ever, and the only person that could defuse the potential mystery. But, first of all, I had to understand what it all meant and how to put the jigsaw together.

A puzzle.

A conundrum.

Chapter Fifty-Three

I discovered that Terry was already in Ireland with Des and Maggie Cullen and would be staying there for a little while, at least until after the funeral. He must have managed to get a flight almost straightaway. I thought again about whether I should try to contact him and say the things that are awkwardly voiced at such times, but decided to wait until it felt right.

If it ever could feel right.

The mood of the office was much more sombre than it had been when the news first came in about Bob being run down and airlifted to hospital.

Understandably, I suppose.

There were a number of people stunned and a few that had met Kay before were clearly affected a little more deeply than the others.

Such a lovely young girl.

So much to look forward to.

I had been awake for so long last night hearing these things clatter around my head that I stepped outside for some air. The yard at the rear of the station was quiet. Cotton wool clouds had pushed their way across the sky and were at least a little more encouraging to see. Most parts of the yard had dried out except in a few areas. Corrigan's car was out somewhere terrifying the neighbourhood. After about twenty minutes of standing around, helpless, I conceded that the best remedy right now was to get on with some work, so I took a last look at the ever-improving skyline and returned inside. As I reached out to the door handle, my mobile phone buzzed and rang in my pocket.

'DI Calloway,' I answered, very wearily and without an ounce of enthusiasm.

'I know who your man is,' said a vaguely familiar voice.

'Sorry, who is this speaking?' I asked.

'You know who it is, you asked me to find him.'

'Sorry, find who?' The connection didn't seem brilliant and I was missing small bits of what he was saying; struggling to hear clearly.

'I can't be specific; I shouldn't even be calling from here.'

Of course; Garron.

I suddenly found some enthusiasm from deep within and managed to pay attention to what he was saying. I needed him to be clearer about what he was talking about so I tried to help him out a bit.

'OK, just confirm who you are.'

'Who the fucking hell do ya think it is? Father Christmas?'

'Mr Garron?' I asked knowingly.

'Yeah.'

'So, who have you found?'

There was a significant pause and I could hear some movement at his end of the line, as if he was walking or changing position in some way.

'The fourth man.'

'I see. Are you going to tell me his name?'

'No, not here. But you don't have to panic, he's gonna be safe enough.'

'How do you know that?'

''Cos, I know where he is and I'm pretty sure "laughing boy" doesn't.'

'That hasn't stopped him so far though, has it?' I asked.

'I know where he is and he'll be fine. If I need yer help I'll ask for it.'

With that the call went dead.

Garron had said his piece and hung up.

If he needs my help. Who does he think he is?

I conceded that he probably didn't think he was Father Christmas but I wasn't at all satisfied with his call. He had found the fourth member of the group but didn't want to tell me where he was or even his name. For now, I would go along with it but very soon Mr Garron was going to be telling me the full story. He said he couldn't speak where he was too. I couldn't really work out what that was all about. Maybe it was just his way of saying he knew something that I didn't. Maybe it was time to get heavy with Mr Garron and get a warrant. Then he would be obliged to tell me. I needed a coffee and went back inside to contemplate the conversation and decide what to do about it.

Chapter Fifty-Four

Rose Hill parked her Nissan and gathered up her favourite old leather briefcase. The sun was shining across the Essex sky as she walked the short distance to the home of Joyce Bladen. Parker Avenue was quiet as usual. She knew the area fairly well and often used the local shops. Most of her adult life had been spent in and around Chelmsford since her parents moved to the area from Chingford, situated on the outskirts of London. Joyce Bladen was one of many elderly people on her list of needy folk who were unable to manage very well for themselves, or even manage at all sometimes.

Rose had studied hard to gain the skills she needed to become a qualified registered nurse, with the acquisition along the way of her Nursing and Midwifery degree prior to attending university to graduate as a district nurse. She undertook an advanced clinical assessment course and had been working in her field of expertise for the last five years. She took a great deal of satisfaction from helping people like Joyce Bladen; those less fortunate. She had been attending to Joyce regularly for several months since her care was transferred from the departing district nurse and onto the books of Rose Hill.

Her mother, Helen, had been a midwife for many years, having done her training back in the 70s when things were very different. The path to becoming a successful midwife didn't seem to have so many hoops to jump through, as far as Rose was concerned, but still her mother had lectured her on how wonderful it would be if Rose could remain as a midwife just as she had done. She told Rose repeatedly about two of her deliveries that served as stories that she would relate to anyone who would listen to her for long enough. The first was that of a lady who came into the delivery suite at Whipps Cross Hospital where she worked in London, near to Leytonstone. Rose had heard the tale numerous times about the Frank Breech lady. The Frank Breech is where the foetus is in the usual breech position with its bottom low down in the cervix but with both legs straight up beside the baby's head instead of them being only 'knees up'. Rose usually switched off by the time the story reached the finer details of the birth. The second story went on a little longer and involved a young girl who had been abused by her father and wouldn't allow anyone other than her husband to touch her, especially in 'those places'. Helen Hill painstakingly explained how she had gained the girl's confidence and managed to assist in delivering the baby without any further difficulties. All very interesting in many respects, but Rose had been the audience one too many times.

Rose always thought that Derek Bladen was a predictable old man. She knew what he was thinking long before she knocked on the front door. As far as she was concerned, he was one of those men that failed miserably to hide his intentions with implausible stories.

She could see right through him.

Rose opened the gate that led up to the front door and as she did, Derek opened the front door, coat on, walking stick in hand.

'Hello, Rose, is it your day today?'

'Yes, Mr Bladen, the same as every day at exactly the same time,' she said with more than a hint of a condescending tone, albeit not strictly accurate.

'Ah well, I forget, you see. Anyway, go straight in, won't you, love?'

On most days of the week Derek Bladen grasped the opportunity, with both hands, to get some fresh air as soon as Rose arrived to take care of his wife. Rose would be there for anything from an hour to two, depending on the tasks she was to perform on a given day, and Derek always made the most of it. The older district nurse, Mrs Arnold, would be along in the evening and Derek would be nowhere to be seen. Rose was his favourite because she didn't lecture him about how best to care for his wife. Rarely did he have to attend to his wife these days since the district nurses were on board with the care she needed. If the truth were known, he didn't really want to be if he could possibly get away with it. Rose would bathe Joyce, change the bed and rub her legs with moisturiser in order to help with circulation, as she was almost entirely immobile under her own steam. Her condition had worsened gradually over the years and Derek had slowly retreated from the fight, thinking only of his own degenerative disease.

'Well, I'll just be popping down to get a paper, Rose.'

'Have a nice walk, Mr Bladen,' she said with a knowing smile.

Derek Bladen wore a sort of holster with his oxygen bottle in it and a length of tubing attached to a therapy mask. It accompanied him whenever he went out, just in case he needed it.

He usually did.

'Take your time,' Rose said to him and patted his shoulder.

'Thank you, Rose,' he said and smiled back at her.

The Visitor knew Bladen's routine only too well and today he had decided to pay him a little call, a sort of reminder that he was still around even after all these years. He had seen the nurse before, coming and going like some sort of Florence Nightingale character. He knew her routine too, but she wasn't important to him.

Very sexy, he thought, but not important.

Derek Bladen walked slowly, careful to avoid any precariously lifted paving slabs forced up by the roots of old trees. It wasn't so much the added weight of his oxygen cylinder strapped across his shoulder but the natural, slow and steady drumbeat of degradation that weighed heavy these days. The 400-yard distance that he needed to cover to get to his first port of call felt like 400 miles to Derek.

Arriving at the newsagent's, short of breath and with his legs a little wobbly, he held on to an advertising stand outside the shop for a moment. He could see that inside the shop there were only about three or four people; not too crowded. He didn't like to enter crowded places for fear of getting knocked over. Once he was on the floor it was a job for him to get up again, even with help. After a few minutes' rest he stepped up onto a small ramp and with careful, deliberate steps, made his way inside. He liked this shop. The Cypriot man who ran it was always very pleasant to Derek and allowed him to rest on a stool for as long as he liked. He made his way past the cold-drinks cabinet and the magazine rack, being extra-careful not to allow his oxygen cylinder to knock into anything. The newspapers were situated halfway down the shop, out of view of the counter, separated by a row of cards for birthdays and other occasions. He reflected that he didn't really have anyone to buy a card for these days apart from Joyce, and he could barely remember to do that.

He concentrated on the headlines of the various newspapers. This was something he always did before choosing one. Derek didn't select the same newspaper every day; he varied his choice based on the headlines that appealed to him the most. Often, he wished he would just pick one that he knew he had enjoyed before, but it was a routine that he was in and he didn't have much else to do. Next would be the visit to the butcher's shop window. He wouldn't go in; he would just look at the cuts of meat from the window. He reached for his chosen newspaper and was aware of someone close behind him, presumably looking at the cards. He felt a little nudge in his back but took no notice. Then he felt the close presence of this person, so close he could feel them pressing against him. Derek steadied himself and half-turned around towards whoever it was. All he could make out was a dark coat of some sort; he couldn't see a face, but he could hear a voice.

'It's not over till I say it is. Do you understand?'

Derek didn't understand anything that was going on in the friendly newsagent's shop. The voice in his ear spoke again, clearer and more like a demonic voice in his head; something that he wanted to simply switch off, but there was no way of switching this off.

'You know who I am, Bladen, and I have not forgotten what you did to my family. I have never forgotten, and I'll make sure you remember what you did all those years ago.'

Bladen felt an uncontrollable shudder building up inside him; his whole body felt as though his skin was stinging, paralysing him to the spot, hurting him and yet strangely numbing. He felt his blood pressure rise and fall; his legs trembled. He thought he was going to collapse there and then but somehow, he realised that he couldn't fall. He was being held up by the man in the big, dark coat who was making sure Derek registered every word.

'When I'm good and ready I'll come for you just like the others, do you understand? I know you know better than to call the old bill 'cos it won't do you any good now, Derek. It's too fucking late for you,' said the demon.

Bladen wasn't able to answer; his fear was at an all-time high and he began to shake.

'Now why don't you get on back to that sweet little nurse and ask her to make you a nice cuppa. Eh? Do you think about her, Derek? Do ya? I bet you do,' his voice was filled with menace and torment.

Derek felt the person brush abrasively by him as he headed for the door, knocking him forwards into the shelf of newspapers. He saved himself with an outstretched arm, hurting his hand as he did so. He looked around, watching him leave. Then at the last minute, just as the dark-coated threat was heading out and down the small ramp, he turned his head and looked back into the shop.

Derek got a real good eyeful of him.

A dark-blue hooded coat and a bushy sort of beard and eyes that he recognised from the distant past.

Derek wouldn't be going to the old bill.

* * *

Rose answered the door just as Derek put his key into the lock.

'Blimey, Mr B, you're back early. You alright?'

'Thought I'd come back in case it rained,' wheezed Derek.

'Not supposed to. I've never known you be in a hurry to come back like this, are you sure you're OK?'

'I'm fine,' he lied.

Rose wasn't so sure but let it go. Derek ambled slowly into the sitting room and dropped his oxygen cylinder down onto the sofa, but it bounced and ended up banging on the floor, followed by his holster, which slid from his shoulder as it fell, causing Rose to come running in to see if he was alright.

'Gordon Bennett, Mr B, what you done now? Here, let me pick that up for ya.'

Derek sat on the sofa trying hard to get over the shock of what had happened at the newsagent's and breathing with some difficulty.

'You wanna use this when you're puffed like this; you look as though you've been running. Now let's get this rigged up and you can have a sit while I get you a cuppa,' said Rose.

Derek could feel the shock wearing off now. Knowing that he was back home and that the front door was locked made him feel a little more secure. Rose fiddled with the cylinder and rested it on the sofa next to Derek. He tried to control his breathing and stop himself feeling light-headed and nauseous.

'Oh, what you done here, Mr B?' said Rose, 'All tangled up.'

She straightened the tubing that had the therapy mask attached to it.

''ere hold on. It's got a ruddy great knot in it. How have you managed to do that?' she said, frantically feeding the tube back through

Syrup and Cyanide

itself and twisting it round, 'There, that's it. Right, c'mon, let's get this on you and you'll feel better. You must try not to get it knotted or you won't be able to use it, will ya?' she explained.

Derek knew instantly just how the knot had got into the tubing and precisely who had put it there.

No old bill.

Chapter Fifty-Five

I had gone down to sit in my car, away from the office upstairs, in order to take another look at Bob's photos in peace, where I would get no distractions. I took a shifty look around the yard where I had parked. I found myself studying the windows upstairs and spinning my head around to check on the back gate. I probably looked more suspicious than ever. I turned the laptop on. I had charged it up recently, so it would be fine for as long as I wanted right now. The screen lit up the interior of the car to some degree as it came to life. Password?

i g l o o

Once more, I was in.

I clicked on the folder marked 'Photos', which made me flush with guilt once more as though I was wrong to be intruding. The four folders sat in front of me again, like a kind of Pandora's Box or some similar version. I decided to go through them in order in case I had missed anything the first time. A lot had happened since then too, unfortunately, and I needed a refresher. The first folder opened on my command and contained a strange picture; strange to me anyway. It showed nothing more than a group of walkers with their backs to the camera, seemingly walking away in the distance along a well-trodden path towards a monument which was possibly on the top of a cloudy hill. Certainly, it was on high ground and the grey and black canopy of cloud that seemed to be drifting threateningly in the background looked quite ominous, to say the least. Heaven knows what that was about. The second produced a picture of a small boat, similar to the sort that might be found on a park boating lake.

Someone was in the boat, asleep by the look of it, or dead. Probably asleep though; their face turned away from shot. I had no clue who the person was. It wasn't Bob, that's all I could be sure of for now. Thirdly;

a rather poorly taken photo of a couple. They were dancing. She was open-mouthed and looking at the camera but it was too blurry to see her features clearly. The man had his back to the camera. I didn't expect these random photos to have a connection, necessarily, but I would revisit them again soon and see whether there was any way I could link them all. I continued to click away and opened the next, the fourth. Here I found myself looking at somewhere that I recognised immediately but simply could not fathom what it was doing here. It was a photo of The Fallen Oak public house taken from across the market square. Bob must have taken a shot of it when we first paid John Garron a call. I didn't know. I couldn't remember. I stared at it for a few seconds, taking in the detail of the building and trying to work out whether there was anything else about the picture that I was missing. It was another one to return to later. I closed the laptop and put it on the back seat under a tartan blanket, out of sight. I would take it home and probably leave it there somewhere. Before I could get out of the car my mobile phone rang; it was Terry.

'Hi Terry,' I said in a subdued manner, not knowing how to start the conversation and deciding to let him take the lead.

'Hi, guv, is it convenient to talk? I can't be long.'

'Yeah, of course. How are you?' I asked clumsily.

'I'm getting there, I suppose. I just wanted to get in touch, that's all.'

'No problem, mate. You can call whenever you like, you know that.'

'Thanks. Listen, guv, I'm gonna be over here for a while. I'm helping Kay's parents with all the arrangements and, as you might imagine, there's gonna be a shed load of interest in the funeral at this end, what with her being so popular around here.'

'Yeah, I bet. Terry, I'm so sorry.'

'Yeah, thanks. I still can't believe it. I can't think straight enough to work any of it out yet.'

'Yeah, well you take it steady, Terry. Just remember that you can call any time. Is there anything you want me to do for you? Anything to check on at your place?'

'I don't know. Maybe you could just have a look around in case you think of anything or see anything there. My mate next door at number 6 has a key. He'll look in anyway but just in case. Just explain and he'll let you in.'

'I'll go around tonight and see him. Listen, Terry. Is there any news about what actually happened, I mean the …?'

'… The plane? No, not yet. It's still being investigated. They said they'll be in touch but who knows when that'll be. I'm just trying to keep an eye on Des and Maggie, you know, helping out where I can. It's not easy, I can tell you that. The pair of 'em are wrecked,' Terry explained, his voice showing signs of the immense pressure that he must be under simply coping day to day.

'Oh, mate, I don't know what to say. The guys here are all shell-shocked too and send their best to you. They are talking about a collection but don't know what to do with the money. Will there be flowers or some other beneficiary?' I asked.

'There will be flowers alright, Kay loved them so Maggie is determined to make sure there are plenty for her. Guv, I can't talk any more, I'm sorry.' His voice was breaking up even more now and he was clearly very emotional.

'Terry, it's OK. Just don't forget to look after yourself too, OK?'

'I'll let you know about the flowers etc. as soon as I can. Thanks for talking, I'll be in touch.'

With that he was gone.

Chapter Fifty-Six

I rang the bell three times before I could hear someone inside moving what sounded like a bicycle in the hallway. The door was half-glazed with frosted glass so I couldn't really see in very well. A couple of choice words were uttered as the cycle slid down the wall against the legs of its owner with a bit of a clatter. When the door partially opened I met with a red-faced guy who was trying his best not to completely fall over the bike which was at an awkward angle against his legs.

He apologised for keeping me waiting.

'Sorry about that,' he said.

'No, I'm sorry to disturb you. I'm Dave Calloway, Terry's work colleague, and he said that you have a key to his place. I was wondering if I might be able to borrow it for a moment. I spoke to Terry earlier and he said you'd be able to let me in,' I explained.

'Yeah, sure. Can you hang on a minute while I get this bloody bike off my leg? My fault really, I should take it through to the back but I can never be bothered. Seems to be in the way wherever I put it lately.'

He wrestled his rather fine-looking road bike out of sight into a room towards the rear of the property which, going by the glimpse I got of what was beyond the hallway, appeared to extend quite a way back. The front had been recently painted and still had a cardboard sign by the front step telling all comers that the paint was wet. I suspect it had been dry for several days. There was a Victorian feel to the property with large round bay windows, and a grid in the small front garden that gave me the impression that it may have been a coal shoot at one time or another. I believe that Terry had mentioned that he had a cellar where he kept all sorts of rubbish.

'I'm Stan, by the way, Stan Hollis. Here we go,' he said in a rather flustered and slightly out-of-breath way.

'Lovely, thanks. I'll pop it back in a bit.'

'That's OK, take your time, I'm going out in a minute so just put it through the letterbox, would you?'

'Right, I will and thanks again.'

I took the key and made my way out of one front gate and into the next. All the houses along this road sat up high from the pavement as if they were full of importance. Once through the gate I strode up the two deep steps towards the front door and put the key into the lock. The heavy door obediently opened and I closed it behind me.

After stooping to collect the most recent post I walked slowly along the passage and turned left into the front room and looked around generally. I didn't know what I was looking for particularly but at first glance everything seemed to be tidy and in order. The carpet was a royal blue with no pattern and the suite was a sort of ivory cream colour. He obviously had a liking for old, antique-looking furniture too. The fireplace had been stripped back to expose the bricks and a cast-iron wood burner sat handsomely in the centre of the space. Above it was a big, impressive chunk of walnut which served as a mantelpiece. It had a couple of photos on it that were not in any frames but just leaning against the wall.

Terry's parents, would be my guess.

I went through into the kitchen which again was quite large and seemed to have been installed fairly recently. Either that or he spent all his days off polishing and cleaning. Some mail had been abandoned on the kitchen table and a mug was sitting, tea-stained, in the sink. I realised that washing up would have been the last thing on Terry's agenda at the time.

I rinsed it out and left it to drain while I wandered back out to the hall and climbed the stairs. I felt like I was being nosy, but I only had to do this once and having found everything in order, I would just lock up and go. On the landing I saw three more steps heading up to my left that led to a closed door. I would take a look at that in a moment. Immediately to my right was an open door that led to the main bedroom. The bed was unmade and one or two items of clothing were strewn onto the floor around the bed. Again, it must be a case of Terry throwing some things into a bag or case and heading for the airport to get his flight to Ireland. I shuddered to think of how he must have been feeling at that point. Maybe he had no feelings left to express by then.

The attached en suite had a bathrobe on the floor which I picked up and hung on the door before glancing into another smaller bedroom which contained nothing more than a single bed and a small chest of drawers. I considered making my way back downstairs but could just imagine Terry asking me if I had fed the hamster or goldfish or cat or something, so I went up the three steps and opened the closed door.

No hamster, goldfish or cat.

A study, instead.

This time the desk wasn't antique-looking; it was painted white and unsurprisingly had the usual keyboard and computer screen placed centrally on it. A large mug contained pens and highlighters and there was a photo in a frame of Terry in uniform. It looked as though it had been taken a few years ago when he had attended his passing-out parade from the police training school. I turned my gaze to the window, which shared a view of the garden, and noticed that it had been raining lightly outside. The houses to the rear were at least 150 metres away and were screened from a clear view by several large beech trees. I imagined that it must be nice to watch the trees alter throughout the year. When I turned to complete my circumferential scan of the room I came face to face with a large picture that completely and instantly held my attention.

I went cold and it rapidly became apparent who I was looking at.

She was dressed in her running kit, green and white, and was clearly at one of her athletics meetings with a large stadium in the background. Her vest showed the number one; what else? She proudly held a couple of medals in her grip and was smiling broadly. There was no writing on the picture or the frame to tell where she was or at which actual event. I wasn't even certain that she was in this country, so it could have been anywhere, more or less. All that was visible in the picture was the stadium with a few hundred spectators. Her long golden hair was tied back in some fancy arrangement that she must have adopted when she ran.

I expelled my sadness in a long, drawn-out sigh and I turned to leave the room. As I stepped towards the door I noticed an A4 writing pad on the computer desk and the word 'INVESTIGATION' in block letters at the top of the page. Somehow, I had missed it at first glance. Underneath were numerous notes that I recognised as those taken by Terry when we visited John Garron at The Fallen Oak. He had written up those he scribbled on the day and had added various comments to them. I read the quotations from the things Garron had said at the time. Terry was certainly thorough. His words began to describe the inside of the pub too. He was accurate in his assessment of it; how it looked and how many people were there. The décor and the pictures; it was all there. He had even made notes about where we left the car and what was on view at the rear of the pub, just in case we needed it, I suppose. His account was quite interesting, and he had also noted things about the alleyway at the side of the pub that led from the front to the rear.

The filthy litter.

The old, fragile cellar door and the dirt-covered green door that provided a side entrance to the building.

I was downstairs and reaching for the door handle with Terry's spare key in my hand when I realised that I should probably take Terry's folder along with me for reference. Once I got to the car I sat for a moment and glanced at Terry's written description that noted that the door was 'covered with years of dirt', which in all honesty could be said for most of the pub, certainly the exterior. I considered that the dirt had gathered over time and realised that it was now time for me to uncover some more dirt, and to take a much closer look at the characters on Bob's laptop too, when I had the time. Although I had no inkling where that would lead, I felt that the straws I was grasping at were becoming a little more substantial. Now I didn't just want to talk to Bob; I wanted to question him.

Fifty-Seven

The end of another tiring and stressful day was just around the corner and would be celebrated with a drop of red wine before walking the short distance to her parents' house. The wine bar was within a quarter of a mile and the late-afternoon temperature was just about right for a stroll. She had been on her feet all day but now the pace was a lot calmer and the walk wasn't a problem.

More of a leisurely amble.

Schoolchildren were gathering at a bus stop after their football match in the park. Parents were manoeuvring vehicles that could barely fit on the narrow school driveway, such was their size; 4x4 after 4x4 bullied their way through as if, elephant-like, they were trampling everything in their path. She often wondered whether they were really necessary, often questioning whether it was a matter of want or need. She knew the answer.

A flock of starlings shot across the sky above her and made her jump, sending a chill down her spine. By the time she looked up they had gone, over the houses and towards the park in search of somewhere to roost for the night, no doubt.

Gillins wine bar was quiet and the first sip of red went down a treat. She wasn't a drinker but there was something soothing, almost medicinal, about that sip. She sat quietly on a sofa for two and noticed him look in her direction as soon as he walked in. He was quite tall and came over to where she sat and began to chat, just like that. Taken by surprise, a little, she simply chatted back; after all, where was the harm in that? He had had a long day too, or so he said. His demeanour was very nice and he had a way of telling a joke that she found amusing every time. Not what she would have expected of herself.

Not like her at all.

Being picked up in a wine bar, or anywhere for that matter, was not what happened to her. It was a combination of her aching feet and the instant relaxation that the red wine gave her that had meant she was just going to sit there and enjoy a bit of company that wasn't going to be too demanding of her. Just chill, she told herself. Anyhow, she quite liked men with beards and Mum wouldn't mind if she was a little later than expected. The car ride back to her mum's house was again out of character for her but she had had a couple more reds than she intended to and her feet were still complaining, so a ride to Mum's seemed sensible in the end, in comparison with the trudge along the High Street and back past the school. She didn't fancy being squashed by one of those cars the size of a bull elephant. She leaned over to drop her bag onto the back seat and caught him looking at her legs out of the corner of her eye.

So, what?

Which way is he going?

Why this way?

They had only been driving for five minutes but she began to feel very uneasy and realised that she didn't even know his name. They had talked so much that it never cropped up. She started to think of how she could get herself out of the car without aggravating him in the meantime. He had stopped smiling and cooing at her and was much more focussed on something. The something worried her more and more as the trees and houses drifted by in a blur, all too quickly.

Why did I get in the bloody car?

Stupid cow.

When the car stopped, abruptly, without any real warning, she thought he was simply going to dump her out and drive off. Leave her to walk back like some kind of stupid boy's prank.

If only.

She felt him lean across to her. His left hand was tightly gripped on the base of her seatbelt so that it couldn't be released. She flinched as his right arm wrapped across her breasts and held her throat, causing her some pain and making her feel queasy; nauseous. She felt herself going pale as the colour drained quickly from her face; her legs began to quiver beneath the dashboard and she wanted nothing more than to be at her parents' house, safe and sound. He pushed his right hand between her legs with such force that she screamed, but it wasn't very loud. As hard as she tried, nothing came out. Not that there was anyone to hear her attempts. She was breathless, engulfed in a welter of panic. Then, instinctively, she slapped his bristly face as hard as she could, grabbing at his cheek, immediately terrified of the consequences of her actions; too late.

It was all happening so fast.

Like a frenzy.

Her head banged against the side window as she strained to create more space between them but there was none left. She couldn't feel the door handle but without the seatbelt being freed she was stuck anyway. She closed her legs tightly together and shifted in her seat, lowering her hand down onto his and trying to prise the immovable grip from the seatbelt release. It was hopeless. She decided to dig her nails into his hand but ... gloves.

When the fuck did he put those on?

Then all of a sudden he did something really weird, making her gasp with shock.

He used her name. Rose.

He *knew* her name.

He was saying something, but her head was so full of terror that she couldn't understand what it was. He kept staring hard, right through her. She heard him say 'sex' and she felt a panic building within her from deep down, like a volcanic eruption that had brewed and then exuded, explosively and without control. She flailed at him with everything she had but mostly missed with each panicked attempt to strike him, and then suddenly she had no strength left to even think.

A very solid punch in her side took her breath away, causing her muscles to tense ... no – worse.

Pain ... so much pain.

Her side was hot and wet. She couldn't breathe properly. She felt herself want to vomit as her mouth dried and then ... blackness.

Chapter Fifty-Eight

To my surprise, Bob was sitting up in bed looking at a TV that was fitted to an extendable swinging arm affixed to the wall at the rear of his bed. The daylight was pouring through a dusty window, at least as best it could, as I walked over to him, but before I could speak I heard a voice behind me.

'Hello again.'

The ward sister I had spoken with once before had followed me in and stood at the foot of the bed.

'Hi. Big improvement, I see.'

'Can I have a word? Mr Calloway isn't it?'

'Yes, Dave Calloway. Is something the matter?'

I half glanced at Bob as Sarah Goodman and I sidled away from his bed. Bob didn't seem to notice. She walked around the corner and out of sight of Bob's bed. I followed her back along the corridor that I had just come in from, side-stepping a tea trolley, and into a side room; a different one to the one I had been in previously.

'Sorry about that, Mr Calloway, I just needed to have a word with you before you saw Mr Hand.'

'Of course, is something wrong? He looks a lot brighter; sitting up at least.' Sister Goodman smiled sweetly and spoke softly as if she didn't want anyone to hear what she had to say, even though she had closed the door behind her. She invited me to sit down and perched herself opposite me on the other side of the only desk in the room. Her dark-blue uniform was as crisp as I remembered from before and her hair and minimal make-up was perfect. She turned to pull a blind down a little, having noticed me squinting at her; averting the glare of the morning sun rising above the hospital building opposite.

'I'm glad I caught you. I shall be off after today for a couple a days, and I was wondering whether you would be coming in.'

'I should have been in sooner but you know how it is with things these days, the time seems to vanish before you know it,' I explained feebly.

'Yes, quite so,' she said with perfect diction.

Before she could resume, my mobile phone buzzed and rang rudely in my pocket. I gave my apologies and took a look at it. I had missed a call from the DCI and he had left a voicemail for me. I had just put the phone down on the desk when an immediate text message landed and caused it to buzz and spin on the shiny wooden surface; shiny more through years of wear than years of polish.

'I'm so sorry. I must just look quickly,' I said, a little embarrassed by the poor timing.

I opened the text message from Corrigan that simply read:

Get back to me … urgent.

I decided that I would listen to the rather lovely Sarah Goodman before I got involved in whatever the DCI wanted, as I was keen to learn about Bob.

'It's OK, I understand. Mine does it all the time which is why it is on silent,' she said.

'Sorry, please carry on,' I said, wondering whether I had been admonished or not.

'Right then. Firstly, I have to say that although Mr Hand is sitting up and watching the TV and appears to be a lot chirpier, we are still monitoring him very closely and have a few concerns about his recovery at the moment. He is responding better and will follow commands most of the time but he is having a great deal of difficulty with his speech. I think that the injury has left him very confused about his whereabouts and his understanding of what has happened to him too. He can become quite anxious when he is pressed to answer these things. I have tried to get him to write his name, or anything really, but he has shown great difficulty with that too. Head trauma can be a very complicated affair and people will respond in different ways to it as far as their recovery phase goes, so I'm not over alarmed, but I think we will need to concentrate our efforts a little more. You are very welcome to sit with him and please do talk to him about things he will be familiar with such as work or hobbies, just don't expect the response to be as you might expect at the moment. It'll take time.'

I had already decided by the time she got halfway into her little speech that if ever I was ill, I wanted Ward Sister Sarah Goodman to look after me.

'Thank you, I'll be careful with him.'

Immediately I thought that that sounded like I was going to play with a new-born puppy or some other fragile object instead of the rough and ready Bob Hand.

'As long as you understand. Call me if you want me for anything.'

A dinner date? I thought to myself.

Chapter Fifty-Nine

I was halfway across the hospital car park thinking about Bob and his world of clouded confusion when my phone sang out again. This time it wasn't Detective Chief Inspector Corrigan.

'DI Calloway.'

'I've been trying to get hold of you. Don't you have a signal or something?'

'I'm at the hospital in Romford, must be the building. What can I do for you?'

'Not a lot but I might be able to do something for you.'

Games, always games.

'Why don't you try me then, Mr Garron?'

'I've seen him, yesterday; walking past the pub, as bold as brass.'

'Who?'

'Who d'ya fucking well think?'

'Why don't you tell me?' I persisted.

'Oscar.'

'And where is he now?'

'Don't know, but he ain't far away. I'll find him and let ya know.'

'OK. What about the other guy, the one you are keeping an eye on?'

'He's safe enough, I told ya not to worry about him.'

'It's my job to worry, Mr Garron. I'd appreciate an address at least.'

Garron went quiet as if he was choosing whether to tell me or not. Ultimately, he chose not to. He signed off with a dismissive 'I'll tell ya when I know,' and hung up.

* * *

As soon as I walked into the office Corrigan appeared like something out of a kid's pop-up book, bounding out of his office and heading straight towards me with a look of great importance written all over his face.

'I want you out investigating a murder. A girl's body was found this morning but she was probably killed some time before. Anyhow, go and see what you can find out, will you? The address details are on your desk waiting for you to finally show up,' he said, very condescendingly.

I could see a memo sitting in the centre of my desk and walked over to it.

'Where have you been anyway?' he enquired.

'The hospital. To see Bob.'

'And?'

'He's not so good. They're still treating him with kid gloves and monitoring his recovery. He was sitting up though.'

'Ah, well I suppose that's something. Anyhow, get yourself off and let me know what you find out.'

'OK, I'm on it,' I said complacently.

I left the office with the memo screwed up in my hand and made my way down the back stairs to the yard where I had parked up not fifteen minutes before. I had only had a quick look at the address details, so studied them again.

Writtle.

Where the hell was that?

Even a postcode had been added at the end of the memo, so I gratefully put it into the car's navigation system. When the helpful voice told me that my destination was only three miles away I realised where Writtle was, and that I should have known it in the first place. As I drove out of Chelmsford, I soon began to recognise the road and realised that I had been out this way before several times. I was being guided down a long lane and could see the Essex countryside all around me. The road was spattered with clods of earth and pitted with a number of potholes. I turned left at the next junction and could then see a police car parked diagonally across a gateway and some traffic tape in place, stretching from one side of the entrance to the other. The constable that watched me approach was one of the women that had attended to Doreen Calderwood after the vicar, Martin Brookes, was discovered at St Dominic's. She studied me hard, trying to place the face and then she must have realised who I was.

'Hello, sir, fancy seeing you here this fine morning,' she said cheerfully.

'Hello again. Forgive me. I don't remember your name.'

'Jill. Jill West. Pity we aren't meeting under more pleasant circumstances, sir.'

'Who else is here, Jill?'

'SOCO are here and the forensic pathologist, otherwise it's just the usual; photographer etc. She was found by a man out for an early morning dog walk; says he saw a car last night coming out of here and leaving the gate open. One of our lot is with him now, getting a statement.'

'Right, thanks. Do me a favour would you? Radio down there and let them know I'm here. I want to have a look before they start moving anything around.'

'Yes sir.'

The track down to the quarry was covered with loose dust so I walked along a patch of grass to avoid getting the dust all over me. It dawned on me that I should watch where I was treading too if this was a dog-walking spot. Fortunately, the morning was still and the wind wasn't swirling around and blowing clouds of dust everywhere. After about 200 yards I could see some silhouetted shapes in the distance, further down below me. I headed down a slope that cut the corner and saved some time. It wasn't so steep there either. A variety of weeds had been able to grow here quite happily, undisturbed by human intervention. Discarded drinks cans and bottles littered the path and an area of burnt ground suggested it could be a place for kids to come and sit and talk, maybe have a crafty smoke by a small fire before they returned home with a mouthful of strong mints and a well-rehearsed set of innocent faces. As I lost the sun I was able to focus better and could see the SOCO team were standing together to my left in a cluster. A man in a white coverall, whose dark charcoal suit beneath it was well protected from the dirt, came towards me from below as I got down to a piece of flat ground. I nodded to the SOCO team and raised a hand as they responded in much the same fashion. They reminded me of a sci-fi scene; a group of stormtroopers having a break between filming their scenes.

'Good morning, Inspector, I'm Doctor Frost. I'm afraid it looks to me as though the poor thing has been dead all night long. That's only an approximate timeframe, you understand, but I'll find out the nitty gritty at a later stage, I'm sure.' He chatted almost nonchalantly, as if he had known me for years.

'Any idea who she is, Doctor?'

'Not yet. At least no-one has told me. Come down and take a closer look.'

As inviting as he tried to make it sound, it wasn't the best way to start the day. I followed his footsteps a little further down into the quarry and could clearly see the figure of a woman. She was lying mostly face down with her legs crossed over; one bent at the knee. She had one arm under her and her hair was matted and partly floating in a huge clay-coloured puddle of grainy sand and sediment. She had no coat on so wasn't prepared to be out at night, alluding to what the pathologist thought about her approximate time of death. Her top was pale blue; rucked up around her chest and darkened by her own blood. She had black trousers and one shoe visible. She was filthy; mud and clay all over her as if she had been rolling in the stuff.

'She didn't die here, Inspector; no massive haemorrhage, you see. She was dead when she was unceremoniously dumped here, I'm afraid. The wound on her head would have caused a huge puddle of blood at the time and even now it would have been clear to see where it had been, but there isn't one. The ground where she is lying is completely clean, in a manner of speaking.'

The clay and grit disguised a wound to her right side which on closer inspection revealed a nasty stab wound to her body, below her ribs.

'It looks as if the weapon, presumably a knife, had entered here and ripped in an upward movement at the same time. Whoever did this to her certainly meant it to cause maximum damage. There is a dried bloodstain that's smeared around her tummy and around her back but as I said, there's no evidence of any on the ground. It looks like a deeply penetrative knife wound to me and if it didn't kill her, then the blunt traumatic intrusion on her head surely did,' he said in a matter-of-fact, pathologist sort of manner.

He repositioned himself, careful not to slip into the puddle that she presently occupied, and using a stick that he had found nearby, guided it under her hair and raised it up to reveal the sickening damage to her skull. The dent on the side of her head was big enough to get a baby's fist into.

'I do rather wonder whether this mess was caused by a hammer or some such article but I shall find out when I have her to myself a little later. All will be revealed, Inspector.'

'Rather you than me,' I said.

'You'll be there, won't you, surely? I expect you'll want to witness the puzzle unfold for your investigation. I'll get someone to call you later.'

'Yeah, sure. One more thing. Has anyone found any items belonging to her nearby, like a bag or phone or whatever?'

'Your people have had a good look around but so far they've come up with nothing. Nothing on her either. I've already looked but I'll look again.'

I arrived back at the gate to the quarry wondering whether I really wanted to attend the pathology lab, but felt that he was probably right with regard to the investigation.

Jill West was still standing beside her car.

'What's it like down there, sir?'

'It's like a dirty puddle with a dead girl in it. Not nice, Jill.'

Her lips tightened and she said nothing. I asked whether the police officer had finished with our unfortunate dog-walker and she confirmed that he had. Apparently, the gentleman didn't have his glasses on when he happened to see the car come whizzing out from the gateway, so his description was a little sketchy to say the least. Jill told me that the statement was already back at the station and being processed into the never-ending system. Once I could find out who this poor girl was I could get on with joining the pieces of the jigsaw. For now, I decided to make my way back to the station and see how the initial digging for information was coming along.

Corrigan would be keen to see me too, and I him, I'm sure.

Breakfast was the first thing on my mind once I had driven out of the gate and soon took precedence over calling in at the station before I had time to think about which way I was heading. I didn't often eat out during the morning but I hadn't had a lot before I went to the hospital so I was ready for a top-up. There was a garden centre that I had passed on my way and it seemed like a good idea to make use of their cafeteria.

I was pleased to see the car park wasn't all that busy and my chances of a quiet breakfast were looking favourable. I sat with an Americano coffee and a B.L.T. sandwich to keep me company. The cafeteria was almost all mine, which was nice, except for an elderly couple at a table behind me who were in deep conversation about what to put into their hanging baskets and whether the colours would complement each other. A little bit of peace was just what I needed to give my brain a chance to catch up and put things in order. I thought, again, about Bob, which drew my thoughts to his laptop and the pictures thereon. That soon merged with the prospect of attending the pathologist's laboratory and the awful image of this girl flat out in a cold and filthy puddle.

Enough thinking.

I settled for staring ahead into no-man's-land and allowing my mind to drift so that I could just enjoy the breakfast.

* * *

An hour later I parked the Mondeo in the station yard and, feeling the benefit of my coffee and sandwich, went upstairs to face whatever came along next. Due to the nosy-neighbour grapevine, our dog-walker's wife had telephoned some friend of hers who in turn telephoned another, and before I had bitten into my sandwich a family member had turned up at the scene. They had found their way into the quarry through another gate and before anyone could stop them, had witnessed the grisly sight up close and painstakingly identified the unfortunate girl. As a consequence, things appeared to be moving along sweetly when I got back to my desk and I was immediately filled in as to the name of the girl reported missing last night.

Rose Hill had been a district nurse and carer for the elderly in the area. She was 38 years old but looked younger to me when I saw her earlier. She hadn't returned home to her parents' house after work. She was expected to come around for the evening with the option of staying, or so the story goes. During the previous day she had been carrying out her usual duties and visiting those addresses on her daily list. The initial findings from her parents suggested that Rose hadn't got a boyfriend and wasn't seeing anyone that evening, as far as they knew. They were adamant that she would have said so otherwise. A list of her movements was made available from the previous day and I could feel some door-knocking coming on. I would have loved to have given Bob that job and I could just imagine his reluctant face. With Terry out of the picture for a while longer I chose to do some of it myself, and thought it would also serve as an opportunity to catch up a bit more with Jill West and her colleague, who I had discovered was Allison Gutteridge.

I would try to remember her name.

Chapter Sixty

Her blood had soaked into the seat and floor like a sticky, gluey mess. The Visitor drove as sedately as he needed and as quickly as he dared without drawing attention to himself.

No mistakes.

Just get out of here.

Two police cars passed him; just a coincidence, he told himself. Even though they were not blazing blue lights he still shuddered deep inside. He had discarded his gloves into the boot of the car as well as the fleece top he had worn. He could smell her, taste her on him. His trousers needed burning too. It had even run down his leg and soaked the top of his sock. As he got further from the scene of the carnage that he had left behind, his mind began to twist in turmoil.

Why had she made him do it?

Why didn't she do as she was told?

He knew it was a stupid mistake and now he had to quickly cover his tracks. He hadn't touched her at all without the gloves, not even an introductory handshake, but he knew there were ways and means of placing him there. He reflected on how careful he had been with the others and he knew she was never part of this. It had been a surge of lust, a cloud of red mist.

Shit. A fucking mistake … not supposed to happen.

So stupid. Stupid, bloody cow.

He glanced down at the handbrake and could see the strands of drying blood hanging from it like stalactites in some damp and stagnant cave. The headache he had developed was getting worse and the pressure was building, the more he thought about what he had done. He had not prepared himself for this at all and began to feel the nausea rising in his chest. He just lost his cool, that's all. It was something he usually had control of, he thought. Sweat was running down his cheeks and dripping from his nose. There was no feeling of achievement like there was with Grainger, Brookes and Elms.

This was different; this wasn't supposed to happen.

There was no plan, but he had watched her, followed her, fancied her.

* * *

Jill West had offered to drive but I told her I'd meet them both there. I'd only be a few minutes behind them. Writtle was its usual quiet self; the school hustle and bustle was over for another few hours. Before we left I had looked over the addresses that Rose had called on and, as there weren't too many we decided to stick together rather than split up. I pulled in behind Jill's car and could see her and Allison standing beside it. I had a list of the houses that Rose had frequented yesterday and they were all within a few streets of each other, according to a map of the immediate area that I had asked Jill to print off and bring along, so we started at the top of the list with a Mrs Butterworth. Her account of Rose was that she had only been coming to see her for two weeks but she seemed a nice girl. It soon became apparent that Mrs B was far more interested in telling us all about her fall last winter than concentrating on whether Rose had mentioned anything to her about her plans later that day. I was absolutely sure that Allison had clearly said that we were investigating a murder but it still didn't distract Mrs B from wishing Rose well and hoping that she would be back on her feet again soon.

'Surely, they're not all gonna be like that, are they, sir?'

'Let's hope not, Allison. It'll be pretty hopeless if they are,' I said.

The next three doors we called on were a dead loss in as far as no-one was in, or at least no-one answered. I wondered whether they could hear us knocking for a start. I put a card through each letterbox to say we had called, with a request that someone call the phone number supplied.

'This'll be over with quicker than we thought, at this rate, sir,' commented Jill with a smirk.

'Yeah, but it won't help, will it, Jill? We need to get an angle on this before it starts to go cold,' I responded.

'The last two are down the same road; why don't me and Jill do the one down the end and see you back at the cars?' suggested Allison.

I couldn't find a good reason why not. We weren't exactly getting much from this pleasant little walkabout. I agreed and the girls wandered off ahead of me which left me with Mrs Bladen to talk to. As I went through the gate I thought I saw a light flicker on in the hall. Perhaps she had seen me approaching. I knocked and rang the bell, hoping to force an answer this time. When the door opened, a man peeped around the door chain and looked me up and down suspiciously. As I opened my mouth to speak he was already ahead of me.

'No, thank you,' he said abruptly and began to close the door.

'Sir, I've come from the police headquarters at Chelmsford, could I have a word please?'

The door paused in its movement and a hand began to draw it open again. The cautious pair of eyes peered once more through the gap and gave me another careful once-over. He looked to me as though he was about 75 to 80 years old, wearing the creases of old age on a pale, defensive face. Without speaking he closed the door to as he fiddled with the door chain, finally opening it fully. I introduced myself formally, showing my warrant card, and established that he was Mr Bladen.

'Sir, I'm terribly sorry to disturb you but I'm investigating an incident and would like to ask you some questions, if that's OK?'

'I suppose so. Do you need to come in?'

'I think it would be best, sir.'

Mr Bladen stepped aside and ushered me into the living room. The room was quite musty and had the sort of appearance that only served to confirm that the people who lived here were indeed elderly. The furniture looked almost antique and the wallpaper was heavily patterned with motifs that I recognised from my parents' house many years ago. In fact, it dawned upon me that the whole impression it gave me was not too dissimilar from that of Doreen Calderwood's house up in Laurel's End; cosy and quaint. Mr Bladen sat himself down in what I imagined was his favourite chair, the arms of which had worn over time. A newspaper rested quietly beside it and a mug of tea or coffee sat half-drunk on a small table within his reach. As I looked around I noticed a large black clock on the mantlepiece which looked as though it had been carved directly from a coalface. The television was on but it had been muted, probably when I knocked on the door. It was when I turned to speak to Mr Bladen that I saw the oxygen cylinder standing in a cradle between his chair and the wall. He followed my gaze.

'That's my third lung, Detective Inspector. The other two don't work so well any more,' he said with a combination of a grimace and a smile that caused his face to contort, showing more wrinkles than Sid James.

'Oh, I see. Good job you have it then, it must be a godsend.'

'I've had it for a while now, unfortunately. Anyway, how is it that I can help you today?' he asked.

'I need to ask some questions about Rose Hill, your carer.'

'She's not my carer; she's my wife's, although she is very good to me too. She's a lovely girl; I do hope she's not in any trouble, Inspector?'

I do hate it when the conversation gets to this point and I have to shatter the poor man's day.

'Sir, there is no easy way to say this but Rose was found earlier this morning. I'm sorry to tell you, but she's been murdered.'

There, I said it.

Mr Bladen stared at me, allowing the reality to set in, and once it had he slumped back into his chair, his eyes glistening like a thousand stars, his face worryingly ashen; drained of all colour.

'Oh, my Lord. Not our Rose. Oh, dearie me,' he said breathlessly.

'I'm sorry, sir. As you can imagine, it's very important that I ask you some questions in order to be able to start my investigation.'

'Oh dear, Inspector. Joyce will be upset,' he said; tears rolling down his cheeks.

'Joyce is your wife, I take it?'

'Yes. She's in her room asleep. She doesn't get out any more, and is bedridden, you see. Besides, she won't be able to tell you any more than I can, that's for sure,' he explained.

'Right, I see. Mr Bladen.'

'You can call me Derek, Inspector,' he insisted.

'Thank you. Well then, Derek, can you first of all confirm for me that Rose was here yesterday afternoon?'

'Yes, she was here doing her usual chores and looking after Joyce. She came along a bit later than usual, about half four it was. I usually go out when Rose comes but she had left it a bit late so I didn't bother.'

'Did she mention anything about what she was going to be doing or where she would be going after she had finished here?'

'No, I don't think so … oh, hang on, she did. It was when she was leaving she said she was off to her mum's house. That was about six o'clock. Yes, it was, 'cos the news came on.'

'Did she say she was going anywhere else beforehand?' I asked.

He gave this a good think, his expression in a daze, and finally decided that she hadn't mentioned anything about going anywhere else. He said again what a lovely girl Rose was and then sat motionless for a least a minute while I scribbled down some of the details. When I looked up at Derek again he was reaching for his oxygen mask and untangling it, straightening out the tubing and offering it to his face.

'Just need a puff,' he said, looking my way again.

'Are you alright?' I enquired.

'Yes, yes, this is what I have to do, you see. The gaps between puffs are getting shorter the older I get, it seems. Have to take it out with me too. Bloody nuisance really. I used to be fit once, would you believe? Did a bit of sparring, that sort of thing.'

'These things catch us all up in the end, Derek. May I ask you whether you know of anyone who may have wanted to cause harm to Rose?'

He allowed this to process in his brain and began to shake his head slowly but there was an element of concern on his face, something troubled him.

'I can't think of … I don't know, Inspector. I can't believe it. Her mother must be devastated … oh, dear,' he said as the tears flowed.

'Do you know whether she had a boyfriend, did she ever say?' I asked.

'She never told me. She was a private girl, really. Never talked much about what she was up to or where she was going, but she was always a good girl. She doesn't deserve this.'

Derek began to cry again and I thought that he had probably helped me about as much as he could for now.

'Well, I'm going to leave you to it but I might be back, or maybe one of the other officers may call at some point. I hope you won't mind that.'

'No, of course not, Inspector. I wish I could be more helpful and hope you get the fucking bastard that hurt our Rose. Her mum will be so upset.'

His eyes welled up with tears for Rose once more and I insisted that I would let myself out. I even remembered to remind him to put his door chain back on when I'd gone. I left Derek Bladen 'having a puff' and trying to come to terms with what had happened to Rose Hill.

As I closed the gate at the front of the house I noticed that Allison and Jill were standing beside their car looking at a notepad. Jill spotted me coming along.

'Did you have some luck, sir?'

'Yeah, someone was in and we had a little chat. Not much to gain from it though. How about you two?'

'Both answered but the first one was as deaf as a post. It was difficult to say the least, and I don't think she signed either. Asking her wasn't easy but we're both pretty sure that was the case. The second one was a gentleman who had had Rose coming to see him for two months but he didn't know a thing about her movements after his visit so we drew a blank on both really.'

'OK. Well, thanks for coming out. I guess we'll have to hope something significant pops up soon. Maybe they'll find the car; we could learn a lot from that. I'll see you back at the madhouse later, thanks.'

I sat in my car and wondered where I went from here. Whoever killed Rose Hill drove a dark-coloured car and had enough blood on the seats to wring out and fill a bath. His clothes, presuming it was a male, would be stained too. I was assuming that she was killed in the car but she may not have been. It does appear that she was transported to the quarry in the car so it could be that she was in the boot. Either way, there would be evidence of blood. I checked the time on the dashboard and it was already 3 o'clock. Where the day went, I had no idea. I looked at my phone and saw there was a missed call and a voicemail. I interrogated it and listened to the message.

This is a call for Detective Inspector Calloway. My name is Carly Thomas and I work with Doctor Frost at the Forensic Pathology Unit. I tried to call you earlier but didn't get a reply. Doctor Frost met with you earlier this morning and invites you to come along at 3.25 this afternoon. He said you will be aware of why. Please call when you get this message.

I let out a big, tired sigh and decided to give the Forensic Pathology Unit a call. When a young lady answered I began to explain that I was responding to the voicemail.

'Ah, yes, DI Calloway. This is Carly, I left you the message.'

'Hello. I should be on my way any moment but it'll take another thirty minutes before I get to you. Please give my apologies to Doctor Frost, won't you?'

'Of course, but he is a stickler for punctuality so don't be surprised if he starts without you,' said Carly.

'That's OK, I'll catch up when I get there.'

I was secretly hoping that with any luck he'd have most of it done before I wandered into the clinically cold laboratory.

* * *

The Forensic Pathology Unit was at the far end of a long corridor and down a couple of flights of stairs. A number of double doors led me deeper and deeper into the bowels of the hospital. It was so much cooler down here than it had been up on the higher levels. The air was quite refreshing thanks to the air-conditioning units. Finally, I saw the FPU straight ahead of me and tackled the final set of doors with a sense of achievement. I could see a lady I took to be Carly through a clear window, sitting in an office with her eyes firmly fixed on a computer screen. I knocked gently on the glass and she beckoned me in with a smile and a wave.

'Hi, I'll let him know that you're here. Would you like a coffee?'

'No thanks, I'll wait till after I've seen the doctor, I think.'

'Not squeamish are you, Detective Inspector?' she said with a coy grin and clearly enjoying the tease.

'No. I'll just wait for a bit, thanks,' I said without any conviction.

I was quite sure that I didn't have Carly fooled for a moment. She stepped out of the office through another door at the other end of the long, slender room. One side of the room was walled and housed several cabinets that were standing up like a phalanx of soldiers on parade. The opposite side was mostly tinted glass that softened the shine from the steel trolleys. Looking through, I could see Carly come into view and glance across in my direction, still adopting the same coy grin. Doctor Frost came into view from the other side of the room and in between them both, half-covered by a white sheet, was the naked body of Rose Hill.

Forensic pathologist Morrison Frost looked at me and gestured that I should join him and Carly. I tried to look eager and slowly followed the path between the desks and cabinets that Carly had taken, exiting one room and entering another with a noticeably tranquil atmosphere. In all honesty it wasn't a matter of being squeamish at all; I just preferred to deal with people that were alive.

'Glad you made it, Inspector. I've already started but I'll explain to you what I've found so far and that isn't very much.'

'Nothing?' I asked.

'Well, I suppose not exactly nothing, but not anything more than I was expecting to find initially. I've had a good look at her wounds and the nasty lacerated puncture beneath her ribs was definitely made by something closely resembling a knife. It had a serrated edge to it too, hence the amount of damage inflicted to her when it was forced upwards; tearing the skin and muscle in its path. There is significant damage to her liver, which would have accounted for a considerable amount of the blood-loss. The head trauma could have been caused by a hammer. There does appear to be a ball-and-socket type of devastation suggesting that the article of choice was rounded. So maybe he used a ball-peen hammer with a rounded end to it, or something else. Either way, he meant to kill her, that's undeniable.'

'Did you find anything on her person?'

'Nothing in the pockets of her top and nothing of interest in her trouser pockets either. I have, however, had a good look at her hands and specifically under the fingernails. As I'm sure you know, that's something that we pathologists do routinely in these types of cases of suspicious death,' he said.

'Yes, I know. So, did you find anything?'

Doctor Frost looked over to Carly and gave a little nod in her direction. She walked over to me with a small clear jar in her grasp and held it up for me to look at. I wasn't sure what I was supposed to be seeing in the jar; it looked empty to me at first glance. I held the jar and looked back at the doctor with a quizzical look.

'What am I supposed to be looking at?' I asked.

He was already in the middle of cutting into Rose's body as he mumbled his recordings to himself into a tiny microphone that he wore. Several trays were lined up beside where Rose lay on a stainless-steel trolley, ready to hold the organs that he would remove, weigh, measure and send for tests later.

'What do you think you're looking at, Inspector?'

I turned the jar for a closer inspection.

'Fabric?' I asked.

'That's what I thought initially, Inspector, but I was wrong. What you're looking at certainly looks like some kind of thin strands of fabric but it isn't at all. Have another go.'

The items in the jar were very small and black, almost resembling hair that had been cut off at the ends, almost like whiskers. I offered another blind guess.

'Is it hair?'

'Yes, it is. Well done, Inspector. Unfortunately, it's not come from Rose's killer.'

'Are you telling me it's animal hair?'

'No, it's human alright. It just isn't his.'

'How do you know?'

'Gum, Inspector. Gum,' he said.

'Gum?'

'When the strands went for analysis the results that returned told me: one, it was human hair and two, there were traces of a gum that had been used to adhere it to someone's face or head. In short, a false beard or moustache or wig of some sort. Sorry. Perhaps you're looking for a man who wears a hairpiece,' he suggested.

'Or a man who wears a false beard,' I added.

Chapter Sixty-One

I got home to find that Oscar the cat had left a present for me right outside the back door. I was lucky not to tread on it. No sign of the most likely culprit, as usual, though. I topped up the bird table and wondered whether I was simply playing into his hands, or paws perhaps. I could have been tempting his victims into his lair all this time. I could feel him watching me from somewhere deep in the undergrowth of the garden or maybe underneath the wild and spiky brambles that had invaded over the fence and now occupied an area beside the shed, providing him with a perfect spot from which to plan his next assault on the innocent. Inside the kitchen again, I made myself a cuppa and temporarily submitted to the rigours of the day as they washed over me. Sometimes I wanted to shut it all out until the arrival of the next day caught up with me, exploding into action with all the tenderness of a starter's pistol. But right now, I felt it was time to reflect and let the information that had intruded into my memory be reorganised into some semblance of usefulness.

I dragged my reluctant body into the living room and sat down on the sofa, and smiled again at Ana's drawing. A reminder of happier times. The pencil lines were so fine and delicate, just like their creator. I rested my head and closed my eyes and was met by the image of Rose Hill lying in that clay-stained grave; pitiful and alone. Devoid of answers, I wondered what had happened to her after leaving Derek Bladen's house. There wasn't exactly much CCTV to choose from in the village so it would probably come down to circulating some photos of Rose around the local shops and bars and talking to people some more. I would get Jill and Allison on it in the morning; first thing. Being able to place Rose somewhere in Writtle after her last call of the day might lead us to where she was heading, or more importantly with whom. For now, I tried to clear my mind and start to reassemble the fragments of the day.

Rose Hill had no ID on her at all. No phone. No money. Just the clothes she lay in; soaked with muddy water and as cold as death. No items had been reported as found near the scene even though we knew that her mother had since confirmed that Rose would have had her district nurse's bag with her after finishing with Mrs Bladen. Logical, I suppose. She had only one shoe on and the other had not been discovered up to now. It was believed that she had been driven to the scene in a dark-coloured car, which wasn't an enormous amount of help, but it was something. Maybe her shoe was still in the car even if the rest of her items weren't. The M11 motorway cameras had not given us anything to get excited about, just a few hundred dark-coloured cars with a whole host of number plates to check. A nice job for someone.

Doctor Frost had discovered human hair under her fingernails. It wasn't hers and it wasn't the killer's, according to him.

'Gum,' he had said.

Adhesive to stick it to a face.

Whose face? That was the question.

The haunting thought of the prospect of a false beard brought me right back to Oscar. Although it hadn't been confirmed that it was him, someone was seen by Mr Haroldson in Plaistow outside Stan Elms' house at or around the time when he was killed on his allotment, wearing a hood and with a dark beard protruding into view. The eyewitness at the hit-and-run where Bob was knocked down reported seeing a man who had a hood and a beard driving the car. Now human hair and gum has been discovered under the fingernails of Rose Hill. If there was a connection, I had to establish what it was

Why should Oscar exact his revenge for the murder of his brother and also kill Rose Hill? Why her? Why, also, would he target Bob? I rubbed my eyes until they almost fell out of the back of my head and swung my legs onto the sofa. The cushion beneath my head worked its magic within thirty seconds.

Chapter Sixty-Two

'There's someone to see you in Corrigan's office.' Turning around, I saw Haley Chambers, who worked on the ground floor and dealt with a lot of Personnel and Human Resources admin. She was pointing towards the DCI's door, as if I didn't know where to find it. Intrigued, I laid my jacket over the back of my chair and continued to his office. The door was closed so I knocked once. The voice of DCI Corrigan tolled out loudly and I let myself in. Much to my delight and surprise, I saw Terry Brush sitting with his back to me at Corrigan's desk.

'Terry, when did you get back?' I said with a degree of excitement.

'Hello guv ... last night, late. I didn't ring 'cos I thought you'd be asleep.'

'Blimey, mate, it's good to see you and I'm so sorry about ...'

'Yeah, I know, guv. Well, what have I missed?'

Terry would no doubt talk about Kay and the funeral and all that stuff at a later point in the day or whenever he was ready, so I left the awkward pause hanging in the air and moved on.

'You know, more of the same really.'

'You'll have to get me up to speed, guv. I've been telling the DCI how I'm raring to get back to it.'

'... and I've been telling him to take his time but there seems to be no stopping him. What do you think, Detective Inspector Calloway?'

I was a little taken aback that the DCI was asking my opinion rather than making the decision for himself but in a way, I was glad to have the chance to get Terry back on the case.

'Listen, Terry, if you are absolutely sure that this is what you want then I'll welcome you with open arms, mate.'

'I'm ready. I've been ready to get back to it for days, actually. I felt I should stay a bit longer with Des and Maggie after the funeral but as time went on I knew what was right for me. I'm definitely ready,' he pleaded.

'Right then, that settles it. Detective Inspector, you can have your detective sergeant back,' said Corrigan, beaming, almost triumphantly.

Terry and I wandered off to get a coffee, passing numerous people who clearly felt uncomfortable and entirely uncertain of what to say to him. Terry just smiled at them and spoke normally, which seemed to ease their awkwardness. We sat down at one of the tables in the canteen.

'I've been getting a lot of that this morning,' he said.

'Yep. I guess they don't know quite what to say.'

'I know they mean well. It'll pass,' he said.

I didn't want to seem unfeeling so I held back talking about the case and its latest developments, but Terry was straight on to it, as expected.

'C'mon then, guv, what's to be done first?' he enthused.

'OK, then. First, we find out where Jill West and Allison Gutteridge are hiding. I have a job for them. Then we take a trip out to pay a call on Rose Hill's mother. I'll tell you as much as I can about it all on the way. So, c'mon then, bring your coffee. Let's get this show on the road.'

Chapter Sixty-Three

I had been told that the number plate check on the M11 had proved fruitless so far. He probably stuck like glue to the country roads and besides, the car would be long gone by now. We would be lucky to ever find it, I suspected. Jill and Allison were now busy gathering all they needed to take with them back to Writtle to set about their task of circulating photos of Rose Hill amongst the shoppers and general public to establish a sighting of her with the driver of the elusive dark car. Terry and I had quite a discussion on the way to visit Mrs Hill; filling him in on the bits he had missed. Terry had even spoken of Kay's funeral and in quite considerable detail too. Apparently, there were more flowers than he had ever seen before, as promised. Maggie Cullen had really gone to town but then nothing could ever be enough for her beautiful daughter. Terry described how the streets of the immediate neighbourhood were lined with people paying their respects to the girl whose career they had followed and whose friendly demeanour they had taken to their hearts. Kay's medals and trophies were displayed in the hearse on both sides of her coffin. She couldn't take them with her, but they were there on the home straight. Her club colours adorned the top of the hearse by way of a running vest that had been affixed to a stand which faced to the front and had one word stitched onto the vest: Leggy. Terry stopped talking, quite abruptly, and I glanced across to him. His tears mimicked mine and we both decided that we would talk about this another time. It was going to be difficult enough talking with Rose Hill's parents as it was, without thinking about Kay. I parked the car nearby their house and reaffirmed with Terry that he was OK.

'Are you, guv?' he responded. I smiled at him as his well-made point struck home.

'It's so good to have you back, mate,' I said.

'I need to be here, guv. I need to be doing this. I'll be fine.'
Something about him told me he was right, too.

Helen Hill was much more composed than we had just been but her husband had gone out with some old friends; he needed the break, she said. The sitting room was painted white and had few pictures on the walls but it was clear to see that someone, presumably her, had a fascination for collecting commemorative plates. Various different sizes of plates, all for different occasions, almost filled one wall and were gradually on a takeover mission of the rest.

'Wow. Is this your hobby, Mrs Hill?' I said, trying to break the ice.

'I suppose you could call it a hobby, that's not what my husband calls it though. I started about fifteen years ago and it just went from there; can't help myself. I've got more boxed in the small room and every so I often I circulate them so that there are not always the same ones up on show. Do you like them?' she said, enthusiastically.

No, I thought.

'Yes, they are lovely, quite an impressive collection, eh Terry?'

'Yes, impressive,' he said unconvincingly.

'Still, I don't suppose you came over to see these. You'll be wanting to talk about Rose, I expect. Would you both like some tea, Inspector?'

'That would be lovely, thank you, Mrs Hill.'

'Oh, do call me Helen, everyone does,' she chuckled and drifted off into the kitchen.

After another silent exchange of knowing glances, Terry and I sat and were pondering the best approach when she returned with the tea. Terry prepared a new page on his A4 folder, which reminded me that I had removed the folder that I found in his study when I called in at his flat and met the very flustered Stan Hollis. I would own up later. It was almost impossible not to be distracted by the invasion of plates on the walls as we looked over some of the notes that I had made when I met with Jill and Allison for the little session of door knocking in Writtle. Disappointingly, that didn't reveal a great deal. Helen Hill appeared suddenly with a dinner plate of her home-made flapjacks and insisted that we try them. She didn't need to ask twice. She began to relate the story of how she came about finding one of her plates when she was on holiday in Norfolk as my phone alerted me to a text message, allowing me to make my excuses and create a break in her story.

It was Jill with a glimmer of hope.

Her text told me that she and Allison had had a bit of good fortune and managed to confirm a positive sighting of Rose with a man around the time that we were interested in. I texted my brief reply, telling her that I would call her as soon as I was done here. I knew I could confidently leave her and Allison to follow this up in the meantime. For now, it was time to tackle another flapjack and make some headway with Helen Hill.

'Helen, I need to talk to you about Rose. I appreciate that this must be hard but it's imperative that we establish what happened as soon as we can.'

'Yes, I know. I'm OK, I've cried all my tears out for the moment. What do you want to know?'

'Thank you. I'll try not to go over the things that you've already discussed with the other officers but I may need to hear certain things again, if you don't mind?'

'That's OK,' she said, solemnly.

Terry jotted patiently as I went over the regular questions regarding her friends and the circles in which she mixed. Helen confirmed that Rose hadn't mentioned anything about her meeting someone. She explained how Rose was quite predictable and how she fully expected her to turn up around six-thirty to seven that evening. She explained how she had been looking out for Rose's car and how she hated seeing it sitting outside now since it had been collected and returned. It soon became evident that Helen Hill hadn't got anything more to add to the snippets of information we already had. I was going to have to look elsewhere for answers. Terry asked a few questions, the answers to which led us nowhere productive, and we wrapped it up at Helen Hill's house. Helen showed us to the front door.

'Well, thank you for your time, Helen, and please give our condolences to Rose's father when he gets back,' I said.

'I will, Inspector, but actually he's not Rose's father. I don't talk about it much and he's always been such a good man. We never told Rose either, but we got married just after Rose was born and it's a sort of secret really, you understand?'

'Oh, I see. Erm ... Mrs Hill ... Helen, I really do need to know who Rose's father is, so could you tell me, please?' I asked, as gently as I could.

Dave Copson

Helen Hill looked quite uncomfortable and a little flushed. She looked at me as if she was trying to decide whether I could be trusted with her secret, whether she could bring herself to open an old wound that had been stumbled upon after thirty-eight years. Helen breathed a sigh and put her hand on my arm.

'It was a long time ago, Inspector. We were just foolish people in those days. I hadn't met my husband yet and I went out with this chap a few times. I'd known him when I lived in Chingford and one night I made the mistake of my life. Of course, it feels like the best thing I ever did now, having Rose,' her eyes welled a little; the tears had regrouped and were ready to flow again.

'I understand. Who is he, Helen?' I asked again.

'Oh, I don't suppose it makes any difference now … only to me. We'd been up here for quite a few years before I happened to set eyes on him one day. Imagine my surprise when I found out that he lived here too. I didn't speak but I think he recognised me. Anyway, his name's Derek. Derek Bladen.'

* * *

I didn't speak until Terry and I got back into the car. Terry had been reading about my visit to Derek Bladen's house and he recognised the name as soon as Helen mentioned him.

'You know what, guv. If you had said "your husband" instead of "Rose's father" we might never have found that out.'

He was right too.

Derek Bladen was Rose's father.

I asked Terry to turn to the page where I had taken notes at Bladen's house. With this new bombshell at my disposal, the more I read, the more I understood. No wonder Derek Bladen was in such a state of shock. I continued to recap what I had written. I sat with my head on the headrest and tried to think about my chat with old Derek. There had to be something to glean from what I had written. Nothing jumped out at me.

'Guv … Bladen never gave you any reason to suspect that he had a connection to Rose … I mean, did he say anything that's not in the notes?'

Terry was right.

278

It was what I didn't write down.

I closed my eyes and pictured myself back at his house in Parker Avenue, sitting in that musty old room, him with his oxygen tank by his chair. His third lung, he called it. Terry stayed quiet while I thought and then slowly, things began to fall into place. Derek had been stunned and I didn't really think anything of it but he was shell-shocked beyond what I might have expected, come to think of it.

'*Not our Rose*'. I took that to mean him and Joyce, his wife. Obviously, it wasn't. He referred to Rose's mother being devastated. He said 'must be' and then later he had repeated '*her mum will be upset*', and I hadn't thought any more of it. I didn't consider this at all.

What else did you say, Derek? What else?

Think, think.

I pictured him again with his 'third lung' as he puffed away recounting when he was younger, fitter. He said something else.

Got it.

Sparring ... he said he did a 'bit of sparring'.

I turned to Terry and he gave me a look that said 'you've got it, haven't you?', and he was right, I hoped.

* * *

We drove through the village and were fortunate enough to see Jill and Allison outside a shop. I pulled up in the only available space and tooted the car horn once; Allison noticed the car and came across the road. She told me that they had spoken with a person who was working at a wine bar on the evening that Rose went missing and had positively identified Rose as a woman he saw sitting in the bar. Someone else had served her but he didn't know who it was. At least we could now place Rose at the wine bar at the appropriate time. The description of the man she left with was reasonably pleasing but I knew it couldn't be trusted to be accurate with regard to Doctor Morrison Frost's discovery of the affixing gum that accompanied the black hairs he found under Rose's fingernails.

As expected, the man had a beard.

They spent no more than thirty minutes sitting and talking before they left. The man was dressed in dark clothing; nothing stood out as very memorable. I was heading to Derek Bladen's house but decided to let Jill and Allison go to pay him a call. I filled Allison in on what I had learnt from Mrs Helen Hill and said that I would catch up with them a little later and to call me if there was anything to add.

'Terry, what d'you say we go and have another little heart to heart with John Garron? I think Bladen might be our missing link, our fourth man, so to speak. We'll get some more out of him. If Garron is keeping an eye on what Oscar is up to, as he says, then Bladen will be OK for a bit longer, and there's no guarantee that Oscar has him on his list; we're surmising that. If he had, then surely he would have killed him before now, like the others.'

Terry nodded his approval and we set off back down to Whitechapel for a quiet word, but this time I would establish precisely who it was that Garron said he was protecting and find out some more about the movements of Oscar. The car's digital display told me it was 14:55 as I rang Garron and told him to stay put.

Chapter Sixty-Four

Debbie and Kim were so ridiculously excited, they were like a couple of silly schoolgirls, giggling and playing daft games as they travelled on the underground on their way home from London's West End. Their day had begun far too early as far as Debbie was concerned but she knew that Kim would be head over heels with anticipation and fully expected the early start. After breakfast, Kim carefully made her way upstairs to get ready before Debbie had even realised that she had left the table. She called out to her to wait but Kim was already at the top of the stairs and had clearly got there safely; Debbie's heart was in her mouth. She cleared away the breakfast things and joined Kim upstairs. The next thing on the agenda was doing Kim's hair and eventually her own. Nothing too fancy for either of them, so at least that saved some time. Once they were ready, they sat patiently waiting for the taxi to arrive. At least, Debbie was being patient; Kim was on fire.

The tube train journey from Piccadilly Circus to Hornchurch with one change at Embankment was energised by the adrenaline rush that had been zooming through their veins all day long. Kim had needed much less help than usual today but Debbie knew that she would be flat out all day tomorrow as a consequence. The day that Debbie and Kim went 'up West' to use the theatre tickets that Kim's Uncle John had given them for Kim's birthday had finally arrived. They had been to Queen's Theatre on Shaftesbury Avenue to watch the matinee production of *Les Misérables* and Kim had sung all the way through at the top of her voice. Kim had been buzzing all yesterday evening and had put on the dress that her uncle had bought for her birthday. She looked simply pulchritudinous and Debbie spent the whole evening telling her to be careful not to mark it.

It had been a slow, determined walk for Kim on the way out of the theatre and back to Piccadilly station but it was all worth it; she had had a wonderful time and for Debbie, that was what had mattered the most. If she had to carry Kim all the way home she would have been prepared to do it so long as her beautiful girl had a fantastic day out.

The monotony of the clackety-clack of the train trundling over the rails and across the junctions in its dark and mysterious underworld soon began to take its toll on Kim. At first, she went a little quiet and not quite so talkative and then Debbie noticed that Kim had snuggled up to her a little more, and before long Kim had nodded off with her head on Debbie's shoulder. Debbie was quietly comforted by the fact that Kim was getting some rest and hopefully this would mean that she would benefit enough to find the strength she would need to get home and complete a very tiring but incredibly happy and memorable day.

* * *

He boarded at Tower Hill and cast a shady look up and down the carriage, choosing to sit near to the doors. His breath smelt of booze and he displayed a dishevelled appearance; unshaven and grubby. His short journey back to Stepney Green wouldn't, in reality, take too long but would drag in his mind like a growth clambering undetected inside him. He put his dirty boots up on the seat in front of him and looked further along the carriage at the empty souls all dozing and sullen, as though misery itself had poisoned their bodies.

Then he saw her.

A filthy grin appeared.

Maybe the ride back to Stepney wouldn't be so bad after all.

He worked out that they were most likely going back to Hornchurch and so he only had a few stops to have some fun. She looked a twat in her fancy dress, like a fucking stupid doll, he thought.

Make-up … huh.

She'll never get a shag off anyone, not in her state.

But she was asleep so perhaps the other one would be his target tonight.

The sister.

* * *

Syrup and Cyanide

Debbie pulled her angel close and rested her head onto Kim's.

What a day.

What a show.

She would tell John all about it and invite him over for dinner so that Kim could give him all the details. She would go off like a huge firework as soon as he walked in and definitely before he took his coat off. He would be so delighted that the day had gone well and that Kim had had such a wonderful time. Debbie could smell the perfume that Kim had chosen and nuzzled even closer. She thought of John and loved him all over again for making the day possible.

* * *

He decided that it was time to shift from his fortuitous viewpoint to a seat a lot closer to her. Maybe even next to her. He wanted that but didn't want her to make a scene. Near to her would have to do. Then the games could begin. He smirked at the thought of something that had just entered his head, something to prey on her mind.

What a stroke of luck this was.

Debbie yawned and as she did, she glanced to her left and saw someone move seats. He was sitting slightly adjacent to her now but she wouldn't stare; it was rude. She looked down at the floor and wondered why anyone would move seats; surely, they were all the same. All just as grimy and full of bacteria and heaven knows what else. She decided that she didn't really want to consider what might be on the seat that she occupied after all and turned her head towards Kim, kissing her softly on her forehead, not wanting to wake her just yet. Debbie studied the nail varnish that Kim had put on for her this morning and noticed again how beautifully she had done it. Debbie had bright red and Kim's was crimson to match her dress and her shoes.

She looked gorgeous.

The man sitting across from her had slid his foot close to Kim's, but Debbie didn't want to try to move Kim's foot for fear of waking her earlier in the journey than she really wanted to. She just looked down at it, noticing the mud on his boot. Her eyes travelled subconsciously up onto his trousers and she could see how disgusting they looked. She wondered if this man was a tramp.

Don't look. Don't draw attention to yourself.

The train had already called in at Aldgate East and was now approaching Whitechapel. It was nearly time to leave his mark for Garron. The train's engine decelerated and he knew he was close. Then the brightness appeared and the colours from the advertising on the walls blurred like a smeared rainbow. The high-pitched whirring of the train as the brakes were applied and the feeling of being drawn towards the driver's cab excited him. Finally, the doors opened and luckily for him most people in his carriage got off. He got up, ensuring that his leg rubbed against Debbie's as he rose from his seat. He didn't look at her, not yet. Why spoil the surprise? He stood at the open doors and paused, looking out onto the platform. She would be hoping that he was getting off here but, no chance. The fun was about to begin. As the doors started to close he swiftly rushed back to the seat almost opposite to Debbie. He looked her in the eye and waited for the penny to drop.

Hoped he was getting off, thought Debbie. Now he's staring at me. Who the fuck does he think he ... she froze, instinctively holding Kim even closer, but as gently as she could.

Christ, it's him again. That bloke who was looking up at the window that night.

Her throat dried and she couldn't swallow. Tears of fear welled up in her eyes, her pulse rate was tachycardic at over 120 beats per minute and her legs felt like jelly. Her head swam with a sudden sickly feeling. She wanted to call out to the passenger at the end of the carriage but she couldn't manage to make a sound. She just stared at his ghoulish expression. Then he moved his hand along his thigh towards her and left it there on his knee, poised like a rattlesnake waiting to uncoil its deadly venom. His hand was filthy; his nails were long and demonic. She stayed completely still and watched him. She began to think of what she had in her bag that she could use to spray in his eyes but she knew she would never have the chance.

Fucking great, he thought ... she's shitting herself.

His boot touched her foot, marking her shoe slightly. She pulled it away and he smirked. He lifted his hand sharply upwards and startled her. He was enjoying himself now. He moved his boot again and she drew her foot further away.

Not long now.

He could feel the train decelerate as it approached Stepney Green and prepared himself for his final move. The timing would be crucial, not too early and not too late. He continued to stare at her as the train entered the station and the light from it once more brightened the carriage. The brakes were on and his moment was coming ... wait, wait. The train stopped and paused before the doors opened. Still he sat, grinning at her, his boot now treading on her foot; just a little pressure. The train gave a hiss and he leapt towards her, shoving his right hand between her legs and up her dress, his left hand grabbing her hair, forcing her head hard against the window behind her. Kim's head shifted slightly.

'Say hello to Johnny boy for me,' he said and licked hard on her face from her mouth to her eye. His beery tongue touched her teeth and left her face wet. The tip of his tongue pushed at her tightly closed eye. He kissed her softly on the tip of her nose.

She whimpered pathetically.

Perfect.

Now the timing.

The doors were about to close as he ran from the train, just getting off before they closed tight. He stood momentarily on the platform looking in at Debbie and Kim and then turned and disappeared into one of the tunnels that would lead him to the ticket hall and out of the station.

As the train lurched onward, Debbie reached tentatively for her phone.

It was 18:40.

Chapter Sixty-Five

Jill's text informed me that they had got everything they needed for now from Derek Bladen and his treasured secret. She didn't go into any further details but I bet he was more than a little shocked at the reason for their visit. I parked the car at the rear of The Fallen Oak; the rusty old burnt-out wreck had gone to its grave, leaving an oily stain as the only reference to its dreaded existence. I grabbed Bob's laptop from the rear seat and ventured in through the front doors of the pub with Terry once more. The afternoon clientele gave us no more than a disapproving sneer. Nothing more than we would have expected to receive, judging by my previous experiences. The scruffy youth behind the bar stumbled over his badly-rehearsed words and told us to go through to the back. He looked very uncomfortable with his task of inviting us through and did it with as little sincerity as possible.

The room where Bernie met his grisly end all those years ago was empty aside from the dated furniture that we had witnessed on the last visit. We walked a little further down the corridor and found Garron sitting in a smaller, even dingier excuse for a room; one table and three chairs, with him occupying one of them. Being a man of few words, Garron simply nodded at the two available seats and we took up the invitation to sit.

'You want coffee?' he asked in his deadpan way.

'Yes, why don't we?' I replied.

Garron got up and walked out without a word, returning after another minute as we embraced the usual gritty atmosphere.

'It's coming,' he said.

I did wonder whether it was a prudent move to have bestowed such a responsibility upon the youth that we encountered before but I guess if it was awful we didn't have to drink it. I put Bob's laptop on the table and Garron gave it a hard stare.

'What d'ya want then, Inspector?' he asked.

'I think it's high time that you let me know who you are protecting from the hands of Oscar, don't you?'

Garron looked at me and then at Terry and then gave another look at Bob's laptop. He was weighing up how to respond so I jumped in ahead of him.

'You see, the gentleman in question could be at risk and we wouldn't want anything to happen to him, and seeing as he isn't in the best of health perhaps we should ensure that we have his best interest at heart. What do you say, Mr Garron?'

I left this comment hanging precariously in the air and watched Garron's face blush, just a little. It would have been almost unnoticeable if you weren't looking for it.

Finally, I got a reaction.

'How d'ya know?' he asked.

'Pure chance really. Nothing for you to worry about. All I want you to do is confirm his name for me.' I looked at Garron and gave a quizzical expression, awaiting his reply.

Before he could respond the coffee arrived, and had the appearance of something from that had been dredged from a swamp. The youth retreated without speaking.

'Well?' I asked.

'Bladen,' he said.

'Thank you. Now tell me what connection there is between Bladen and the others; Grainger, Brookes and Elms.'

'They were just some blokes who hung around the pub and played a game of darts, back in the day.'

'Hung around the Repton Gym too, I wouldn't be surprised to hear. That right is it?'

'Yeah. Sometimes.'

'Of course, you were there too in those days, weren't you? It's strange how you couldn't remember him though. Maybe you just needed me to jog your memory, eh?'

'Yeah, perhaps,' he said.

'Well, Mr Garron, let's see if I can jog your memory a little further.'

I opened Bob's laptop and Garron watched closely, as if it was some kind of sleight-of-hand magic trick. I asked Terry to start it up and scribbled something on the corner of his folder.

'That's the password,' I said.

'Really?' Terry said with a half-smile.

'Yep, that's the boy.'

'Well I never,' he said.

Garron sipped at his coffee and put the mug down on the table with a bit of a thump.

'Wanker,' he shouted.

'Not to your taste then, I assume?' I said.

Garron wiped his mouth with the back of his hand and I noticed the scar he had on it.

'Nasty,' I said, pointing at the scar. 'How d'you get it?'

'Don't remember.'

'I think I would remember how I got a scar like that one, looks like something got stuck in your hand,' I said.

'Yeah, well, it's better now.'

Terry had the laptop ready and slid it across to me, interested in what might be coming up next.

On the way down here, whilst Fleetwood Mac entertained on the CD player, I had been turning things over in my mind. I had thought about the photos on Bob's laptop again. I thought about the group of walkers and wondered who they could be, and began to take a wild guess.

I drew up the photos one by one and decided to start with the walkers. Turning the screen to face Garron, I asked. 'Recognise them?'

He raised his eyebrows and looked over the top of the screen at me.

'So?' he said, being as helpful as ever.

'So, do you know them, Mr Garron?'

I brought up the photo of the sleepy chap in the boat next and showed it to Garron. I didn't spend any time on this but just watched his expression, which was non-committal to say the least. Next it was the turn of the couple dancing. He studied it and nodded as if to say 'next'. The Fallen Oak was next. His face was beginning to crack into a puzzled look but he still kept his lips tightly closed. Although he wasn't saying much, I could hear him loud and clear. Seriousness clouded his face, like he had just been picked out of a line-up.

'Who's that then? Which one enjoyed a dance?' I asked.

Garron looked over the screen again and back down to the picture of Daniel Grainger. It had come to me in the car and the more I thought about it, the more I realised exactly who the woman was: a younger Louisa Grainger.

Garron said nothing. I turned the laptop back around to me.

'Well, isn't that a coincidence, Mr Garron?' I said.

He stared like a rabbit in the headlights awaiting its final fate. The cogs were turning in his head; calculating and making snap decisions. I wasn't really so bothered about Garron and his ways, I was more concerned with what these photos were doing on Bob's laptop and whether Oscar had any more surprises in store. In the meantime, I had an opportunity to try to make sense of some of it.

'Your pub, Grainger, your friends. So, tell me about the walking group.'

'They used to be my friends before ...' he said, giving a tired and bored sigh. He sat up straighter and picked up the cold mug of coffee deciding, wisely, not to attempt any more of it.

'Fucking shit,' he said, giving the mug a look of distaste.

'I'm not sure it's that good,' I said.

Garron scratched at his chin and just as he was poised to speak, the youth showed up in the doorway, interrupting his train of thought, saying something about a phone call on his mobile that he had left behind the bar. Apparently, it had been ringing over and over.

'Alright, I'll be done in a minute ... and, Jamie ... your coffee was bollocks,' he shouted after him, as the unfortunate Jamie made his way back to tend to the bar. Composing himself, he carried on where he left off ... 'Look, I don't know why there's a photo of the pub. But I know that the photo of the walkers are the four of 'em; Grainger, Brookes, Elms and Bladen. Christ knows why you've got 'em though.'

'So, did you take the photos?' I asked.

'No, not me, but I think I know who did.'

'Oscar?' I asked, blindly and with a degree of desperation.

'No, it weren't him. It was your mate, the copper. He used to go walking with 'em sometimes. He must have told yer all about it.'

Terry and I looked at each other, trying not to let Garron see the surprise in our faces. There was a silence that filled the room, stifling the air; thick like Jamie's rank coffee. Garron knew from the first moment I tried to surprise him with the photos that I had no idea about

Bob being involved in some odd way. He had studied my face just as much as I had studied his.

He played me and he played me well.

'You wanna ask him about it. Your mate,' he said.

'I would if I could but he's in hospital and he's unwell, not up to this sort of thing just yet, unfortunately.'

'Ah, what a shame,' he said.

'What would you know about that, Mr Garron?'

'Nothing, Inspector. Give him my best.'

I sat and thought about what we had just discovered and asked another poser.

'What sort of relationship did Mr Hand have with you and your pals in those days?'

'Nothing much really. I knew he was around and that he went about with the others from time to time. He knew me and I knew him but that was about it.'

Bob knew Garron all along?

'Did he know who The Crew were?' I asked.

'He knew. Didn't have anything to do with 'em though. Not directly.'

'What do you mean by that?'

'I mean he never hung about with 'em. He was friends with the others but not in a big way, just knew a lot of faces, I guess. He came in the pub sometimes, not a lot. The pub was busy in those days so I couldn't keep up with when everyone came and went, know what I mean?'

I thought I knew what he meant. Now I had a lot more to think about and I was desperate to talk to Bob, but there was no immediate guarantee that I would be able to in the foreseeable future, so that was out.

'So how come Grainger's wife is on there, dancing? Did they take their wives with them?' I asked.

'Huh! No, *they* didn't, but Grainger couldn't go for a shit without her hanging around outside the bog waiting for him. They used to tell him over and over to get rid of her, but 'course he didn't listen. He was too scared anyway. The bloke couldn't move without her traipsing around behind him. Old cow,' said Garron with a roughness in his voice and a snarling expression.

'Not your favourite then, I take it?' I said, as Garron shook his head and grumbled something under his breath.

I continued with Garron and asked a more direct question. 'Where do you think Oscar is hiding?'

'Could be anywhere around here. There are lots of places he could be. Down by the river, squatting, in an old derelict. It's anyone's guess.'

'Do you reckon he knows where Bladen lives?'

'I doubt it. Still alive, ain't he?' he said cockily and gave a condescending smirk.

I turned the laptop and closed the lid, handing it to Terry. So now I knew why Louisa Grainger appeared in the photo. I also knew that the picture of the walkers was the four of them but unfortunately, I also knew that I couldn't talk to Bob about it just yet. That thought in turn reminded me that I should try to have another chat with the lovely Sarah Goodman and check on Bob's condition, for the sooner I was able to glean some information from him the better.

We left The Fallen Oak at around 7 p.m. that evening and could hear Garron on the phone as we pushed open the front doors and experienced the pleasure of some booze-free air. It sounded as though he was getting an ear-bashing so we were not too unhappy to leave him to it. We could hear him raising his voice even as we walked down the side alley and past the old green side door.

'Someone's getting it,' said Terry with a chuckle.

'Yeah, lucky for them, eh?' I said ironically.

* * *

Back at the station I sat and typed a lengthy email to Trevor Eaden at Plaistow nick. I made sure that he was up to speed with the latest about Derek Bladen and Rose Hill but I didn't say a word about Bob and the recent developments. I had still got to have that conversation with Corrigan and I wasn't really sure where to start with that one. Terry placed a cup of coffee on my desk and wandered off to speak with someone further down the office. I muttered a stifled 'thanks' and took a sip. I knew it wouldn't burn my lips 'cos Terry always put too much milk in, but I put up with it. As I sat pondering the thought that Bob knew these people all along, I began to wonder what was stopping him from telling me. I couldn't see that knowing them from days gone by was a crime. He knew Garron too but still played that game of his in the pub the first time we went to talk to him, as if he worked out that it was Garron sitting at the bar by checking the picture of him that he had on his phone.

He was just a bit too familiar with him.

My mind was rapidly back-tracking now to where this all began.

St Dominic's and the Revd Martin Brookes.

He knew him too. So, was that why he was on the scene before I got there? Then something came to me as I rubbed my eyes. Of course, he knew him. Why didn't I think of this earlier? It was when I asked who the unfortunate vicar was and Bob said his name. I knew there was something odd about that. He said Martin Alan Brookes before we had established he had a middle name. So, I bet he knew about Grainger two years before as well. It was Bob who had introduced me to Andy Potter at the pub that night when I found out about the ace of clubs that was found in Grainger's shoe. Bob probably knew all about that too. So, it was as if he was helping me to catch up but still holding back. The more that I puzzled, the more came to light and the more my head spun. Did he already know where Martin Brookes previously worked and that the four of them used to frequent the gym in Bethnal Green?

He must have done.

So why, Bob?

What the hell is going on?

And why the hell had Garron been 'keeping an eye' on Bladen? Why should he care?

Chapter Sixty-Six

My alarm clock told me it was 04:14 when I woke suddenly. I hadn't slept with any sort of quality but now it was all over, no point even trying to drift off again. I didn't get my head onto the pillow until 01:35 and had spent each hour checking the time, hoping it was going to show me that it was nearer to six, but no such luck. I had spent the previous evening thinking about what the conversation with Garron had all meant and what the consequences of it would prove to be.

I thought I knew Bob Hand.

Did I?

My house phone rang and I picked up the handset next to my bed without questioning why it was ringing at such an unearthly hour.

'Guv, sorry to call but I can't stop thinking about this situation with Bob.'

'Nor can I ... and you haven't woken me, I've hardly slept.'

'Nor me. We're gonna have to try to explain this to Corrigan, ain't we?' said Terry.

'I've been wondering about that too. I can't think clearly about that conversation just yet, let's see how we feel about it in the morning.'

'Are you suggesting that we don't tell him, guv?'

'I don't know what I'm suggesting right now, Terry. Look, get some rest while you still can. I'll talk to you at the station in a few hours, OK?'

'Sure, guv. Nite.'

* * *

Oscar the cat sat in the early-morning sunshine on top of my shed like some kind of regal prince, master of all he surveyed. He sat squinting and washing his face. He probably had a better sleep than I did, and he certainly looked a lot fresher than I did too. I finished my breakfast and, as hard as I tried not to, I repeatedly kept thinking about how to deal with the difficult conversation with Corrigan. I tried to imagine the different outcomes and hoped to be able to decide what to do before I got to work. I knew that I was finding it difficult because I felt that I should protect Bob. I began to think again about what he had done that was so wrong; nothing actually wrong as far as I could tell up to now, apart from not declaring his previous contacts, which would not go down well in an investigation. I could feel that I was becoming less and less inclined to say anything just yet but I could only hold off for so long before I got myself into hot water. I needed to dig a bit deeper first, then I would tell him. Terry would go along with it, I was sure.

I glanced fuzzily out into the garden and saw Oscar the cat skulking along the top of the fence like some kind of thin, hairy lizard. Sleek and so low that his legs were barely visible. He had spotted a squirrel of all things, and was homing in on it like a deadly stealth missile, becoming quicker with every tentative step. However, there was only ever going to be one winner in this particular battle of wits and predictably, as soon as Oscar surged forward, the squirrel leapt clear, leaving Oscar clinging precariously to the top of the fence before he finally lost his grip and plunged unceremoniously into the garrya bush below him. He reappeared decorated in seed and as fluffy as a pom-pom, wearing that stupid look that cats wear as if to say *'I meant that'*.

I knew that I had to get myself one step ahead of the real Oscar and make him look stupid too. Unfortunately, that was proving to be difficult. He was out there, and I wanted to know where. He was killing for fun and I was beginning to feel like I was being left behind in this particular chase. Corrigan wasn't impressed, poor Bob was in all sorts of trouble, Terry had lost Kay and I'd just about had enough of Garron and his silly attitude. At times like this when it was all getting on top, I missed Ana more than ever. And yet, how could I subject her to this? Listening to me go on about how unsuccessful I was. Maybe that was why she wasn't here, after all. As I wandered into the living room I knew that the first thing to do was to desist with these thoughts. They did no good and helped nobody, least of all me.

Chapter Sixty-Seven

The shock of seeing him again on the train had precisely the effect that her tormentor had desired and had sent a fearful dread through her. It had been an immense challenge but she had somehow managed to get home without Kim realising that anything was wrong. Her false façade had been something she had reluctantly had to rely on in the past and she used it to its full effect. The well-rehearsed guise had bought her some time whilst she got Kim settled into the living room and made them both a cup of tea. 'Popping upstairs,' she called, and hid herself away in the bathroom, trembling and gushing silent tears. She had slid slowly down against the bathroom door with her hand covering her mouth to prevent any tell-tale sounds that she was weeping and sobbing uncontrollably. She fumbled hastily to press the quick-dial button on her phone. She had spoken to him briefly from the train but needed her big brother so much right now.

His bloody phone was switched off for the night.

* * *

Garron's visit the next morning was again filled with consternation and he said little more than necessary to comfort his sister. Holding her protectively, his head was a tortured combination of rage and worry. Quietly, he whispered to her ensuring that his words were out of earshot from Kim, who was watching TV in the next room. Apparently unconcerned with the intrusion into their lives that was made once more by the man on the train, she laughed at *The Big Bang Theory*. She had no trouble working the DVD player, having ensured that it had been set to record her latest favourite programme before leaving the house, even though Debbie always double-checked that the correct timings had been entered into the machine's memory. When Uncle John appeared, Kim, as expected, tried to speak all her words at once, such was her excitement and her eagerness to tell him all about what a fantastic day they had had in theatreland. The tiredness conceded to alacrity as Kim's enthusiasm overwhelmed the room. It was as though someone had dropped a lit match into a box of fireworks. Kim wasn't expecting to see her Uncle John quite so soon, but this was perfect. The magic of the Queen's Theatre and the songs were all fresh in her mind as well as the thrill of riding on the London underground. She recited the whole day in rapid-fire. The set, the costumes, the applause, and even that she fell asleep on the train on the way home. Debbie's eyes met John's.

'Deb, I'll come by again soon. I've got some business in the next few days but you know you can call me any time, eh?'

'What if I can't get ya? Your phone ain't on at night is it? What if he comes here, John? What will I do?'

'He won't, Deb, he's had his fun for now.'

'He bloody touched me,' she said, tears running again. 'What if he gets in the house?'

Garron felt certain that that particular phase had already been and gone but it would do no good letting on. He thought about the mirror which now resided upstairs in the pub; out of sight, out of mind; out of Kim's mind.

'Just don't go out without locking up first, right? If yer think you've seen him again, call me straight away, yer got it?'

Debbie nodded and hugged him close before finally releasing her grip on the man that she had come to rely on the most since her husband was taken.

Another bloody mystery.

Sometimes she didn't want the answer.

It was getting towards lunchtime and both she and Kim needed to get something to eat. Debbie locked the front door and double-checked the window locks in the kitchen before returning to the living room and passing through it, avoiding any eye contact with Kim until she had managed to wipe her face again, to do the same at the back of the house. The garden was peaceful and silent and yet to Debbie it was full of sinister creatures and things that were trying to get into the house.

Terrifying things; dirty and unshaven.

She could smell *him* everywhere.

She turned away from the door that she had already checked twice and screamed as she bumped straight into Kim, who had followed her out of the room. Kim squealed and grabbed at Debbie, who went cold from head to toe.

'Jesus, you scared me.'

'Sorry, Mummy. I just wanted to ask you something.' said Kim, innocently.

'Oh, God. Sorry I made ya jump, darlin'. What is it?'

Kim looked hard into Debbie's eyes, almost peering inside her head.

'Who was that man on the train?' she said.

Chapter Sixty-Eight

The search for the car that Rose Hill's killer had used was getting us nowhere fast. No-one had come forward to report seeing them together other than the bartender, who had recalled taking little more than a sideways glance in their direction when the drinks were served. The cameras in the bar were off, awaiting some repair or other. A photofit of a featureless man with a beard was never going to get off the ground either. CCTV in the area had drawn a blank, which wasn't too surprising as the coverage was limited, to say the least. The laborious process of eliminating hundreds of dark-coloured cars that had travelled along the motorway around that particular part of the day was both necessary and unproductive. Jill and Allison had continued to press on with the difficult task of finding someone with more to offer than 'No dear'. Morrison Frost, the pathologist, hadn't got any more for me than the human hair with a trace of gum on the end, and Rose Hill's bag, missing shoe, phone or any other substantial sorts of ID appeared to have vanished, along with my hopes of talking to Bob about the serious implications that rattled around my head, according to Sarah Goodman at the hospital.

My visit to see Bob, who was asleep throughout my fairly brief stay at his bedside, turned into a chance to chat with Sarah Goodman instead. I caught her eye as she busied herself at the nurse's station and asked if I could have a moment of her time. Without telling her why I needed to talk to Bob, I impressed upon her that it had become even more important that I did so as soon as I could. She suggested that we got a hot drink from the small cafeteria that the on-duty nurses tended to use at the end of the ward, away from the pandemonium of the main cafeteria on the ground floor of the building. I walked beside her along the ward and through a set of double doors that were being held open by a porter. As I reached the doors and smiled at him for holding the door open, I was almost run down by a trolley, which was entering the ward from the other direction and turned out to be the actual reason why he was holding the door. I stepped back, treading on Sarah's foot, and found myself apologising to her and the porter at the same time and wishing that I had not made a fool of myself. She didn't flinch but it can't have been painless. The trolley squeezed past me and left me pinned to a wall as Sarah continued down the corridor as if nothing had happened. I caught her up as she turned left and reached the cafeteria ahead of me.

'Tea, coffee?' she asked.

'Oh, I'll have coffee please. Sorry about your foot, is it OK?'

'It'll live. Anyway, I'm used to being trodden on in these busy corridors. Don't worry about it.'

We sat at a small table with just enough room for two people; our knees almost touching. Four or five nurses in various shades of blue were chatting at the counter as we arrived. They chirped and giggled but didn't stay long once we got there. Maybe they didn't want to make their extended tea break too obvious to the ward sister.

My impatience at the thought of waiting any longer to quiz Bob prompted Sarah to explain one or two things about Bob's current condition more clearly, so that even I could understand, although she didn't put it like that at all. She explained that the events that follow a significant brain injury should be treated as a marathon rather than a sprint.

'The cognitive effects of a brain trauma are what I want to explain to you firstly. The types of injuries we see are far-ranging and our patients respond in a variety of ways, depending on the severity of the trauma and the location of the injury,' she calmly explained.

'So how bad was Bob's injury?' I asked, assuming that it wasn't exactly good.

'Let's face it; he was hit by a car so it was significant. In other words, the impact he experienced was bad enough to cause a great deal of swelling initially and that in itself can create a number of problems. It is only as the swelling reduces that we begin to learn how badly the trauma has affected our patient. In the case of Mr Hand, the reduction of the swelling is only the first step. Now, over the past couple of weeks, he has already gone through a number of stages towards recovery but that still doesn't mean that we know precisely how things will turn out just yet. For example; the skills that you and I take for granted every day are not necessarily going to be such a walk in the park for him. We have to consider his speech, his memory, his concentration levels and his understanding of carrying out relatively simple tasks.'

I almost said 'sounds like Bob' but thought better of it, in the circumstances.

'Are you saying he might not recover all of these things?'

'I'm sure he will continue to make progress but I have to stress that we need to be patient. Communication alone is often quite challenging and then there are things like his emotional state and depending on how he improves, we have to consider how we can provide help a little further down the line; but for now I should forget about trying to talk to him about anything too demanding.'

'I see. OK. Well thanks for explaining that to me. I guess I know where we stand now.'

'Yes, for now, but don't think the worst. Mr Hand has a real chance of a full recovery in time. What is it that's so important anyway?' she asked.

'Ah, just work stuff actually.'

'Well, that can wait then, can't it?' she said with a smile.

'Yeah, it'll have to,' I said, as my head replayed the conversation I wanted to achieve but couldn't have.

After a quick coffee and an even quicker chat about what was on my agenda for the rest of the day, Sarah made her excuses and my precious moment alone with the beautiful Sarah Goodman was at an end. We wandered back to look in on Bob, who was still asleep, and, after thanking her for her time, I left her to get on with her busy schedule.

I drove away from the hospital feeling down. On the one hand it was because my mate was lying trapped in his own body, and on the other because I couldn't get to the information that he held within his frail and fragile brain. I stopped at a set of red lights and watched a young mother, who could have been no more than 16 or 17 years old, struggle with a small pushchair laden with shopping bags. Two little swinging legs at the front told me her responsibilities in life had come along sooner than she would probably have chosen. But then, in a way, she did choose, I suppose. As I drew away from the lights that were now displaying a more favourable colour, a torrent of rain began to drum hard above my head. The windscreen wipers were just about able to keep up with the downpour that was running down the windscreen. It was almost as if I had driven under a waterfall. The rain bounced on the road and pedestrians could be seen scuttling about through the watery scene. Huge puddles had formed very quickly and cars were inadvertently spraying and showering those caught unawares. I drove sedately along towards Chelmsford nick. The radio was tuned to Classic FM and provided the sort of calm I needed right now in order to make another attempt at thinking clearly about what to do next. It's strange how thoughts come to you, out of the blue, when you are least thinking about them, and as I tootled along through the rain-drenched streets, the downpour seemingly relentless, I remembered where I had seen the man lying as if he were asleep in the boat; the one from the photo on Bob's laptop. The clothes he was wearing were precisely those that I saw in the photo that Doreen Calderwood had of Revd Martin Brookes; the one that I had borrowed from her and not really done a great deal with other than look at it for a while. So, I presume that Martin's photo had been taken following a walk with the others.

What did she say?

Epping Forest; that was it.

Chapter Sixty-Nine

As his breath lingered for no more than a couple of seconds in the doleful night air, the stratocumulus clouds wafted silently across the sky, broken only by a few, occasional, crepuscular rays of divine-like beams.

The Visitor stood watching.

He could see a shadow moving about inside.

He could feel the predator within him stirring again like an incendiary emotion as he peered through the darkness towards his prey.

No disguise this time.

The dark boiler suit reflected his mood. A black woollen beanie hat was turned inside out to hide the emblem on the front, eliminating any chance of identification. A serrated knife, the one that killed Rose Hill, the memory of which still tore at his soul, was housed in one of the deep pockets on the inside of the suit and a whole lot of hatred swirled around in his head. He shook his head in an effort to discard the thoughts of killing her.

Why did you have to struggle?

Memories from the past tormented and plagued his ability to think as clearly as he wanted to, but either way, it was time.

Retribution was going to be his.

As luck would have it most of the streetlamps were out; saving energy no doubt and making it much easier to go unnoticed. The house looked innocent enough and had no idea what it was about to witness. The curtains were closed at every window that looked out onto the street. A single light from a back room emitted a gentle glow from the front door and out towards the modest front garden. The passage had no light on. The evening had been mostly dark for a couple of hours; the clocks having been turned back to accommodate the autumnal ritual, plunging those dank and chilly early winter afternoons upon the neighbourhood. A single car came towards him as he stepped softly into a shop doorway and turned his face away from the street, avoiding any reflection from the lights illuminating him, until it had rumbled on by and out of harm's way, returning an eerie silence to the area. Now that the regular beat of rhythmic street life had prepared itself for bed, it was his turn to come out to play.

The Visitor unfastened a button halfway down his boiler suit and slipped his hand inside. The thick, strong handle of the knife felt comfortable in his grip. His heart raced a little as he momentarily held on to the weapon, squeezing it in his hand, eager to put it to use.

It would be busy tonight.

He checked the time on his mobile phone, not really knowing why. What difference did it make? He had as long as he needed. The hard part had been in the planning and now he was within reach of one final showdown. He pondered, ephemerally, and considered the run of circumstances that had steered him on this destructive path. A path that had developed in his mind like an uncontrollable invader; haunting him across the years and driving him on for revenge.

First Grainger; then Brookes and Elms. He knew he couldn't alter the path of devastation to his family but he could distribute the punishment.

Chapter Seventy

As I drove through the back gates I could see that the heavy rain had flooded the yard and that the swirling wind had blown a large dustbin across from one side of the yard to the other and into Corrigan's car. The offending bin was lying on its side with its contents strewn under and around the car. The man in question was out there inspecting the damage; his white shirt clinging to him as he wiped the rain from his face. I parked up and got out with my jacket shielding the worst of it from me.

'Who's supposed to make sure these blasted bins are secure?' he shouted.

'No idea, sir,' I said as I hurried past him and found some respite under a covered parking area.

'Well, when I find out I'll have their guts for garters,' he yelled as he swiftly joined me out of the rain.

'Much damage?' I asked.

'Enough. Fucking things. I told someone about these bins only last week, but I can't remember who it was. When I do, they'll be for it, I can tell you.'

We scuttled in out of the storm, which was far from predicted, according to the local news earlier today.

'I heard the bloody thing clang from my office. It sounded like a bloody riot was going on out there. Anyway, where have you been hiding?' he said.

'Been to see Bob.'

'How's he getting on; up and about?'

'Hardly, sir. I had a word with the ward sister and it looks like it's gonna be a while before he's on his feet.'

'Oh dear. Oh well, do keep me posted, won't you? In fact, step into my office later and give me the full run-down, would you?' he said, dripping rainwater onto the already grubby carpet that led us to the rear stairs.

'Yes, sir, of course,' I said, deferring an awkward conversation just a little further into the future and sparing myself the effort of going over all that Sarah Goodman had conveyed to a wet and grumpy officer. Later he would, in all probability, be dry and, hopefully, less grumpy.

Upstairs, I found Terry at his desk with an A4 pad in front of him.

'What're you up to?' I asked.

'Actually, I'm doodling some thoughts, guv.'

'Really? Anything you'd like to share?'

'If you like,' he said, casually nodding.

I put my sodden jacket on the back of my chair, pushing it across nearer to the radiator, and went to stand beside Terry. Looking down onto his artwork I could see a couple of topical names straight away. Our four walkers, individually listed, Garron, Oscar and a string of lines that seemed to be more of a jumbled spider's web than anything constructive. I wasn't sure where this was going at all, if anywhere.

'So, what does all this mean then? Anything?' I enquired.

Terry sat back in his chair and let out a soft sigh. He dropped his pencil down on his desk and drummed his fingers on his laptop case.

'I'm just running it through my head again,' he said, running his fingers through his hair before he continued. 'Let's accept that the four of them did for Bernie in the back room of the pub and by some miracle Oscar got away. Well, that was about twenty years ago, wasn't it, so why would he wait all this time before appearing from wherever he's been hiding to start his revenge? I mean, it's a long time.'

'Maybe he's been out of the country and decided that it would be safe enough to come back now that the whole thing has been all but forgotten,' I offered.

'Perhaps. What about Garron then?'

'What about him?'

'Well, why hasn't Oscar done for him too? Surely, he must have been involved in some way; he knew all the others in those days. Oscar must suspect that Garron had something to do with it all, surely? He must think that Garron set them both up. And what was in it for him, anyway? I mean maybe he got his own friends to do the job while he stayed all sweet and innocent but what was his share of the spoils?'

Terry's onslaught of relevant questions got me thinking too. Oscar, clearly, hadn't killed Garron off and we never really got an answer to all those scars and bruises he was sporting a while back.

The nasty scar on his hand.

He never had explained it properly.

'Terry, what was it Garron said about his friends?'

'What d'ya mean, guv?'

'Check the notes that you took when we were at the pub recently, let's see what he said.'

Terry dug out his notepad from a desk drawer and began to flip through the pages, muttering as he did.

'Here we go. You asked him about the photos that showed the pub and the others etc. and he said ... "They used to be my friends" ... so?'

I looked at the notes and read them again, but I wasn't happy.

Something was missing.

There was something else.

I racked my brains and started to pace up and down. Terry watched me and glanced up and down to his notes.

'What?' he said.

'Shut up a minute,' I said, a little too sharply, 'Sorry, gimme a sec.'

I walked very slowly and deliberately and placed myself back in the pub with Garron. The bland and grubby room, the undistinguished coffee and the unanswered questions that were a common feature of conversations with Garron. I could see his face, the cocky expression that accompanied him whenever I had asked him anything ... but he wasn't wearing that grin now. '*Your friends ... your friends ...*'

'Read it again, Terry,' I said.

'They used to be my friends,' he repeated.

As I turned away from Terry's desk once more and traced my steps again up and down the office floor, the proverbial penny thudded into place. I waved my hand in the air, clicking my fingers loudly. '... before', he said 'before'.

Before what?

Before the night they did for Bernie?

Before what?

'Listen Terry, let's just run this thing again. Let's agree that Oscar is back and killing those that he blames for the death of his brother, dealing the aces as he goes, after all at least that much makes sense. I know we've run into no-man's-land chasing clues about the deaths of Grainger, Brookes and Elms but Bladen is still alive and maybe on his hit list, but we don't know whether he even knows where he is yet. I agree with you that Oscar must suspect that Garron set the whole thing up or at least had something to do with it ... even we think that, but when I first met Garron he had cuts and bruises on him so maybe he had had a visit from Oscar, but he didn't kill him. Garron certainly wasn't interested in talking about his wounds.'

'Perhaps Oscar doesn't see him as one of those who actually did the killing so he just roughed him up and spared him,' said Terry.

'Perhaps ... Could be. When I went to the pub with Bob, Garron said something about Oscar and Bernie having some diamonds on them the night the killing took place. The four of them must have taken the goods away as well as killing Bernie. After twenty years they will be long gone. Garron said that The Crew had done a job somewhere in Essex and come away with some stones.'

'Divided by four on that night, I guess,' said Terry.

'Yeah. Although what was it you said a moment ago about Garron? You said "What was in it for him?"'

'Yeah, so what about divided by five? But, if that's the case then wouldn't Oscar have killed him too?' Terry asked.

'I really don't know, Terry. Maybe not if he somehow knew or suspected that Garron hadn't been one of the gang that actually killed his brother, but I'll tell you what I do know, my old mate ... I think we've spent too much time chasing Oscar's shadow when we might have been better to have been chasing Bernie's ghost. Have a dig around and see what you can come up with about a jewel robbery in the 90s. He said some people got hurt. See if you can find a report on it from those days in the press or maybe go through the archives of the Essex local rags. It'll be there somewhere. It could easily be another dead end but let's give it a go. Let's start chasing ghosts.'

Chapter Seventy-One

I sent an email to Andy Potter asking him if he could recall anything about an incident at a jeweller's shop around twenty years ago. Andy wasn't linked directly to Essex but he may remember something from that time; it was worth a shot in the dark. Whilst I was at it I emailed Trevor Eaden at Plaistow in case anything else had turned up regarding the Elms murder. I felt that I was still reaching out into the unknown and hoping to clutch on to a lucky break. I didn't expect any such event to be forthcoming but it was all I could do for now while Terry got on with his own particular digging into the annals of the Essex press.

When I stepped into Corrigan's office I felt a sense of unease. Not that that was entirely unusual but this time I felt that I was under an extra pressure. From the moment I had learnt that Bob had known Garron and the others all those years ago and had not told me a thing about it, I had carried a secret around with me. It was one I wished I had never discovered. It was one that I couldn't discuss with Bob either. There were so many questions I wanted to ask him and yet, if what Sarah Goodman said was anything to go by, I still didn't know whether I'd ever be able to talk to Bob on a frank and level playing field.

What a bloody mess.

'Take a seat, Detective Inspector,' offered Corrigan.

As I sat down at his desk with its perfectly laid-out clutter, I made a decision that I knew I could quite possibly live to regret.

Say nothing.

I told a genuinely concerned Nicholas Corrigan all I could remember about how Bob's injury might affect his future lifestyle, depending on how his improvement progressed. I gave him the general run-down that Sarah Goodman had eloquently passed on to me over coffee when we sat, touching knees, at that inadequately small table. It was the closest

I was likely to get to her too, I felt. Corrigan was pleased that Terry was busying himself looking into the Essex incident to see what we might be able to turn up and enthused about how he was developing with regard to his work ethic etc. It was around this point that my interest began to waver and I found myself nodding in agreement without being entirely sure what I was agreeing with. My eyes must have glazed over because suddenly I was aware that he had stopped talking and was looking straight at me, as if he was anticipating an appropriate reply. I sat and didn't know whether to smile or not, but fortunately the awkward moment passed quickly and before I knew it I had been excused and was soon out of his lair and back at my desk. Terry didn't notice me at all, engrossed as he was on the telephone and scribbling furiously on his A4 pad. I had a quick look at my email inbox to check whether a reply had come in from Andy Potter or Trevor Eaden, but there was nothing other than something from Corrigan referring to some policy that I would no doubt browse and delete later. I decided to grab a coffee for Terry and myself in the hope that when I got back from the canteen he might be off the phone and have something of interest to discuss.

Chapter Seventy-Two

The decision to open the door in response to a faint, almost unheard knock was a bad one. It was not something he would usually do. It was probably nothing; probably the wind moving something about in the front garden, but he chose to take a look anyway.

Probably nothing.

He peered around the door and looked out towards the street. It was all quiet. He began to close the door when he stopped and noticed that the gate was open. Someone must have come in earlier; maybe it was when that leaflet had been posted through the letterbox advertising the new Indian restaurant just around the corner.

More crap for the recycle bin.

Better close it.

No-one else would be calling tonight and he wouldn't be answering the door if they did. As he stepped out onto the path it began to rain a little. A flicker of sheet-lightning caused him to turn his head again sharply towards the transient brightness which lit up the front of the house. He looked up at the darkening sky as the heavens rumbled their mood. Hurriedly, he closed the gate as the thunder echoed around the sky and turned back towards the front door, which had seemingly blown open further than he remembered it being when he stepped outside. Back inside, he cursed at the weather and made his way along the dimly lit passage towards the back room. The television was churning out some garbage about the latest 'it girl' who had flaunted her ample breasts on an equally ridiculous reality series, much to the amusement of the pathetic, giggling presenter.

Must turn that off.

He didn't reach it though.

An immense pain filled his head, followed swiftly by a curtain of darkness.

* * *

Finally, Terry was off the phone. I put the coffee down beside him and asked him whether he had had any joy with the Essex media.

'Well, there was a robbery alright. All the details seem to fit with the period and there were definitely some jewels taken. Not a huge amount by today's standards but enough in those days. The guy said that one of the security blokes was quite badly beaten although I don't have the full story of the severity of his injuries, but it all fits otherwise,' he said.

'OK, so that sounds as though it could be the job Oscar and Bernie did. Anything more from that at all?' I asked.

'Yeah, it was at Hornchurch at a smallish shop, by all accounts. A midweek day. According to this chap there were no witnesses to it from outside of the shop and no-one has come forward to say they saw them leave, so there is no idea about a car or anything.'

'How many people were in the shop when it happened?' I asked.

'There were three men with the delivery of diamonds, and a shop owner and a girl too. It appears that she got badly injured as well.'

'Any names of these people?' I asked.

'He gave me the girl's name and said he would look into the others and call back in about an hour or so. He remembered her because she was nice looking, or so he said. He visited her in the hospital or something. Typical ain't it, remembering the pretty girl and forgetting the blokes, names, eh?'

'So who was she?'

'She was 17 years old at the time and her name was Kim Fisher. I think he must've fancied her, the way he went on about her.'

'OK, well done, mate. That's a good start. Once he comes back to you, get addresses for these people too, just in case we need them, will you?'

'Yep, of course, guv.'

Promises, Promises

'Where the hell have you been?'

'Fucking bus didn't come. I had to trot all the way down the street past those horrible flats.'

'Them flats are alright. Never been any bother that I know of.'

'Yeah, well I don't like 'em. Anyway, where're the others?'

'Grainger can't get a pass, the fucking ponce, and Elmsy reckons he's got family round or something. Pair of tossers.'

'You wouldn't be saying that if Elmsy was 'ere, I know.'

'Bollocks.'

Eagle Place had seen its fair share of trouble, although nowadays it was considered safe enough since the hardened gangland had diminished and handed the manor over to the 'wannabe crooks'; those that made all the right noises but didn't have the bottle to carry any of it out. The Stag and Talbot was full tonight. It was the perfect choice as a venue for Bladen to call a meeting. Not so noisy that you had to shout but with enough going on that no-one took any notice of what anyone else was talking about. He also liked the open fire at his back. The refurbishment looked like a waste of money, as far as he was concerned; could hardly tell the difference, although it was prudent to acknowledge how it made the place look brighter even if it didn't. The flooring had changed from hardwood blocks that were laid out in a herringbone design to some kind of hard-wearing surface. It might be easier to mop and sweep but he didn't like it; no character, he said. A number of things had altered since the days when he came in here more regularly, before he became a regular at The Fallen Oak and before the gym days. Girls used to do a bit of stripping some years back, usually on a Friday and Saturday night, but that was before the publican fell in love with one of them. His penchant for Tae Kwon Do put two men in hospital when they got just a little too close to his precious Madeline on one particular Saturday night; the last of the stripper nights and the start of a temporary decline in custom, but *they returned as soon as the happy hour was introduced. Grayson Stoner was not a man to mix it with unless you had a death wish.*

'Well, well, Martin Brookes and Derek Bladen. Where are yer boyfriends, in the bog shagging?'

'Good evening, Grayson, nice and busy tonight, I see,' said Bladen.

'Yeah, punters everywhere. So where are they then?'

'Grainger can't get a pass and Elmsy is busy with family stuff.'

'Huh, Grainger I can understand, he always has been under the thumb, but Elmsy I expect better of,' said Stoner.

'He'd be here if he could, I'm sure, Grayson. Anyway, how is the lovely Madeline this evening?' asked Bladen, a little unwisely.

Grayson Stoner put his enormous hand onto the shoulder of Derek Bladen and squeezed firmly, just sufficiently for Bladen to feel uncomfortable.

'Just being polite, Grayson,' said Bladen, almost apologetically.

'Yeah, well she won't be getting her tits out, if that's what you're thinking.'

'I wasn't, Grayson. Honest.'

The calloused and heavy hand lifted slowly from its resting place and patted Bladen solidly on his back with just enough force to cause him to jolt forward in his seat. Stoner turned away without another word and made his way back to the bar.

'What the fuck?' said Brookes.

'He's on something. I ain't seen him like that since the time he busted those two geezers for trying to touch her. He's on something, I tell yer. He's insanely jealous, yer know? He thinks someone is sleeping with her, and fortunately he thinks I'm not.'

'Jesus, Derek,' said Martin, trying to stifle his outburst.

Martin Brookes rolled a cigarette and tutted to himself quietly. His hands showed the signs of an involuntary tremble. He had only just got over the effects of the killing of Bernie, albeit the nightmares returned occasionally when he allowed them to seep back into his troubled mind. He wished Elms was here. He always felt that nothing bad could happen when Stan Elms was around. His faith in Stan Elms took a huge wobble that night at The Fallen Oak when the shotgun blasted, but he still believed in him.

'So, why'd yer call us here tonight then?' he asked.

'I was really hoping everyone would be here, especially Grainger.'

'Why especially him?' asked Martin.

''Cos the little prick has been talking, that's why.'

'About what?' said Martin.

'What d'you fucking think he's been talking about? He's been making promises on our behalf behind our backs. Promises that we will not be keeping. He's been doing deals without asking first, not that I would have agreed to it anyway. He's a mouthy little … Now we've got trouble.'

'What's he said, Derek?'

Bladen paused just long enough to turn his head left and right in order to ensure that no-one was near enough to hear him. He let out a long, slow sigh; his expression wore a serious and concerned look, his eyes narrowed and his voice lowered to a barely audible level as he leant forward towards Brookes, beckoning him to do the same.

'He's promised a share of the goods and it ain't happening.'

'To who?'

'Who would you not share the goods with, Martin?'

Martin knew Grainger liked to boast and enjoyed whispering about things, but never thought anything of it. Now he wondered what he had been saying. Martin kept out of the way; he didn't have anything to do with any unsavoury sorts if he could help it, but Grainger was a creep. What Derek Bladen was saying made sense to Martin. Grainger was the weak link; he'd do anything to cover his back. This job was too big for Grainger, but it was too late … and it was too late for the rest of them now too. Martin knew you couldn't make promises like this and then expect to withdraw them without repercussions, and repercussions were not what Martin wanted. He looked around the pub and could feel the sweat running down his back, just like he did on that night. The same trickle of perspiration that had woken him up night after night as it ran down his face. He knew he would have to look over his shoulder forever and hope that his faith would not desert him.

Chapter Seventy-Three

Terry Brush was never happier than when he was rummaging around in search of information. I glanced across to him and had to admire his enthusiasm and the urgency with which he made notes on his pad. I didn't know precisely what he was scribbling away at but I expected I'd find out before long. As I watched him, I found myself thinking about Kay Cullen and how the two of them should, if there was any justice, have had so much time together to plan a future. The thoughts made me feel very sombre, to the point where I was almost lost in a dream world. I felt a cloak of sadness engulf me but was snapped out of it when my laptop alerted me to an incoming email from Andy Potter.

Hi mate, just wanted to let you know that I do recall the incident but I don't have anything worth knowing to add. Sorry. Good luck.

Good luck indeed.

I could do with some of that.

Terry seemed to come to the end of his scribbling session as he dropped his pen down onto his desk. He stood and approached with a page of A4 in his hand.

'Right, guv, I've got the names and addresses of the people that were at the jeweller's in Hornchurch. At least, these are the details from Hornchurch Police Station; they may well have moved on since, of course. Do you think they'll be any use to us?'

'I'm not gonna hold my breath but you never know. Let's have a look at them,' I said, taking the page from Terry and beginning to scan down it.

The three that delivered the goods all used to live in London at various different locations. The man that worked at the shop was from

Colchester in Essex and the girl was local. The passing of nearly twenty years placed each of the men somewhere in their sixties. The girl was in her teens at the time of the robbery and so I expected her to still be around. Whether she would have any clear memories of the day or anything useful to say was anybody's guess. All I knew was that she had been badly injured by all accounts. I sat and pondered the scenario again. Thinking back to the time of the robbery, I assumed that as no-one had ever been arrested for the crime, the injured people had also never known who was responsible, and if we were right about this then one of the guilty parties may well have returned and be causing more chaos. If we got him … when we got him, we could pin this on him too and that might be of interest to them. I looked at the page of names and addresses again and realised that the girl's address was only about half an hour away down the A12 so I suggested to Terry that we take a trip over there in the morning and just have a chat, providing she lived there.

Chapter Seventy-Four

On the way through to Hornchurch, Terry opened up a little more about his highly emotive spell in Belfast. He went into detail about the atmosphere in Kay's parents' house during the days leading up to the funeral. He couldn't count the number of awkward silences where no-one knew quite what to say or how to say it. It was, as he described it, harder to know how to cope with than anything else he had ever experienced. Even harder than his first interview before being accepted into the police, he joked. That was something I liked about Terry. As awful as it all must have been, he could still rustle up a joke; albeit tongue in cheek. The hordes of people that were waiting at the church when he and Kay's family arrived left them all virtually speechless. The church wasn't much more than a mile from where Kay's parents lived and even the huge number of messages of sympathy that had arrived in many forms, whether they were hand-written letters, emails, text messages or the bombardment of touching messages that landed on Facebook and other social media sites, could not have prepared them for the heart-wrenching sight that they saw before them outside the church.

The street either side of the path that led up to the church entrance, including the pavement opposite, was lined with people who variously fell into the category of neighbours, friends, people Kay had worked with, or simply the local people who had all heard about the terrible loss that the Cullen family had had to endure. Terry's words were flowing in such a way that I could tell he desperately needed to tell his story and I was aware of how much good this was probably doing him to get it off his chest, which is something he had very likely not done too well since his return from Belfast. I wished in a way that our intended destination was a little further away so that he could keep going and considered whether he would notice if I stretched it out a bit longer by driving round until I felt he had finished. He didn't miss much and would probably suss me out, but I was tempted, nonetheless.

I sat in arrant silence as he painted a picture in such detail of the inside of the church. It was a good job that the A12 was quiet so that I could slow down and just point the car and listen. It might have been better if we were settled at my house with a few beers for accompaniment, but it wasn't for me to choose where and when Terry was going to share these innermost and very personal thoughts. I barely managed much more than a token nod or grunt as he unloaded the details of the service and by the time he had finished I felt as though I had been a witness to the whole day. When Terry finally fell silent I glanced across at him, wondering whether he was OK, and was met by his watery gaze.

'Thanks, guv,' he said.

'I didn't do anything, mate.'

'Yeah, you did. You kept quiet,' he said with a broad smile.

Chapter Seventy-Five

It was with a little trepidation as to whether this venture was going to be worth our while that I knocked on the front door at the address that Terry's homework had led us to. I hoped that Mr and Mrs Fisher would still be living here.

'Who is it?' said a cautious voice.

'My name is Dave Calloway, I'm a police officer. Would it be possible to speak with you for a moment?'

'I need to see some identification. Hold it up to the glass,' requested the voice.

'This is my warrant card. I'm Detective Inspector Calloway from Chelmsford and this one belongs to Detective Sergeant Brush. Could you, perhaps, open the door?' I said, holding Terry's card up to the glass next to mine.

'Hold on.'

I could hear the door being unlocked and hoped we would at least be allowed in for a chat. When the door opened slowly there was evidence of more caution. The lady peeped her head around the door, which only opened as far as the door chain would allow. She looked us both up and down before taking the chain off and opening the door wide.

'What's happened?' she said, with a worried look on her face.

'Nothing that we know of. We would just like a word. We are hoping to talk to Mr and Mrs Fisher, would you be Mrs …'

'Yeah, why? What's wrong?'

'Nothing's wrong. We just would like to have a quick chat, if that's OK? Could we come in, maybe, if you don't mind?'

Mrs Fisher stepped aside without a word and we entered the hallway. She invited us to follow her into the living room and offered us somewhere to sit. Before I could begin to explain our intrusion, she stepped back out to the foot of the stairs and cocked her head slightly and listened for a second or two, before coming back in and sitting down opposite us.

'Can you keep your voices down? My daughter is asleep upstairs,' she asked.

'Of course,' I said, abiding by her request.

She sat without speaking and was clearly not entirely comfortable that we had shown up at her front door, but I suppose it could be a bit disconcerting when two police officers turn up out of the blue as we had.

'As I said, there isn't anything to worry about. We have been investigating a particular case and it just might be that in doing so we have discovered some information about an event nearly twenty years ago that involved your daughter. Kim, isn't it?'

'Yeah, that's right,' she confirmed.

She sat with her eyes wide open and almost in anticipation that something terrible was about to happen or be said. I assured her again that we were only here because of a coincidence but she was still quite nervous of our presence, so I thought it best to get to the point.

'Mrs Fisher, is there anything you or Kim could tell us about the incident at the jeweller's all those years ago?'

'Oh goodness, well, I wasn't there and I never talk about it with Kim, so I don't think so, no,' she said.

'Maybe Kim could …' I began.

'No. You can't,' she said, abruptly, shaking her head.

I gave a sideways glance at Terry and asked her why.

''Cos we don't talk about it. Not ever. I won't,' she explained.

'What if I came back another time when Kim was awake and …'

'No, you can't. Look, Kim isn't very well some of the time and it would only make her worse.'

'In what way, Mrs Fisher?' I said, trying to use as much tact as I could muster to deflate her anxiety.

'Well, when it happened Kim was hurt, badly hurt. She spent a lot of time in hospital and it hasn't been easy, Inspector. She's had a lot of difficult times and she's gone through so much since then. Not just the injury either. She's got a lot better than she used to be but it's something that isn't spoken about. It's not gonna happen, I won't allow it. I don't care what ya say. I refuse.'

Terry and I were slightly taken aback by the stance that she had taken over this incident, although if it really did cause her daughter so much stress then it was understandable, I suppose. I began to feel as though there may not be very much to gain other than, perhaps, that we could be assured that the incident that involved Kim all those years ago was the same one that Bernie and Oscar had been a part of. Remembering to keep my voice lowered I continued to press for any glimmer of information that may possibly be of use.

'Would you mind telling me what you know of the incident, as far as you can remember?'

'It was a robbery. That's all I know. My baby got hurt and the nightmare began ... and just kept getting worse for a long time. Whoever did it got away with some diamonds and never got caught. That's it.'

Terry jotted away at his notepad and once he had caught up he looked up at me with an expression that appeared to be questioning whether there was really much need for us to stay any longer. I tended to agree but just wanted to see what reaction I got from her next.

'I believe we may know who was responsible for the robbery and for causing Kim's injuries,' I said quietly, and left that comment hanging in the air for a moment or two.

'D'ya know who did it?' she blurted out.

'Maybe. We have still got to do a bit more digging but it's possible.'

'Bloody hell,' she said raising her hand over her mouth.

'Is your husband going to be home any time soon? I'd like to talk to him too,' I said, having noticed a photograph that had been framed and was sitting on a wall unit on one side of the room behind where she sat.

Her face changed from one of surprise to one of sorrow very swiftly. She turned in her chair to look at the photo that she realised I had spotted, and looked back at me, simply shaking her head without speaking. I wondered whether they had divorced at some point, without questioning whether a photo would still be on display. Before I could think of how to broach the subject she spoke.

'No, he ... was killed. Hit-and-run. It was about five years ago now. No-one was caught for that either.'

Now I knew what she meant earlier when she had referred to Kim as having gone through more than just the injury and the consequences of that. I immediately felt sympathetic towards her. She really had hit on hard times. First, having had her daughter sustain these injuries, and then to lose her husband so abruptly.

'What was your husband's name?' I asked.

'It was Brian … and I'm Debbie, by the way.'

'I'm sorry to hear about that, it can't have been easy, especially with Kim to look after.'

'No, it wasn't; still isn't really. The neighbours have been good to me and my brother has been a rock, so I get by one way or another.'

'Is your brother near?'

'Not really, he lives in London, but he keeps a check on me and Kim. She's his special girl, y'know?'

I nodded and smiled, unable to grasp the full extent of that level of family trauma.

'Good job he's around for you then,' I said.

'Yeah, he looks like Brian too. Makes me jump sometimes,' she said with a smile as she held the photo in her lap, cherishing it.

At that point Kim could be heard calling softly to her mum from upstairs and instinctively Debbie jumped up and called back to her, dropping the photo in its frame as she did so. I reached down to pass it back to her but she was already halfway out of the living room and heading for the foot of the stairs, calling once again to Kim for her to stay where she was and wait for her to come up, explaining that she wouldn't be a moment. I placed the photo back in its rightful place and made sure it sat straight.

His face smiled back at me.

He held my gaze for a few seconds before I turned towards the hallway and offered our apologies for turning up without warning, promising to keep her informed of any developments that might be of interest.

'Mummy …' called Kim.

'We'll show ourselves out, be sure to lock up, won't you?' I said.

'Now you sound like my brother, he's always worrying after me,' she said with a little chuckle.

* * *

With Kim settled downstairs wrapping herself around a mug of hot tea and engrossed in whatever the TV had to offer prior to the lunchtime news, Debbie perched herself upon a stool out in the kitchen, clutching her mobile phone. She spoke as soon as he answered.

'I've had a visit from two coppers.'

'You what? What did they want?' he said.

'They wanted to talk about when Kim was attacked at the shop.'

'Really. What did yer say?'

'I said I didn't talk about it to Kim. I don't know anything anyway, really. They said they might know who did it and who the robbers were.'

'You sure?' he said.

'' Course I'm sure, they've only just gone. And they wanted to talk to Brian so I had to explain, y'know?'

'Did they say who these robbers were?'

'No, they're still working it out or something. Kim was upstairs so she don't know they was 'ere. I ain't telling her, 'course.'

'What were their names, Deb? Did they say?'

'Yeah, one was Brush or something and the other one was Galloway, I think. Something like that. I didn't really take any notice. Why? D'you know 'em?'

'No ... If they come back you tell me, right? And don't go talking about me either. It's none of their bloody business,' he urged.

'No, I didn't. I didn't mention you, honest,' she said, biting her lip.

Traitor's Gate

The fog that had drifted lazily in overnight from the east end of the river had already obscured the view of London Bridge from where he sat on the embankment, not far from St Thomas's Tower and Traitor's Gate. Whilst he waited, he looked blankly out onto the old river and pulled the collar on his overcoat up around his neck, resisting a shiver in an effort to stop the cold, misty air seeping in where it wasn't wanted. A thin ownerless dog scampered by with its nose down to the ground, stopping only to inspect a bin for anything palatable. It turned its attention to a discarded drink can that had spewed its contents out onto the well-trodden path. A quick sniff and the dog's interest waned as it found a paper bag down by the embankment wall to investigate, before scurrying off out of sight around the side of the castle. He checked his watch and knew he would have to wait a little longer before Derek Bladen showed. He had got up and out early this morning and cursed Bladen's choice of venue, but couldn't deny it would be quiet. It was alright for him as he didn't live far away but for Stan Elms it had meant a drive from Plaistow to the Tower, but he decided not to make a big issue of it.

Elms' long grey coat and charcoal-black trousers were topped off at both ends by a pair of black shiny brogues and a mop of black shiny hair that looked more like he had tipped a tub of tar on his head and styled it, swiftly, before it had set. His tall, upright stature carried it all off nicely. As he sat huddled on the bench he gazed across towards the south bank and watched a barge gently making its way out of town and under Tower Bridge. No need for the bascules to tire themselves and make any extra headroom for the little slender barge. The bridge looked ever more impressive, encompassed by the drifting fog. He studied the bridge, in awe of its majesty, and recalled how it had worn a more lacklustre appearance before the repaint for the Queen's jubilee in '77, and tried to picture the scenes of the old bridge laden with horses and carts that used to trundle across in an era way before he was born.

Footsteps interrupted his daydream and turning, he saw Bladen approaching from around the Tower. Elms rose to meet him and simply nodded in the direction of Tower Bridge, suggesting that they should walk.

'Alright?' *said Bladen.*

'Cold, thanks to you, actually.'

'I told you half past nine, didn't I?'

'Yeah well, you should know I'd be early. I'm always early,' *offered Elms with a grunt, as he drew his collar up once more and moaned that he'd have put a thicker jumper on if he'd known it was going to be so chilly.*

The pair walked along towards the bridge as Bladen wrestled two warm pasties out of his pocket, offering one to Elms.

'What's this, a peace offering?' *said Elms ungratefully.*

'No need to be so grumpy. Get it down yer. Anyway, you're the one who's moaning about being cold.'

Stan Elms allowed the pasty to warm his chilly hands for no more than a few seconds before jamming the first bite in and wincing as the heat from it burned the top of his mouth.

'Blimey, that's hot,' *he said.*

'Serves yer right. You should learn to take yer time. You might know it'd be hot. Full of good stuff, these are; expensive mind, but nice. Anyway, I ain't dragged yer down 'ere to talk about pasties.'

As Elms continued to battle with the pasty they made their way towards St Katherine's dock, which gave Bladen the time he needed to run the plan through his head once more before going over the finer details with Elms; details that he had rehearsed in his mind several times. He didn't have any doubts about Stan Elms' ability to follow the plan, simple though it was, but the others would have to be coaxed along and Bladen knew that Elms was the man that they would follow without question. They stopped before they entered the docks then turned back towards the river and wandered down as far as they could, before resting against the embankment walls. Elms was busy demolishing his pasty which gave Bladen the chance to speak between bites.

'Look, I know you're sick of hearing it, but this'll be the last time we go over it, OK?'

'Fine,' *said Elms casually, as he turned to rest one elbow on the wall and screwed up the bag the pasty had come in, stuffing it into the pocket of his coat. Derek Bladen hesitated, half turning his head as a man on a bicycle rode by, and having watched him go, he wiped his mouth with the back of his hand and spoke.*

'*I don't want any mistakes, right? You keep an eye on the other two and make sure they don't lose their bottle. We can't afford for this to go wrong, it don't bear thinking about,*' he said.

'*I'll sort the other two out. They won't go against me. Is that van still ours, by the way?*' said Elms.

'*Yeah, that's all taken care of.*'

'*And the driver, you sure he's up for it?*'

'*Yeah, he'll be there, don't worry. Have you got the tools ready?*'

'*All in the bag. I'll put them in the back of the van on the night and we can dish 'em out. I'll be bringing something of my own too,*' said Elms.

Bladen looked up at Elms with some uncertainty at the thought of what he might have in mind, but he decided to leave it at that.

'*Also, I've had a thought about how we can make sure that they don't have a clue who we are.*'

Elms reached into his coat and brought out an example of one of the devices he had got for them all to use.

'*This little darling is a voice changer,*' he said, putting it on the wall in front of Bladen.

Bladen looked at it and picked it up with a quizzical frown.

'*What'd ya do with it?*' he said.

'*It's easy. See this box? Just make sure it's fixed onto the inside of the boiler suit that you'll be wearing and then have the little wire come up into your mask. There's another clip here that will secure this bit on the inside of your mask. Make sure it's near your mouth and then it'll do the rest.*'

Derek Bladen's expression told Stan Elms that he liked the idea as he switched it on and spoke into the tiny microphone. The voice he heard was certainly nothing like his own. Just the job, he thought, as he nodded his approval and grinned with anticipation at Elms.

'*Terrific. That's just right. Nice one,*' Bladen enthused.

Stan Elms looked out across the river to the south side and spotted a young woman jogging along the embankment; her hair was blonde and flapped around behind her like the tail of a comet. She seemed to glide effortlessly along without a care for the chilled morning air.

'*Oi, you wanna pay more attention to what we're doing. Never mind watching the girls go by. I don't wanna be standing 'ere shivering all day. Stick this back in yer coat and bring 'em all along on the night. Speaking of which, let's go from the start and then we can clear off,*' said Bladen.

'*Right, yeah, OK,*' responded Elms, who had had enough already.

'Right, listen ... we'll meet round the back of the garages near my place at 10.30. The suits will be in the holdall that I'll bring with me and the tools will be in the bag that you're gonna bring. We'll get changed in the back of the van and fit the voice changers into the suits. We need to be around the corner from the pub at about 11.30 and then we'll make sure everyone knows what they're doing and we'll wait. We'll go in when I tell you to. Grainger will stand guard at the front and bang on the door if there's trouble, which we'll deal with at the time. The van will stay opposite so we can get straight out and away when we're ready. The rest of us go down the alley to the side door, which will have been left unlocked from earlier when Garron went home or wherever he's gone. From there, we go in tooled up and get stuck into 'em. See how that goes but either way we come away with the goods. Anything else?'

'It all sounds OK apart from the bit that we don't control,' said Elms.

'What d'ya mean?'

'We don't know how they're gonna react when three blokes wearing masks and carrying weapons suddenly storm in to spoil the party. Especially as they're expecting some ponce with a briefcase full of money for them to take away and count. Surprise, surprise, he don't exist, thanks to a beautiful piece of work on the telephone by our chosen driver for the night.'

'They'll turn as white as ghosts and shit 'emselves, with any luck. But remember, we have to make sure we hit 'em hard and fast so they don't have time to think about what's going on,' said Bladen.

'I think you'll find you can rely on me for that bit. If we're doing this then we're doing it properly. Those pair of shits have had it coming for years. I ain't messing about, I warn yer now, and you better be right behind me. Those bastards are 'aving it, you can be sure of that. I've been looking forward to getting stuck into that pair one day, and that day is approaching fast,' said Elms.

Bladen knew Stan Elms was right, that they deserved everything they had coming, but what bothered him was not knowing how far Stan Elms would go, especially when he was wound up and let loose. This was risky for a number of reasons but Bladen still thought that the main risk was Grainger. He had his doubts about Brookes too but knew that they were both fully aware of what the consequences would be if either of them let the side down now. He turned around and looked up towards the Tower, its flags coated in the moisture that was still blowing in along the river, and decided that they had hung around for long enough. The fog seemed in no particular hurry to lift and he had said what he came here to say.

Stan Elms was already walking slowly back towards the Tower.

Chapter Seventy-Six

The house was pretty much as I had remembered it apart from the four or five extra people present. Even with them here, there was hardly a sound save for the routine interruptions of some dull mumbling amongst the occupants of the hallway. Terry was out there talking to two rapid-response paramedics who were making phone calls and doing all they could to get Joyce Bladen out of here and into hospital. Her condition wasn't terribly serious or immediately life-threatening but she was desperately in need of proper care. She had been left completely unattended to by her husband, Derek, for a number of hours following the last visit from the evening community care worker. The odour that hit the nostrils of the returning district nurse on Monday morning, who had been let in by the lady next door, wasn't unfamiliar to her; not in her line of work. What it did was ring loud alarm bells with her. She was adroit enough to ensure that Mrs Ling, the kind neighbour, didn't enter any further than the front door and insisted that she would look after everything from here on in.

When Terry and I had arrived, fifteen minutes earlier, she was sitting outside on a chair that Mrs Ling had provided for her. The police officer that had beaten us all to it had begun taking notes regarding what she had done and what she had seen whilst he waited for the ambulance to get there, at which point he would hand over everything he knew so far about the incident to them. After a very brief chat with her, just enough to give us the gist of what we might expect to find inside, we had ventured in.

From the front door, all I saw was a door left ajar in front of me. I knew from my previous visit that it led through and into the rear room where I had chatted with Derek Bladen. Terry closed the front door in order to prevent prying eyes looking in. As I toed the door gently open I already knew I was going to witness yet another murder but the scene that presented itself to me looked a lot more like something from a horror movie.

The body of Derek Bladen had clearly, at least to some extent, been tortured.

Whilst Terry was trying to sort out the dilemma concerning Mrs Bladen, I stood alone, a few feet away from the man that I had chatted with when I broke the sad news about Rose Hill. He was sitting, slumped in his chair that faced the TV, with his head lying as far back as it could possibly go. The plastic tubing that fed the oxygen from the cylinder to the mask had been tied very tightly around his neck.

He had cuts too; to his face and arms and another couple to his torso. Deep and deliberate.

They had run with blood at some point, soaking his shirt and trousers; as had the wounds to his face and head. In his mouth I could see something like a rag or handkerchief, no doubt to muffle any cries of pain. My eyes were dragging in every bit of the sordid picture before me. His hands looked as though they were broken, judging by the huge amount of swelling. Something wasn't right about his nose. A hideous puddle of clotted blood sat balanced on his top lip. I looked closer and could see that the small piece that divides the nostrils had been sliced open. My human biology days reminded me that it was called the columella.

Heaven knows where I dragged that from.

I kept on looking for whatever else may have been done to him.

And I kept on finding more.

The question that initially bothered me was why there was a need for the murder to be so cruel and callous. What was it that Derek Bladen had done to deserve this degree of gratuitous violence? Oscar must have hated him the most of all. Maybe Bladen was the one who orchestrated the whole thing. Maybe he set up the killing of Bernie and Oscar, albeit Oscar somehow escaped his fate. Or was there more to it? As I pondered this, standing next to the gruesome sight in front of me, the living-room door opened slowly and a familiar face popped around the door.

'It's only me,' announced Morrison Frost, the pathologist. He was suited in his white coverall.

'Good morning, Doctor.'

'I wondered whether I might meet you again. Oh golly, what on earth has been going on here?' he said as he carefully swapped places with me and stooped to take a closer look, 'Hmmm … that's nasty.'

I watched silently as Doctor Frost went about his business and mumbled constantly to himself, as if he was talking to me, but I was sure that he wasn't. Terry popped his head around the door to let me know that Mrs Bladen was going to be taken out of the house by the ambulance crew at any minute. He glanced up at the pitiful sight of Derek Bladen, grimaced a little, and said that he would make sure the door was kept firmly closed until she had gone. I confirmed what a very good idea that would be.

I turned my attention back to the busy pathologist as he peered and prodded and went about his routine inspection, still mumbling contentedly to himself. He was paying attention to Bladen's hands and fingers and periodically he would nod his head and mumble something else to himself. Then he began to study the knife wounds on Bladen's arms and body, measuring them with a small ruler, and started nodding again. He let out a loud sigh and half-turned towards me.

'His hands have been broken by something pretty solid, similar to a hammer, I'd say, and these cuts have been made by a knife with a serrated edge. Actually, they remind me of that girl. What was her name? Hill? No connection, I suppose, Inspector?'

I looked back at Dr Frost and gave a non-committal smile as the jigsaw pieces thudded into place in my head.

'I reckon he's been like this for something in the region of ten to twelve hours and not much more,' he continued. 'Of course, I am only basing this on my external examination. I shall know more when I see him again, you understand? It's just a best guess for now, Inspector. Who found him?'

'The district nurse did, this morning,' I said.

'Well, that'll be what we call the legal time of death. I assume you have a time recorded? It'll have to go on the death certificate, you see?' he said.

'Yes, we do.'

'Good. I'll do my best to give you a more accurate time in due course. For now, as I said, it appears that he died around twelve hours ago.'

'How do you tell?' I asked.

'There are various ways and a lot more things for me to learn about him yet, Inspector, but I tend to rely initially on the jaw and thigh method. You see, as you know, rigor mortis will gradually take place once someone has died and by gently moving the jaw from side to side and pushing a finger into the thigh, it will help me get a basic idea of the timeframe. You see, if the jaw is stiff and the thigh is not then we can fairly reliably say that he is in the first twelve hours of rigor, but if the jaw is stiff and the thigh is hard then we are probably looking at the second twelve-hour timeframe. But that is all very well for now; like I said, when I see him again shortly I can establish a lot more for you. For now, I think we can safely say he is dead. I'll make some arrangements to get him removed.'

'So, the jaw is stiff then?' I asked.

'Yes, look.'

Morrison Frost held the tip of Derek's jaw and tried to move it from side to side in order to prove his point for me but as he did so the rag that had been stuffed into Derek's mouth fell out onto his chest and rolled down into his lap.

'Aghhh ... Ghastly thing,' he said as he moved a foot back so as to avoid any possible contact with the blood-soaked rag.

I tried to avert my eyes from the rag but for some reason they seemed intent on studying it. No matter how much I genuinely didn't want to look at it my eyes disobeyed my brain. It was suddenly clear to me that Morrison Frost seemed to be studying something else.

'Now what is that?' he asked himself out loud, once again.

I couldn't see what he was looking at properly but all of a sudden, I wanted to know. Doctor Frost grabbed a pair of tweezers from his bag and began to slowly and very deliberately prise something from Derek's mouth.

'Hmmm ... what do you make of that, Inspector?' he said as he turned towards me with something held by the tweezers.

Something I recognised immediately. I could see it was patterned on one side with a blueish outline. I knew what it was.

'Good Lord. The ace of bloody diamonds,' said a frowning pathologist, looking up at me with a confused and quizzical expression.

Chapter Seventy-Seven

The manhunt for Oscar was now in full flow. I had sent an email out to DI Trevor Eaden and he assured me that he would take charge of the situation from his end. Every available resource would be put to good use and although London is a huge place, Oscar would have to be extremely careful and, as time went on, extremely lucky to evade capture. What didn't help was that Corrigan wanted to know how I had let him get to Bladen. I tried to explain that whilst Bladen was one of the four men we thought might have had something to do with the events at The Fallen Oak all those years ago, we still had no proof of it. No-one had ever come forward. There was nothing out of the ordinary from the crime scene at the pub to help us at all either. Even Garron didn't convince me completely. He just painted a picture that seemed to fit. I always felt more circumspect than confident where he was concerned. All I knew was that Oscar was back and causing chaos. The only slim consolation I could think of was that there didn't seem to be any need to expect any more revenge killings. Oscar had completed his rout, as far as I could see.

Half the force in London, to coin a phrase, were on the lookout for Oscar, and although he may have once used the East End as his main stomping ground, he could be anywhere now. He was like the invisible man. The ports and airports were on alert too. At least if I could keep him in the country we might have a chance, but with a pretty hopeless ID for him and very little to go on, it wasn't necessarily going to be straightforward. The SOCO team that had been working at the house of Derek Bladen didn't have an awful lot to be excited about initially either.

No forced entry.

No prints.

Nothing yet.

The front door was closed when the district nurse arrived and was undamaged. Not a single rogue fingerprint was discovered anywhere. Oscar would surely have had blood on his clothing and in his car, exactly as for Rose Hill's murder. Maybe he surprised Bladen. Bladen was old and not in the best of health and therefore would be easy enough to push out of the way and manhandle into the back room. The images of Derek Bladen pushed their way into my mind again. The last moments of his life must have been abhorrent.

The word had spread to all the police stations in the Essex force, just in case he had stayed local, but I doubted it. He would have probably scooted back to hide amongst the throng of London and sought sanctuary, once more, in the depths of the East End. The M11 CCTV was also likely to offer nothing we didn't already know. In all honesty he could've gone in any direction but the East End was my bet. Guesses were still all I had and I reflected on the time that I turned up at St Dominic's Church, where poor Martin Brookes was found in a puddle of blood by Doreen Calderwood, partly because I had seized the opportunity to reunite with Bob Hand. Who would have thought that Bob would end up as he has? The more I thought about that the more I was haunted by the unanswered questions that I wished to pose to him. By the time I could talk to him it would probably all be over. I felt guilty again that I had not been to see Bob for a little while and made a note on my phone to get to see him soon, which by happy coincidence might just mean I could spend a bit more time chatting to Sarah Goodman. We would see, I guess.

Chapter Seventy-Eight

I had to admit that apart from one or two differences of opinion, I had actually developed a liking for Oscar. I watched him skulking through the borders, head low and with eyes that darted to and fro at every movement that any unsuspecting bird made as it flitted across the garden just out of his reach and into the safety of a neighbouring tree. I wondered who actually owned him. I had never given it a thought before. I couldn't imagine him playing the part of the cosy lap cat, but maybe he did. Perhaps he was some old lady's best friend and the terror of the gardens all at the same time. I averted my gaze from the events being carried out in the garden and looked down again at the travel page in the weekend supplement and allowed my mind to drift and take me to sunnier places on a city break. Lisbon, Rome and Barcelona were displaying an array of colour and warmth and I could almost smell the flowers as I became enveloped by the beautiful, picturesque scenes in print before me. As ever, any reference to Portugal reminded me of happier times when Ana lived with me. My stomach knotted slightly although the emotional discomfort had subsided a great deal over time and I was able to reflect on those days with a slightly wistful smile instead of a tear or two.

I had one hand holding my mug of tea and gently and dreamily raised it to my lips. Suddenly and in complete synchronicity, my peace was shattered by the combination of a horrendous clatter at the back door and an awful din that emanated from my mobile phone. The pile of logs that I had chopped into smaller pieces a few days ago had been knocked over and had fallen against the back door, hitting a steel coal bucket as they careered down the back steps and rolled onto the grass. A number of panicked birds reached for the skies and a certain cat could just be seen almost flying over the fence as he bolted to safety in a fit of panic. Tea dripped all over the magazine and onto the kitchen table as I leapt off my stool, spilling most of it over my hand. Cursing loudly and not knowing which dilemma to deal with first, I instinctively grabbed at my phone with my dry hand and fumbled to answer it and cease the infernal noise. Using the less-favoured hand to do the simplest of tasks is always a challenge, but I just about managed it without dropping the thing.

'DI Calloway,' I answered.

'Guv, it's Terry. Sorry to disturb you on a Sunday but something just came up.'

'How come you're at work today? I thought you were going out somewhere, weren't you?'

'I was, but it all got cancelled ... anyway listen.'

'Hold on. Is it you who's been messing about with my ring tone again? The bloody thing nearly gave me a heart attack ... and I've spilt my tea all over the bloody Sunday supplement. I'll find out, so you may as well tell me now,' I ranted.

'It ain't me, guv, I swear,' he pleaded, trying his best to get a word in. 'Guv, I think we might have something.'

My attention was abruptly steered back on track as I sat on the stool again, trying to avoid the tea stains that had run off and trickled onto the floor around my feet.

'What do you mean, mate?' I asked in a much quieter tone.

'We've had a report of a car that's been found and it fits the description of the one from the Rose Hill murder. Don't know for sure but it could be. You might wanna come and have a look at it,' he said in his adrenaline-fuelled way.

'Can't you just get it brought in so the forensics team can go to work on it? There'll be Rose Hill's blood for a start if it is that car,' I said.

'Guv, there's something else.'

'What else?'

'It's got a body in it.'

I surprised myself at the speed with which I was out of the door and into my car. Terry blurted the directions for me to find the address and promised to meet me there. Apparently, it was going to be another chance to meet Morrison Frost, the pathologist, who was also on his way. The local bobbies had secured the scene and by the sound of the location, it was unlikely that too many people were going to inadvertently stroll by anyway. I was heading towards a single garage that was situated behind some old disused factory units. My understanding was that it had only been discovered because someone's Yorkshire terrier had squeezed its way under the up-and-over door, which had been bent at one corner, allowing the inquisitive canine to go sniffing around in hot pursuit of a rat. When the dog refused to come out, its owner managed to force the door open and found more than just his nosy dog and the accompanying rat.

The sight of a police car parked at the entrance to the industrial estate confirmed for me that I had found the right location. One of the huge gates was closed but the other was hanging by just the lower hinge and leaning precariously over. Nature's wilderness had taken over and sprouted young saplings in various locations. Tufts of grass had pushed their way through the cracks in the concrete slabs and a number of items had been dumped on the site over the years. Lying beside the gated entrance was a sign that read 'Martin & Sons'. Spray paint specialists, according to the faded writing on the sign. Once I was close enough to see the single garage, I spotted Morrison Frost dressed in his white coverall as he stepped out from the garage and back in again, busying himself and probably mumbling contentedly in his usual fashion.

Terry would be another fifteen to twenty minutes before he arrived and I could only imagine how much he would like to have been here first. I stopped, got out and ducked under a piece of traffic tape that had been primitively tied across between two spindly trees. One of the constables nodded and I continued towards the open garage. Looking in, I could immediately see a car. It was dark in colour and may have been the one we had all but given up on finding. The number plate at the rear was missing and one of the rear tyres was completely flat. Doctor Frost was leaning into the rear passenger compartment about fifteen feet away but I couldn't see what he was doing. I didn't enter as I had already been told that he didn't want anyone else in there. I saw him lift his head and noticed that he was wearing some kind of respiratory mask with a canister attached to it. A bright searchlight was turned slightly towards me and prevented me from being able to look in that direction for too long. I decided just to wait for him to emerge. Apart from a few constables and a sergeant who were standing behind me, there was no-one else around. Although I half-expected Corrigan to be here or on his way.

Nothing to do until Doctor Frost had finished his initial exploration. As I shielded my eyes and peered into the garage once more, he raised a hand and gestured to me. I took it to mean he was on his way out and sure enough, he began to amble out towards me.

'Don't come too close, I'm contaminated,' he said dramatically.

I didn't need to be told twice. He began to tell me what he had found out so far from our cadaver.

'He is a male. I should say he was in his fifties, at first guess. Cause of death is most likely due to his throat being slit and he has a number of other wounds too. I'll find out for sure though, you can depend on that, Inspector,' he said predictably.

'Is there any ID on him?' I asked.

'Nothing that's jumping out at me, no. Mind you, that's about the only thing that's not jumping out,' he said.

'What do you mean, jumping out?'

'He's alive, Inspector. Not with human life but with other kinds. Insects, I mean. His body has begun to putrefy and insects like to lay their eggs in dark secluded spots, and they've found plenty to choose from on him. His abdomen is quite swollen and he's showing a number of heavily blistered areas; can't see everything, of course. Not yet, Inspector.'

Rather him than me, I thought, as I listened intently.

'What about the inside of the car? I'm also interested in whether there are any signs of blood, possibly in the front passenger seat.'

'Way ahead of you, Inspector. I discovered several areas of bloodstain, most notably between the front seats; it's all over the place really. What I'm confused about is why there is so much of it in the front when matey boy was almost certainly left to bleed out in the rear of the car,' he said.

'Could it be old blood?' I asked, hopefully.

'It could be but I won't be able to determine that accurately for you here. There are ways and means though. You see, blood has proteins and the time-related degradation of blood proteins reflects the age of the bloodstain, so with any luck we can pinpoint how old it is.'

'That would be helpful, Doctor, thanks. How long has he been dead?'

'About ten days, I'd say, going by what I could see in there. His feet are bound together by what resembles nylon string and one of his arms is broken, going by the extent of the deformity. Oh, and another thing, Inspector, the knife was serrated; ring any bells?' he said as he wandered back into the garage.

I'd left my mobile in the car, so I began to make my way back across to it in order to ring Terry and see where he had got to, but just as I got to the car I heard Doctor Frost calling me again. Looking over to where the sound had come from I saw him beckoning me across to him. I left my phone where it was and went to speak to him again. I got to the garage and could see him waving me to come further in. Going by what he had said about his discovery I reluctantly stepped towards the car. For the first time I could see the man and I knew what the doctor meant by putrefaction. The smell was not at all pleasant and the last thing I wanted to do was stay in there any longer than I needed to.

'Just quickly, look at this, and don't touch anything, not him, nor the car,' said Morrison Frost as he held the man's arm aloft, pointing at his hand.

'What is it?' I asked with my hand cupping my mouth and nose as much as possible, doing my utmost not to focus on the hordes of flies or inhale any more than was absolutely necessary.

'It's a nail that appears to have been driven into the back of his hand, holding a postcard in place. It was behind his back so I hadn't seen it until now. It says "Welcome to Bratislava". What do you make of that?'

All I wanted to do was get out of the garage and away from the dreadful odour of death. I retreated with the doctor's words rattling around in my head. I took a few breaths of fresh air before I consciously began to collate this information. As I considered each piece I could feel something building inside me and this time it wasn't vomit. It was a sense of understanding for the first time in months. I broke into a trot as I approached my car, not really knowing what to do first. As I stood by the Mondeo I saw Terry's car driving towards me from the gated entrance. I ran over to his car and before he could get out I found myself trying to unload a host of thoughts all at once.

'It's Oscar. I'm sure of it. Bratislava … Eastern bloc. The stab wound in his hand,' I garbled.

'Whose hand? What are you on about?' said Terry.

'In Garron's hand, the stab wound,' I said.

'Guv, slow down.'

I held my spinning head and tried to organise all the thoughts that had arrived out of the blue and all at once. Terry had got out of his car and was looking at me with a very concerned expression.

'I'm alright. Now listen. It's making sense now, I think,' I said with no real conviction whatsoever.

'Guv, slow down and tell me what's going on.'

'I think Oscar is in that car. He's been dead for about ten days so he couldn't have killed Bladen. The doctor has said that his throat has been slit with what looks like a serrated knife, the same style that tortured Bladen and similar and possibly the same as the one that killed Rose Hill. He's got a postcard stabbed into the back of his hand just like the wound that Garron has on his hand. He must have returned the favour. Oscar gave him that injury when he was covered in battle scars the first time me and Bob saw him. Oscar didn't kill Bladen ... oh my God, what if he didn't kill any of them? Not Bladen and not Rose, if it is the same knife. The car seems to have a lot of bloodstain in it, according to Doctor Frost, so what if some of that belongs to Rose Hill but Oscar didn't do it?'

'Then maybe Garron did ... but why, guv?' said Terry.

'He knew all the others right from the start and he was directly involved in Bernie getting murdered, or indirectly at least. He set it up, they did the job ...'

'... and then they hung him out to dry and didn't share the diamonds ... and he's held the grudge ever since? Really?' offered Terry.

'Could be, Terry, but we're still missing something. Can it just be about the diamonds and a grudge that he's held for twenty years? Oscar didn't kill Bladen and let's say he didn't kill Rose. If that's so then it completely breaks the chain. It's all right in front of us and we can't see it.'

I leant forward onto the roof of Terry's car and closed my eyes, trying to get things reorganised into a sensible timeline.

'Guv, you remember when we were back at the station and we started chasing "Bernie's ghost", as you called it? Well, why don't we try that again?' said Terry.

Terry had a good point and we weren't getting any further right now, so we sat in his car and methodically worked it all through from the start again.

'OK, I'll start,' I said. 'Twenty years ago, Bernie and Oscar did the job in the jeweller's at Hornchurch and came away with some diamonds.'

'Then, through whatever means, Bladen, Brookes, Grainger and Elms found out about the exchange that was supposed to take place at the pub.'

'But that was a set-up and they didn't just want the diamonds; they wanted to kill Bernie and Oscar too, although Oscar got away,' I said.

'Right, and for whatever reason, Garron never got his share for his part in the deal and when Oscar surfaced after all those years, Garron used him as a scapegoat, painting him as the vengeful brother and systematically taking out his own revenge on the others.'

'But why, Terry? Just for some diamonds twenty years ago? There's gotta be another reason.'

'OK, well what about that girl who got hurt in the shop?' said Terry.

'Kim Fisher? What's the connection?' I asked.

'Dunno, really.'

C'mon, c'mon, c'mon … think …

'But I do,' I said, 'Remember that picture that she dropped on the floor … the Fisher woman, Debbie … the one I picked up. She said her husband resembled her brother … that's it. I knew that face was familiar, but when she said it was her husband I didn't think any more of it. He does look like her brother. He's the spitting image of Garron,' I said, turning to Terry who was already looking straight at me, agog.

'And that makes Kim his niece. His niece was badly hurt by Bernie and Oscar and so he was only too pleased to help give the four of them the chance to rob them, but when they killed one of them that was a bonus as far as Garron was concerned, unless he knew they were gonna kill 'em both,' he said.

'And he did want a share of the goods … to use the money to help Kim with her treatment; maybe from abroad, who knows? Could that work?' I asked.

'But he didn't get anything and the grudge ate away at him as he watched Kim suffer for all those years. What d'you reckon, guv?'

'It's gotta be bloody close, mate,' I said.

'And,' Terry added excitedly, 'if Garron killed Rose Hill, that could've been another way at getting back at Bladen, couldn't it? She was his daughter after all and maybe Garron knew it.'

'Surely killing her was going too far though, Terry?'

'Maybe he didn't intend to but things got out of hand. Doesn't matter now, he's done it.'

'Yeah, looks that way,' I said.

'But, guv? What about Bob?'

'What about him?'

'Well he was hit by a car that was, according to the eyewitness, being driven by a man with a beard,' said Terry.

His words hung in the air like the foul smell of Oscar's decaying corpse. I let them travel around my tired brain for what seemed like an age.

'And it wasn't Oscar, was it? Oh shit. I don't know what Bob does know in that confused mind of his but whatever it is you can bet Garron doesn't want it coming out. That's why he ran him down. But he hasn't finished the job, has he? Bob could still let the cat out of the bag.'

'Right, and he won't be leaving anything to chance; not now it's gone this far. We'd better get over there. He's gonna need protection. I just hope we're not too late. You go, guv. I'll make arrangements for that Debbie Fisher to be picked up and taken into her local nick to see what else she has to say, and I'll get DI Eaden to arrest Garron at the pub, that is unless he's had it away on his toes already,' said Terry.

'Good lad, Terry. Keep me posted ... and call Corrigan for me, would you? He'll be glad that we've got something positive at last.'

On leaving, I caught the eye of Doctor Morrison Frost, staring disapprovingly as my Mondeo spun its wheels on the gritty concrete, creating a cloud of dust that wafted towards him.

The Fatal Flaw

The Fallen Oak darts team was expected to win the semi-final tonight. They had seen off the team from Eltham easily enough at their place and been bragging about it for over a fortnight. The double top that had been required to seal a place in the semi thudded in dead centre and was the trigger for a mini eruption. Several punches were thrown, albeit not many of them found their intended mark. A couple of glasses were broken too but the short-lived turmoil was soon under control. The teams shook hands and briefly pondered a rematch across the water, but it was all talk and probably best avoided. The result was in the bag and was phoned through to the match organiser at the Stag and Talbot. They were already out, beaten by a team of old blokes from the local Salvation Army who had entered the competition at the last minute; nobody liked to disappoint them.

There was a good two hours left before the team from Bethnal Green were expected to put in an appearance, so it was quiet at The Fallen Oak. Just a few of the regulars sitting quietly, chatting and watching the world go by outside. Some of them had become a part of the furniture over the years and had occupied the same seats in the same corner of the bar through thick and thin. The atmosphere should be good tonight and John Garron was looking forward to a full house. The beer sales could always do with a bit of a boost and he knew that the steady drizzle outside wasn't going to prevent the punters turning out for the semi-final of the darts.

The front door opened and in walked Daniel Grainger, shaking an umbrella and getting some abusive language for his troubles as the spray of droplets showered someone sitting near the door. He apologised and made his way to the bar. He had his darts in his pocket. The flights were new and sported a sparkly motif that he believed brought him luck in the recent matches he had played. He thought that since changing them he had found a run of good form. He'd need to be on form tonight; letting the side down would be unthinkable.

Grainger ordered a pint and sat on a barstool and waited nervously. It wasn't only the thought of the game that was on his mind.

Upstairs, John Garron was lying on a bed and reading the sports pages of the Evening Standard. *West Ham had won away from home last night in an insignificant cup game and he was engrossed in the report. He was smartly dressed in a dark suit and didn't intend to get his hands dirty tonight. He had organised the bar staff so that he had plenty of them to cope with what he expected to be a busy evening. The darts evenings were popular and he wanted the team from Bethnal Green to see that he ran a successful pub business. Their own landlord played in the team and Garron wanted to create a certain impression.*

Shelley could be heard clipping and clopping up the stairs towards where he lay. Garron fancied his chances with her later. She had obliged in the past and he was hopeful. He put the newspaper down beside him on the bed and waited until she appeared in the doorway. Shelley was only 22 years old but she was no slouch when it came to life in the fast lane. She had acquired a lot of wisdom from her torrid upbringing and knew how to handle herself with blokes like Garron.

He was the boss and the boss wanted her.

She had on a black satin pencil skirt, sheer tights and high heels. A red woollen jumper with beads and a bra underneath that left little to the imagination. Her mates had embraced the grunge era but Shelley liked the sexier look, and tonight was no exception. She swaggered provocatively into his room and stood at the end of the bed and slowly licked her lips, which got his full attention.

'Everything ready downstairs, is it?' asked Garron.

'Of course, would I ever let you down?' she responded sexily.

Garron liked what he was hearing, or more likely the way it was being said, and patted the bed beside him. Shelley looked at him with a smile and stepped around to one side of the bed. She put one knee onto the bed and leant towards him, grinning with her perfect white smile. Garron raised a hand up to her and pulled her towards him by the arm with a strong, masterful grip. Shelley liked Garron but he was sometimes a little too rough for her liking, and she held her position without lowering herself fully, resisting his advance, for now. Garron sat up and met her mouth with his, still holding her arm tightly, pressing his lips onto hers. Shelley didn't resist for long. She didn't want to turn him down completely and have him bark at her for the rest of the evening in front of all the customers. He did that once before and she regretted it then. The kissing was fine but she knew it wouldn't stop at that. She could feel Garron's hands on her, pulling her skirt up to her bottom and beyond. She was lying on top of him before she knew it. He forced one leg between hers and rolled her over with ease. Then he heard a creak on the floorboards just outside the bedroom door. He looked up over his shoulder and saw Daniel Grainger standing in the doorway with a stupid grin on his face.

'Did I tell you to come up here?' said Garron with anger in his eyes.

'No but I thought ...'

'No, you didn't fucking think, did yer?' bellowed Garron.

Shelley took the opportunity to swing her legs off of the bed and tidy her skirt. She was already halfway out of the room before she heard Garron.

'... and don't think I'm finished with you either,' he said.

Shelley scooted past Grainger, pushing him aside as she went. Her footsteps clattered down the stairs as Garron's attention turned to Grainger.

'I said wait for me downstairs, didn't I?'

'Yeah, but I thought ...'

'Shut it.'

Daniel Grainger was already on edge without all this on top. He stood motionless and waited to be told what to do next. If Garron told him to jump out of the window he would have to consider it.

'Get in here and shut the door,' ordered Garron.

Grainger did as he was told and sat down on a chair that was situated by the bed. Garron propped a pillow up at the head of the bed and lay against it, his face a mix of emotions. Grainger was the one who had instigated the meeting but he didn't feel as though he had any control of it. He had let his tongue slip again and Garron had become a thorn in his side ever since. Grainger hoped that none of the others turned up early.

'Are your shower ready for this?' asked Garron.

'Yeah. We've got everything in place. The boys are ready.'

'You mean Bladen's got everything in place?'

'Yeah,' said Grainger, sheepishly.

'Who's driving for yer?' Garron asked.

'The Joker, I told yer.'

'What's he got to say about it, then?'

'Who? About what?' said Grainger blankly.

'About my share, of course. Bladen ... what have you told him?'

Grainger felt his insides twist and tumble. He already had a nauseous feeling and he needed to be cool, but he wasn't.

'I ...' began Grainger.

Garron gave him a stare and Grainger knew the game was up.

'You haven't told him, have yer?' said Garron.

'I will tonight, after the match. It'll be no problem,' said Grainger.

Garron looked up at the ceiling and let out a sigh. He stood up and walked across to the window that looked out onto the market square. Turning to face Grainger, he cracked his knuckles, which didn't do anything for Grainger's already knotted stomach.

'I don't care whether you tell him or not, actually, but what I do know is that I'm gonna get my share. Is that crystal, Grainger?'

'Of course, Mr Garron,' said Grainger, as he started to show further signs of weakness; fidgeting in his seat and wishing that he had never mentioned the possibility before talking to Bladen.

'You know why I want it, don't yer, Grainger?' said Garron.

Grainger knew but didn't know whether to bring it up. He wished he had never brought it up in the first place a week ago.

'Yeah, but …'

'But nothing, you little wanker. I am gonna get my share or I'll kill the lot of yer. You got that, Grainger?'

Daniel Grainger had 'got it' loud and clear. He shuddered at the thought of telling Derek Bladen what he had let them in for. He tried to recall how it had come about that he had promised Garron a share of the diamonds without first talking to the others. Brookes wasn't much of a problem but Bladen and Elms would kill him themselves. They were so close to it now that they couldn't just pull out, not that Elms and Bladen would ever do that at this stage. When he had spoken to Garron he had let his guard down seriously. What began as a bit of 'brown-nosing' on his part had ended as a deal between them that he had no right to make and absolutely no courage to cancel.

Garron was hard to say no to and once he had got a sniff of the opportunity to take a share he was impossible to shake off. Grainger was suckered in, well and truly. He sat looking at the door and wanted desperately to get out of the room and return downstairs, but he didn't dare move until he was told to. Unfortunately, for Grainger, Garron wasn't quite finished with him. Not just yet.

'You just make sure I get what I want. I'll deal with Bernie and Oscar another day,' he said, turning back towards the window and continuing.

'You know what they did to my Kim, don't yer?' Grainger didn't want to answer.

This is the last thing he wanted Garron to be talking about.

His mood was getting darker and darker by the minute.

Grainger was aware of the silence but didn't know what to say for the best. He decided on saying nothing as Garron turned sharply towards him and strutted across the room. Before Grainger could react, Garron had him by the throat, his fingers pressing painfully into Grainger's windpipe, lifting him out of his seat.

'They nearly killed her, the bastards.' he shouted, 'I never said kill her, did I?' Garron's eyes were filled with evil and Grainger was frightened.

'I'm having my share, Grainger, but it's not for me, you know that, do yer? Kim needs help and I'm gonna make certain she gets it, do you understand?'

Grainger did but could barely speak. He just shook with fear.

'Don't you let me down, Grainger or I'll come for yer … all of yer. Got it, have yer?'

Before Daniel Grainger could summon the right answer to try to defuse Garron's anger, he found himself striking the wall with the back of his head as he fell to the ground with Garron above him, still threatening and cursing, although Daniel Grainger could no longer work out anything Garron said. He shut his eyes and cowered against the wall. He could feel himself shaking. Tears welled in his eyes and he bowed down in anticipation of a punch to the head, or maybe Garron would bring his knee up into his face.

When the bedroom door slammed, shaking the doorframe, Daniel Grainger had wet himself.

Chapter Seventy-Nine

Although my journey to the hospital was brief it allowed plenty of time for me to ponder the scenario that was unravelling in my head. If we were right about this, then Bob might be Garron's final problem. I tried to imagine his pain at seeing his beloved Kim suffering in hospital and then tried to imagine how that had festered in his head for all these years. His sister, Debbie, had also gone through an awful time, caring for her daughter and being torn apart by this dreadful situation. I was just thinking about how her life had changed so dramatically, and all the years of looking after Kim, when the photo of her husband hit me again. He looked remarkably similar to Garron although it was out of context when Terry and I were talking to her. But now it started to throw all sorts of thoughts into my mind.

The resemblance.

The hit-and-run accident.

Or was it an accident?

Could it be that someone tried to get rid of Garron but made a fatal mistake? If that were so, then Garron would have had to witness even more terrible tragedy for his sister and the fact that someone had killed Kim's dad at a time when she and Debbie needed him most.

Christ.

He would have wanted Bernie and Oscar dead for what they had done to Kim but it didn't quite work out the way it was planned ... if it was ever part of the plan ... and then there were the diamonds, or lack of them, for Garron and his anger over being snubbed by Bladen and his pals ... treated like a mug. He must have held it all back and stored it in some dark corner of his mind, and then when Oscar showed up, I guess he couldn't suppress it any longer. That must have brought it all flooding back; Kim's pain, the need for retribution ... not only on Oscar but the others too … and what an opportunity to start his revenge. 'Revenge is a dish best served cold' they say … and this was very cold. With Oscar back on the streets it all naturally pointed to him. Perfect.

The revenge for his brother's murder.

Garron must have wished he could've got his hands on him for all those years. And then he returned … and I bet Garron couldn't believe his luck.

As I pulled the Mondeo into the hospital car park, my thoughts turned back to Bob. It was still a mystery as to what it was that he hadn't told me and now couldn't. I walked through the reception and spotted Doctor Aziz, who was the doctor that I had originally spoken to about Bob's condition when he was first admitted. He spoke first.

'Hello again. Mr Callahan, is it?' he said.

'Calloway, Dave Calloway,' I corrected.

'Ah yes, please accept my apologies, it's been a while since I've seen you here.'

'I've been in and out although not as much as I would have liked to. How are you?' I asked.

'I'm fine, thank you. I'm as busy as ever, of course. Are you going to see Mr Hand now?'

'Yes, just on my way. Have you seen him yourself lately?'

'I'm not working at that end of the hospital so it's been a while since I saw him, but I have heard that he's coming along nicely,' he smiled, and nodded, which I took to mean he wanted to get on with his work and so the niceties were over for now.

I took the hint, leaving him to carry on with whatever it was he was doing, and continued up to see Bob and to speak with someone about my concerns for his safety, given the latest on the Oscar case. As I walked along the corridor towards the ward I could see that the double doors in front of me were closed. A young nurse with iridescent hair was standing by them and chatting to an elderly couple who I suspected were here to collect someone, judging by the bags of clothes that the gentleman was holding. As I approached, the nurse broke her conversation with the couple and took a step towards me, raising one hand up.

'I'm sorry, sir, you'll have to wait for a few moments, we've got a bit of a situation going on. Shouldn't be long though,' she said, smiling in that 'caring nurse' way.

'What sort of situation?' I asked with concern.

'Erm … there's just a bit of cleaning up to do. Won't keep you too long now,' she said hesitantly.

'Some old gal has been sick,' said the elderly gent with a chuckle.

'Oh, glad I missed that,' I replied, smiling to him.

Great, I thought. But at least I hadn't had to be witness to it. I noticed a few seats in the corridor behind me and went to sit for a moment.

'You visiting?' said the elderly gent, making small talk.

'Yes,' I said.

'Don't like hospitals, do you? They give me the willies. When I'm on my last legs they can flush me down the toilet, I'm not coming to one of these places … full of sick people,' he said with a nod and a wink and a croaky chuckle.

I nodded back and smiled politely, not thinking of anything more to add.

To my left I caught a glimpse of a familiar face: Ward Sister Sarah Goodman. She had just come out of one of the side rooms and was straightening some paperwork that she was holding. She looked towards me and smiled. My stupid heart skipped a beat as I rose from my seat and started to wander over to her for a quick chat.

'Hello again,' she said.

'Hello. How are you?' I burbled.

'Fine, thank you. Are you here to see your friend?'

'Yes am I. I shall need to speak to someone in charge too, though,' I added.

'Oooh, sounds interesting,' she said with an inquisitive look.

'You could say that, but I'll go to see Bob first; check on how he's doing.'

'I think you'll see a bit of difference,' she said.

'Really?'

'Yes, he's saying one or two words and has been doing much better in the cognitive skill tests we've been running just lately. Remember not to expect too much from him, won't you? He tires easily.'

'Yes, of course. Thanks,' I said, as I noticed that the doors were now open and began to make my way towards them.

As I wandered behind the elderly, bag-laden man I heard Sarah Goodman call out again.

'Inspector, he might not be in his bed. A moment ago, he was on his way to the toilet,' she said.

'He's walking around?' I asked.

'Yes. Not completely unaided but we've got him up and about a lot more. I think you'll be surprised,' she said with another bright smile.

'Great. Thanks,' I said and continued on.

I sat patiently beside Bob's empty bed and stared around the ward at the comings and goings. The odour of pine disinfectant hung in the air as nurses and porters skilfully guided trolleys and wheelchairs around the signs that read 'DANGER WET FLOOR'. I looked at Bob's chart and decided quite quickly that the squiggles and lines on it didn't really mean very much to me. I checked my mobile phone in case Terry had left me a message, but it was once more devoid of a functional signal.

Did he get Trevor Eaden's team over to The Fallen Oak?

I hope Garron was there.

I expected that he may have had something to tell me but maybe my signal went adrift as soon as I got into the hospital building. Looking back towards the end of the ward, I saw that Sarah Goodman had turned up at the nurse's station with her armful of papers and was counting them into three separate piles. As I watched her, I began to wonder how long Bob was going to be before the nurse brought him back to his bed. It was an untidy mess, which seemed to fit quite well with Bob, generally. With nothing better to do for a few moments, I began to straighten it up a bit. As I pulled the covers up towards the pillow, Sarah Goodman appeared beside me.

'Want a job, do you?' she teased.

'No, I was just ...'

'It's OK. I was just thinking that it was time this lot was made to look like a bed again instead of a jumble of rags. Got it into a right old pickle, hasn't he?'

Sarah undid my efforts by drawing the blankets and sheets back towards the foot of the bed; obviously she had a plan, whereas I didn't. She picked something up off the bed and put it onto the small table that was used for Bob's dinners and drinks. She moved around me to fluff up Bob's pillows and as she did so I reached across the bed and moved a cable that had fallen onto it; one of those that comes out of the wall behind the head of the bed.

'Are you OK?' said Sarah as she looked up at me. 'Inspector?'

I was momentarily frozen in time; somewhere between disbelief and realisation; but lost, stunned and paralysed. From the bedside table I had picked up a playing card that on one side displayed the Joker but also had blue colouring on the rear.

'No ...' was all I could utter ... 'Sarah, call the police ... tell them to get a message to Detective Sergeant Terry Brush. Tell him ... Garron's here ... at the hospital.'

'What?' she said.

'Sarah, just do it ... get them to tell Terry Brush that Garron's here ... quickly ... do it now,' I urged.

Sarah Goodman began to scamper around the bed with a frantic look on her face, almost pale with a sense of some kind of startled shock.

'Sarah, where are the toilets? Did you see who took him?' I shouted.

'His friend took him. Down to the left.'

'Did you get a look at him?' I said as I dodged around trolleys and people, heading for the toilets.

'Just a man with a beard,' she said in all innocence.

'Jesus Christ,' I blurted.

'Don't think it was,' said Sarah as she disappeared behind the nurse's station and towards the nearest telephone.

Her sharp humour bypassed me completely as I tried to think straight and formulate some kind of plan in my head. Then a horrific thought almost stopped me in my tracks.

What if Bob is dead?

Chapter Eighty

Sarah had got through to the police and although I didn't know it, the cavalry were on their way at break-neck speed. Terry received the message via the radio in his car as he headed towards the hospital to talk to me about how his conversation with Corrigan had gone, and to give me the news that Garron was not at The Fallen Oak when Trevor Eaden's men had arrived unannounced and in numbers. He had stopped very briefly to place his blue light onto the roof of his car and recommenced his journey to the hospital at a much faster rate. He had also tried to call me on the hands-free kit but with no luck at all.

I reached the door to the male toilets and stared at it for a moment. My heart was racing and I knew that there was a distinct possibility that I might be too late.

Would I find another dead body or would I come face to face with a knife-wielding John Garron?

I looked around me for something that I could use to protect myself if I needed to. A paramedic walked towards me. I spotted the handle of his torch sticking out of one of the pockets on his cargo pants and asked if I could have it. Those things that the paramedics used were solid and made of strong stuff. After I explained who I was and gave him a précis of the situation I was in, he handed it to me and offered his help. He was a large, sturdy chap of over six feet tall and, in the circumstances, I was in need of all the help I could get. I warned the paramedic that Garron may be armed and placed my hand gently onto the door handle, hoping and praying that it wasn't locked. I put just enough pressure on it to move the handle.

It was locked. He had to be in there.

'I'll do the door. Not much strength to 'em,' whispered my new friend, by which I took him to mean he would barge it open.

I had no choice but to use his help if I was going to be able to save Bob. I really didn't want to endanger this man and knew how foolish my on-the-spot decision was, but he looked as though he was capable of making short work of the door and I was desperate to get it open. I didn't like it and I didn't know where Terry and the back-up were or how long they would be, presuming Sarah had been successful, so I made my decision. I told the paramedic that as soon as he hit the door he had to get himself to one side and let me by, and was not to go inside. It was a rubbish plan but I was out of time. Garron would kill Bob if he hadn't already, and it was now or never.

The paramedic nodded that he understood and stepped a few paces back across to the far side of the corridor. He stood, braced and looked at me with his eyes on stalks, waiting for me to give him the nod. I held the torch tight and paused to let my brain catch up with this impossible situation. The plan was ... there was no plan, other than to get the door open and hope Bob was still alive, and that Garron didn't kill me instead, or as good as ... *Nightmare.*

I glanced down the corridor, hoping to see Terry hurtling towards me with an army of officers kitted out in riot gear, but all I saw was the frightened face of the lovely Sarah Goodman and a host of onlookers.

'Wait,' said my paramedic colossus. 'Have you got any pepper spray?' he asked.

'No.'

'Shit. That could've been handy,' he said.

We braced ourselves again and he prepared to charge the door. I was hoping that this would surprise Garron sufficiently to allow me to get to him. I was about to give the paramedic the nod when Sarah appeared holding her hand out.

'Here,' she said softly.

'What is it?' I whispered.

'Antiseptic spray.'

'Antiseptic spray?'

'Yeah, but he won't know it's not pepper spray if you spray it straight at his face,' she said.

She was right and I had nothing else to use. It could work and buy me enough time to catch him off guard ... enough time to hit him hard with the torch and overpower him. One more look towards the end of the ward told me that Terry was not in sight. Bob's life was on the line and time had now run out. Garron had Bob and I could only hope that I wasn't going to find another traumatic and bloody scene like the one at Derek Bladen's house.

'Ready?' I said to the paramedic.

'Ready,' he said, red-faced and eager.

'Go.'

He hit the door like a train and not only did it open, it all but ripped from its hinges. A loud bang echoed around the corridor and fragments of wood splintered into the room. My paramedic friend fell flat onto the remains of the door with an ungainly thud. I followed, stepping on him and spraying antiseptic into the air before I could really see clearly where Garron was standing. I shouted 'pepper spray' and waved the stuff around causing numerous droplets to fill the air and land onto the two body shapes in front of me. Then I could see Bob to one side and I could also see Garron, who was flinching and trying to protect his eyes. I still couldn't be sure as to whether Bob was alive but right now the priority was Garron. He seemed to have been caught by surprise after all and probably hadn't known we were outside. As I focussed through the haze of the spray and raised the torch in readiness to strike, Garron spun around and grabbed hold of Bob.

He was alive.

My attack halted when I realised that Garron was holding a knife. *The knife*, I expect … the one that killed Rose Hill and Oscar and was the cause of so much of the damage to Derek Bladen. His face was shining from the spray as his eyes met mine. His breathing was heavy as he struggled to compose himself. He managed to half stand and half lean against the far wall as he trod clumsily on the pieces of wood from the door. He had one arm around Bob's chest and the other was forward, threatening to use the knife. His steely eyes burnt harder into mine but he didn't speak. He seemed to be trying to work out just how he was going to get out of this entrapped dilemma that had intruded, so inconveniently, upon his dystopian world.

'Give it up, Garron. The place is full of police,' I said, hopefully.

'I'll kill him,' he said, desperately.

I took a better look at Bob and his exact position. Garron had tied a cord which came down from the ceiling around Bob's neck. It was wrapped around two or three times and was slowly strangling him.

Bob's face was ashen, his circulation was severely compromised and his eyes looked blank and lifeless, but he was still alive.

This time Garron had chosen an apparent suicide.

My paramedic friend was back on his feet and standing just behind me.

Garron spotted him and must have further realised that his situation was grim.

'Get him out of the way,' he demanded.

'You can't go anywhere, Garron,' I said.

Now that I knew that Bob was alive I had a few extra seconds to think. I had to get Bob safe and ensure Garron didn't harm anyone else in the meantime. My foolish and desperate plan had endangered the life of the paramedic and if things went 'pear-shaped' I would be in a huge pile of trouble.

Another couple of minutes should be enough time for Terry and his back-up officers to arrive. I had to get him talking.

'Why did you kill Rose Hill? She had nothing to do with it,' I said.

'She was …' he began.

'What … Bladen's? Was that the idea? You killed her because he hadn't given you your share of the diamonds? You wanted to use the money to help Kim, didn't you? So, was that how you repaid him?'

'You don't know what it's been like,' he shouted.

'You killed 'em all, didn't you? Grainger, Brookes, Elms and then Bladen. Made you feel better, did it?'

'They deserved it,' he said.

'No, they didn't. Nor did Rose Hill … We found Oscar this morning too. Bet you enjoyed killing him, eh? Revenge for the beating he gave you … was that it? Or more revenge for Kim?' I said.

Garron glared at me. I had definitely touched a nerve. I wondered, momentarily, whether I had gone too far. He looked as though he was going to turn all his pent-up anger on Bob and finish him.

I could hear footsteps approaching along the corridor and quickly glanced out of the door. My paramedic friend nodded at me which was all the confirmation I needed to know that I had company. I turned my gaze back to Garron who had clearly heard the same sounds. This was the moment where it could have all gone wrong. If he was going to try anything drastic, it was going to be now. I looked up at the cable and for the first time noted that it was red. It was the alarm that any patients in difficulty could use to alert the members of staff. On the wall where Garron stood was a siren. If Bob's body went any lower, the strain on the cable would activate the siren.

Terry had arrived and a number of armed officers were standing close by in the corridor. It was a stalemate. Garron's day had gone from bad to worse and yet he still held the advantage because he had Bob's life at his mercy. Terry was standing very close to the toilet door but still out of Garron's sight. From what I could gather, everyone was ready to over-run Garron and it was simply a matter of picking the perfect moment. I knew we had to act pretty soon as the longer we waited the more chance there was of Garron reacting to his impossible situation. If he killed Bob then there would be no chance of the information he held ever coming out and yet, in a very strange way, I didn't know whether I wanted to know.

'Let him go, Garron. It's over now,' I said.

He altered his position and gripped Bob by his dressing gown, holding the knife in front of him. He didn't have what I would call a firm hold. I glanced to the officers who were standing close beside me, just around the remains of the doorframe, and gave a look that said 'this is it'. They responded by nodding their heads and edging very gently forward.

It was time.

Garron was finished.

'Go,' I screamed as I leapt forward, but not towards Garron, who was flailing his huge knife at me, but at Bob.

I dived down and performed a rugby tackle around Bob's waist, allowing my weight to fall to the floor. Bob's body tore from Garron's one-armed grip and stretched the alarm cord downwards. The alarm yelped loudly in Garron's ear as the cord tightened around Bob's throat, causing the fittings on the ceiling to come down, still attached to Bob by his neck. The room filled with dust, and broken ceiling tiles covered Bob and me. All I could hear was a lot of yelling as the armed officers stampeded into the toilet to overcome Garron. I was covered in dust and debris from the collapsed part of the ceiling but could appreciate that a number of officers were on top of Garron. I could only see black uniforms lying on the floor in a heap but I knew he was under there somewhere. Someone was grabbing at my shoulders and lifting me backwards and out of the doorway. I held on to Bob and dragged him along with me away from Garron. When I managed to turn myself over, I could see Terry.

'You alright, guv?' he said, shouting above the awful din from the alarm.

'Yeah,' I said, a little stunned by the sound of the frenetic screaming and shouting coming from the toilet.

'Is he alive?' said Terry.

'Yeah, I think so. Get him out of here, will you, Terry. Get him a doctor.'

White-coated saviours milled around Bob and he was quickly whisked away into a side room as the chaos began to subside very slightly. I stood and dusted myself down and leaned against a wall, catching my breath. I saw the black uniforms begin to back out from the toilet towards me and had to squeeze myself to one side in order for them to have the space they needed to fit themselves and Garron through the crowded area. They were carrying John Garron, who was handcuffed and unconscious. I had no idea what had happened once I hit the floor with Bob in my arms but I knew it wasn't going to be a favourable outcome for Garron. Terry followed the armed officers down the corridor.

'Guv, I'll see you when you get back ... and guv ... nice one,' he said with a smile and a thumbs-up.

I knew that what I had done was pretty stupid and very risky. I reflected upon the fact that I had endangered my life and that of the paramedic but what could I do? If I had waited for the appropriate back-up Bob may well have already been strangled by Garron or may have suffered irreparable damage in the process. I realised that I needed to get some water to quench my dry mouth, which had been invaded by antiseptic spray and years of dust from above the ceiling tiles. I was covered in small pieces of broken tile and looked an absolute mess, but it was over. I got him before he got me.

Chapter Eighty-One

Looking like I had just done a hard day's work on a building site, I sat and shared a coffee with Sarah. I explained as much as I could to her about how this dramatic situation had come about and apologised for the dreadful commotion. Amusingly, she admitted that she had thoroughly enjoyed it, but asked me not to mention that to any of the hospital 'big-wigs'. I promised to keep it quiet for her. Sarah explained that the doctors had confirmed that Bob was not in any danger with regard to his immediate condition but that several checks would be carried out to establish exactly what effect his traumatic experience had had on him. The transient restriction to his breathing was a huge concern but until the results from the scans and tests were back we had to hope for the best. Sarah hoped that Bob had not struck his head in the struggle and I hoped that I had not made things worse. She was worried about the possibility of any bleeding on and around his brain, which could set him back considerably in his recovery. As we chatted about the rather exciting and dramatic morning, she reminded me of something I had mentioned to her before.

'Inspector, what was it that you were so desperate to talk to him about?' she asked.

'Erm … well … it's only work stuff really.'

'Oh, sorry if I'm being nosy, I didn't mean to be.'

'No, no, it's Ok. Erm … well … It's just that I think that Bob knows something about the investigation we've been doing and I've been wanting to talk to him about it but, of course, once the accident happened … well, everything changed, I guess. I may never find out.'

'I see. Well, he's going to be here for a while longer, I'm sure, so if you think I can help then please don't hesitate to ask,' she said.

'Thank you, Sarah … and it looks as though I'm going to be in and out of here for a while longer too, doesn't it?' I said.

'Yes, it does, but I'm sure that I can cope with that, it'll be nice to see you popping in,' she said, smiling broadly as my heart skipped all over again.

Sweet Dreams

Debbie watched the skeletal trees brush to and fro across the Lenten moon from her bedroom window. The unyielding night frost clung to the garden fences and coated the unruly ceanothus like a cloak. A sudden chill ran through her as she stared out onto the garden which, in turn, stared bleakly back. She felt as though she had just been plunged, naked, into meltwater.

It was just after 2.30 a.m.

She was still dressed in the clothes she wore yesterday.

The days since John's trial had rolled by slowly. She couldn't believe that it was a whole year ago. It seemed like the weeks and months had slurred into one timeless suffering. Everything was so different now. She worked, she cooked, she cleaned, she cried, and most of all she wondered why.

Why had he not told her, not trusted her?

She was his sister and could've helped him, just as he had always been firmly by her side through the nightmares that had punctuated her life. She had reflected upon this over and over and never found any solace or answers.

He did what he did.

Loneliness and emptiness were her constant companions now.

It had all come out in the trial; all the dreadful details. Debbie had watched it all, and every word she heard had tormented her repeatedly over the ensuing months, although she knew she hadn't absorbed all of it. Much of it bounced off her and was filed away; she hoped, forever. As the nightmare unfolded in court, Debbie had the feeling that she had already read this chapter. It didn't feel new. It felt as though it was just a matter of time before she became haunted by another ghost.

Why didn't he talk to me?

It wasn't unusual for her to be awake at this time of night.

But tonight, everything was different.

Tonight, a new, terrifying door had creaked open.

Kim slept quietly in her room; no longer did she cry herself to sleep. No longer did she sit downstairs shaking and whimpering. Debbie hoped that time would be a healer once again; time and perhaps a miracle or two. She looked down at the piece of paper in her hand as a tear trickled its way down her cheek.

Just another wound to deal with.

Another test of her resolve.

Over the past year Kim had altered considerably. Debbie could tell more than anyone. Kim had been poleaxed by the shock of her Uncle John going to prison. It was impossible for Debbie to stop the news getting into the house and impossible for her to concoct any sort of story about him simply going away.

How could she expect to fool Kim indefinitely?

Debbie knew that he wasn't coming back for a very long time, if at all.

Probably never.

She had sat down with Kim and tried to explain it all to her but without telling her everything. In fact, Debbie spent most of the conversations tripping herself up on what was true and what was appropriate to tell Kim. The first few months were the worst. The tears and the spontaneous questions were expected but Kim's reversion back to the miserable days of depression and unpredictable behaviour were hard to manage. There were some days when Kim hardly spoke at all and others when she didn't seem to stop. Somehow, they got by. Somehow ...

Part of Kim's way of helping her mother to cope was to spontaneously volunteer to help out. Sometimes it was a welcome gesture but on the days when Debbie needed quiet it was overbearing. Debbie would bite her lip to stop herself snapping at Kim. Kim's energy levels ranged from a slothful lethargy to a torrent of hyperactivity.

Debbie quietly made her way downstairs; sleep was not a viable option right now. As she passed Kim's room she glanced in. Kim was sleeping peacefully; at least one of them was. Debbie made herself some tea, curled up on the sofa and unfolded the piece of paper that she had discovered earlier that evening. She had read it several hours ago but maybe if she read it again the words would be different.

Maybe she misunderstood.

Maybe she'd got it wrong.

It was in an old pack of cards; the ones that Monica Heathcote had given Kim to take home from the hospital. The girls would make up games with them. The two of them played day after day, prompting the nurses to make jokes about a gambling syndicate. Kim would laugh like a drain at this, which would start Monica laughing, and before long the nurses were laughing too. It never mattered that the joke was old, to Kim it was simply funny and in those days it was so comforting to see her happy. Monica was Kim's best friend whilst she was in hospital. She helped Kim's recovery more than she ever knew. Monica was nine months further on in her treatment than Kim and had fewer complications to deal with from the start.

The old, creased pack of cards that had fallen behind the wardrobe in Kim's room hadn't been played with for a few years and Debbie had forgotten all about them. The last time Debbie could remember seeing them was one time when John was here. Kim was drawing on the cards and marking them so she knew when her uncle was holding the aces. She found it so funny. She coloured in the Jokers too. She used to say that they were her and Uncle John, but Debbie couldn't find them in amongst the cards and assumed Kim had put them somewhere or lost them. Kim had wanted to have a game with Uncle John on her birthday but he said they should hurry and cut the cake before her friends ate it all. Debbie remembered how Kim had giggled and taken his hand, leading him to the kitchen to smuggle out some cake out before anyone else realised.

Debbie had been reaching underneath the wardrobe to fetch out an old rucksack that Kim had once used for school, which had been flattened and laid under there, out of sight and cloaked in dust. A couple of discarded CDs were right at the back against the wall and beside them, covered in a thick layer of cobwebs, was a pack of cards. She prised them out with the vacuum cleaner attachment and was going to ask Kim whether she wanted them any more, when she spotted a piece of paper that had been folded and tucked into the pack. Curiosity got the better of her but now she wished that she had disposed of them straightaway; saved herself from even more pain. Debbie couldn't explain why she put the pack of cards in her pocket and why she went downstairs to unfold the paper, leaving Kim to continue ferreting about in her room, but she did, and when she read the words she instantly became numb. Her legs became weak, forcing her to lean against a wall before sliding to the floor. She trembled when she realised the full impact of what it meant. Sweat brimmed on her eyebrows as the past raced back towards her, steamrolling its horror over her. When she realised that Kim must have read it too, she was physically sick. The words that Debbie read weren't real. Surely this was something she was imagining. She had been incredibly strong for so long but right now she could barely stand.

* * *

My darling Kim,

I never knew that you would be at the shop that day. I didn't mean for any of this to happen the way it did. I hope that when you are better you can forgive me. I thought you were out with your dad. If I could turn the clock back I would, you know that.

You will be better soon. I know you will. Please forgive me.

All my love,,

Uncle John xxxx

The tea was cold but not as cold as the ice that ran through her veins right now. She got up with no feeling in her legs and subconsciously stepped across the room; not thinking. Debbie knelt in front of the wood-burning stove and took the pack of cards out of her pocket. She opened the front of the stove and placed the pack of cards loosely on top of a piece of firelighter, spreading them in a pile over it. Instinctively and without taking her eyes off the cards, she reached to the side of the fire and took a match from the box and struck it. Debbie touched the flame to the firelighter. The light from the fire flickered across her face and around the room. It burned brightly as the cards blackened and curled. She tossed the letter onto the blazing mound and closed the door to the stove. As Debbie quietly ascended the stairs she could still see the reflected light from the fire dancing on the walls, but nothing registered in her mind. Her face was blank, her eyes were dead. She walked into Kim's room and bent down by her bed. She gently teased Kim's tousled hair from her face, kissing her softly on her forehead, and whispered.

'I love you, darlin'. Sweet dreams.'